Praise for *The View from Here*

"A warmhearted yet clear-eyed look into what brings people together and what tears them apart, this makes a delightful case for shaking off childhood roles."

—*Booklist*

"Warmhearted and a perfect beach read."

—9 to 5 Toys, "Best Summer Books"

Praise for *Sailing Lessons*

"If you are a fan of sisterhood-themed beach reads by Nancy Thayer and Elin Hilderbrand, then McKinnon's latest engaging standalone needs to go on your summer to-be-read list."

—*RT Book Reviews*

"McKinnon writes with such imagery that you can almost smell the salt in the air."

—Booked

Praise for *The Summer House*

"Sure to appeal to fans of Elin Hilderbrand and Dorothea Benton Frank, *The Summer House* is an intriguing glimpse into a complicated yet still loving family."

—*Shelf Awareness*

"Charming and warmhearted."

—PopSugar

"McKinnon bottles summer escapist beach reading in her latest, full of sunscreen-slathered days and bonfire nights. Fans of Elin Hilderbrand and Mary Alice Monroe will appreciate the Merrill family's loving dysfunction, with sibling rivalries and long-held grudges never far from the surface. This sweet-tart novel is as refreshing as homemade lemonade."

—*Booklist*

Praise for *Mystic Summer*

"When two roads diverge . . . take the one that leads to the beach! Hannah McKinnon delivers a charming gem of a novel in *Mystic Summer*. I adored this book."

—Elin Hilderbrand,
#1 *New York Times* bestselling author of *The Identicals*

"Hannah McKinnon's *Mystic Summer* is a heartwarming story of lost love and the against-all-odds chance of finding it again. . . . *Mystic Summer* is a lovely summer beach read that will keep readers turning the page until the very end!"

—Nan Rossiter,
New York Times bestselling author of *Summer Dance*

Praise for *The Lake Season*

"Seasons of change take us home to the places and the people who shelter us. Well-told, and in turns sweet and bare, *The Lake Season* offers a compelling tale of family secrets, letting go, and the unbreakable bonds of sisterhood."

—Lisa Wingate,
nationally bestselling author of *Before We Were Yours*

"Hannah McKinnon's lyrical debut tells the story of a pair of very different sisters, both at a crossroads in life. McKinnon's great strength lies in her ability to reveal the many ways the two women wound—and ultimately heal—each other as only sisters can."

—Sarah Pekkanen,
New York Times bestselling author of *The Wife Between Us*

"Charming and heartfelt! Hannah McKinnon's *The Lake Season* proves that you can go home again; you just can't control what you find when you get there."

—Wendy Wax,
New York Times bestselling author of the
Ten Beach Road series and *The House on Mermaid Point*

Other Books by Hannah McKinnon

The View from Here

Sailing Lessons

The Summer House

Mystic Summer

The Lake Season

For Young Adults (As Hannah Roberts McKinnon)

Franny Parker

The Properties of Water

In loving remembrance of my brother, Joshua Goodwin Roberts.
Whose bright sun set too soon, but whose wake runs deep with
laughter, memory, and spirit.

Message in the Sand

◆ *A Novel* ◆

Hannah McKinnon

EMILY BESTLER BOOKS

ATRIA

NEW YORK LONDON TORONTO SYDNEY NEW DELHI

An Imprint of Simon & Schuster, Inc.
1230 Avenue of the Americas
New York, NY 10020

First Emily Bestler Books/Atria Paperback edition June 2021

EMILY BESTLER BOOKS/ATRIA PAPERBACK and colophon are trademarks of Simon & Schuster, Inc.

For information about special discounts for bulk purchases, please contact Simon & Schuster Special Sales at 1-866-506-1949 or business@simonandschuster.com.

The Simon & Schuster Speakers Bureau can bring authors to your live event. For more information or to book an event, contact the Simon & Schuster Speakers Bureau at 1-866-248-3049 or visit our website at www.simonspeakers.com.

Interior design by Yvonne Taylor

Manufactured in the United States of America

1 3 5 7 9 10 8 6 4 2

The Library of Congress Cataloging-in-Publication Data is available.

ISBN 978-1-9821-1457-2
ISBN 978-1-9821-1459-6 (ebook)

Message in the Sand

PROLOGUE

Nestled in the woods and wetlands of Saybrook, Connecticut, was a secret. It was discovered one flawless summer day by a young mother walking in the woods with her two boys. At first glance it appeared to be an ordinary turtle: nothing to get excited about in those parts. For most, their populace spanned the region as far and wide as the roots of a hundred-year-old oak span a forest floor. In Native tribe folklore, the turtle was sacred, a symbol of good health and long life. Ambling through waterways in shelled solitude, the small speechless creature likely did not know that. But in one corner of one western town, a rare species traversed the wetlands furtively: the red spotted turtle.

It had always been rare, but development had hastened its scarcity. As farms turned to neighborhoods and habitats disappeared, so, too, did the spotted turtle. But still, in dark nooks at the edges of deep lakes or silent swamps, a small number carried on, discovered only on occasion by those adventurous few who delved deep into thickets to make its acquaintance: of those, the young mother who fell in love with the garnet dapples on the shelled creatures.

Who treasured the shy reptile and the green spaces where it lived. Whose older son would carry on with the same love of deep thickets and quiet green shrouds where he, too, could live on in solitude. A seeker of sanctuary.

One

Wendell

A man who'd dwelt every one of his thirty-nine years in Saybrook, Wendell Combs had seen more than a few untoward things in his time. For all its open-faced New England charm, he understood that even quiet hill towns like his own hid their share of unpleasantries behind the virtuous lines of their cobblestone walls. Still, a lifelong bachelor who'd never seen the wisdom in pulling his gaze away from a good thing, he hadn't hankered for what may have lain beyond the town's bucolic boundaries. What was the point? Like the three generations of Combses before him, Wendell knew what he liked, and he liked what he knew. Saybrook had long been a hamlet in the Connecticut hills of Litchfield County, where most of the faces you nodded to at the local market or gas station were the same ones you'd been passing in those very places since childhood. Tucked in the fertile valley at the base of the Housatonic watershed, whose dormant farmlands ran as deep as the tributaries that spawned them, Saybrook seemed to turn a sleepy eye away from time. It was what had drawn the city folk from their noisy urban sprawl and set them scrabbling over the George Washington Bridge and up the Saw Mill River Parkway to cross its borders. Just an hour shy of the wiles of the Big Apple, Saybrook may as well have been a world away. But no matter, the city had come to it.

That morning, hours before most had even stirred in their downy beds, Wendell had risen and climbed into his truck with Trudy. He, too, could have used a few more hours of sleep. After eight years being back home from his tour in Afghanistan, Wendell felt he should've been able to silence the dark memories that found him in the night. But last night's had been worse than usual, and around four a.m. he'd abandoned any hope of rescue via the strategies Dr. Westerberg had pressed him to try in therapy and staggered out to the screened-in porch. There, he collapsed into the Adirondack chair until the rivulets of sweat dried between his shoulder blades, his hands stopped shaking, and the sky lightened. He still thought of Wesley every day, but it had been a long time since the dreams had been that bad.

Now, with one more night behind him, he drove through the sleepy town center. There were only two main roads in town, both owned by the state, and designated so by double-yellow lines and bright signage. All the rest were of the windy scenic sort, as rural as the hills and private lakeshore properties that made up Saybrook. Back when Wendell's father was the mayor, he used to joke that if you blinked as you drove through, you'd miss the village center. His father had been gone a long time, but little had changed. Historic houses lined the main street, their windows still dark. The New England charm of the tiny town center was not much interrupted by commerce, aside from a gas station, a coffee shop, and the sole restaurant in town that served good burgers but lousy pasta. There were two churches: a sweeping modern design for the Catholics and a traditional white chapel for the Protestants. Wendell wasn't much for religion, even though his mother had tried, but he supposed the Protestant church was where he'd end up if he had to go. These days, that was of little concern to him; quietude in the great outdoors was the only religion he needed.

Beside him in the cab, Trudy slept on as they passed the stately brick library, the playhouse his godfather had built, and the historical society museum that resided by the library in an antique red barn. Where the two main roads converged at the only stoplight in town, he turned left. The village market was the only thing open, its small parking lot already crowded with pickup trucks whose drivers were probably standing in line at the market deli counter for a fried egg sandwich and cup of coffee. Across the way, the school was closed for the summer, its colorful playground equipment gleaming in the early-morning sun like spit-polished shoes.

A mile north, Wendell swung his truck off the main road and onto Timber Lane, toward the Lancaster place. Here the road narrowed, its paved median void of painted yellow lines. People who lived in this town knew to stay in their own lane, at least the ones who'd grown up here. Trudy lifted her nose from the folds of her blanket and peered out from beneath heavy lids at the scene rolling by. Wendell rested a hand atop her head, and almost immediately, the basset hound resumed her wheezy snore. They passed Lonny Hastings's dairy farm. The lights were on in the milking barn. When Wendell returned, hours later, the cows would be out in the pasture. Just past the dairy, farmhouses dotted the hill on both sides, their windows shadowy. Outside the driver's window, the first rosy glimmer of the new day emerged. Wendell glanced at it. It surprised him, the fuss people made over a sunrise: snapping pictures and posting them on all those social media sites. No different than the cardboard sign affixed in the center of town inviting residents to experience *sunrise yoga!* down at the lake. Wendell shook his head. For him, dawn marked the beginning of another day, an hour after he'd had his first cup of coffee before he drove up to check on the Lancaster place, and two hours before he'd stop at the market for his second cup. He didn't need to snap a picture.

• • •

At the crest of the hill, the sun burst in full on the horizon, and Wendell pulled the tattered brim of his John Deere cap lower on his forehead. He glanced in the rearview mirror. His blue eyes shone back at him. Honest eyes, his mother used to say. Eyes that once knew the ins and outs of almost every front door and backyard in this town. Though some people in town complained there were fewer locals and more transplants from the city. It was nothing new. People bought weekend places, had kids, and moved here full-time. Knocked down walls and put up fences. Expanded. Improved. Wendell didn't pay it much mind. As his father used to say, when he was sitting behind the first selectman's desk at town hall, it was how things went.

At a dense grove of pine trees, Wendell turned left onto a gravel driveway and stopped at the gates. The simple wooden sign at the edge of the drive was so discreet you might miss it if you weren't looking: *White Pines*. Wendell stopped at the gate and punched in the security code: Alan trusted him with that, as with most everything else on the property, a fact that Wendell harbored little sentiment over. It was business.

At the end of the gravel drive, the big gray house rose up. It was early yet, but he was surprised not to see Alan's Jeep Wagoneer. Despite his choices of vehicles—a Ferrari, a Porsche, a vintage T-Bird—all covered and stored here on the estate, Alan favored the old wood-paneled Jeep for daily use. But this morning the Wagoneer's spot by the barn was empty. Wendell put the truck in park and Trudy sat up, her expression little changed in wakefulness. He held the door while she lumbered across the seats and hopped down. "Come on, girl. Time to get to work."

As Wendell waited for Alan to come down from the house to go over the day's schedule, he took inventory of the equipment.

The Kubota was running low on gas, as were the weed eaters, but they could wait. It was the Scag he was here for. He grasped the orange handles and maneuvered it down the ramp and outside. Today he'd mow the acreage that Alan referred to as the western lawn, where his wife, Anne, kept a vegetable garden. She'd once told Wendell that he need not think twice about it—that patch of dirt was hers to bother with. Even so, Wendell made sure the hoses were hooked up properly and the water ran through the irrigation system he'd built for her. Each year he took pleasure in spying a flash of red tomato or the orange orbs of pumpkins in fall. He especially enjoyed seeing Anne, her straw hat pulled neatly over her blond hair. Wendell appreciated hard work in any form, but he'd dare to say there was something artful in the tended rows of lettuce and gently woven pea lattices. Broad stalks of Brussels sprout arced over leafy pepper plants, and beneath them all the tangled vines of squash wove their way through the underbelly of the garden like secrets. By midsummer it was a dazzling array of texture and color that Anne tended to as lovingly as she did her two daughters, lending a sense of wild beauty to a property that was otherwise hedged and trimmed and shorn from one immaculate corner to the next. He loved it when the girls joined their mother, filling small baskets with whatever was growing. Often Wendell caught himself gazing wistfully in the direction of the garden. But at this hour of the day, the yard was quiet.

As he rolled the Scag mower to the edge of the lawn and started it, a flicker of movement by the house caught his eye. Wendell looked up, but it was not Alan. It was Pippa, the younger of the two girls, pushing her bike across the top of the driveway.

As a rule, children were largely mystifying to Wendell, and Anne and Alan's two daughters were no different. The younger one, who had a shy streak, kept as close to the house as she did to her mother. She was a sprite of a thing, all elbows and kneecaps and fine-spun golden hair, fairylike. But Lord, did she have a set of pipes on her, which he'd had occasion to hear when her temper was piqued or she was overcome with something particularly delightful. Today seemed of the delightful variety, he was relieved to note as he watched her skip with reckless abandon across the yard, singing loudly and out of tune. She stopped suddenly by her mother's garden gate and disappeared in the greenery. The tall stalks of gladiolas shook violently as she rummaged through the rows, until she finally emerged with a handful of picked flowers that Wendell was pretty sure she ought not to. Wendell glanced at Anne, bent over the house beds in the shade. He would never say anything, of course. Caretakers existed in the background.

The older one, Julia, was a different story. She was in her early teens and a curious thing, always lurking about like a cat. Perched in a tree branch with a book or hopping down from a fence, catching him by surprise on his rounds. Despite his better efforts to steer clear, the two had had a few memorable run-ins.

Earlier that spring, while mowing the upper fields, he'd come across her crying at the base of a dogwood tree, cupping something gray and tufted in her palms. "You have to help it," she'd cried, holding her hands out to him.

Wendell was used to coming across wildlife in his line of work, if not weeping little girls, so he took the bird gently from her. It was fully feathered, just a fledgling.

"Well?"

He turned, and Julia's eyes locked expectantly on his. They were the same arresting blue as her mother's. Wendell glanced across the field toward the house, but neither parent was around. "All right," he said hesitantly. "Let's see what we can do."

Julia had remained fixed by his side as he considered the tree the bird had fallen from, eventually pulling himself up into its dense branches in search of the nest. Nearby, a gray swallow chided them loudly. "She's not happy with us," he said, pointing her out. "Must be the mother."

"But we're helping."

"No," he said. "To her we're predators."

Julia bit her lip. "Then you'd better hurry up." He'd paused, glancing down through the crisscrossed limbs at her insistent face. Much more like her father, he decided.

They'd returned the baby bird to its nest and, as far as Wendell knew, to safety. After that, Julia began popping up during his workdays. Swinging her leg over a fence rail. Peering around the corner of an open barn door. Most often she found him in the stable, where her horse, Radcliffe, was stabled. Each time, "Whatcha doing?"

Wendell made it a practice not to interact with his client's families. It kept things clean. Besides, he had no kids of his own and had never wanted any. They were as baffling to him as the wider world beyond Saybrook, a world he saw no point in acquainting himself with any more than necessary.

It was true what others said about him: that Wendell preferred the company of animals to people. Animals did not bother him, nor ask for more than what they required. And when he looked in their eyes, he saw an instinctual certainty about life that he recognized: the need to survive. But horses—like children—were another matter altogether. The fact of the chestnut horse had forced his path to cross with Julia's more than once. Radcliffe was clever and stubborn, just like his young owner, and after the matter of the little bird they'd rescued, Julia began to seek Wendell out when things went awry.

On a particularly gusty day a few months earlier, he'd been surprised to see the two heading out for the fields. "Windy days make for frisky ponies," he'd cautioned. "You may want to keep to the safety of the riding ring today."

But Julia had already made up her mind. "I'd rather ride in the field," she'd retorted, urging the horse into a brisk trot. Not five minutes later, she came stomping back on foot, red-faced and covered in grass clippings.

Wendell knew enough about females to keep his gaze fixed on the hay bales he was busy stacking. He did not look up when she huffed into the barn and slammed the door. "Need a hand?" he asked finally.

Out of the corner of his eye, he saw Julia swipe at the mud stains on her britches. "No." Then, her eyes filling with tears, "Maybe."

Wordlessly, he went to the tack room and scooped some sweet grain into a bucket. In the doorway, he glanced back at Julia, who seemed poised to retreat to the house for a bubble bath. "What're you waiting for? He's your horse."

After a sharp look, she followed. It had taken half an hour between the two of them, but eventually, the little beast had been caught. Since then, Wendell seemed to have risen in Julia's estimation as more than a curiosity who worked on her father's property. And though Wendell preferred to be left alone, he was surprised to find he did not entirely mind her occasional presence.

But there was no time for distraction today. The Lancasters were hosting the annual gala that evening, and there was much to be done. Alan's Jeep rumbled toward him, and he rolled down the window as he pulled up alongside Wendell. "Good morning," he said. "What a day, what a day."

Wendell was used to Alan's vocal affection for his property. It extended beyond the ownership of the estate; Alan was in love with the land.

"It is, Mr. Lancaster. What's first on the schedule this morning?"

Alan rested his elbow on the window. "Wendell, I admire your work ethic. But a morning like this is to be admired. Look at that sky! Not a cloud."

Wendell cleared his throat and glanced up obligingly. The truth was, he saw in this property exactly what Alan Lancaster did: the lush greenery, the watery shadows around the pond, the thrilling flash of white-tailed deer or wing of osprey. Having grown up in this town, Wendell didn't just see all of what Alan saw, he felt it. And ever since his tour of duty, he needed it.

The sky overhead was sharp and cloudless, and with some hesitation, Wendell allowed his eyes to wader across its expanse. It was a luxury he did not often allow himself. Wendell knew it was better to stay busy—to keep moving, his hands working, his brain planning. He did not allow himself to soak things in, as Alan suggested. Because then his mind wandered, and when that happened, the ability to control what filtered through it might slip. Wendell held his breath as his gaze traveled: There were the treetops, branches reaching like a woman's slender arm. The light was gauzy and soft at this hour, and Wendell began to relax, to let his breath out. Suddenly, in the distance, an egret launched itself gracefully off a weeping willow, and Wendell followed its slow sweep across the lake. Alan was right: the morning was nothing short of spectacular.

But as he watched the egret glide across the water, the sky began to blur at the edges. Wendell blinked. He tried to focus on the egret's silhouette, but it, too, began to flicker. And before he could stop it, the scene before him flashed away, replaced suddenly by Wesley's profile. There he was, against the sky. All twenty-five years of him, staring off in the distance as if he, too, were watching the egret's descent. Wendell recognized the strong set of his jaw, the determined gaze. Exactly as he'd looked the last time Wendell saw him in Afghanistan. Wesley turned his way and, seeing his big brother, grinned like an eight-year-old. Then disappeared. Wendell braced himself, shook his head against the memory.

Alan misunderstood his expression. “Stops you in your tracks, this view. Doesn’t it?”

Wendell blinked, forced his tongue to work around the sandy confines of his mouth. “Yes, sir.” He met Alan’s gaze and prayed his own was steady, but inside, the wave of nausea crested violently in his gut.

Alan looked at him curiously. “Feeling okay, Wendell?”

Wendell ran a hand across his brow. “Yes, sir. Just a little warm.” He peeled off his sweatshirt, willing the nausea to subside, to climb down the burning walls of his insides once more. The first waves were always the worst. Thankfully, Alan did not press him.

“I have to run in to town,” Alan said, passing him a piece of paper. “Here’s what Anne has set out for us today.” He looked apologetic. “The damn gala is upon us.”

But even as he said it, Alan Lancaster’s eyes twinkled. Wendell knew how it went: Alan in his black tie. The man loved nothing more than hosting people he cared about or who also cared about the land, the town, his mission to preserve it. He did not shy away from crowds but entered them with a glass raised and a clever remark on the tip of his tongue. His laugh was rich and infectious, his intentions honorable enough, as Wendell saw it. Though his friends often gave him crap for thinking so, accusing him of going soft. Going to the *other side.* Wendell didn’t care.

All Wendell cared about was doing his job. Doing it well enough to be left alone, to be welcomed back here where he could try to do something good, however small or simple, and contain the dark well within him.

Two

Julia

Julia crouched on a mossy rock and dipped her bare foot into the stream while she waited for him. The water was ice-cold, a welcome respite from the muggy June day, and it was one of the many things she loved about this hidden spot among the wetlands behind her family's field. In the distance a tree branch cracked, and she looked up sharply. Was it him? She waited, holding her breath, as she scanned the dense grove of trees for movement. Sam was late, and they didn't have much time. The annual gala was starting in a few hours, and she was supposed to be home helping her mother arrange flowers.

A moment later, there was another snap of branch underfoot, and Julia stood. When a lone doe emerged from the shadows, she let her breath out in a wave of disappointment. He'd said he would come.

Sam Ryder lived a mile up the road, but their properties abutted in the rear, and just recently, they'd taken to meeting up in the woods. He was supposed to be here. Not because he'd said he would be or because she'd lain awake for many of the last summer evenings, thinking about him and wondering if the time was right. But because from the moment she'd woken up this morning, she'd known: today would be the day she kissed him.

Between the dense greenery came a sudden shadow of movement, and Julia's chest pitter-pattered as a small fawn trotted out of the thicket. The mother deer paused, gazing over her shoulder at it, then sharply about for predators. She stiffened when she locked eyes with Julia, not twenty feet away. Julia had grown up in these woods, and she knew better than to make a sound. She let the doe study her, slowly sinking back down onto the rock, where she remained while the animal sized her up. *It's all right, mama,* she thought.

The fawn, impulsive and unaware, bounded up beside its mother, all gangly legs and elbows. It had not noticed her, nor the warning flare of its mother's nostrils, and in a fit of play, it began to buck about in an ever-widening circle until it had unwittingly closed the distance between itself and Julia and halted smack dab in front of her. Julia held her breath.

For a frozen moment, the two stared at each other. The fawn's eyes were bright pools of surprise, its inky nose so close that Julia could hear its intake of breath. The mother snorted a sharp warning, breaking the spell, and bounded off with a flick of her white tail. Startled, the fawn leaped after its mother. In that fleeting moment Julia closed her eyes and thrust out her hand, and just when she feared she'd missed it, the tips of her fingers brushed against the fawn's sleek pelt. Julia's eyes flew open. There was a swift crash of branches and shaking of undergrowth. And then the streambed went still, the only sound the gurgle of water swirling its distant way to some unseen estuary. Overcome, Julia tipped her head back and laughed out loud. Sam had not come after all, but it no longer mattered. Here, the magic was everywhere.

The ding of her phone broke the silence. Julia reached into the back pocket of her cutoffs and retrieved it. Her mother wanted her home to get ready for the gala. She cursed and sprinted for the trail home.

. . .

Back at the house, Julia sneaked around to the rear of the house, slipped through the mudroom and into the grand farmhouse kitchen.

"Better watch out. Mama's gonna get you!"

Her little sister, Pippa, was seated at the kitchen island, all gussied up in a pink tutu-skirted ensemble, swinging her legs back and forth off the barstool as she licked whipped cream from a large silver spoon. She smiled wickedly through a white mustache.

As if on cue, Eliza, their mother's right hand stepped out of the pantry with a mixing bowl. Julia halted. "Miss Pippa, your mother's going to get *you* if you spill one drop of that on your party dress," Eliza warned. Pippa scowled.

Eliza was their mother's assistant in all things, from the administrative duties for Anne Lancaster's charity work to assisting with the events themselves, as she was tonight. Now she regarded Julia's mud-splattered knees and shook her head. "Lucky for you, your mother is dealing with the jazz band, who was also late. Better hustle." She winked.

"Sorry, I lost track of time." Julia raced for the stairs. Up in her room, she kicked off what her mother still referred to as her "play clothes" and ran into her adjoining bathroom.

In the mirror, a wild-haired woman-child stared back at her. Julia's eyes were as dreamy blue as her mother's but almond-shaped like her father's: discerning, he liked to say. Her hair was another story. Blond and thick but prone to tangled rivulets, like the streambed she'd just abandoned. She swept it impatiently from her face with a brush, wondering if Sam was standing by the stream waiting for her right now. Or if he hadn't come at all.

It wasn't like they were an official couple, she reminded herself.

But what she and Sam shared was so much more than what the other girls at school, who had *real* boyfriends, talked about. Those couples went to movies and out for pizza. Sometimes they went to a party, which meant dealing with beer and maybe weed. Sometimes they hung out at each other's houses to watch Netflix, which was also code for alone time. And then there was the question about whether there'd be pressure to fool around and, if you did, what *that* would mean.

Julia and Sam did not do any of those things. And yet lately, it was starting to feel like they did so much more.

It had started only one month ago. Sam Ryder was like any other boy from school, unremarkable in the way boys you'd grown up with since kindergarten were. By the time you graduated, you'd seen just about every boy pick his nose, fall down in PE class, or lose his lunch during the spelling bee. Sam was smart enough to take honors classes, though probably not as smart as she was. He played baseball. He was quiet. To be honest, she'd never paid him any mind. There was no reason to. Until Miranda Bennet opened her big mouth.

Julia had been sitting in the high school cafeteria with her best friend, Chloe, and some other girls. That week a new girl had arrived at Saybrook High, a lacrosse player, like Chloe, and Chloe had invited her to join their group lunch table. Miranda seemed nice enough, if a little loud and dramatic. Despite how much she followed Chloe around, Julia wasn't worried. Theirs was an impenetrable friendship. It was well known that Chloe and Julia were like one. They didn't do anything or go anywhere without each other. That day, when Miranda joined them at the table with her lunch tray, she let out a low long whistle. "Okay, so who is that?"

Julia looked up. Sam Ryder was making his way through the maze of lunch tables, headed for the baseball team table. His floppy hair hung across his eyes, and as he went past, he looked up at the girls and flipped it out of his view. He was wearing one of his typical checkered flannel shirts. But the breadth of his shoulders beneath was wholly new to her. It was like seeing him for the first time.

Chloe stirred her chocolate milk with her straw. "That's Sam. He's a sophomore, too."

Miranda grinned at them. "Someone needs to introduce me. He's hot."

Julia was shocked to hear Chloe go along with her. "Pretty much." Not that she disagreed with Chloe but because neither of them had ever discussed Sam before. How had she not noticed him?

As the other girls considered the shade of Sam's blue eyes, Julia remained silent, studying his retreating figure. When had his shoulders gotten so broad? Had he always walked with such confidence?

Suddenly, Sam was everywhere. Julia passed him in the hall between algebra and bio. It turned out they shared a study hall, something she hadn't paid any attention to before. He'd always ridden her bus, as they lived just a mile apart on Timber Lane, but usually, Sam stayed after school for sports. Now that the baseball season was over, he was back on bus two, and when he plopped down in the seat in front of her, she found she couldn't take her eyes off his wheat-colored head of hair the whole way home. Worst of all, Sam, who had always smiled and said hello in the past, didn't seem to notice her one bit anymore.

By the last week of school, during study hall, Julia couldn't take it anymore. Summer vacation started in a matter of days, and who knew when they'd cross paths next. Before she could second-guess herself, she rose from her desk and headed across the room. She'd pretend to get a piece of paper. Maybe a tissue. As she passed his desk, she glanced down. She didn't need an excuse anymore. "Oh, wow."

Sam looked up. There were those eyes, under that straw-colored flop of hair. He squinted. "What?"

"Your painting." She indicated the small watercolor on his desk. "It's . . . amazing."

"Oh." Sam sat back and regarded his work. It was a landscape of a green field, with a large hillside rising on the horizon. Through the peach-colored sunset she could see the faint lines of his original pencil sketch. "Thank you."

Julia stood a moment longer, entranced by the watercolor. He was really good. "I didn't know you were into art."

Sam shrugged. "It's just something I like to do. This is for my open studio final. I'm kind of behind."

Julia stared at his lips as he spoke. Then caught herself. "When's it due?"

Sam smiled. "Yesterday." He didn't seem concerned.

"Oh, well. Then I should let you get back to it."

Sam nodded as if that was probably a good idea. Feeling suddenly awkward, Julia turned on her heel and made a break back toward her desk. She realized too late, after sitting down, that she hadn't gotten herself either a piece of paper or a tissue.

On the bus ride home, she sat near the rear, knees tucked against her chest. When Sam boarded the bus and walked by, she hunkered down. He probably thought she was an idiot. Worse, maybe he'd forgotten about her comments altogether. To her chagrin, he sat in the seat right behind her, and he didn't say a thing.

They were almost home on what seemed like a painfully long hot ride when Sam leaned into the aisle and tapped the back of her seat. Julia almost jumped. "Did you recognize the view?" he asked.

Julia blinked, confused. She looked out the bus window. "The view?"

Sam shook his head and smiled. "No, dummy. My painting. Did you recognize it?"

"Oh." Julia was taken aback by his playfulness. Before she could say anything, Sam reached into the leather portfolio between his knees and pulled out a flat board canvas. He tilted it toward her.

"Oh my gosh. Is that . . . ?"

Sam nodded. "Your place, White Pines. It's the view from my house."

Julia felt something inside her chest swell. Of course it was. Sam's property bordered her own in the back, and each house was set on a small rise. Between them was a lush green meadow surrounded by wetlands. It was one of her favorite views in the world, even though she saw the reverse from her house.

"Weren't you supposed to hand it in?"

"I'm going to tomorrow. But she'll probably fail me, it's so overdue."

Julia shook her head. "She's crazy if she doesn't give you an A. It's the most beautiful thing I've ever seen." Then she winced. What was she *doing*?

But Sam didn't laugh. Instead he held her gaze, the corners of his mouth pulling back in that boyish way.

Then the brakes hissed, and the bus lurched to a stop. He slipped the painting back into his portfolio and stood. "See ya."

Julia watched him walk down the bus aisle. He said goodbye to their driver, Kathy, whom everyone else forgot to say goodbye to. When he stepped down the bus stairs, Julia stole a peek through the window. Sam walked up the driveway, his stride long and easy. He didn't glance back.

Julia didn't see Sam the last couple days of school. He wasn't in study hall and didn't ride the bus for some reason. Then it was Friday, the last day of school before summer.

Julia boarded the bus and sat near the back, in the same seat. Minutes later, to her immense relief, Sam climbed the bus stairs and headed down the aisle toward her. But he was staring at his phone and walked right past her. She couldn't tell which seat he took, but she knew it wasn't directly behind her like the last time. Clearly, he was not interested in talking to her. And she was too much of a wimp to turn around and say anything the whole way home.

When the bus finally stopped at his driveway, she heard him stand and gather his things behind her. She was mad at herself for letting the opportunity go. But it was too late to say anything now, so she stared straight ahead as his footsteps grew closer.

"Hey."

Julia's head snapped as he stopped by her seat. He held something out to her. "You were right."

It wasn't until she took it from his hand that she realized it was the painting. By then Sam was already halfway down the aisle. Julia flipped the painting over. It was graded A. And there was a note beside it in pencil: "You seemed to like this, so keep it. Maybe you can come see the real thing."

She jerked her head up just as the bus pulled away from Sam's driveway. She pressed her hand to the glass window. Sam raised his in return.

She pulled her phone out and looked him up on Snapchat. "How about tonight?"

After that, they began meeting up. Walking up to Sam in the middle of the field made Julia feel suddenly shy. It was one thing to bump into each other at school or on the bus. It was another to plan it. But seeing Sam sitting on the big boulder in the middle of all that greenery relaxed her. When she reached it, she clambered up and sat beside him, staring at the horizon. "It's good, but your painting is better."

He turned to look at her, and she could feel the weight of his gaze. "You know, my mother really liked that watercolor. I had to come up with a lie when she asked me where it was."

"She did?" Julia spun around to face him. "Oh, God, I feel terrible!"

"You should. It was her favorite."

Julia smacked him on the arm. "I'm giving it back."

"Nah, she's got plenty of them." Sam chuckled. "I just wanted to see you squirm."

After that, they met almost every night. They found a large rock by the lake's edge where they could see a blue heron's nest in a weeping willow. When it was particularly hot, they met by the stream, where the shadows were cool and the ground mossy. Once she caught a small brown turtle with garnet-red spots on its shell that she'd never seen before. "Look at that," she said, handing it gently to Sam.

"I've never seen one like that," he said, examining it in wonder. "It must be rare. Let's put it back by the water." As Julia watched him return to turtle to the mud, she couldn't think of any other boy who would appreciate such things.

"What do you two talk about?" Chloe demanded when Julia would call her to report back.

"I don't know. Nothing. Everything."

It was true. Sometimes they just sat and listened to the peepers. Sometimes Sam brought her a snack, like the perfectly ripe plum he once pulled out of his pocket, took a bite out of, and wordlessly handed to her. She'd never tasted anything so sweet. Sometimes they joked about school friends and gossip. Sometimes it was more serious, like a few nights ago, when they sat on their rock and he told her he had to go to Saratoga Springs soon to visit his grandfather, who was dying of cancer. "He's my favorite relative in the whole family. I don't know what to say to him." Sam's voice broke. "I'm not sure I want to remember him like this."

It was the first time Julia had taken his hand. She pulled it onto her lap and squeezed it in her own. Sam's hands were softer than the buttery leather reins on Radcliffe's bridle. It hardly sounded romantic, but as an equestrian, she found nothing more satisfying to the touch than the smooth braids of leather woven between her fingers. Until that moment when Sam looked at her and squeezed back.

Now, as she got ready for her parents' stupid gala, Julia found it hard to keep Sam out of her thoughts. Hurriedly, she pulled her hair into a loose ponytail and dabbed on lip gloss. If it weren't for the mint dress, and the freckles starting a dangerous trail across her nose, she'd almost say she looked pretty. Almost. She hurried to her walk-in closet and selected a pair of white sling backs which were tricky to walk in but made her taller. Before dashing downstairs, she grabbed her phone off her bed and sent Sam a text: "Sorry I couldn't stay, but my parents have that thing tonight. How about after?"

As she trotted downstairs, she could hear the house already buzzing. The patio doors had been thrown open, and notes of music trailed inside like birdsong as the jazz band warmed up. Her family was gathered in the archway between the living room and kitchen, apparently waiting for her. Her mother sounded impatient. "Where is Julia? We need to take the family photo." Eliza stood at the ready with a camera.

Julia groaned. Before every party, her mother went crazy with the photos.

"I'm coming!" But no one heard. At that moment, Badger, her father's beloved Irish setter, bounded inside with a look of wild glee on his face and a trail of muddy pawprints in his wake.

Her mother threw up her hands. "That dog! He was supposed to be crated."

"He was." Julia's father, a crisp vision in white linen, lunged just in time and secured Badger's leather collar. He scruffed the dog playfully, his tanned face crinkling with joy as Badger wagged against him. "How'd you escape, Houdini?"

"Alan, your suit," her mother protested.

"It's all right, honey. I've got him." Somehow her father managed to steer Badger through the kitchen and into the rear mudroom without getting a speck of dirt on himself. "Come on, you mangy mutt." Her father's patience knew no bounds.

Anne shook her head and turned to Eliza. "I swear, if it came down to me or that dog . . ." It was then that Anne noticed Julia standing in the doorway.

Julia wasn't sure what to expect from her mother; she'd seen the towering vases of hydrangeas lined up on the tables outside, knowing she hadn't had a hand in a single arrangement. She deserved an earful.

"Well, well." But her mother's expression softened when she noted the mint-green dress. She crossed the marble tiles in no time and planted a kiss on Julia's forehead. "Oh, honey. You look lovely." Pippa was skipping in small circles around them, swinging an overstuffed drawstring purse, which flew out of her hand and landed with a sharp thud on the floor.

Their mother spun around. "Pippa Mae, dare I ask what you're hiding in that handbag?"

Pippa snatched up her purse and pivoted away, but Eliza caught her midskip and spun Pippa around to face her mother, as if presenting a gift or a felon, Julia was not sure. "Show your mother."

Their mother shook her head as she emptied the contents of the purse across the island counter. "Oh, Pips. Really, now." Julia stole a peek over her shoulder. There were two gray rocks, one that looked like a real toe-breaker if dropped. A feather from the chicken coop. An open bag of M&M's, half melted. A leaking sparkly purple gel pen. And a miniature brass sculpture of a sailboat that their father immediately scooped up from the pile as he returned to the kitchen sans Badger. "Hey now, I've been looking for this for weeks."

"But I need all of it!" Pippa wailed, her eyes roving territorially across her loot. She was such a little hoarder.

Julia hid her smile as her mother dumped it gently into a small pail that Eliza miraculously procured from thin air. "We'll save it for later, honey. Your purse is a party accessory, not a backpack for a two-week excursion."

With everyone finally accounted for, Anne's eyes flashed. "Picture time," she declared. Even their father slumped a little.

Eliza gathered the four of them in the living room by the bay window. Behind them, the afternoon light was pink and still promising, casting a rosy glow on all four Lancasters. Julia leaned in to her mother. "I'm sorry I didn't help with the flowers," Julia whispered. "I lost track of time."

Her mother regarded her with a knowing smile. She looked vibrant, her blond hair swept up elegantly, eyes twinkling. "You were out in that swamp again, weren't you?"

Julia stiffened. How her mother seemed to know everything confounded her.

But if her mother knew it had anything to do with Sam Ryder, Julia was given a reprieve. "It's all right, baby girl. Next time."

Julia felt her insides relax. Anne Lancaster was a rock, a force of nature. But she bent and flexed gracefully like the reeds in their wetlands, sure of her position in the family. Despite the fact that her mother sometimes drove her absolutely crazy, somewhere deep in her bones Julia ached to be just like her. Love could be so conflicting.

Julia watched her mother's gaze flicker toward the bay window, where suddenly, the first guests alighted on the patio in their summer whites. The women looked like cranes, stepping gingerly in their heels across the flagstones. "Hurry! Everyone smile for the camera."

Pippa wriggled in between them, her recovered purse repacked, and accidentally stomped Julia's toes with one of her block heels. Julia yelped.

"Sorry," Pippa squeaked. At that moment Badger galloped through the kitchen, somehow sprung from his crate once again and awash with fresh mud. Upon locating his people in the formal living room, he spun on his hindquarters and thundered in, antique tables and lamps wobbling in his wake. "No!" Anne cried. "Stay down!" The family braced themselves, but it was too late.

Badger leaped into their fold, knocking against Pippa's tulle skirt, dragging his muddy tongue across Alan's face. Everyone sidestepped and shouted. The camera flashed once, then again, and Julia's father roared heartily, "Let the party begin!"

Three

Roberta

Roberta Blythe opened her mailbox and peered inside. "Ah! Something for both of us." At her feet, Maisey thumped her black tail expectantly.

Each time the UPS driver delivered a package, he left a dog biscuit in the mailbox for Maisey. Lately, Roberta had been shopping online with such frequency that the dachshund had come to expect something whenever they got the mail, which Roberta was more than a little ashamed of. She handed Maisey the biscuit and withdrew her package: the shape and weight of the hardcover book inside made her heart feel light. If a little guilty.

Despite the fact that Roberta believed in small business and loathed the Internet, she'd recently buckled and done something she'd sworn she'd never do: she'd made peace with Amazon. It had taken her years to arrive at that commercial-giant juncture, but ultimately, it was bigmouth Jimmy, from her physical therapy class, who was responsible.

Since her knee surgery back in February, Roberta was confronted by the likes of Jimmy Barkhausen three times a week at the orthopedic rehab center. All through the winter and spring, she'd been forced to listen to him rave about the many things he found inspiring (he was one of those expressly grateful types who thrust his good cheer on people), one of which was Amazon. According to Jimmy, it had changed his life. As with most things Jimmy said, Roberta initially tuned it out. If pressed, she supposed he was likable enough, a retired attorney, which gave them something in common, since she herself had been retired from the probate court bench for a good fourteen years now. But Jimmy talked too much and treated the rehab class like something of a social club, a place to hunker down and chew the fat. Roberta didn't want to hunker down with anyone, let alone chew the fat. She wanted to get in and get out of there. It was no secret that many in town considered her a bit of an introvert, which suited her just fine.

As Jimmy had railed on about the wonders of Amazon, a business so diversified that it sold everything from toilet paper to good literature, Roberta had focused instead on her rehab exercises. Her knee was healing nicely from ACL surgery. Nicely enough, she hoped, that she wouldn't have to keep coming back to rehab three times a week to do these god-awful stretches. The few occasions Roberta left her house, her errands took her to only three places: the local IGA market, the pharmacy, and the town library. And those she visited during off-hours, so as not to have to see people.

So when Jimmy mentioned that he didn't even have to get in the car and drive to the mall for jeans or to the pharmacy for his favorite brand of aftershave, it captured her attention. She tipped her head slightly in his direction on the trampoline in the corner. It was what he said next that made her put down her weights altogether.

"You ever hear of that book *Where the Crawdads Sing*?" Jimmy shouted. The shouting irked her more than anything. "Been on the bestseller list for weeks." Roberta nodded. She didn't need Jimmy Barkhausen to tell her that. She'd read it twice already, then recommended it to her sister. "Well, my wife has been trying to get it from the library for months. So, I got on the Amazon [*the* Amazon:

further annoyance], clicked 'add to cart,' and surprised her with a copy the very next day. Good Lord, she loves that book."

Books. Books were Roberta's one true thing. Her love, her escape, her habit, her weakness. Roberta coursed through books like caffeine addicts tossed back a triple espresso. It was how she spent her days and nights, when not cooking or walking Maisey or talking to her sister, Gina, on the phone. Roberta may have been an introvert, but she was no fool. She'd known Amazon sold books, but she was a devotee of her local library. What she couldn't procure from the library, she treated herself to from an adorable indie bookstore two towns over, though only on special occasions. But that summer her beloved Saybrook Library was under renovation, and the bookstore was a bit of a drive to keep up with her habit. "Next-day delivery!" Jimmy shouted from across the room.

That same afternoon Roberta logged on to her computer. It took only a moment to create an Amazon account. The array of options was staggering. Sinister, even. Who were all these merchants? Could she trust them? Before the sun set, she'd not only filled her cart, she'd compiled a bestseller wish list. She clicked the latest Hildebrand release. It was half-price and brand-new. *All right,* she told herself before committing altogether. This was temporary. To tide her over during the library renovation. Oh, but there was Ann Patchett's latest release! And so it happened that Roberta Blythe came to have a book a day delivered to her mailbox. To absolve her conscience, she still drove two towns over to the indie bookstore every month. And when the library reopened in the fall, she'd drop the Amazon account like a bad habit. In the meantime, there was no use beating herself up. These were the things she told herself.

Now, as she closed the mailbox and held the new book against her chest, the rumble of an approaching truck caught her attention. Roberta recognized the blue Ford right away: Wendell Combs. She lifted a hand in greeting.

Wendell's mother, Charlotte, had been a dear friend of Roberta's right up to the end. It began as an unlikely friendship, as at first glance neither woman had anything remotely in common with the other. But that was life in a small town: no one escaped with just one glance.

Roberta had been in the IGA market scouring the produce section when she heard a shriek. At the end of the aisle, by the dairy case, stood Charlotte Combs. Roberta followed the young mother's gaze to a lone shopping cart with two boys. Standing up in the cart was the younger one, whom Roberta guessed was about two years old. In his clutch was an empty egg carton, and below, on the linoleum floor, the remnants of the entire dozen. But that was far less concerning than what he did next: still standing in the cart, he threw his hands up overhead and wobbled precariously.

To Roberta's horror, the toddler lurched over the edge at the same time the mother screamed, "Wendell!"

Quickly, the big brother spun around and threw out his arms. In that instant the little one fell into them, and the two flopped to the floor. There was a terrible thunk as the older boy's head fell back against the linoleum, followed by crying.

Charlotte reached her boys first, scooping up the little one, then falling to her knees beside his big brother. "Darling, are you all right?"

Roberta had reached them by then, and Charlotte looked up at her. "Here!" Before she could say a word, Charlotte thrust the younger boy into her arms. He paused in his tears to regard this stranger and then howled louder.

Charlotte ran her hands over her older son's head, inspected his hair, fretting. "Wendell, you brave, brave boy."

Roberta watched Wendell's mother help him up. He put a hand to the back of his head. "I'm okay, Mama. It doesn't really hurt."

Charlotte turned to Roberta and exhaled with relief. Roberta was taken aback momentarily by her glow; she was quite beautiful. "Thank you so much," she said, relieving Roberta of the boy. "This is Wesley." She blinked at the messy floor in dismay. "The egg breaker."

The two had exchanged brief introductions as Roberta waved over the deli boy and sent him to fetch a mop.

"It's my fault," Charlotte said, swiping a lock of blond hair back into her ponytail. "I never should've stepped away from the cart."

Roberta regarded her sympathetically. So many parents came through her courtroom with less regret over far bigger issues. "It happens to the best of mothers," she reassured her.

The deli boy returned with a mop and bucket on wheels. "Oh no, I can't allow you to," Charlotte said. "This is our mess." Without warning, she thrust Wesley back at Roberta; he eyed her warily but, thankfully, this time did not howl. To everyone's surprise, Charlotte relieved the boy of the mop. As she mopped the floor with brisk, efficient sweeps, Roberta got a good look at both boys. They had large cornflower-blue eyes like their mother's and thick brown hair that must have come from their father.

"Thank you again for your help," Charlotte said when she was done. She eyed Roberta's tailored suit and white blouse. "I hope Wesley didn't get any egg on you."

"No, no. It was no trouble at all," Roberta said, stooping to pick up her small basket of vegetables. It looked lonely compared to the teeming cart Charlotte strapped Wesley into and took hold of.

As she made her way down the aisle away from the little family, Roberta heard her name. She turned.

There was that smile again. "Are you free this Thursday night?"

Roberta fumbled with her basket. "Free?"

Charlotte pushed her cart closer. "I host a bridge game. You must come."

"Oh, I couldn't possibly."

Charlotte grinned. "Don't be ridiculous."

If anyone had taken the time to actually notice Roberta, they might have called her several things. But "ridiculous" was not one of them.

Charlotte was not taking no for an answer. "We start at seven. Do you play?"

She did not, but from then on Roberta spent every Thursday evening at Charlotte's dining room table with a group of eight women who seemed to like being there. Roberta had learned there was no denying Charlotte Combs.

But Roberta was a quick study, and she found herself almost enjoying the group, despite how vastly different they were from her. All were married and mothers. Janice Garvey was a high school English teacher, and Marie Dennis worked at the town clerk's office, but the rest stayed at home with their young broods. It was exactly the kind of group that normally would have set up the hair on the back of Roberta's neck. Roberta preferred her own company. She held zero interest in the exchange of Crock-Pot recipes and found idle chitchat migraine-inducing. Nor did she have a spouse to complain about, something many in the group approached like a sport. In fact, as far as Roberta could tell, the others behaved as if they'd been sprung from some domestic prison for the night. There was spiked punch and finger food and always some kind of baked-good contribution. Roberta did not bake. But she allowed herself to partake in the offerings. It was the eighties and the entertaining was easy, if completely foreign to Roberta.

As the weeks passed, Roberta found herself holding her breath in anticipation of Charlotte's bridge club. To her surprise, the women did not make her feel one bit excluded. If anything, Roberta felt somewhat revered. Of course, that had much to do with Charlotte, who had artfully set the tone from the beginning, causing Roberta to blush. "This is my dear friend Roberta, and she's kind of a big deal. She's a judge." Which set off a wave of exclamations across the room. But what rang loudest in Roberta's ears was what Charlotte had called her: "my dear friend." Besides her insufferable sister, Roberta had never had someone to call a real friend. Forget one as stylish and irresistable as Charlotte.

When the game nights ended, Roberta found herself lingering after the others left. She was drawn to something about Charlotte Combs's house: perhaps it was the effortless glamor that Charlotte gave off, from her red flared pants to the gold cuff bracelets she favored—so different from Roberta's sensible loafers and bland suits. Maybe it was the warmth of her home, a stately antique farmhouse that, upon closer inspection, defied subtlety: a purple velvet Victorian fainting couch in the corner, silver candlesticks on every table, heavy damask curtains the color of an August moon. Pops of Charlotte's urban upbringing winked throughout the farmhouse like hidden treasures for the discerning eye. Even her husband, Alder, someone Roberta had thought of as just another politician, was intriguing. He rarely made an appearance at the all-female card game, but when he did, Roberta could feel the ardor he held for his wife. It filled the room as surely as the tall man himself.

Roberta didn't get invited to many parties, but she knew enough not to be one of those who overstayed their welcome. So she made herself useful. Against Charlotte's objections, she'd station herself at the kitchen sink, rinsing the diminutive crystal punch glasses that Charlotte told her had come from her parents in New York as a wedding gift. "They don't come out much," Charlotte confided. "Oh, they love the kids, of course. But they never really understood what drew me out of the city full-time." Or Roberta would wrap the leftover food on platters and tuck them carefully into the fridge. "Bertie, really. You don't need to do this." But Roberta did. No one had ever called her Bertie before.

After, Charlotte would invite Roberta to the living room for a cup of tea; Charlotte would curl up on one corner of the sofa and tuck her knees under her chin, childlike. She was a waifish thing, and despite her tanned complexion and the strong arms that swept the boys up like they were weightless, Roberta noted a fragility to her.

"What did you think of Penny's news?" Charlotte asked wearily one night. Penny Leary had stunned the group midway through the game with the sudden announcement of her impending divorce, a move that led to a heavy hush in the room before a flood of questions. Roberta remained silent, but she ached for Penny Leary. Divorce was not new, of course, but in a small Connecticut town in the eighties it wasn't the norm. As for Roberta, divorce cases didn't come through her courtroom, but often the fallout did, in the form of custody hearings and financial cases. She'd listened in silence as Penny poured out her heart and then stopped abruptly and turned to ask for a refill of punch. Despite the hugs and advice offered, the evening had turned solemn, and there was no repackaging it after that. The game had ended early, and as the headlights went on and cars backed down the driveway into the night, Roberta imagined the others rushing home to hug their husbands. To make promises. To seek assurances. In case Penny's situation might be contagious.

"It's very sad," Roberta mused, staring at her own ringless left hand. "Unfortunately, I hear plenty of domestic cases in my courtroom. Though I'm sure it won't come to that," she added quickly.

Even Charlotte seemed down, her bright spark dimmer than Roberta had seen. She sipped her tea, then stood abruptly and crossed the room to the bar cart. "Want some in yours?" she asked. Roberta watched as she poured some brandy into her cup.

"Oh, no, thank you." Roberta had to drive home. She also had to get up and work the next morning. She watched as Charlotte returned to the couch.

"You know something?" Charlotte asked.

"What's that?"

Charlotte let her head rest against the back of the couch. "We're a lot alike, you and I."

Roberta clutched her mug. She didn't know what to say to that. Oh, she longed for it to be true, but she hadn't the faintest idea what Charlotte was getting at. They just weren't.

"We are," Charlotte said, lifting her head to meet her friend's gaze. It was as if she could read Roberta's mind.

Roberta cleared her throat, shaken. "How's that?"

Charlotte hesitated, then smiled sadly. "We're both outsiders here."

Roberta stiffened. This was not what she'd expected to hear. *No,* she wanted to cry out. *You are on the inside. You've brought me to the inside, too.* A feat Roberta had, her whole unexciting life, thought impossible. "What do you mean?"

Charlotte lifted one shoulder. "This town. It's a happy little town, for sure. But they stick together, they do. We didn't grow up here. We're not like them, and we never will be."

It was the first time Roberta had heard Charlotte utter anything less than plucky. She, who invited everyone into her home, who insisted they stay and play awhile. Who turned up the music and kept the conversations going. Who made a complete stranger like Roberta feel like a part of an established gang. Roberta realized she had fallen in love with Charlotte in a way that she had always wished she could fall in love with herself. The person she wished she could see, *could be,* when she looked in the mirror as a fourteen-year-old girl and saw the freckled nose and the dark blunt bangs that framed a perfectly forgettable face. In Charlotte's company, Roberta felt she belonged, like she was seen. Now, to hear her refer to the both of them as outsiders split something deep within that had only recently healed.

"But everyone here loves you," Roberta began.

Charlotte laughed, softly at first, then gruffly as she sat up and loosened her ponytail. Her blond hair fell about her shoulders. She shook her head. "Love. What a curious thing to call it."

She rose then, and Roberta, feeling unsure of herself, stood, too. Charlotte closed the space between them and Roberta held her breath. Maybe it was the brandy. Maybe something Penny Leary had stirred up. Charlotte stopped in front of her. "Good night, Bertie. Thanks for coming." She relieved Roberta of her mug and brushed her cheek with her lips. "I'll call you in the morning."

Roberta drove home with her insides mixing. She'd never known anyone like Charlotte Combs. When she rested her head on her pillow that night, she felt as uneasy as she imagined all the wives at bridge had felt that night after Penny Leary's confession. But Roberta feared losing Charlotte.

Charlotte did call in the morning. Her voice was bright and crisp on the line, like usual. "Bertie! How'd you like to come by next Saturday? It's Wendell's birthday."

And just like that, Roberta's equilibrium was restored.

Their friendship went that way from then on. A visceral necessary thing that Roberta treasured. Roberta grew to know and love the boys. She attended family gatherings and sometimes even holidays. Their lives, different as they were, became interwoven as much by their friendship as by the nature of being neighbors in a small town. Eventually, she began to catch the scent of what Charlotte had warned her about: they were not like everyone else. But it would be years before she really understood what that meant.

Now, as Charlotte's oldest boy pulled up alongside her in his blue truck and rolled down his window, Roberta smiled. "Wendell. How are you?"

His blue eyes smiled back. "Doing fine, thanks, Bertie. How about you?"

"Oh, I'm hanging in there, as much as an old lady can."

Wendell didn't say anything, but his eyes crinkled kindly. He'd always been a quiet boy.

"How's work at the Lancaster place?"

"Busy. The gala is tonight." He leaned out the window. "Why aren't you in your gown?"

Roberta smiled. The gala. She'd never been, though an invitation appeared in her mailbox around this time every year. She knew it was Wendell's doing. "Going to have to miss this year," she said. "My tiara is still at the jeweler being polished."

Wendell nodded. He didn't expect her to attend any more than he would've himself, though she appreciated the invitation every summer.

"Quite the controversy this year, with the land acquisition disagreements in town," she said. "Has it had an impact on attendance?"

Wendell shook his head. "No, ma'am. Party is larger than ever." It made Roberta wonder. For a small town, recently divided over the very land use the party was raising funds for, she couldn't imagine where the supporters came from. She wondered if they were pulling friends from New York. She hoped not. Last year the *New York Times* had listed Saybrook as New England's "best-kept secret." She loved the *Times* but really wished they hadn't: locals wanted to keep it that way.

"Wendell, when can you come for dinner? I'm not getting any younger."

Roberta felt a duty to issue such invitations: she'd promised Charlotte to keep an eye on her boys. And after what had happened with Wesley, well . . . Roberta wouldn't allow herself to think much more on that. It was the only time she thanked God Charlotte wasn't alive to have to endure that.

As Wendell glanced uncomfortably over her head at the treetops, she prepared for the usual polite refusal. "Now, I know you're busy, and this time of summer is especially so. But what about an early dinner next Saturday on my patio? I grill a mean steak."

It was all a lie. Roberta was a vegetarian, and the only thing she grilled with any measure of success was corn. No matter; if she could get the boy to come over, she'd set him to the task. Men seemed to like to be in charge of primal things like fire and red meat.

"All right, Bertie. Dinner would be nice."

Roberta almost fell over. That was the thing: Roberta knew Wendell Combs was as much a loner as she was, but it *would* be nice. Not just out of obligation to his mother's memory. He was the one person in her life Roberta worried over.

She wagged a finger between them. "Was it the red meat?"

He laughed, and she rapped the hood of his truck. "Six o'clock, next Saturday. Don't make me wait."

Back inside, she put the kettle on for tea and considered the ticking grandfather clock in the corner. Roberta had lived alone the whole of her adult life; never married, never had kids. She'd been retired, as she told people, nearly fourteen years. These days there was nothing but time.

What she didn't tell people was how much she missed her job as probate judge. Having never had a family of her own, Roberta had thought of her work in the family court system as serving the greater *family* of her local county. The work was not pleasant, no. There were drawn-out custody hearings, the ones that pressed against her heart the hardest. Long-settled divorces that reentered her courtroom over revocation of rights. Disputes over trusts and estates. That was the thing about family court: the families who entered her courtroom barely qualified as such.

As gritty as the work could be, it filled her with a sense of purpose in preserving family. Not having one of her own was an advantage, in her mind. Roberta was unbiased. Her empathies did not automatically tilt in the direction of the young mother because she had been one herself. She did not pretend to possess knowledge of how difficult it was to balance the caregiving responsibilities with the funds available in a family bank account. Exempt from long nights nursing a sick child, caring for an elderly parent, or covering for a drunk spouse, Roberta had unprejudiced opinions. While other colleagues might have considered her personal lack of family experience a hardship in her line of work, Roberta believed it lent her judgment clarity.

For twenty years she'd been elected to office. That meant something. And she'd have stayed on as Saybrook's judge for many more, if things had gone differently.

If five-year-old Layla Bruzi's custody case had never come through the door of her courtroom. If she'd only listened to her gut.

Judge Roberta Blythe did not always get things right; over her esteemed career, there had been a handful of cases she might have ruled on somewhat differently when new evidence came to light. And there were a couple of cases she later had to revisit. But the Bruzi case was neither. It was the one that had not just ended her career; it was the one that would haunt her for the rest of her life.

Four

Wendell

Preparations for the gala had consumed Wendell's day. The White Pines lawns had been mowed so pristinely they appeared as a rolling green carpet just vacuumed. Not so much as a leaf tumbled across their lush sprawl. Freshly trimmed hedges draped in white lights flanked the driveway, leading a twinkling path up to the main house. Smartly dressed valets stood by in the circular drive awaiting incoming guests, and behind the main house, the peaks of white tents soared against the remnants of blue sky like sails. Wendell followed the cobblestone walkway to the rear of the house, noting that his crew, Jerry and Hank, had done a sound job power-washing and sweeping. He was pleased to see that the patio setup was complete. It had seen a lot of traffic in the last twenty-four hours. The event company had carried in and arranged all the tables and chairs, along with electrical cords for speakers and lights. There had been some minor disruption to the adjacent garden beds, but thankfully, Wendell's crew had seen to a final tidying of every nook and cranny. As he was ticking off the last items on his to-do list, the party planner, Josephine, started hooting from the top of a ladder at the edge of the garden: "You! Over here." Wendell glanced up to where she teetered on the top step, in orange heels, no less. "There's a problem!"

In Wendell's opinion, there was more than one, but he was not about to waste his breath. Josephine Applegate was apparently some kind of big deal in Litchfield County. She seemed to be under the mistaken impression that Wendell worked for her. "I need you," she called, though he was already moving in her direction.

Wendell looked up to where Josephine was hanging Japanese lanterns. He really hoped she wasn't stringing them too tight; the pear tree leaves were delicate at this time of year. "What seems to be the problem?"

Josephine grasped the nearest lantern and shook it urgently. "There's no power." Her eyes were wide and frantic.

Wendell was used to this. The Lancasters, who were a much bigger deal than the likes of Josephine Applegate, made entertaining look effortless, but no matter how laid-back they were, their event planners were not. He could never understand why people got so worked up over party decorations. "I checked the lines earlier. It may be a fuse."

Josephine stared down at him. "And?"

At this proximity, Wendell noticed her lips were the same shade of orange as her ridiculous shoes. "And I will check on that for you."

"Right now, yes?"

Wendell would have very much liked to leave Josephine Applegate teetering right where she was. But although he did not work for the likes of Josephine, he did work for Alan. And he knew this would upset Anne, which meant it would upset Alan. Without another word, he turned on his heel.

"Wait! Where are you going?" she shrieked.

He didn't reply. At that moment what bothered him more than Josephine Applegate was that he'd have to go through the main house. In all the years that he'd worked for Alan Lancaster and his family, Wendell had made a point to stay out of the house. As he saw it, his job was to manage what was on the outside. Whatever happened on the inside was up to them. But the Lancasters, being who they were, made that difficult. They were always trying to bring him into the fold. Once, when Alan was away, Wendell had helped Anne carry in a large tufted sofa that the furniture company's delivery truck had inexplicably unloaded and left in the driveway. She'd been so grateful for his help that she'd asked him to stay for a lemonade. It was homemade, just like his mother used to make when he was a boy, and the fresh pulp and grit of sugar on his tongue almost brought tears to his eyes. The memory and the kind look in Anne's eyes were too much; he'd gotten out of there as fast as he could.

Another time, after Alan had deduced that Wendell had no family of his own, they'd invited him to Thanksgiving dinner. Wendell had been flummoxed. He had one good suit, and he hadn't worn it since Wesley's funeral. He could not imagine being more out of place than at their sweeping walnut table, laden with crystal and fine china and candlelight. Alan and Anne would preside at either end, as cemented in their happiness as one of those wedding-cake-topper couples. And the girls. For some reason those little girls had always followed him around, though Wendell could not for the life of himself imagine why. At least on the estate he could avoid them, walk faster, stay busy. But there would be no escaping them in their own living room.

Wendell dreaded the invitation right up to Thanksgiving morning, almost begging off with an excuse of stomach upset. But he was honest, if nothing else. The meal had been rich and hearty, the family's conversation boisterous, and by the time dessert was served, he'd almost begun to enjoy himself. But after, when the girls ran off to play outdoors and Alan carried out a tray of steaming Irish coffees by the fireplace, Anne had asked about his own family. Wendell felt himself sinking into the buttery recess of the leather armchair, struggling to keep his breath even. He'd choked down the rich drink and excused himself abruptly, burning with shame as he pulled the front door closed behind him. He could not mix business with pleasure, he chided himself on the drive home. For him, there could be no pleasure.

Now he knocked on the front door. No one answered. Alan had told him to come and go as he needed that day, so, reluctantly, Wendell let himself in. He headed through the foyer, keeping his head down. He really hoped it was just a matter of resetting one of the breakers in the fuse box. He was just about to turn down the hall for the basement door when Anne caught sight of him from the kitchen. "Wendell! Come in."

He froze, looking down at his work boots, then up at Anne. She was a vision in a slip of a white dress, her hair pulled up and her face aglow. But there was a furrow in her brow. She pointed to a half-collapsed tripod in front of her. "Would you please give me a hand? I can't get the darn thing to stay up. And Alan and the girls aren't even dressed for the family photo."

Gingerly, Wendell joined her, praying he had stomped his boots hard enough outside not to track any dirt. He caught a flurry of pink dash by. There was the little one, Pippa, in a fancy dress. She grinned at him, then ducked behind her mother, who was still focused on the buckled tripod. Anne tugged at one leg, then the other, her cheeks flushed. "This stupid thing." She was not quite ready to hand it over, and so he stood to the side, trying to keep a straight face. "Oh, hell." She stepped away and blew a tendril of hair out of her face, looking suddenly like a little girl herself.

"May I?" he asked.

"Please. But if you can't get it to work, I get dibs on smashing the damn thing." This time he did not hide his smile.

There were clips on each leg she hadn't noticed, but he fiddled with them a good while, so as not to show her up. "It's tricky," he fibbed. Then he extended the legs and screwed each clip tight, almost afraid to meet her gaze.

She cocked her head. "Well."

"You would've figured it out, I'm sure . . ."

"Liar." But Anne recovered quickly and laughed. "Thank you. Now don't let me keep you from whatever it is you were trying to do."

Wendell headed back down the hall and into the basement. Sure enough, there was a blown fuse in the box, a simple fix that filled him with relief. It was when he passed the living room on his way out that he stopped in his tracks.

By then the whole family had gathered in the living room for the photo. Eliza, Anne's assistant, stood behind the camera and the tripod he'd helped set up. Wendell watched Pippa wiggle and fidget. Julia stood beside her mother in a summer dress, a foreign creature out of her usual riding clothes and jeans. She was as tall as Anne and threatening to be almost as beautiful. Wendell appreciated the slight curl of teenage disdain to her mouth as Eliza directed her to smile "like she meant it." Alan seemed as unperturbed as he was thrilled by all of it, arms wrapped tightly around his three girls, that crazy dog of his leaping about at their feet. Frozen, Wendell took it all in.

"Smile!" Eliza instructed one last time, and when the flash went off, Wendell saw stars.

Outside, he scanned the scene with military-like focus. Tall vases of hydrangeas had been set on each linen tabletop. The musicians were setting up in the gazebo. A faint plume of smoke billowed from the catering tent, delivering the scents of the lavish summer menu, causing his mouth to water. What pleased him most was that none of it could compete with the spectacular view of White

Pines. Beyond the patio and all its trappings were the rolling fields, green and gold. Crisscrossed by the occasional tumble of New England stone wall, the view was tamed, then wild again, and it left Wendell with a deep sense of peace. It was the best tribute to an evening devoted to land conservation, and though Wendell was not a political man, the ruralness of his hometown mattered very deeply to him. He felt good about his contribution.

He was on his way out when the first guests trickled in. There was Donald Hungerford, the town's first selectman, and his wife, Estelle. The position had changed a good deal since Wendell's father held it, but Don was a fair man who worked closely with the citizens of Saybrook, and Wendell liked him quite a bit. Right away Wendell recognized the president of the bank, Tim Gordon. The man had donned a white tux, dressed more formally than most. Tim had denied Wendell a home equity loan when he first inherited the family farmhouse and wanted to repair the roof; Wendell had been fresh from Afghanistan without a job or savings. On the way out of their meeting, Clara Wintonberry, the longtime bank teller who'd been friends with his mother, averted her gaze before marching back into Tim's office. A day later, Wendell got a call that there'd been some kind of error and the loan had been approved.

The guests were really flooding in now, and among them Wendell spied the chairwoman of the historical society, Gloria Rose; the library director; and the head of the Candlewood Lake Authority. They were as known as some of the celebrity-caliber weekenders of Saybrook: the choreographer of the New York City Ballet, a morning news anchor from NBC Studios, a journalist for the *Wall Street Journal.* They were regulars, and while Wendell knew none of them personally, thanks to the size and nature of Saybrook, he knew many of them. He had to give it to Alan Lancaster: the man drew everyone from every corner, and he was as well connected as he was respected. From years of watching his own father, Wendell could appreciate the challenge of that achievement.

When he was sure things were going as planned, he stole away down a side path to the lower barns and climbed into his truck. Wendell adjusted his rearview mirror. In it was the shimmer of the setting sun and the white tents and the twinkling lights. The upper pasture sparkled with row after row of shiny cars. The party would roll late into the night, possibly into the early-morning hours of tomorrow. His work here was done.

Back in his own driveway, Wendell breathed a sigh of relief as he pulled up to the house. When he cut the engine, he sat a moment, staring up at the farmhouse.

He'd inherited it years ago, after his father passed away, but it still felt strange to him, the only surviving member of his family.

From the beginning, Wendell hadn't been sure he'd wanted it, so full of memories it was. But he kept it up, at first in memory of his mother, and later as a sense of obligation to his father. And it was worth a pretty penny now, sitting on ten acres of land just outside the town center. Over the years, he'd had more than a few offers for it, several times from out-of-towners who happened by it on a Sunday drive. Those offers were met with the same reply each time: a blank look from Wendell and the squeak of hinges as the door swung shut in their faces. He was not a rude person, but it got under his skin every time. Wendell did not need the four lofty bedrooms that spanned the whole of the upstairs. Nor did he need the open kitchen with the original woodstove or the wraparound porch or the formal parlor his mother had insisted be added to the side. But even less did he need other people's money or opinions.

True, it was the place where his mother had died. It was also the last place the whole family had been together, before Wesley had gotten it in his head that he needed to enlist in the National Guard and serve his country overseas. Wendell did not believe those were the reasons that rooted him to the property, but he also couldn't say they were not. One thing he'd learned since being in Afghanistan: there were some questions that did not require answers. Sometimes you just did what you thought was the right thing in the moment. Sometimes that was the only thing you could do.

He made his way down the side walkway to the back door and into the kitchen. Nothing in the house had changed since his childhood, and he liked it that way. The kitchen wallpaper was a blue chintz design his mother had favored. He hung his truck keys on the same rack his parents had used by the door. Wesley's room was as he'd left it: navy blue walls, pine bunk bed. In the downstairs parlor, which his father had used as an office, the mahogany desk still stood in the corner. How many meetings had his father held at that desk that Wendell overheard as a child?

As first selectman of Saybrook, Wendell's father had always been a fair man, in his son's estimation, but it was different viewing a man through a child's eyes than as an adult. He'd been a politician, and even fair ones had to bend and flex, he often told Wendell.

Of all the memories of his father managing negotiations, there had never been more than the year before the breast cancer took his mother away from them. Charlotte Combs had fought long and hard, but in the end, when the cancer had won, she'd insisted to the doctors that she come home to die. On her terms, she'd said. As devoted as Alder was to Charlotte, he could not escape his work at the town hall entirely. As life would have it, he was also wrapped up in a town development project involving a particular piece of open space that Charlotte was very fond of, called the Town Meadows.

The Town Meadows was a place Charlotte had taken her boys

all throughout their childhood: to sled down its hills and skate across its pond in winter, to picnic in summer, and to hike its wooded trails in the fall. Her favorite thing to do was to take the boys fishing and hunt for spotted turtles. For hours she'd crouch at the pond's edge, showing the boys how to locate them among the rocks and cattails. The spotted turtles were so rare they'd been feared almost extinct, but they'd begun to thrive in recent years in that section of protected parkland.

That summer, however, a developer from Hartford had made the town an offer to purchase it. A sprawling suburban development, the first Saybrook had seen, was proposed dead center in the meadows. The woods would be felled and the pond drained. Thirty-six lots for a series of vinyl-sided boxy Cape-style houses, each as uniform as the one before it, would fit the tract-style pop-up neighborhood. Not many in town were happy.

Despite her frail condition, Wendell's mother was among the most outraged. "They cannot dig up that field and fill it with such ugliness. You cannot let them, Alder," she'd cried from her bed. "What about the turtles?"

"Yes, darling. The DEP is on it. They've got state biologists coming in to do a count."

Wendell's mother was not done. She propped herself up on shaky arms. "Those turtles are special, Alder. You must fight this."

Wendell could see the pain in his father's face as he tried to placate his wife. "It's all right, darling. The development will probably never get passed, even if it does come down to a vote. Now, let yourself get some rest."

Wendell watched as she collapsed against her pillows. His father stayed beside her, pressing a cold washcloth to her forehead as she fretted. When she finally settled, his father came out to the hall looking weary. He always looked weary these days after being with her.

"I have to go to that meeting tonight at town hall," he told Wendell. "Look after your mother."

Wendell could not believe his father was leaving for a meeting. Their mother was fading before their eyes, especially in recent days, and he feared being alone with her almost as much as he feared the ticking of the clock.

"Are you going to stop the development?" he asked.

"It's not up to me, son. I'll do my best. But it's a board vote, and I'm just one."

"But what about Mom's turtles?" Wendell's childhood memories with his mother ran strong through those meadows. He might not otherwise have felt as passionate about them as she did, but given her poor health, preserving them was about far more than preserving the turtles.

His father loosened his tie. There were deep bags under his eyes. "There are some things your mother doesn't understand."

Wendell was too respectful to voice his disagreement, but his father was dead wrong. Despite the hundred ways her body was failing her, there was nothing wrong with his mother's mind.

Later that night, when his father came home, Wendell passed their room on his way to bed. On the other side of the door, he heard his mother's whispery voice. She'd insisted on staying awake until his father returned. "Jane McNeill called. She said there was a vote tonight."

Jane McNeill was a friend of his mother's and a town busybody. But he could tell by the look on his father's face when he came home that Jane was right. Wendell paused, waiting for his father to say the right thing. Through the crack in the door, he watched him sink onto the edge of the bed. "Jane McNeill doesn't know what she's talking about," he said softly. "Don't you worry, I'm taking care of it."

His mother looked up at his father, a mere bird beneath the

blankets, and Wendell waited for her to say more. But her eyelids fluttered. Wendell watched his father take her hand and press it to his lips. The look on his face made Wendell swallow hard. "Get some rest, my love."

There had been a vote. Later, Wendell would learn that money was exchanged and the aforementioned DEP file was buried, along with the plight of the spotted turtles. But if his father could not protect the turtles, he did everything he could to protect his wife. Wendell was never sure how he managed it, but he held the contractors off and out of the town meadows all through that spring, as his mother grew sicker and sicker. Permits were stalled. Paperwork was misplaced. And all the while Charlotte Combs faded.

She'd been laid to rest in the cemetery for just a week when the first dozer clambered up the grassy flank of the meadow and broke ground. Somehow his father had kept them at bay just long enough. Wendell supposed that was love.

Five

Ginny

Could a thirty-five-year-old woman ever really go home? Ginny turned the radio down as she crested the final hill to Saybrook and slowed to take in the view.

Ahead, the sun hovered over the horizon, casting everything beneath it in a bath of gold. Ginny couldn't help it: the idyllic view took her breath away now just as it had years ago, and she steered her VW Beetle to the side of the road so she could take it all in. Flanked by rolling green hills on either side, Candlewood Lake shimmered like a silver ribbon in the distance. The small village of Saybrook stretched along its shoreline. "It's nice that some things don't change," she whispered to herself, sliding her sunglasses up on her head.

She could trace her entire childhood at the base of this hill. White church steeples and red barns jutted out of the greenery. There was Main Street, dotted by familiar shops: the Hickory Stick bookstore, Haven's Bakery, and Sacred Grounds coffee. Among the quaint village shops was her parents' real estate business, Feldman Agency. Though she couldn't see it from the hilltop, outside the village center were the library and Saybrook Elementary, where she'd gone to school. Beyond, tucked among the New England greenery, looped a tangle of rural country roads that she knew like the back of her hand: leading to the homes of childhood friends, the town beach, the winery at the northern point on the lake. All of it glittered in the late-day sun like a promise, and Ginny tried to reassure herself that it was a sign. A grown woman could go home. Even if she didn't really want to be there, there was nothing like summer in Connecticut's lake region.

Reluctantly, she put the car in drive and pulled back onto the main road. Time to face facts. The rental cottage she'd arranged for the summer was only five miles from her parents' place and right on the water. She loved her parents, but there was no need to press her already questionable luck and cram in together under the same roof.

"I don't understand," her mother had complained. "You have a perfectly good bedroom waiting for you. I even left all your high school posters on the wall!" Which was precisely why Ginny would *not* be staying with them. Aside from the far more important fact that her father was still recovering from heart surgery. A small detail her mother had sprung on her mere weeks ago, a week after the heart attack and days after the subsequent surgery. "He's fine, really. It was a bit of a scare, but we didn't want to worry you. Nothing a double bypass couldn't fix."

Ginny had been shocked. Not just by her mother's casual and late sharing of such dire news but by the realization that they hadn't wanted to *bother her* with it. "What?" her mother had asked in an exasperated phone voice when Ginny questioned why on earth they hadn't told her right away. "We knew you were already coming home. Why add to your stress?" It had left Ginny speechless.

It didn't matter that the doctor said he was in otherwise good shape, that he could expect a full life ahead of him with some dietary tweaks and a little exercise. If her parents had truly believed the news of his heart attack was best kept a secret for her own well-being, what did *that* say about the state of her life?

True, Ginny was in a bit of a transition, as her therapist had defined it. She had left her fiancé, her job, and her apartment in Chicago and driven halfway across the country to return home. But she was not a train wreck. The past year had been the real train wreck, when her fiancé of five years finally admitted that he was not just pushing off the wedding yet again—he actually did not want to get married at all. He was happy, however, to stay together and continue to live together as they had been the last four years. "It's just a piece of paper, Ginny. It doesn't mean anything." But the problem was, it did. To her. For five years she'd waited for Thomas to set a date. After all, he'd been the one who had proposed! At first he'd wanted to save up more money. Then, when they found a great deal on the Lincoln Park place, they couldn't afford to turn it down. So the wedding was delayed another year. "I want you to have the kind of wedding you've always dreamed of," he'd insisted. Which was kind of funny, really, because unlike plenty of brides, Ginny had never been caught up in the idea of a dream wedding. All she'd dreamed of was marrying Thomas. And so it went, year after year, while they attended the weddings of all their friends, and Ginny began dreading the repeated question, "When is it going to be your turn?" The wedding showers gave way to baby showers, and by then Thomas questioned if it even made sense to host a wedding. "Then let's elope!" Ginny had said. But after further consideration, Thomas would say something like "We'd miss having our friends there" or "My mother would never forgive me," to which Ginny thought, *What about me?*

That spring, when they'd returned home to their one-bedroom apartment from a friend's housewarming party celebrating new digs out in the suburbs and new twin babies, Ginny had tossed her purse on the couch and confronted Thomas. "We're never getting married, are we?" He'd looked perplexed, then offended. But when pressed, Thomas could give no real reason. They'd sat on the couch, shoulder to shoulder, staring out the window of their perfect one-bedroom, and split a bottle of wine. "It doesn't have to be this way," he'd said when she suggested moving out. "Then give me a date, Thomas," she'd countered. "Any date. Anywhere, you choose. Just give me a date in the next six months." When he couldn't, Ginny told him it was over.

After that, they'd listed the apartment. It took only a week to find a young couple happy to pay the full ask, while Thomas slept on the couch and Ginny stayed late at work, since, as it turned out, it really was the perfect apartment for a newlywed couple. Just not for them.

Ginny took advantage of her real estate connections and had just begun scouting rentals, in a rush to find a new place, when her boss called her into her office. "I'm sorry, but we're downsizing."

"I thought we were merging?" Ginny sputtered. She'd been working in commercial real estate in the city, for Cooper and Hayman, the second largest firm in Chicago.

"We are, but I'm afraid there isn't room to keep everyone. The new partners aren't willing to let me bring more than two agents with me." At least she'd looked pained as she broke the news. "You are one of my best. I'm sorry, Ginny."

The timing couldn't have been worse. But as she cleaned out her desk, Ginny picked up a small framed picture of her parents sitting on their family boat back home in Saybrook. Looking at it in that moment, it had occurred to Ginny that Thomas had not been her only problem. As much as she'd initially loved Chicago, her heart wasn't in the city anymore. She'd outgrown the bar scene and the nightlife. Her friends had all moved out to the plush suburbs of Highland Park and Hinsdale. She had no real connections in the city, outside of colleagues. And now she had no job.

The following week, as she and Thomas packed their belongings and divided up furniture, Ginny's mother had called with the news. "I don't want you to worry," she'd insisted. "There's nothing you can do here, and besides, you have enough going on in your life."

That was the problem. After a decade of throwing herself into her career, investing in the perfect urban home, and waiting for the promise of marriage, Ginny had absolutely nothing going on in her life. She'd played by the rules, and hard, and yet here she was, empty-handed. Without thinking, she blurted out, "I'm coming home."

"You're what?"

With the exception of the odd Thanksgiving holiday, it had been years since she'd been back to Saybrook. Her mother would have clicked her heels and done a backflip if she could have, but now she sounded wary. "No, honey, don't be ridiculous. Your father is on the mend, and the agency is just fine."

But Ginny knew she was fibbing. "Oh yeah? Who's running the show if you're home taking care of Dad and Dad is home recovering from a bypass?"

"Sheila. She's more than capable."

Ginny scoffed. "Sheila can barely answer the phone." It was true. The woman made a lovely grandmother to her sixteen local grandkids, but she couldn't work the fax or figure out the scanner and, according to Ginny's mother, hadn't sold a house in three years.

"Let me come help for the summer," Ginny said. "Just until you and Dad get back on your feet, and until I figure out what I want to do next."

Her mother paused. Ginny knew it was killing her. Her mother had petitioned for Ginny to come home ever since she'd left town over a decade ago. She left guilt-inspiring voicemails each holiday and sent passive-aggressive gifts, like the maple syrup from the local farm: "Since you've probably long forgotten what your childhood was like." But that was when everything was going well and everyone was in good health. Now, in a pinch, her mother did not like to accept help. "It's really not necessary, dear. We can manage."

But suddenly, Ginny wasn't so sure she could. For the first time since she'd left Saybrook, she had a pressing urge to go back. "Mom, please. Let me help." She did not say, "It would help me."

"Oh, honey. If you're sure." There was what Ginny thought was a teary pause, and then she was back. "Well, you'll be pleased to know that Sarah Dickerson is back in town. Wasn't she in your grade?"

Ginny rolled her eyes. "Sarah Dickerson was a jerk. Remember she stole my bike in second grade?"

"Oh. Well, she makes a decent cup of tea. She opened the cutest little café over in Bridgewater. And, of course, Wendell is still here. But I suppose you already knew that."

"Mom." Ginny did not know Wendell was still in Saybrook, though, if pressed, she couldn't imagine him anywhere else. In fact, she'd spent the first five years of her decade away trying not to imagine a single thing about Wendell. And then it didn't matter anymore, because Thomas had come into her life and by and large filled that void. In the beginning, at least. And not that there was any real *void,* per se. "It doesn't matter who's in town. That's not why I'm coming back."

"What?" her mother said, somewhat defensively. "I thought you should know."

"Mom."

"Sorry." Then, after a sigh, "But in case you're wondering . . ."

"Not wondering."

The other end of the line went uncomfortably quiet. Ginny could picture her mother pressing her lips together. Trying to bite her tongue. "Wendell is single." And failing.

"Got to go, Mom."

Within a week of selling her Chicago apartment and saying goodbye to the last decade of her life, Ginny had packed the car feeling the smallest flicker of hope. She was going home to help her parents with their firm and figure out her own next steps. It wasn't forever.

But as she turned east, Ginny's second thoughts began to whir along with each passing mile. By the time she'd crossed into Connecticut, the second thoughts had begun to whistle. Now, as she sailed down the last hill into Saybrook, they clanged like an alarm.

The sole stoplight in town was red, and she rested her head wearily on the steering wheel as she waited. She'd go to her parents' place first and say hello. Then she'd pick up the keys for her lake cottage and go check it out. Baby steps.

When she looked up, the light was still red. To her right, people were sitting outside Sacred Grounds drinking coffee at little tables. To her left, shoppers meandered along Main Street. Across the way was her parent's brick-front realty business, with its black shutters and cranberry-red door. Ginny stared at the wooden sign over the door, Feldman Agency, and a sense of nostalgia washed over her. It was a picturesque night, and she felt her breathing even out. A faded blue pickup truck crossed in front of her into the coffee shop parking lot. She didn't see many trucks like that in Chicago, she thought as she waited.

The truck door opened. It was a guy about her age. Rather fit and good-looking. *Well, maybe there's hope,* Ginny mused.

As the light went green, he turned her way; it was Wendell Combs.

Six

Julia

Julia slid her bedroom window up and perched on the window seat where she had a full view of the patio and gardens below. The party was almost over, and it had been nearly perfect. She was proud of her parents: after the controversies in town, the rumor had been that no one would come this year, and her family had proved them wrong.

Her father would be so pleased. She'd always known the Land Conservation Board was an important cause to him. But until this summer she hadn't known there were rumors throughout the community that he was also the largest donor. God, her parents could be so tight-lipped.

"Discreet," her mother had corrected her when she'd asked about it.

It annoyed Julia to no end. "I'm old enough to know things," she complained. "If you'd just tell me." Julia wasn't sure exactly how much land her family had purchased and donated back to the town over the years, but she'd come to realize it must be a lot.

She'd first learned of it that winter when she overheard a conversation during their Christmas party. Olivier Garrison, a neighbor and head of the Planning and Zoning Commission, had commented on her parents' gifts to the town a little too brashly over his snifter of brandy. "One hundred thirty acres on Wakeman Hill! Donated in full. Can only imagine what a pretty penny that cost you."

Her father's modest expression didn't waver in the firelight. "I can't say I know much about that." But one look at her mother's averted gaze, and Julia realized Mr. Garrison knew exactly what he was talking about.

"Oh, come on. Friends don't keep secrets," Mr. Garrison went on, clapping her father on the back. "I bet it was a nice write-off . . ."

Mrs. Garrison had placed a tactful hand on her husband's shirtsleeve and lifted her glass between them. "Well, *whoever* made the donation, it was terribly generous. The whole town will benefit."

Until then, Julia had simply thought of her parents as occasional volunteers, not much different from any of her friends' parents. They attended benefits. They supported local organizations. A few times a month, her mother helped to deliver meals to elderly citizens who were housebound. But it was overhearing that conversation as she sat on the back staircase that winter night when she fully understood their quiet contributions to the town. "Whatever you believe in, Jules, you have to get behind it," her father once told her. "Put your resources into it. I don't mean money. I mean your energy, your time, your voice: whatever you have. Everyone has something to give."

Since then, the more she paid attention to current events in Saybrook, the more Julia grew to be proud of her parents' philanthropy. But not everyone shared her sentiments.

A growing number in town didn't support some of the Lancasters' efforts. They opposed the increase in town-owned open space and the proposal to change from two- to four-acre zoning, which would increase lot size requirements and decrease new construction. "Open space will increase taxes," someone complained in a letter to the editor in the *Town Tribune*. "This town has always been trees and fields. What we need is more development." Others saw her parents' efforts as a garish display of their wealth: "Outsiders who come in and think they know better. We have plenty of land; what we need is less of them." Worse, some accused them of elitism: "Four-acre zoning is for the privileged. Hardworking blue-collar families won't be able to afford to live here. Are we shutting the gates to Saybrook now?"

Julia showed the letters to her mother. "Don't pay it any mind," she'd said reassuringly. "Your dad is doing good work. You can't please everyone."

Though her parents didn't speak of the local pushback in her presence, Julia had overheard their low conversations in the kitchen after town meetings. When word got out that the anonymous donor who'd hired masons to repave the library parking lot and put in a sidewalk with a handicap ramp was her dad, Julia suffered a few pointed stares in town.

"A bit fancy for Saybrook," one old-timer grumbled loudly enough for the two of them to hear as she and her father walked by. Julia wanted to turn around and ask him if he even knew where the library was, but her father put a firm hand on her shoulder and guided her to the car. "Everyone is entitled to voice their opinion," he whispered. But Julia noticed no one said a word when her parents donated a generator to the town hall, which served as a warming center for citizens during winter storms and power outages. Couldn't people see her family loved this town as much as they did? *Maybe even more,* she thought.

Then came the jokes at school. "Hey, Jules, maybe your dad could spring for a tent with some of those cooling fans?" one of her soccer teammates joked on a scorcher of a game day. "Nah, he can just buy us an ice cream truck," another said. Then, when Julia shot her a look, "What? Everyone likes ice cream."

It wasn't fair. Her parents' contributions were made quietly. There were no shiny plaques with their names emblazoned across them. Not even a handprint in the concrete of the new library sidewalk. Unlike her classmate, Emmy Fletcher, whose family business was slapped across the largest sponsorship banners in town. Julia had once overheard another parent quip, "Fletcher's sign cost more than the donation he made to the Little League." Julia had swung her gaze toward the neon green banner hanging on the fence: *"Lit up!" by Fletcher Electric.* Now, that was tacky.

The success of tonight's gala only confirmed her suspicions: her family's work in town was important. Below her window, the jazz band was still going strong, and the round high-top tables dressed in white linen had been abandoned for the dance floor. There had been grilled tenderloin, cucumber dill salad, steamed clams. When her father stood to make a speech, Julia had sneaked a flute of champagne from a passing waiter's tray. Just as she put the rim to her lips, her mother caught her eye from across the patio and raised an eyebrow.

But then she smiled and waved Julia over. "I guess you're old enough to share a toast with your mother." Julia raised her glass uncertainly, the golden flute swishing.

"To tonight," her mother said, her eyes twinkling. "To you, and to Pippa and Daddy."

"And you," Julia added. They clinked glasses, and Julia took a large swallow. The fizzy rush surprised her, and she sputtered.

"Easy, tiger," her mother warned. "Best to sip."

The champagne was drier than she'd expected, but it left a delicious sweet aftertaste. As they sat side by side, taking in the event and sipping from their flutes, Julia felt an easy warmth spread within her. Around eleven thirty, as the evening began to wind down, her mother suggested she go up to bed. Pippa was long ago passed out in her own bed. So with some reluctance, Julia had said her good nights, found her father in the crowd to kiss his cheek, and come up to her room.

But the night was not over yet. On her way upstairs, her phone dinged. It was Sam. "You awake?"

Now she left her bedroom window open and slipped out into the hallway.

Before sneaking downstairs, she peeked in on Pippa. Her little sister always looked so much younger in sleep, her blond hair fanned out like a wild pixie's across the pillow. Julia bent to kiss her forehead and tiptoed out.

Downstairs, she let herself out through the front door. With the party roaring out back, there was little chance anyone would notice her. There were two valets, both college-aged boys, sitting on the front stoop talking. The cuter of the two looked sideways at her and smiled as she slipped past. That sort of thing was happening more and more, she'd noticed. Julia shot him a smile back and headed for the side lawn. She'd have to go around the party to get to the trail, but she was careful to skirt the shadows, and soon she'd crossed the east lawn and stood at the edge of the woods.

As the band slipped into "Moonlight Serenade," she stole a look back. It was her parents' favorite song, one she'd heard a thousand times in her life. Even at that distance, she had a full view of the gala. Julia held her breath as she watched her father lead her mother to the middle of the dance floor. Others gathered around as the two spilled into each other's arms like water. Their love was so obvious, almost embarrassing.

Overcome by the night, Julia tipped her head back and laughed aloud. Then she spun back toward the woods. Behind her, the party glittered in the distance. Ahead, somewhere in the darkness, Sam was waiting. It felt like the whole world was hers to step into. She tugged her shoes off and ran.

Seven

Roberta

She'd fallen asleep reading on the couch. Something had startled her awake, and when she glanced at the grandfather clock, she was surprised to see it was one a.m.

Somewhere in the distance, the wail of a siren rang through the night. Roberta sat up. The siren rose outside her window, and she fettered the urge to stand up and go look. The firehouse was in the town center, a few miles away. There was nothing to see. But still, it filled Roberta with a sense of unease. It always did. Living in a small town meant it was likely someone she knew.

As the siren rose and fell, it was joined by another. *Fire truck*, she thought. Or maybe ambulance? It was too far off to be sure.

She rubbed her eyes and set her book on the coffee table. Maybe it was a false alarm. Or maybe someone had fallen in their home. As the sirens and trucks drew closer, she stood up and went to the window. She turned out the light. Sure enough, the stark glow of red lights filled the darkness up the road and spilled into her living room. She stood back as one, then another, fire truck roared by her little house. The walls shook with the reverberations. A moment later, an ambulance followed. Roberta stepped away from the window.

It had been fourteen years since she'd been to church, and if anyone asked, Roberta would tell them herself that religion was no longer for her.

But in times like this, her Catholicism rose involuntarily within her like a vine unfurling, and she didn't question it. In the dark, she did a quick Hail Mary. She hoped that everyone was all right. And that wherever the emergency vehicles were headed, they got there in time.

Eight

Wendell

The blast went off and Wendell jerked upright. Back arched, fists clenched, he screamed out in the darkness.

It was happening again.

Eyes wide, he scanned his surroundings. He was in his room, once his parents' room. In his childhood home. He was safe.

As he struggled against the heaving in his chest, Wendell fought to catch his breath. "It's over, it's not real," he repeated silently, like a mantra.

But the sudden roar of a siren outside his window caused Wendell to shudder involuntarily. Sirens: one of his worst triggers.

Heart still pounding, Wendell swung his legs over the side of the bed. The sheet was already soaked in sweat.

The last few years, his night terrors had quieted, and he'd almost allowed himself to believe he might finally have shed the worst of what haunted him. At least the night hours, just so he could lay his head on the pillow without fear of what darkness might bring. And for a while he had.

But lately, they'd begun to creep back in. Nothing like before, thankfully. He no longer awoke standing on the front porch in just his boxers, wondering how the hell he'd gotten there, how long he'd been outside. Nor did he feel like he might choke to death, something that used to happen when his heart raced so hard against his ribs that he passed out. Each time it felt like death was coming. That's what the whole first year home had been like.

Shakily, he stood and went to the bathroom to splash water on his face. This one was not bad, he told himself. It was just a siren from a fire truck. There was nothing for him to do, no one for him to try to save.

Wendell stared at his reflection in the mirror as the sirens grew louder. They were coming closer. He closed his eyes and opened them, forced himself to swallow. "Not for you," he whispered hoarsely to himself.

But he wondered.

He turned out the bathroom light and the bedroom fell again into darkness. A red flicker danced around the edges of the windows, slipped through his curtains. Wendell went to look out.

His family house was set on a green rise overlooking the corner where two roads met: to the side of the house ran a state road, and to the front, a quiet town lane. A series of trucks, lights flashing, were heading his way up the state road. Wendell held his breath as they slowed. One by one they turned sharply onto his lane. Where could they be going?

When the last of the trucks passed, Wendell stood a moment longer, following its light up the hill to where it rounded the corner and fell out of sight. Eventually, the sirens faded and the after-dark sounds of June again filled the night. Wendell closed the curtain and turned back to his bed. He would not sleep. He never could after an episode. But he lay down against the still-damp sheets and closed his eyes.

. . .

At daylight, the birdsong woke him. Wendell sat up, chilled but amazed; he'd fallen back to sleep. He showered quickly, let Trudy outside, and made quick work of breakfast. It was no more than a half hour later that he was pulling in to White Pines.

No doubt Alan would give him a hard time about coming in to work on a weekend, but Wendell couldn't help it. With the gala behind them, it was time to assess the damage. Having the catering and event-planning trucks on the property bothered him; they often did not leave the estate as they found it, and no doubt there would be garden beds trampled, tire marks in the lawns, and areas of grass to replant.

Now, as he turned up the main drive, a young girl outside the main house caught his eye. She staggered across the lawn, then fell to her knees. It was Julia. She heaved on all fours as if becoming sick. Wendell stopped the truck and got out. It was then he heard it: a keening wail, like that of coyotes at night.

The front door of the house flew open, and a dark-haired woman he did not recognize filled its frame. She hurried across the grass toward the child. Something was terribly wrong.

Wendell abandoned his truck in the driveway and began moving toward them. The woman stopped where Julia lay sprawled in the lawn and, after a moment's hesitation, bent beside her, placing her hand on the girl's back. If she'd been jolted by a shock of electricity, Julia could not have lurched more violently. She sprang up like a wounded animal, at the ready, and then ran. A sense of dread had coiled itself in his stomach, and without realizing it, Wendell found himself running, too.

"Julia?" he called. He quickened his pace.

. . .

Upon hearing his voice, the girl halted in the middle of the yard. Wendell did, too. Her mouth hung loose as if stuttered between expressions, her long hair wild about her face. For a ghostly moment she stared through him. Then, like a rabbit, she bolted. Across the yard, away from the woman and Wendell, too. Wendell remained frozen as he watched her tug the barn door ajar and disappear inside. By then the woman had come up beside him, and he turned to see it was the Lancasters' neighbor, Alison Walters. She'd been all dressed up with her husband at the party last night. Now her expression was drawn.

"Alison. What's going on?"

She wrung her hands. "They're gone," she said. "Both of them. Gone."

Alison was talking too fast. "Who is gone?"

"Alan and Anne."

"Gone?" Wendell shook his head. She wasn't making sense.

"They took the T-Bird out for a drive. After the party. The car was found this morning—crushed against a tree off High View." She gulped back a sob. "The poor girls . . ."

Wendell turned and stared at the vacuum of light streaming through the barn doorway, at the golden spill of dust motes roused from the hay-strewn floor. Beside him, Alison went on. "The girls just found out. We wanted family to be here with them, but I only know of one. There's an aunt. She's flying in from London tomorrow."

From inside the barn came the dense thud of a stall door being slammed. A squeak of a gate. Around the side of the barn, Radcliffe's bridled head emerged. Julia pulled herself up into the saddle and swung her leg over his back.

"Julia!" Alison cried upon seeing them. "Please, wait."

There was a flash of chestnut flank and golden hair, and then the pounding retreat of hoofbeats reverberating against the green morning.

The dirt beneath his feet seemed to tilt, and Wendell steadied himself against his senses, the smell of fresh-cut grass fermenting in his nostrils.

Nine

Roberta

Roberta had heard about it that first morning in the IGA market. She was standing in the produce section, selecting tomatoes for a garden salad she planned to make, when she learned of it.

"Their car went off the road up on High View," Mike Lanzi, the market owner, told Sherry Whiting, one of the local realtors. He shook his head sadly. "Such a tragedy. Both good people, both so young."

Sherry put a hand to her mouth and gasped. "I just saw them at the gala! What about the children?"

"They were home," he said softly. "Asleep in their beds."

Roberta tilted her head in their direction, wondering *who* had suffered such a terrible accident.

Sherry turned to her as if reading her thoughts. "Can you believe it? The poor Lancasters."

Roberta had set down her tomatoes and exited the store. *Wendell,* she'd thought.

She'd gotten straight in her car and called him from the front seat. His cell rang seven times, then went to voicemail. Wendell's voice was lilting, like his mom's, and tears pricked her eyes as she listened to the recording. But Roberta did not leave a message. She went home and put on her apron.

Whenever she was stressed, she ate. *A lot.* And since she couldn't very well eat for Wendell (though she'd done a bang-up job trying), she'd made him food. A roasted pepper-cheddar-chicken casserole she figured would fill a man up. The dish was still warm from the oven as she pulled it off the passenger seat of her car and carried it up the walkway to the front door. How long had it been since she'd walked up this path?

Before she could knock, Wendell opened the door. Roberta held up the tray and smiled sadly. "Sorry to drop in, but I wanted to bring you something."

He looked down at the casserole, then up at her in surprise.

"I heard about the Lancasters."

Wendell held the door for her.

They ate together on the porch in silence. After, Wendell mopped the last bit of creamy chicken off his plate and set his fork down. "That was delicious, Roberta. Thank you."

Like his plate, his work boots, she noticed, were polished spotless. She wondered if this was a habit left over from his years in the Guard.

Wendell eased back in his rocking chair. "I don't know what happened up there on that road. It's a terrible corner, sure. But Alan was a skilled driver. From the tractors on the property to the vintage sports cars, he could drive anything. And he was with Anne. No way would he have been going fast."

Roberta stared out at the green undulation of perfectly mowed lawn. It was as crisp as she imagined he kept the lawns at White Pines. "What will become of White Pines and the children?" she asked suddenly.

"There's just one relative, Alan's estranged sister," he said. "Candace Lancaster is her name. She's flying in from London. I guess we'll have to wait and see." Wendell looked down at his teacup, which she realized he hadn't touched. "There's already talk."

"I'd expect nothing less."

Roberta wished people would mind their own business, but facts were facts: the Lancasters were a big name in town.

The Lancasters' fingerprints were all over Saybrook. The library had been founded by Alan's grandfather. There was the village shopping center, with the IGA market, coffee shop and bakery, bookstore, and bank. The town marina, adjacent to the local beach, had recently had new docks put in. As it was, resident boat owners had to put their name in the lottery system just to get a slip. Only the summer before, the Village Playhouse, whose lavish productions were known to draw audiences from surrounding towns, had been revived with cedar shake shingles and a fresh coat of stark New England white paint. If Saybrook had been a charming New England village before, the renovations had delivered the past right to the present, straight out of the history books.

The Lancasters held positions on the Historical Society Board, funded the town's higher-education scholarship committee, served on the Candlewood Lake Water Safety Commission. While all of those boards would certainly survive without them, the Lancaster Foundation was a tremendous investor and supporter.

The first rumor was that the family foundation would maintain White Pines for the daughters, and they'd stay on with the mysterious aunt everyone was wondering about, finish school, and move on with their lives as best as two orphaned girls could. It was tragic, but at least they'd remain in the community and school system, where they were known and loved.

A close second rumor was that the estate would be turned into a nature preserve for the town, and the main house into some sort of museum. This, of course, was popular with many who loved the large property and had always longed for the opportunity to sniff around the gardens and cultivated nooks and crannies of a place many had only heard about from those who were invited or could afford to attend the social events held on the property over the years. As far as Roberta was concerned, there was a lot of nosiness behind that plan. Saybrook was lovely enough, and it was just plain selfish to sacrifice the home of two innocent children for a bunch of busybodies who were too cheap to pay for the garden-tour tickets the previous year. People should be ashamed of themselves.

She really hoped Wendell knew well enough to ignore all the talk. He'd been through enough in his young life as it was.

Later that night, as she sat on her screened-in porch with a book in her lap, Roberta's mind drifted. It had been a long day. As Roberta nodded off to the rhythm of the summer peepers, images filled her dreams. Two little girls in matching blue dresses stood in the middle of an overgrown field, their hair as fair as the bleached summer grass. They held hands, as if waiting for her. Roberta walked toward them. Suddenly, they turned away from her and, in a fit of giggles, disappeared into a small grove of trees. Worried, Roberta followed the sound of their voices. But without warning, the sky darkened. A brisk wind picked up, and out of the corner of her eye, she saw a flash of blue skirt among the trees. The giggling had stopped. "Girls?" she called softly. "It's okay. You can come out now." There was just the wind. She waited at the edge of the field, a feeling of dread growing. Roberta did not want to enter the forest. "Girls?" she called again. Still there was no answer. Somewhere ahead, a branch snapped. Roberta squinted into the shadows as a small figure emerged from the trees. It was neither of the Lancaster girls. This girl had short dark hair, her bangs cut in a jagged line across her forehead. Roberta recognized those bangs. That hollow gaze. She opened her mouth to scream, but no sound came out. There was only a loud crash.

Roberta startled awake. Her book had fallen from her lap and lay open on its spine. She put a shaky hand to her chest. "It's just a dream," she said aloud.

But there was no one there to confirm that. And besides, it wasn't the truth.

Ten

Julia

"I hate her," Julia said. There followed the scratch of pen on paper as Lottie made a note in her little green journal. Who even wrote in journals anymore?

To Julia's consternation, Lottie did not grimace nor look surprised. That was the thing: she never did. Julia wondered if anything she said would shock the middle-aged therapist. She doubted it. Not one hair of her perfectly coiffed bob was ever askew. Her dress shirts always looked starched. Just looking at her put-togetherness was infuriating.

Finally, Lottie looked up from her journal. "That's excellent."

Julia scoffed. "So, hating my aunt is okay with you?"

Lottie took her glasses off. That was another thing: before she said something important, she removed her glasses. As if that were a signal to Julia that she should lean in. Instead, Julia pulled her gaze away and stared out the window.

"Actually, Julia, this is all good. You're feeling something. And you're starting to express it. That's a long way from where we started quite suddenly."

That was a lie. There was no "we" in any of this. Lottie had not had her parents torn out of her life one perfect summer night like a page from an unfinished book. She didn't have a little sister who'd pretty much stopped speaking, who had started to look like the little orphan she was: a rag doll who followed Julia everywhere and climbed into her bed at night to cry. Lottie was not at the mercy of the only adult who'd come forward to take care of them, an aunt she barely knew and from whom her father was long estranged. His own sister! Who had arrived at White Pines, taken one brisk look at the property and the house and the two girls, and looked like she wished very much that she'd never been summoned.

The truth was there was so much to hate right now. The powder-blue T-Bird her father loved so much. The sharp corner of High View Lane. The ancient maple tree that grew at the edge of the turn.

But her aunt Candace was alive and breathing, standing by the kitchen stove where her father should have been each morning, sipping tea from a bone china cup her mother liked. Julia's hatred needed a target. For now, her aunt would do just fine.

"Julia, everything you're feeling is normal. Let yourself feel it, and don't worry if it's not what others might call socially acceptable. Right now isn't about that. It's about identifying what you're going through and forging a way." Lottie set the journal on her desk, signifying that their time was about up. "I'm proud of you."

Julia stared into her lap to hide the tears that pressed at the corners of each eye. Why did this woman have to be so nice? She liked Lottie, or at least she might have if they'd met under different circumstances. If she weren't someone to whom Julia and Pippa were dragged for these last unbearable weeks to talk about the most unbearable thing. Julia didn't want to talk. Talking about it meant that it was real. That she was learning to *accept* what had happened. That she would figure out how to *move on*. But Julia didn't want to do either of those things. She wanted her old life back.

• • •

Julia knew from the moment Aunt Candace arrived that she would not work out. The limo driver had carried her bags up the front steps and into the house, and Candace had followed. There she stood in the foyer, clutching a small gold purse, staring at the girls as if she'd never seen a child. Julia could find no trace of her father in Candace. Pippa had stood beside Julia, squeezing her big sister's hand, the thumb of her other hand jammed into her mouth, something that had started the day they learned of their parents' death. Regressing, Lottie called it.

"It's terrible what happened," Candace said finally, stepping toward the girls. "I am very sorry for you both."

Julia had stared back at this woman who was supposed to be her father's little sister, who had not opened her arms nor offered a shred of comfort, and known instantly just how awful this arrangement would be.

Eliza, who'd been staying with them from that first horrific day, stood behind both girls and nudged them forward. How Julia wished Eliza could stay.

The first night without her parents, Julia lay awake staring up at the ceiling as images flashed in her mind: the way her father's eyes crinkled in the corners when he laughed, her mother's gentle hands in Pippa's hair as she braided it. It did not seem real that they would never experience those things again; it wasn't possible.

Her parents were just here. And they still were. Everywhere in this house and on this property, she felt them. That night she lay awake until her eyelids felt like sand, until the ache in her bones grew dull with fatigue and she eventually fell into a fitful sleep. When she awoke a few hours later, Julia blinked at the sunlight streaming in through her curtains. Her first thought was that her stomach was growling. When had she last eaten? She sat up. And then she remembered.

She'd barely made it to the bathroom before she vomited. When she finished, she stood and rinsed her mouth out at the sink. The girl in the mirror was not the girl who'd done her hair for the gala, standing in this very spot only two nights ago. She was not the girl who'd watched her parents twirl on the dance floor, the last time she would ever see them both alive. Nor was she the girl who'd sneaked back across the lawns, the cold dew beneath her bare feet, after meeting Sam in the woods. The very same night he'd leaned in and pressed his lips against hers: her first kiss. Afterward, she'd raced home, stolen up the back stairs, and tumbled into her bed, thinking of the warmth of Sam's mouth, the tingle of his fingers intertwined with hers. How foolish. How selfish!

It was Eliza who had let herself into the quiet house at White Pines the morning after and broken the news. Poor Eliza, who'd been awakened by a frantic call from their neighbor, Mrs. Walters. The state trooper had gone to the Walters's house after unsuccessfully attempting to rouse anyone at White Pines. The trooper apologized to the disheveled Walterses and explained that he'd been trying to reach a member of Lancaster family, but no one had answered. Of course they had not. Pippa and Julia had been tucked in their beds, exhausted by the celebrations of the night and blissfully unaware of the unfolding tragedy on their doorstep. Thankfully, Mrs. Walters had known to call Eliza. She was the closest thing the girls had to family.

Since then, Eliza had not left their sides. She'd stayed the first two nights until Candace arrived from London. And even a couple after. Eliza rubbed Pippa's back for hours. She washed dishes; she heated up the meals that all the neighbors and friends and concerned citizens of Saybrook brought to their door. And when Julia's and Pippa's grief left them unable to stomach the rich quiches and casseroles and savory roasts, Eliza stepped into the kitchen and whipped up comfort food that they could eat: macaroni and cheese. Buttered pasta. Chicken noodle soup that Eliza brought up on a tray to their rooms. As if Julia were sick; as if this were something she would ever heal from. Those first few nights, Julia heard Eliza's voice, ripe with sadness as she spoke with Candace downstairs in the parlor, explaining the girls' schedules, likes, and dislikes. As if she could teach this strange new relative something about her own nieces that might somehow save them all. In the mornings, Eliza made their beds and laid out fresh clothes. She placed toothbrushes in their hands and ushered them into showers and gently brushed their hair. Throughout the house, she set out puzzles and board games and crayons and paper to distract them. Afternoons, she lured them out of doors to the front lawn and read aloud from picture books on the soft grass under the impossible cheer of the July sun. Mute and numb, the girls followed her through the day like little wards. But Julia knew Eliza could not stay forever.

The morning she packed her bag and hugged them goodbye, Julia's heart ached with fresh rawness. She couldn't bear the thought of being left with her aunt. From the moment she laid eyes on Candace's reedlike appearance, Julia doubted she cooked or ate, and soon enough her suspicions were confirmed. Candace's dishes were a gray meat and potato stew and some kind of lamb roast that Julia attempted to gum down and Pippa only stared at. Their days together were lonely; once they were dressed, Candace ushered them outside: "All right, then. Go play." As if they could. She spent most of her time on the phone, with what sounded like lawyers and board members. Julia heard terms like "executor of the estate," and there were hushed discussions about wills and assets and probate court. Julia didn't care; times like that, she escaped outside to the barn, where she could think and be alone for a few minutes. Whenever Julia returned from the barn, Candace asked her to wash her hands and change her clothes the moment she stepped over the threshold. "Horse smell," she'd sniff, wrinkling her nose. "You'd best shower."

At night, their aunt did not check on them after tucking them in, the way their parents had. And she had little tolerance for being awakened by a child with a bad dream. Very late on the first night the three of them were alone together, Julia's bedroom door swung open. Shielding her eyes from the spill of hallway light, Julia made out two silhouettes, one large and one small, in the doorway. Her aunt's voice was not unkind but also not patient.

"Go on, then, you may sleep with your sister." Since then, Pippa made a habit of coming to Julia in the middle of the night, wordlessly sliding beneath the sheets and curling herself around her big sister. There would be a few hiccups of tears until she settled. Then Julia would flip her damp pillow over, kiss her little sister's head, and pull her in close. She was all Pippa had now. She would have to be both parents to her.

Julia's friends were another story. They did not leave her alone, as her aunt did. They filled her phone with texts and calls, images of flowers and kittens and videos of sappy songs and sunsets. Julia turned her phone to Do Not Disturb. Chloe was the only one she could manage to speak to, and Julia asked her to spread the word that she did not, could not, talk to anyone right now. That she appreciated the outpouring of concern but that she needed to be alone.

But then Mrs. Fitzpatrick appeared at the front door with her arms loaded with flowers and pink boxes Julia recognized from Haven's Bakery. Candace invited them in.

"It's very nice to meet you," her aunt said, accepting the giant vase of flowers. But Mrs. F had eyes only for Julia, and the second she saw her, she unloaded the pastry boxes onto the nearest table and rushed her.

"Oh, sweetie," she said, weeping, pulling her in. Julia fell into the maternal hug, at once pillowy and strong and saturated with warm sadness.

Chloe was right behind her mother, and the two teens pressed their foreheads together when they embraced. "I'm so sorry, Jules. I'm *so* sorry."

Everyone was sorry. Which left Julia in the odd position of telling everyone who said it that it was okay when, really, nothing was. With Chloe, Julia did not say this. She nodded and cried, and swore under her breath, and let her best friend hold on to her.

Candace had stood in the background, watching with a pinched look of despair but also something else. Awkwardness, Julia thought. Pippa, having heard the fuss from her room upstairs, appeared at the bottom of the stairwell, and Mrs. F scooped her up, too. Julia was relieved when her aunt invited everyone to move into the living room to have some tea. What she lacked in maternal instinct, she possessed in manners.

They stayed awhile, sniffling between attempts at normal conversation, but it all felt forced and tiring, and Julia soon found herself wishing they would go. Chloe sat close beside her on the couch, squeezing her hand. They didn't go out to the barn to hang with Raddy, like usual. There was no pulling Chloe up to her bedroom to whisper about Sam's latest text or to giggle about school gossip. When they finally left, Julia stood at the front window watching the car go.

Without warning, her chest smarted with something like anger. Chloe got to go home with her mother. Back to her house, where everything was normal and everyone was accounted. Julia had been there hundreds of times, so she could picture the rest of their day: Mrs. F would make something good for dinner. Chloe and her little brother, Matt, would argue about who set the table and who fed the dog, but eventually, both chores would get done.

Mr. Fitzpatrick would wander in from work in his suit, his tie as loose as his smile. He'd be tired but happy, and they'd all sit down together to eat. *Together,* Julia had thought as she'd watched their car turn around a corner and disappear behind a stand of trees. It only made her miss her parents more.

The only person who did not make her feel worse was Sam. Since the morning after he'd texted. All day, each day. What Julia found she liked most about his messages was what Sam did *not* say to her. Sam did not ask how she was. He did not tell her it was going to be okay. Nor did he press her to reply, which she did only once: "I feel like I'm broken."

His reply came right away: "Because you are. But I'm here for you."

After that, Sam sent her texts instructing her to go down to the lake, where he would leave something for her. He understood she didn't want to see him yet. But still, he found ways to send tidings. There, in the sand at the base of their special rock, he left his messages.

"I miss you," written with a twig stuck in the sand.

"Beauty" next to a small bouquet of silvery bird feathers tied with a red string.

"Hope" etched into the mud beside a puddle filled with wildflower petals.

Each message a secret comfort to her soul.

Between comforting her sister and crying for herself, between trying to eat and trying to sleep, and navigating their aunt, who stood out in their family home like a foreign object, Julia found herself depending on Sam's messages. They were the only things that got her through each day. She woke to them in the morning. And she looked at them one last time before bed. Sam was her lifeline, even if she couldn't bring herself to see him yet.

"Why don't you want to see him?" Chloe asked.

"I can't. I just can't." It was true. There were too many reasons she could not.

First, there was the matter of Pippa, who sensed like a little wild animal if Julia's attention turned anywhere other than toward her. Pippa was skipping and coloring one minute, then sobbing the next. Julia could not leave her.

But it was more than just Pippa that kept her away from Sam. There was the gnawing terrible guilt she felt. He was the reason she'd sneaked out and left the house that night. The last time her parents were alive, Julia had not been sleeping in her room under the same roof, like she was supposed to be. Like they believed her to be. She'd been out in the woods with Sam.

All Julia knew about what happened after she sneaked out with Sam was that a little after midnight, her parents took a drive.

From what Eliza told the girls and the police, the last guests had just left the party, and she'd bumped into Alan and Anne in the front driveway on her way home. They'd thanked her for all her help and said good night. Anne had even hugged her, she recalled tearfully. They seemed happy. As Eliza walked toward her car, she heard Alan say to his wife, "Come on. Let's take a moonlight drive."

Julia would never know if her mother agreed right away or if her father had to work his charm to convince her. It was late, but the moon had been almost full, so full that Eliza said she could see her way easily across the yard to the side field where her car was parked.

Julia was surprised they had gone for a drive. They didn't like to leave the girls home alone, even though Julia had babysat Pippa plenty of times. But those times were different; they were planned. Julia was told where they were going and when they'd be back.

There were goodbyes and hugs. So it made no sense to her that they had just gotten in the car that night and driven off.

If Julia had thought the day her parents died was the worst day of her life, the funeral made her reconsider. The morning of the service, Eliza had come back to the house to help the girls pick out dresses and get them ready. Julia did not care what she wore. For all she cared, she could stand up in front of the church naked. What was the difference? She'd been ripped open and laid bare to the universe. Her limbs weighed a thousand pounds, and she moved through each day doing what she was told. It was easier. She did not want to think. But that day at the funeral home, seeing all the people from Saybrook and beyond who'd come to say their goodbyes, had momentarily jolted Julia back to life.

There was not an open seat in the church, and many of the mourners had to stand against the walls in the back and along the windows. So many sorrowful expressions turned their way when she and Pippa entered the church. Julia could almost feel the weight of them as she processed down the aisle. There was her nursery school teacher, Miss Flynn, dabbing her nose with a tissue in the last pew. The owner of the IGA market, sitting in the row beside the Walterses. Her riding instructor, Heidi, waved sadly from across the aisle as she and Pippa passed. So many of the faces she'd seen just nights before at the gala. Faces that had been laughing and dancing and eating fine food in her very own backyard. Dressed up as they were now, only this time in mourning attire.

As Julia and Pippa followed Candace down the aisle of the church to the front pew, Julia stole glances at those faces around her. Red-rimmed eyes. Pursed lips. The muffled cries that escaped when they laid eyes on the Lancaster girls, as if this were the saddest thing they had ever seen. Julia had wanted to escape. To turn and race back down the aisle, and push open the church doors, and scream at the sunlight, which she could not believe had the gall to shine on this of all days. But she did not. Because when she got to the front of the church, Candace, who'd been blocking Julia's view, stepped aside, and Julia's attention was ripped from the sorrow around her to the two coffins directly in front of her.

They lay side by side, blinding her: the white lacquer, the brass handles, the wave of flowers that cascaded over them. So many flowers that the stems and blossoms overflowed, filling the narrow space between the two coffins, intertwining like hands being held. It was all Julia could do to sit down in the pew before her knees snapped beneath her.

Now, sitting in the therapist's office as Lottie handed her an appointment card for next week's session, Julia realized she was holding her breath again. Something she seemed to do all the time now.

How foolish. What could she possibly be afraid might happen? The worst already had.

Eleven

Ginny

The lake cottage was summer perfection. Oh, it was far from perfect, as far as a dwelling went. The hundred-year-old rental was tiny. And it was perched on a steep rocky slope overlooking the lake whose waterfront access consisted of a hillside staircase constructed of old logs that jutted out at precarious angles the whole way down. Not to be attempted in the dark or after a couple glasses of wine, Ginny noted. Inside, the kitchen was dated and basic: a farmhouse sink, a butcher-block counter, and a behemoth GE Americana turquoise refrigerator that was so prehistoric Ginny looked it up on eBay and learned it was a 1964 World Fair special edition. To her surprise, it still worked, even if it hummed loudly.

At the front of the cottage was a modest half-bath with a pedestal sink, and the only shower was outdoors. No matter, it was on the side of the house with a water view. There was just one bedroom, which narrowly fit the queen bed and antique dresser squeezed into it, but its window was wide and opened to the lake breeze and hillside greenery. The rest of the cottage was open-concept. The pine-paneled walls were painted white, and there was just enough room for a downy sofa in front of a fieldstone fireplace. But what the cottage lacked in newness and size, it more than made up for in character and seasonal charm. The backside of her rental overlooked the lake through a wall of floor-to-ceiling windows, and when Ginny stood in its center, she realized she was ensconced in blue: everywhere was water and sky. An itty-bitty deck with room for two Adirondack chairs and a charcoal grill lay outside a set of French doors, which were the first thing Ginny drew open on the night she arrived. Immediately, a cool gush of lake air filled the cottage, and Ginny hurried from window to window, sliding them up, letting the outside in. When she was done, she unpacked her two suitcases, unloaded into the antique fridge the three bags of groceries she'd purchased, and went to the back bedroom to change. She shed her jeans and slipped into a pair of cutoff jeans and walked barefoot to the kitchen, where she grabbed a beer, cracked it open, and went out to the deck. The lakeside was wooded with evergreen trees, and she tipped her head back and inhaled the pine scent. Somewhere across the water, a motorboat hummed and children laughed. *Summer perfection,* Ginny thought. Spartan and simple, like a new beginning should be.

In the days since her arrival, she'd not had much time to spend at the cottage, but already the space was feeling like her own. Most of her time was spent visiting her parents. Her father was home from the hospital, taking it easy. Ginny had prepared herself for what he might look like the first time she saw him, but to her relief, he was surprisingly chipper.

"I'm not dead," he said when she walked into his bedroom and burst into tears.

"If anyone's going down, it's going to be *me.* Trying to take care of *him,*" her mother countered. It was good to see they were engaged in their usual banter, even if her dad did look a little pale.

“You look good,” Ginny told him, planting a kiss on his cheek.

“I’m just fine,” he insisted. “Now that I’ve laid eyes on you. I hear your mother is putting you to work.”

“Well, it’s the only work I have at the moment,” she said bashfully. She wasn’t sure who was helping whom with this new arrangement.

“Nonsense,” her dad said, squeezing her hand. “You’ll be flying the coop before we know it. I’ll be better in no time. Don’t let us hold you back, you hear?”

She appreciated her parents’ belief in her, but honestly, working at their real estate firm was the only gig she had going. It was an oddly unsettling feeling, being home at her age without a job or place to call her own.

After, her mother had heated the teakettle and called her into the kitchen. “Business isn’t what it used to be for our agency,” she shared in a hushed tone. “I don’t want him worrying about it, but I have to say it’s a good thing you’re here. Think you’re ready to start sooner than later?”

The real estate market in Saybrook was booming, Ginny discovered the next day. Despite that, her parents’ agency was struggling. That morning she rose early, went for a quick jog up the lake road, showered, and got into the office all before eight o’clock. Sheila was already at her desk scrolling through listings. “Oh honey, am I glad to see you.”

“I hear it’s a seller’s market,” Ginny said, after giving Sheila a hug hello. “Big difference from the last time I was home.”

Saybrook had always had a unique market, being a small town not too far from New York City. The good school system and proximity to the city helped, but so did the sense of privacy for artists and professionals looking to raise families or live simply amid the bucolic charm. But inventory was limited, and the market could be slow. Now, according to her mother, properties were flying faster than the agency could list them. "Why the uptick?" Ginny asked, helping herself to a cup of coffee and coming to sit on the edge of Sheila's desk.

"Politics and policies. This past year, the town switched from two- to four-acre zoning as part of the Land Conservation Board's initiative. Which would limit new construction and sales of smaller lots. So people rushed for permits to grandfather their lots in ahead of time, and since then we've had a bit of a building boom."

"Huh." Ginny had read some of the local news articles her mother had sent her the links to, but hadn't thought too deeply about it. "So, I guess that's driving prices up a bit?"

Sheila shook her head. "Or driving locals out, depending how you look at it. People want to subdivide while they still can, and protect the value of their real estate. Now they need four acres to build, and that's too pricey for many."

For the New Yorkers coming into the area, it probably wasn't an issue. But Ginny imagined for the many locals who'd been born and raised here on family farms or large parcels of land, it meant something different. "Are the old-timers upset?" Saybrook was a harmonious town, but there was no denying the polite divide between lifelong residents who could trace their family's town history back several generations and the newcomers moving in.

"Up in arms, some of them."

Ginny could understand it. Her mind flashed back to Wendell. She wondered where he stood on the matter. "But Feldman Agency is struggling."

Sheila shrugged. "It's true. The other agencies in town seem to snag the bigger listings. I guess you could say our marketing strategies are a little old-fashioned. And the three of us are, too."

She winked at Ginny. "But with you back, we'll have some young blood."

Ginny had long suspected her parents were a little behind the times in terms of social media and marketing, and as she looked around the office at the dated equipment and computers, she could see why. First thing, she'd need to take a look at their website and listings.

But Sheila had other matters she wanted to catch up on. "So how are you, honey? I was sorry to hear you called your engagement off."

The mention of the broken engagement caused Ginny's cheeks to flush, though it was nothing to be ashamed of, and it had been her decision. "I'm fine," she said, trying to sound like she meant it. What she did not share with Sheila was that she still had trouble sleeping. That even though her new cottage was cute and cozy, it was not hers, and it was temporary. Ginny had always been a planner; she did not like when plans fell apart, even if they were for the best. "Change is good," she lied.

Sheila wasn't buying it. "Well, you're finally back home, and your parents couldn't be more thrilled. They've missed you, honey. We all have."

A small wave of guilt rose up in her. For years Ginny had been too busy to come home, or so she'd said. Holidays slipped by, then whole years did. Saybrook was too far. Work was too demanding. She and Thomas had limited vacation time. The reasons were plentiful. A handful of times she'd returned home, but she'd always kept the visits short. Occasionally, her parents had flown out to Chicago to spend the odd Christmas or Thanksgiving, but it was never the same, and she knew they didn't understand why she stayed away. After a while, Ginny forgot; but after seeing Wendell in town the other night, she was beginning to be reminded.

Ever since, she'd been unable to stop thinking about him. Wendell was a part of her past that she'd tried to keep there, but at one time he'd been the most important person in her life.

Many in Saybrook thought their years began as high school sweethearts, but they were wrong. Back then she had eyes only for Wendell's best friend, Evan. Evan was popular and outgoing, unlike Wendell, who was just as well liked but shy.

Dating Evan was exciting at first, but about a year in, Ginny came to realize it was Wendell whom she always ended up with. At parties Evan would disappear with friends to do keg stands, leaving her to the side. On nights when she tired of Evan's flirting with other girls, she'd find Wendell in a quiet corner and pour her heart out. He'd listen, careful not to badmouth his friend but always finding a way to switch the subject or say something to make her laugh. It was Wendell who shared her honors classes, not Evan, who skated by on charm over intellect. Once in AP chemistry, when learning about exothermic reactions using marshmallows, she overheated hers. When it blew up, covering Wendell's face in hot marshmallow, he didn't get upset or even embarrassed. Instead, he licked his lips and declared, "I like mine a little less toasted." By senior year, it became clear that Wendell might have had a little crush on her. For her part, Ginny didn't want to admit that her feelings for him were also changing.

But there was one winter night when she couldn't ignore her feelings anymore. New Year's Eve of senior year, they all went to Kerry Grove's party. The whole school seemed to be there, and everyone was wasted. Ginny, who didn't usually have more than one or two drinks, was handed a tall glass of spiked Hawaiian punch. She was halfway across the kitchen to go look for Evan when she felt her limbs start to go numb and her head spin. She went outside to try to sober up in the cold air. There, on the front steps, she found Jake Wilson having a smoke. When he finished his cigarette, he turned to her, staring.

"What?" she asked, gripping the railing for balance. She was starting to get nauseated and wonder where the nearest bathroom was.

"Nothing." Then Jake smiled mischievously. "C'mere." He reached one arm around her and tried to kiss her.

At first she thought Jake was joking; he was Evan's friend! So she pushed him. "What're you *doing*?"

But then he leaned in a second time. "Stop it," she said. But Jake had already pushed her up against the door.

The rush of alcohol mixed with fear swept through her, and she turned her head to yell. Before she could, there was the sudden crunch of footsteps in snow and a flash up the steps. Wendell had sprinted up behind them and tackled Jake, the two of them flying off the steps and into the snowy yard. When Jake popped back up, Wendell leaped to his feet first and socked him in the jaw, sending him sprawling backward in the yard.

"Don't you even look at her!" he shouted, standing over Jake, his fists balled. Ginny drew back against the house, watching the two face off beneath the flood of the porchlight. Puffs of cold air filled the broken space between them.

Jake's nose streamed with blood. He put his hand to his face and staggered to his feet. "What the hell, Combs? You busted my fucking nose."

Then he lurched away from them both and down the driveway, walking unsteadily along the line of cars toward his own.

Wendell looked up at Ginny. The snow around him was flattened, drips of red blood at his feet. He was breathing hard. "Are you okay?"

Before she could thank him, Ginny spun around and threw up in the bushes. He waited until she was done, then came to sit beside her on the step. She was mortified. "Thank you," she said, finally able to meet his gaze. Then, "Please, don't tell Evan."

Wendell stared at her in disbelief. "Evan should've been out here with you. Jake's an asshole."

"He couldn't have known Jake would do that," Ginny said defensively.

"Well, then they're both assholes." Wendell shook his right hand, and it was then she saw the angry red glare of his knuckles under the porch light. Ginny reached for his hand gently, ignoring his wince of pain. She took off her scarf and filled it with snow, then wrapped it around his swollen hand. They sat on the step like that until the party broke up and people began to flood past them. When Evan eventually came out, Ginny let go of Wendell's hand.

Evan pulled his coat up over his shoulders and laughed. "Great party." He looked between them. "Ready to go?"

Ginny stood. "It's late." Wendell didn't move.

Evan put his arm around Ginny. He didn't notice that either of them was upset, just as he didn't notice her red scarf tied around Wendell's hand when he turned to him. "You coming, buddy?"

Wendell shook his head. "Nah, you go ahead. I'll catch a ride."

Evan tipped his head back and blew a stream of air out. "Suit yourself." Then to Ginny, "Freezing my balls off out here. Let's go." Without waiting for her, he started down the driveway.

Ginny hesitated, conflicted. "Let us give you a ride."

Wendell unwrapped her scarf from his hand and handed it back to her without eye contact.

"I've already missed curfew," she went on, stalling. Why wouldn't he just come with them?

"Then you should go," he told her.

Reluctantly, Ginny followed Evan to his car. When they pulled away, she looked back. Wendell was right where she'd left him on the stoop, a dark silhouette illuminated against the snow.

The next morning, she broke up with Evan.

Ever the gentleman, Wendell didn't pursue her right away. Or at all, for that matter. All spring they passed in the hallway, and Ginny wondered if perhaps she'd gotten it wrong. Maybe he'd never felt about her the way she had come to feel about him.

Late that spring, her friends Kristen and Ali dragged her to a house party down by the lake. It was crowded indoors, and the music was too loud, so they found refuge outside on the patio by the water. There she found Wendell playing poker with a couple of other football players.

It took her two wine coolers to get up the courage. When the guy next to Wendell folded and left the table, she plopped down in his empty chair. "I broke up with him," she whispered.

Wendell kept his eyes on the cards as he gathered them "Yeah. A while ago," he said.

It was ridiculous. As if they were picking up exactly where they'd left off on Kerry Grove's front step last New Year's Eve.

Ginny leaned in. "Think I made a mistake?" Her eyes traveled across the patio and landed on Evan's back. No surprise, he was chatting up a freshman girl by the keg.

"Doesn't matter what I think," Wendell said. She watched the bridge of cards flip seamlessly through his fingers as he shuffled. Wendell had strong hands. "Do *you* think it was a mistake?"

Wendell looked up, his gaze so intent that Ginny felt her cheeks warm. She shook her head.

Wendell kept his voice low so the others wouldn't hear, but his message was clear. "Ginny, he's still my best friend."

Ginny blinked. It was not what she'd expected. The words coming out of his mouth did not match the look in his eyes.

"Got it." Mortified, she stood up. It was no consolation that she could feel his eyes on her back as she walked away.

Bored and embarrassed, she convinced her friends to leave. "It's early," Kristen complained.

"I'm tired," Ginny lied. What she was really tired of was pretending to have fun. They climbed the steep lakeside hill to the road above, where everyone had parked. They were almost to the top when she heard someone call her name. "Ginny, wait!"

It was Wendell. She stopped, letting her friends go ahead as he caught up.

"Don't go." He was out of breath, having sprinted all the way up the hill.

"Why not?" The sound of Kristen's Jeep purred from up the street. Ginny had already made a fool of herself; she wasn't going to miss her ride, too.

"I thought about what you asked," Wendell said, standing to his full height. "If I thought you made a mistake breaking up with Evan."

Ginny crossed her arms. "Like you said, it was a while ago."

Wendell looked so uncomfortable that she almost caved right there. "You only made one mistake," he said. Then he reached for her hand.

Ginny felt herself soften. "What was that?"

Instead of answering, Wendell leaned in and pressed his lips against hers. He pulled away slowly. "What took you so long?"

Up to the day they left for their respective colleges, they were inseparable. Nights they skinny-dipped in the lake at the town beach, and days they worked summer jobs, counting the hours until work ended and they could be together. Wendell's father, who had little patience for teenagers and certainly didn't know what to do with a teenage girl, took to Ginny right off the bat. By August, he was setting a fourth place for her at the dinner table each night. Wesley, who spent all his time on the sports fields and who'd paid zero attention to any girl Wendell previously liked, also took notice. Suddenly, Wesley was home all the time. He hung around telling bad jokes, sitting with them in the den watching movies, and trying to impress her with his basketball skills in the driveway. It got to the point where Wendell half-jokingly told Wesley to bug off and find his own girl.

Wesley punched him in the arm. "I don't like her like *that*," he said. "It's just nice having her around. Kind of like before Mom died."

It was true. Ginny brought something back to the Combs' household that had been missing. Wendell only wished his mother had met Ginny; he was sure she would've loved her.

By the time they'd packed their suitcases for college, neither was sure what would come of the relationship. Ginny went off to study business at Providence, while Wendell attended University of Vermont for biology and environmental studies. They stayed together all four years, visiting when they could and spending holidays and summers back in Saybrook, like the old days. By the time they graduated, they didn't just talk about a future; they talked about *their* future.

By then, Wesley had graduated from high school. Still wide-eyed and hungry for adventure, he couldn't settle on a college despite his father's insistence. He'd been a varsity-letter athlete all through school but was just as devoted to his social life. Wesley's grades weren't great; he partied too much. Alder Combs worried about his younger son. Unlike Wendell, Wesley always seemed restless for more. Saybrook had never seemed enough for him, a longing Alder feared he'd inherited from his mother. Perhaps it came from losing his mother at a young age. Perhaps it ran in his veins.

When Wendell and Ginny graduated, they returned for the

summer but planned to move to Boston together at summer's end. Wendell had a contact at an environmental law firm and wanted to save money for law school. Ginny had a degree in business and wanted to try her hand at corporate real estate. But that summer they noticed Wesley was in trouble. He'd deferred college a year earlier and was home pumping gas at the local station. Wendell gave him a hard time about the late hours he kept, partying like he was still in high school, the kinds of company he was keeping. "They're losers," Wendell confided in Ginny after he bailed Wesley out of a bar fight one night and picked him up from a DUI another night. "Wesley's going nowhere if he sticks around much longer. He's going to hurt someone. Or himself." It was true. Wesley seemed depressed, a washed-out version of his bright and funny old self. The final straw came when he lost his job and Alder kicked him out of the house. It took Wendell two frantic weeks to track his little brother down; he was living in someone's basement, drinking through the days. Though she loved him, Ginny worried. Wesley's problems were becoming theirs.

But everything came to a halt the day Wendell shared Wesley's big news. He'd come back home, and he'd sworn off drinking. It seemed too good to be true, but Wesley insisted he had a plan. He was not going to college. Nor was he going to A.A., which they all thought he needed. Wesley had enlisted in the National Guard.

No one was more surprised than Ginny. But it was what Wendell told her next that came as a bigger surprise: "I have to go with him."

"Are you crazy?" Ginny asked. Wesley was starry-eyed and silly. He couldn't possibly understand the kind of commitment the Guard was. He'd never left Saybrook for so much as a week away at Scout camp. He was too sheltered to grasp it. But Wendell? He knew better!

"I know," he said, his voice already full of regret. "But Wesley is a loose cannon. He needs help and he needs structure. If I go, too, I can keep an eye on him."

"And what? Protect him? You can't protect him from himself, let alone from combat." Then, "Oh my God, Wendell. What if you two get sent overseas?"

"No, Ginny, it's nothing like that. It's just a two-year commitment," he reassured her. "We'll do basic training and probably never leave the Midwest."

"But why?" she pleaded. "We have plans together."

"We still do! As soon as I get back, we'll go to Boston. And this will help me pay for law school. Besides, I feel like I sort of left Wesley behind when Mom died. I wasn't there for him. Now I can be."

None if it made any sense to her. Wendell had never shown any interest in the military beyond respect for those who enlisted and served. This was Wesley's doing. This was Wendell's guilt. And this drastic change in plans would keep them from starting the future they'd talked so much about.

"It'll go by so fast," Wendell promised her. "I'll be home for breaks. We'll write and call. This doesn't change anything between us."

With a heavy heart and no small amount of worry, she said goodbye to both brothers later that summer. The Boston apartment they'd been looking at was still available, so she found someone to share it and went ahead without Wendell. Wendell had promised.

Wendell had been wrong about all of it. Near the end of their service, both brothers were called for active duty: Wesley to Iraq and Wendell to Afghanistan. Nothing would ever be the same.

Ginny had been doomed from the beginning. She'd had the misfortune of finding her soul mate at a young age. The man who'd promised he'd come back to her kept his word; but he was not the same man who returned.

Wendell

He still could not wrap his brain around the fact the Lancasters were gone. He'd just seen them at the gala.

The details of the accident were minimal. They'd apparently gone for a moonlight drive. That part didn't surprise Wendell too much. Alan was as romantic about his wife as he was about White Pines. And he loved taking out that old car.

Since Alan wasn't known for recklessness, and since there were tire marks before the car left the road, the findings suggested a deer had simply run across the street, causing them to swerve. It was certainly a common occurrence in their area. But in the end, none of it changed the outcome. Finding out the details wouldn't change the facts, Wendell tried to tell himself. He would not see them again, a fact that pained him more deeply than he thought possible. In the last fifteen years, Wendell had buried every member of his family; though he'd never admit it to anyone, Alan and Anne had become the closest thing he had to one since.

Now, when he showed up early to work as he had since the accident, Wendell remained alert for signs of the girls. Secretly, he feared seeing them. He would not know what to say or if he should say anything at all. Wendell was no good at this kind of thing. It was better to keep his distance, to stay in the background, taking care of White Pines as Alan would want.

Jerry and Hank arrived shortly after, and the three loaded up the Gator with weed eaters and headed down to the lake. That morning they'd trim along the outer edge of the cattails and natural grasses that grew along the water's edge. Alan was adamant about keeping the lake in its natural state, and he preferred to leave all vegetation alone for habitat areas. That way the waterfowl could nest and raise their young in the protective covering of the reeds and thicket. The mist was thick that morning, rising in cottony strands from the water's surface. It was the very kind of scene Alan used to love, and often Wendell would see the man strolling along the lake with his dog in early-morning hours. There was so much he owed Alan.

When he'd first come back from Afghanistan, Wendell did not reenter civilian life easily. His father refused to speak of Wesley, and Wendell, who'd been some fourteen hundred miles away the night Wesley's unit was attacked, could not help but think that there had been some failing on his part to protect his little brother; that his father wondered how one son had come home without the other. It could just as easily have been Wendell. Maybe it should have been.

The moment Wendell's plane touched down, Ginny was back from Boston. But he could not bring himself to see her. It was too painful; he didn't expect her to understand that seeing her now was a glaring reminder of all that would never be. Even at the funeral, where Ginny sat in the pew behind him weeping softly between her parents, and later pressed her hand in his during the receiving line, Wendell could barely lift his eyes to meet hers. He couldn't explain why, but the moment he met her tear-filled gaze a rush of shame filled him. It wasn't fair that Wendell was home in Saybrook, safe and sound, without his little brother. It didn't make sense.

For a while, Ginny refused to give up. She left messages, begging Wendell to at least sit down and talk. Several times she drove to the farmhouse and knocked on the door, while Wendell stayed on the other side holding his breath. On her last night before she went back to Boston, Ginny stood below his bedroom and tossed pebbles up at his window. It was agony. She was leaving in the morning, and there was a nearly full moon, and Wendell had to will himself to stay put. Second to coming home without Wesley, it was the hardest thing he'd ever done. But Ginny was so alive, so full of hope; she deserved someone who had the same to offer. He told himself these things as he lay in the dark listening to her stones plink off his bedroom window one after the other. If Wendell could have felt anything at all, he would've rushed downstairs and pulled her inside and begged her forgiveness. But he was numb.

Once Ginny left, Wendell stuck to his pattern of self-isolation. He hung his National Guard uniform in the closet, stopped shaving, and spent his days rattling around the house. Eventually, old friends stopped calling. Neighbors stopped dropping off casseroles. Upon Wesley's death, his father had retired from his first selectman position, and the two fell into an unspoken agreement of seclusion. It felt as if the farmhouse was holding its breath as he and his father coexisted in silence. Just when Wendell thought he'd lose his mind, he ran into Alan outside the market. Wesley wasn't the only one who'd died while Wendell was overseas. Alan's father, whom Wendell had worked for during the summers, had passed away while he was gone.

Alan was standing in front of the community bulletin board outside the market entrance, and when he saw Wendell, he did a double take. "Wendell, welcome home!" Then, "I was very sorry to hear about your brother."

"As was I about your father," Wendell replied. "He was a good man to work for."

Alan nodded sadly. "Well, it's not the same, is it? He lived to be an old man." Then, "The whole town was very proud of both you boys."

When Wendell didn't say anything, Alan looked down at the flyer in his hand. "Hard to find good help these days." He turned to the community bulletin board outside the market entrance and pinned it up. It was a help-wanted sign. "It was good to see you, Wendell. Please let us know if there's anything we can do for you."

Alan was halfway to his car when Wendell tore the flyer off the bulletin board. "Alan." He held it aloft. "There is something you can do."

The work was draining and the days long, but White Pines was quiet and secluded. Alan liked the idea of a strong young veteran soldier managing the estate. Wendell was quiet, and Alan respected that. Wendell could pour himself into the job and work until near collapse, returning home merely to eat dinner and then fall into bed before rising the next morning to start again. For a while it quieted the dark thoughts in his head.

Eventually, Wendell needed more, and since he wasn't allowing himself the comfort of Ginny or his friends, he found it at the Spigot. It started with Friday-night happy hours at the local watering hole, where he found a dark corner stool at the bar. Sometimes he bumped into locals who offered him a beer or, worse, toasted the memory of Wesley. But the beers were cheap and cold and helped to pass the time. Before long, Wendell became a regular. Most nights after work he'd come in, starting with a bottle of beer and some wings. Ending with a glass of bourbon, neat, and a warm numbness that got him through the night.

At first he was able to keep his growing nighttime habit out of the daylight, but after a while Wendell began to slip. A few times he showed up late and other times hungover. Alan didn't say anything at first. But then Wendell missed a day's work, and once, when Alan came to oversee him cutting a tree that had fallen during a storm, Wendell's hands began to shake so badly that he felt the blade slip. Quickly, he drew it back and set the saw down in the grass between them.

"Take the rest of the day off," Alan said, relieving him of the chain saw.

Wendell sat back on his haunches, trying to compose himself. "I'm just tired."

Alan glared at him. "You almost cut off your goddamn hand. Go home."

That night, Alan pushed the Spigot's front door open. Wendell didn't see him right away. The usual customers were saddled up at the bar when Alan tapped roughly on Wendell's shoulder. "This stool taken?" He pointed to the empty seat.

Wendell gave him a sharp look. This wasn't Alan's place, and he didn't appreciate Alan tracking him down.

"So, what are we drinking?" Alan asked, picking up Wendell's glass and taking a sniff. "Ah. The good stuff."

"Hey." Wendell took his glass back and the two exchanged a look.

When the bartender came over, Alan pointed to the empty spot in front of him. "One for me, too, please."

Wendell was too angry to speak, but Alan didn't seem to mind. Glass by glass, Alan kept silent pace. After his second, he started talking. He talked about growing up as the son of Alan Lancaster Sr., and how hard it was. "He was a great man in town but a tough bastard to live with. My sister never could get the hang of him." It was the only time Wendell had heard him talk about his sister, Candace, and how she'd long hated White Pines. How she'd felt their father favored Alan, as a son, and how that distanced her from the family to the point where she moved overseas and kept little contact. "She's never even met my daughters," Alan lamented, now emptying his third glass. He set it down on the bar and turned to Wendell. "Your turn."

Unable to hide his curiosity, Wendell had been listening to the stories. If Alan wanted to keep talking, that was fine with him. But he had no desire to talk himself. "My turn?" he shook his head and held up his glass for the bartender.

Alan leaned in. "Tell me about Wesley."

Wendell could've turned and punched him in the face. The urge hit him before the thought did. Instead, he pushed his empty glass away. "Not your concern," he growled beneath his breath.

Alan didn't hesitate. "You need to talk to somebody. Whatever happened over there—it's eating you alive."

"What the hell do you know?" Wendell asked. Who did Alan think he was?

"I know my father saw something in you all those summers you worked for him in college," Alan said. His voice was as gruff now as it had been when he took the chain saw away from him earlier that afternoon. Wendell's cheeks burned at the memory. "And I know you've come back carrying a burden that you can't afford to carry any longer. So tell me."

Wendell scoffed. Alan was full of himself, so privileged. "Alan, you don't want to know. You've probably never had a blister on your hand, let alone carried an eighty-pound backpack across a desert in hundred-and-ten-degree heat."

"No, I can't say I have."

"You've never followed your company commander through mountain villages asking civilians where the Taliban is."

"Never have, Wendell."

"Or stayed up all night on watch, bored to near death, only to suddenly hear the firecracker snapping that comes before a supersonic round passes."

Alan's eyes were trained on his. "Go on."

Wendell did not mention how he'd received word of Wesley's death by a suicide bomber while he was coming in from a night patrol. How a helicopter had landed to deliver the news and bring him back to base. What he shared was coming home alone. And driving to Bradley Air National Guard Base with his father in the truck to meet Wesley's remains. "The look on my father's face when he picked me up. I will always wonder if he wished he was picking up my little brother instead."

It was the first time Wendell had said it out loud. And Alan was the only person he'd ever said that to.

"I want you to get help," Alan said when Wendell was done speaking. He rested a hand on his back. "I'll let you stay on at White Pines, but first you have to agree to get help."

Now, eight years later, Wendell still saw Dr. Westerberg on occasion. He was better, thanks in part to Alan's intervention, and thanks to the therapy he'd received. It wasn't just White Pines that had saved him; it had also been Alan.

As the men worked along the lake, Wendell turned the Gator back up to the barn and drove across the southern fields. By then the mist had dissipated in the morning heat, and the view was clear to the main house on the rise. There was no sign of the girls, but as he headed up the hill he noticed a tall figure walking down the upper lawn. It was a woman, and as he approached, she waved.

Wendell pulled up to meet her and cut the motor, careful to wipe his palms on his jeans as he hopped out of the Gator. "Wendell Combs," he said, extending his hand. "I manage the property for Alan." He paused, realizing his mistake.

But if it bothered her, she gave no indication. "Candace Lancaster. Nice to meet you."

She had a slight British accent, Wendell noted with curiosity. "I am very sorry for your loss," he told her. "It's a pleasure to finally meet you."

She nodded. "Thank you." Then her gaze shifted to the green

landscape behind him. "I'm sorry to interrupt your work, but I wanted a moment to speak, if that's all right."

"Of course."

"As you can probably imagine, there is much to be decided. I have come over from London to see to the girls. However, it also falls upon me to manage my brother's estate."

Was Candace Lancaster referring to White Pines or to Alan's will?

"Until we decide next steps, I would like to continue running things as my brother did. You are the general manager, I hear?"

"Yes, ma'am. I'm the full-time manager, though there are two other men who assist me. My schedule is Monday through Friday, eight o'clock to four p.m." He paused. "I've worked here since your father oversaw the property."

"Then you're well acquainted with what needs to be done."

"I am. Right now we're focused on mowing around the lake and trimming the orchards. Alan has an arrangement with a local farmer who comes in twice each summer to hay the upper fields, but that won't be until mid-July, when the grasses come in—"

Candace raised an elegant hand to stop him. "I don't need all the details, please. I'm confident you have everything under control."

Wendell closed his mouth. Something about her abruptness made him wonder whether she was overwhelmed by grief or, rather, did not care to know the details of White Pines. He decided to give her the benefit of the doubt. "Please know I will take pains to make sure everything is taken care of, and I won't bother you with any details unless something important arises."

Candace's sharp gaze pivoted back to his, and she held it appraisingly. The only things familiar to him as far as being a Lancaster were the steely blue eyes, the same as Alan's and their father's. "Very good. Your paychecks will remain uninterrupted during the transition. If there is anything I need to be apprised of, please find me here at the main house."

"I will."

"Tomorrow afternoon, the family attorney is coming by to review plans for the estate. I'd like to invite you to join in that meeting. Does four o'clock work?"

Wendell considered. "That works for me."

"Good." She turned and pointed to the house. "Until then, I'd like the crew to work on the areas surrounding the house."

Wendell scratched his head. The pear trees were next on the schedule, and he'd really hoped to start shearing them that afternoon. "I'd be happy to tidy the house beds for you, but this afternoon I'd planned to work on the orchard. Can the beds wait until later in the week? The pear trees really need to be sheared."

Candace's expression shifted. "My mother's pear orchard? I didn't realize it still existed."

"It does. And it's blooming now. I can take you to see it if you'd like."

She gazed in the direction of the east fields, to where the orchard lay. "I can't believe they're still alive . . ." she began softly. Then she shook her head quickly. "No, thank you. That won't be necessary."

Wendell searched her face. Gone was the moment he thought he'd seen some flicker of emotion. He didn't yet know her plans for the future of White Pines, but he'd thought that showing her the orchard might inspire some sentimentality and give him a chance to get a read on her thoughts. "Then I'll plan to join you tomorrow at four o'clock," he said instead.

She gave him a tight smile. "Very well." Candace was partway up the yard when she halted and turned. "Don't waste time shearing in the orchard today. I'd rather the boxwoods along the front of the house get done."

"Are you sure? Alan liked the orchard done early in the summer."

“That won’t be necessary. What’s more important is the main house. I’d like to enhance the house’s curb appeal, that sort of thing. I’ll explain at the meeting tomorrow.”

“Alright.” Wendell climbed back into the Gator and watched her retreat to the house. It no longer mattered what she explained at the proposed meeting. He already knew. Candace Lancaster had a new plan for White Pines.

Twelve

Julia

Breakfast was plain steel-cut oatmeal. Again. Julia dragged her spoon through the gluey concoction and stole a glance at her aunt across the table. Candace had a cup of tea in front of her and was reading an article in *The Atlantic*. Her father's magazine, Julia thought wistfully. Beside her, Pippa slumped in her chair. "Come on, Pip. One bite."

Pippa shook her head, ever so slightly.

Candace glanced over the top of the magazine. "Don't you like oatmeal?"

Julia watched their aunt squint in disapproval, waiting for a reply. When none came, Julia spoke up. "She does. It's just that we've never had it like this." She glanced down at the bowl of gray mush. Would it have killed their aunt to add a spoonful of sugar? Or some cut pieces of fruit? *Something* kid-friendly. Candace had made an effort, she supposed, but it had never occurred to her to ask the girls what they liked to eat.

Now their aunt sighed. "Well, how does she like it?"

Julia paused. "My mom used to make it with cream and fresh peaches from our fruit trees. But they won't be ripe until—"

"August," their aunt interjected, glancing out the window facing the orchards. "Late-August sun makes the juiciest fruit."

Julia studied her aunt. Candace was a mystery. A complete stranger their father had never talked much about, except to say she'd not liked White Pines the way he had. That she was a city person, and as soon as she could, she'd traded New York for London, where she worked in some kind of finance. Which was why he'd moved his family to the Connecticut estate when their grandfather died and passed it down to him. But now, Julia realized, there might be more to the story.

"Well, how about an egg?" Candace asked.

This gave Julia a measure of hope. She turned to her sister. "You like them scrambled with butter. Right, Pip?" she asked brightly.

"Why don't you let her answer," Candace said.

But Pippa was not going to answer, Julia already knew. Just as she was not going to eat. And the small spark of hope Julia had felt for her aunt extinguished like a candle flame.

"Pippa, would you eat a scrambled egg?" Candace asked again.

Pippa stared at the bowl of oatmeal in front of her as if she couldn't hear.

"Pippa?" she said again.

Julia couldn't stand it a second more. "Can we just get her to eat something first, and then worry about her talking?" she cried.

Candace looked at her sharply.

Julia hadn't meant to snap, but her little sister was not talking, barely sleeping, and eating even less. "I'll make it," she said, rising.

Her aunt did not try to stop her. As she went through the fridge, Julia wondered why Candace had come at all. She didn't know a thing about kids, and she sure didn't seem to want to learn.

As Julia cracked two eggs in a bowl and began whisking, Candace brought her teacup to the sink. For a moment Julia wondered if she'd come to help.

"Julia?" Her aunt's voice was barely a whisper. "At your next therapy session, I think I ought to come with you." Until then, their aunt had dropped them off and picked them up at the front door. Not once had she come in.

"Okay," Julia said uncertainly. She wondered if it was because of the way she'd just spoken. "Is there something you're worried about?"

"Yes. It's about Pippa's bed-wetting."

Julia let out her breath. "That only happened once." She retrieved a frying pan from the corner cupboard and lit the range burner farthest away from Candace.

Candace frowned. "Your mother let you use a gas stove?"

She looked sideways at her aunt. "Actually, my dad did."

If he'd been there, her dad would've taken over for her by now. He loved being in the middle of everything. If you were standing at the stove cooking, he'd appear at your side and start snacking on the ingredients. Then he'd hand you a spatula while he started in on a story. Then, before you knew it, he'd crack the eggs for you and take over the pan. It drove their mother nuts and made the girls laugh.

But there was no threat of that happening from Candace. "Well, Pippa's too old for bed-wetting. I'm going to ask the therapist to draw up a behavior chart or something."

Julia poured the eggs into the pan. "She just needs time."

Candace was distracted by the clock on the stove. "Speaking of time, Attorney Banks is coming by. We have meetings all day. I'd appreciate it if you girls kept outdoors as much as possible, so we may work without interruption."

Julia's stomach fluttered at the mention of Mr. Banks. "Is this about my parents' will?" She'd been wondering when someone was going to get around to telling her what was going on with that. Since Candace's arrival, the focus had been on getting through each day: enduring the funeral, the onslaught of condolence cards and flowers and dishes of food. Just getting dressed and eating breakfast each morning was sometimes almost impossible. But now there was a growing unease about the future. “You said Mr. Banks was planning to meet with us about the will.”

Candace hesitated. “Not today. First we’re reviewing paperwork and going over plans for the estate.”

It was not a real answer. “But what about us? We’re staying here, right?” Julia stared at her aunt for emphasis. “This is our home.”

Candace sighed as if exasperated. “Yes, this is your home. You needn’t worry about that now. When the time comes, we will all sit down and go over next steps.”

It was the same vague answer her aunt always gave when Julia asked. Though she knew her parents had left a good deal of money for her and Pippa, Julia couldn’t help but feel uneasy. “When will that time be?” she pressed.

Her aunt was already heading down the hall toward her father’s office at a brisk pace. “I’ll know more after today’s meeting.”

Julia turned to see if Pippa had been listening, but she was flipping mindlessly through the magazine their aunt had left on the table.

“Here, Pips. I made you eggs.” Julia carried a plate over and set it down gently in front of her. “Extra butter, just the way you like them.” Her insides relaxed when Pippa finally took a small bite. Julia sat down and studied her little sister gingerly forking the eggs into her mouth. No matter how long it took, she’d sit with Pippa until the last bite was gone.

More and more, it was becoming clear that it would be her job to take care of her little sister now. Pippa had never been a bed-wetter. What she needed was some affection, not a stupid behavior chart.

After breakfast, Julia helped Pippa get dressed and steered her outside, as Candace had requested.

"There's nothing to do," Pippa whined, standing in the middle of the yard with her arms at her sides.

"Let's try your bike," Julia suggested.

"Too hot."

"We could take the fishing poles down to the lake."

Pippa sighed and plopped down in the grass. "I only fish with Daddy."

Julia tried to keep her expression neutral. It was true; their dad was the one who used to walk them down the side lawn and across the lower field to the lake on weekend mornings. They'd walk out to the edge of the wooden dock where the family's big red canoe was moored. It was the same one their father had grown up fishing in, he said, and every couple of years, he'd haul it up to one of the main barns and strip it and repaint it the same color of cranberry red. Just thinking of their excursions made Julia smile: she recalled how her dad would kneel at the edge of the dock and steady it for them. The way the canoe rocked from side to side when they stepped down into it, and each time their father would laugh and shake it just a little, to make them squeal. But he never took his hands off the sides, and no one ever fell in.

"Sometimes Mama would come," Pippa said softly. "She made peanut butter and jelly."

Julia looked at Pippa sympathetically as she tried to come up with something to distract her. "I miss them, too." Then, "They'd want us to have fun, Pippa. Mommy and Daddy would want you to play. And fish in that canoe."

Pippa didn't say anything but pulled at a stray dandelion in the lawn.

"Maybe another time," Julia said, glancing down at the lake. What she would have given to have her license. There were three large lakes in Saybrook. She could take Pippa to the town beach.

Maybe try seeing her friends. And Sam. She pulled her phone out of her pocket.

Sam had messaged her that morning, as he did each day, telling her that he was thinking about her. Asking to meet up by the stream. Or on their rock. *Anywhere.* She could almost feel the ache in Sam's message. It was something she ached for, too. It would be so good to talk to him, to have him hold her hand. To feel almost normal for just a few minutes. But then the guilt would come washing back: the fact that it was Sam she'd been with when her parents took their last breaths. That maybe if she'd been home that night, something different might have happened.

And then there was Pippa. Julia glanced longingly at Sam's last message and shoved her phone back in her pocket. "Come on, Pip. Let's go visit Raddy."

Wendell's truck was parked by the barn. Just the sight of the blue Ford filled Julia with a sense of comfort. She used to wonder why he drove an old-model truck, the paint faded across its broad hood. Now she smiled at the familiar dented fender.

The barn was the one place where Julia felt like things were still the same. It was the only place that offered her a sense of safety. As soon as they stepped inside, Raddy nickered and pricked his ears. "Look, Pip. He's happy to see you!"

The smallest smile crept across Pippa's face. Julia went into the tack room and removed the lid from the grain bin. The sweet smell of molasses filled her nostrils as she reached inside and scooped a few handfuls into a small bucket. "Here, give him this."

Pippa hurried over to Raddy's stall door and held her hand up, palm open. Raddy went hog wild for the sweet grain, and Pippa giggled softly as he ate eagerly from her hand. When some spilled from his lips and down her arm, she let out a little squeal of laughter. "It tickles!"

Thank God for Raddy, Julia thought as she sank onto a bale of hay and watched them.

There was a creak in the doorway behind them, and both girls turned. Wendell stood in the open frame, watching them. Julia stood up from the bale of hay, feeling suddenly uncertain.

Wendell was a quiet person, someone she never could quite figure out. But she was sure of one thing: he was a good guy. Her dad had thought so, and she'd seen it herself over all the years he'd worked for her parents. Seeing him now made her eyes fill up inexplicably.

"Sorry to disturb you. I was just looking for the big green garden rake." He smiled at them both, looking like he was almost as glad to see them as Julia felt to see him in the barn.

Julia pointed to the far wall, where a small collection of stall rakes and shovels hung. "It's over there."

But Wendell was distracted by Pippa and Radcliffe. His face lit up as he watched Raddy reach over the stall door and nudge Pippa playfully with his nose, begging for more grain. She giggled and got another handful. "Careful, kiddo. You'll spoil that horse rotten." He watched the two a moment longer, and Julia began to wonder if he'd forgotten about the rake. Then Wendell cleared his throat, his expression turning serious. Julia swallowed hard, sensing what might come next.

"Girls, I want you to know I'm really sorry about your mom and dad. What happened to them, and to you, is just so unfair."

Julia glanced quickly at Pippa, who'd gone still, her hand extended over her head. Julia let her gaze drift to the doorway and to the bright green morning outside, considering what Wendell had just said. "Unfair" was the first word someone had used to describe her parents' deaths that made any sense to her.

"They were such good people, and I . . ." Wendell paused and swiped at his eyes. To her shock, Julia realized it was tears. "I miss them, too."

Julia nodded, forcing back her own tears. It was all such an unexpected demonstration from the Wendell she was used to that she didn't quite know what to say. "Thank you," she said finally.

Thankfully, he relieved them of the moment. "Well, I'll let you get back to fattening that horse up. I have to head up to the house to meet your aunt."

This got Julia's attention. "What for?"

Wendell shrugged. "About my work on the estate, I think."

"Are you sure it's today? She's already meeting with our family lawyer."

"Yes, Mr. Banks. She mentioned that."

Julia's eyes narrowed. "That's weird. She won't let us meet with him, but she's invited you?"

Behind them, Pippa gasped. Wendell and Julia swiveled to face her at the same time.

"Are you being fired?" Pippa's voice was small, but she'd spoken. Julia couldn't believe it.

Wendell smiled softly. "I sure hope not, kiddo."

"She can't fire him," Julia assured her. "Can you imagine her trying to mow the fields? Or muck the stall?"

This caused Pippa to giggle, so Julia went on. "Besides, we wouldn't let her fire him." She could feel Wendell's eyes on her.

"Well, I'd best get up to that meeting," he said. "You girls enjoy the day."

Julia watched Wendell stroll down the path to the big barn. What a surprise adults could be. But what was more of a surprise was how Pippa had talked to him. "Hey, Pips, do you like Wendell?"

Pippa was busy scooping grain into her hands. "'Course."

Julia waited ten minutes. By then Raddy had eaten his fill of grain, and she was almost certain Wendell would have been invited in and the adults would be retired to her father's office. "Let's go up to the house," she said. "I need to use the bathroom."

"I like it out here," Pippa said.

"Raddy's had enough. Wendell's right, you will make him fat. We don't want him getting a bellyache. C'mon. We can play Barbies."

"Really?" Pippa's eyes grew wild with excitement. The promise of playing Barbie was Julia's golden ticket, and it worked like magic every time. It was something the sisters used to do together years ago. Desperate for a playmate, Julia would sometimes allow Pippa to join her in the playroom, but inevitably, she'd get annoyed because Pippa would strip all the dolls naked and mess up the DreamHouse she'd arranged just so. It didn't last long; because of their age difference, by the time Pippa was old enough to appreciate the DreamHouse, Julia had outgrown it. But that didn't mean Pippa didn't occasionally beg her to play. As such, Julia reserved it for dire circumstances.

"Yes," Julia agreed. "If you play Barbies very quietly up in your room—and promise not to come downstairs—I will play with you. But first I have to take care of something."

Pippa was already halfway to the door. "Let's go!"

Back in the house, Julia set Pippa up in her bedroom with the pink DreamHouse, a bowl of crackers, and a glass of apple juice. "I'll be right back," she promised.

Pippa jumped up and put her hands on her hips. "Hey, no fair. You said you'd play, too."

"I will, I will. But I have to do something downstairs first. Promise you'll play quietly up here, okay?"

Pippa scowled. "You better come right back."

Julia put her finger to her lips. "Before you know it!"

Downstairs, she crept through the kitchen and down the hall to her father's study. How many times had she burst into that room to ask a question, share a story, show him a blue jay's feather she'd found by the lake? Now, crouching outside his closed door, she missed him more than ever.

Muffled voices came from inside the study, and she knelt, listening.

Mr. Banks had a deep voice. "I understand your concerns, Ms. Lancaster. Which is why I've drafted this contract as per our previous conversation."

Julia pressed her ear gently to the door to hear Candace, whose voice was much softer. "Good. Please show Mr. Combs where we've made provisions for his bonus."

Mr. Banks spoke softly so that Julia couldn't hear all of it, but she caught the tail end. "Ms. Lancaster proposed a bonus of fifty thousand dollars in addition to your annual salary to tide you over once the place is sold."

Sold? Julia sat up.

There was a long pause.

At first Julia wasn't sure if Wendell was in there. Perhaps they hadn't invited him into the meeting yet. She glanced nervously down the hall behind her.

Then, "Well, Mr. Combs? Can we count on your discretion?" It was Candace talking. "Saybrook is a very small community. We don't want word of our plans getting out before the property is listed."

Julia's heart began to pound. Her father owned several properties in town, from the small shopping center in the village to the gas station. There was no need to panic, she told herself. No one had said anything about White Pines. She leaned closer to the door, straining to hear more.

Finally, Wendell spoke. "As I said before, my word is good, Ms. Lancaster. But I do have one question."

"Yes?" Candace's tone was impatient.

Wendell's was full of concern. "When will you tell the children?"

Thirteen

Wendell

Since the moment Candace had asked him to attend, the meeting with the family attorney had weighed on him. So much so that the night before, he'd had the strangest dream about it. In the dream, Candace called and said he needed to come to White Pines immediately for an urgent matter. Fearing something terrible, he hopped in his truck with Trudy. Upon his arrival, the sky grew dark and clouds tumbled overhead. No sooner had he run up the front steps than the front door swung open. Candace met him on the threshold. "Hurry inside," she whispered, glancing up at the stormy sky. Wordlessly, Wendell trailed her to the rear of the house and down a long dark hallway until they reached a closed door at the very end. She beckoned him through it. Inside, the office was dimly lit, the walls paneled in rich mahogany. Seated behind a large antique desk, an older gentleman looked up at them over his spectacles. Imposing shelves of books lined the walls behind him. Wendell stepped inside, and the door shut behind him.

The man gestured to a ladder-back chair. "Sit." Then he pushed a thick manila folder across the desk.

Hesitantly, Wendell opened the file to find a stack of loose-leaf papers. *White Pines* was typed in boldface across the cover sheet. Wendell thumbed through the pages behind it, all of them blank.

When he looked up, the man was gone. Candace sat in his place. "It's yours," she said.

"All of it?"

She nodded and handed him a brass key. It was small and tarnished, with a fancy scrolled handle.

Then she escorted him out of the office, back down the hall, and to the front door. This time she stepped through it. "Good luck," she said without looking back.

"Wait!" Wendell followed her outside. The sky had cleared, and the sun spilled through. He scanned the bucolic view that unrolled before him: the barns at the bottom of the drive. The silvery span of lake to the west. The shadow of woods behind it. He stood blinking on the front steps as Candace disappeared down the driveway.

When he turned back to the house, the door had shut. Wendell tried the handle, but it was locked. At first Wendell panicked. But then he remembered the key. Carefully, he slid it into the lock. There was the slightest click. He was just about to turn the key when he awoke.

All day leading up to the meeting, the dream had stayed with him. It was ridiculous, of course. White Pines would never be bequeathed to him. There were Julia and Pippa. And Candace. Knowing Alan, there was just as much chance he'd leave his worth to charity. There was no way on earth Wendell factored in to any of it.

And that was fine with him, as long as he kept his job. These days, it was the only place where Wendell felt any sense of peace in his own skin. The veteran who'd returned from his tour with the National Guard may have looked and sounded the same, but the old Wendell Combs was long gone. Without White Pines, he could not imagine what he would do.

Finally, four o'clock came, and as Wendell knocked on the front door, he tried to push the strange dream from his mind.

The door opened almost immediately. "Ah, right on time," Candace said. "We're meeting in Alan's office. Follow me."

Wendell and Alan had always held their meetings on-site: outdoors in the fields, or along the lake, or inside one of the barns. Never before had he been inside Alan's office, and as he entered, he allowed his gaze to wander discreetly. It was not the dark mahogany-paneled room he'd dreamed. Rather, it was light-filled and airy, with vaulted ceilings. A scrolled circular metal staircase led up to a small loft at the far end of the room, flanked by windows. A cozy nook, he thought, imagining the Lancaster girls. There were built-in bookcases along the wall beneath, and floor-to-ceiling windows along the adjacent wall, filling the room with the outdoors. Candace directed him to two leather armchairs seated across from a chesterfield sofa, where a middle-aged gentleman stood from his seat. "Geoffrey, this is Wendell Combs, our property manager." The two men shook hands. Wendell appreciated his strong grip and easy smile. Candace took a seat in the armchair adjacent to Wendell's. "Well, shall we get down to business?"

Geoffrey spoke first. "Mr. Combs, I'd like to start by saying that Alan thought very highly of you. He said as much in our many conversations over the years whenever we discussed White Pines."

At the mention of Alan's name, Wendell stared down at his calloused hands. His nails were trimmed short and scrubbed clean. But there was no denying the recent extra hours of labor to keep the place in good standing. He had hoped Alan would be pleased. "Thank you. It was a pleasure to work with Alan."

Geoffrey continued, "As you can imagine, this has been a trying time for the family. While they are of course grieving, there remain significant details to be sorted out as far as the future of White Pines is concerned."

Wendell shifted uncomfortably in his chair.

Geoffrey opened his laptop and began scrolling. "As you may

have already guessed, Candace has been assigned guardianship of the children." He paused and looked up over his computer at both of them. "As we work through next steps for the family, we must also consider the future of White Pines." He turned his attention to Wendell. "This is where you come in.

"The management of White Pines is also to be passed on to Candace. While Alan and Anne very much enjoyed living here with the children, Candace's life remains back in London. As such, she has expressed a desire to return there with the children as soon as possible."

So she would not be staying. And neither would the children.

Wendell sat back in his chair, stunned. He'd thought the estate would be left to the girls in some kind of trust. It was their home. And he knew how much Alan and Anne had loved the place. Candace's arrival had somewhat cemented that idea in his mind, though he realized now how foolish it was to make such sweeping assumptions. Of course she would have her own life across the pond, as Geoffrey said. But couldn't she have put that somewhat on hold for the time being? Until the girls had a chance to adjust and grieve?

He turned to Candace. "The girls are moving to London?" Wendell was not sure of many things when it came to women, but he would bet his life that Julia would hate this plan. Julia was already fifteen. In just three years, she'd be a full-fledged adult. Surely something could be worked out to keep the place for the children until then?

Candace cleared her throat. "What's best for the girls now is to move on with their lives and start a new chapter. My life and my work are in London. The girls will adjust." She said this last piece as if the girls were an afterthought. "Is everything all right, Mr. Combs?"

He knew what she was implying. None of this was his business.

But he couldn't help himself. "Alan and Anne would have wished for the kids to move overseas?" Wendell turned to Geoffrey, trying to get a read on his thoughts.

"It's complicated," Geoffrey allowed. "The will was drafted many years ago, before Pippa was born, in fact, and when the family lived in New York. The provision made at that time was to leave any children in Candace's care."

None of it made any sense. From what Wendell had gleaned of the siblings' relationship, Alan and Candace were long estranged, no matter what an old will may have stated. He looked at Geoffrey imploringly. In addition to being their attorney, Geoffrey was Alan and Anne's longtime family friend. Wasn't he meant to also represent the children's wishes?

But Geoffrey seemed intent on focusing on Wendell's role. "What Candace needs your assistance with is the running of the property."

Wendell bit his lip and turned his attention to Candace.

"Mr. Combs, you know this estate better than anyone else. I would like to propose a deal with you."

"What kind of a deal?"

She chuckled. "A legal one, fear not."

That wasn't what Wendell feared. He'd just learned the children were being sent off to Europe. What was in store for him and the future of White Pines promised to be just as dire.

"My plan is to ready the house and outbuildings for sale. Geoffrey and I have discussed a few options and met with a broker; at this time, we are looking into subdividing the property and selling it off as parcels."

"You're going to sell White Pines?" Wendell tried to keep his voice neutral, but his heart was already racing. He closed his eyes, willing one of his episodes to stay at bay. *Not now,* he thought. *Just let me get through this meeting.*

Candace seemed surprised by his question. "Well, they can't stay here alone. And the proceeds will go to the children eventually, anyway, so why would I keep it?"

Why, indeed.

"A subdivision will likely take more time, but it will also be more lucrative. Not everyone wants the responsibility or can afford the expense that comes with a sprawling hundred-acre estate."

Wendell couldn't believe what he was hearing. They were going to cut up White Pines and sell it off like spare parts. Visions of lines bisecting Alan's beloved property filled his head.

"My wish is to return to London as soon as possible. But our plan for White Pines will likely take time. It requires the combined efforts of surveyors, engineers, and the application for numerous permits with Saybrook's town regulatory boards." Here she paused. "That said, I have asked Geoffrey to come up with a contract that would keep you on as estate manager until that work is complete, the properties are listed, and the sales procured. There would be some changes, of course, to the detail of your work. But it would maintain your current position for the time being."

Wendell's head was swimming. "I see. You want me to stay on as White Pines is broken down and sold off."

Candace brightened. "Yes. There's really no reason for me to remain here during that time. With Geoffrey's oversight, the real estate broker's direction, and your management, I feel the estate can be settled while I am in London." She paused, cocking her head slightly. "Would such an offer be of interest to you, Mr. Combs?"

Wendell met her gaze, trying to keep his own steady. His haven here would no longer exist. He gripped the wooden armrests.

Candace must've misunderstood his hesitation. "If it's your salary you're concerned with, please don't be. Because of all your years of hard work here, I am also including a bonus once the sale is finalized."

"Yes," Geoffrey interjected. "It would be amiss not to mention that Candace has been extremely generous to you, Mr. Combs. We recognize that this tragedy impacts you as well, and eventually will require you to seek employment elsewhere, so Ms. Lancaster proposes a bonus of fifty thousand dollars in addition to your annual salary to tide you over once the place is sold." He grinned as though this were wonderful news.

Finally, Wendell found his voice. "I would like very much to stay on at White Pines as long as possible."

Candace nodded approvingly. Seeing the relief on her face, Wendell realized he had just agreed to help her do the very thing he feared most: get rid of White Pines.

"Then it's settled," Candace said, turning to Geoffrey. "I believe Geoffrey had drawn up a contract that outlines the terms as discussed. You may take a couple of days to think this over and have an attorney review it."

"That won't be necessary," Wendell said, looking between the two of them. As awful as the proposal was, it bought him more time at White Pines.

"There is one last thing," Candace said.

Wendell studied her expression, wondering what more she could possibly drop on him.

"We'd like you to be discreet."

Enough was enough. A plume of defensiveness rose up inside him.

"What Candace means," Geoffrey explained, "is that this is a private family matter. While the listing of the house will be public, of course, we ask that you not speak of any of the details we have discussed here today. Specifically, plans regarding the estate, the children's future, or anything to do with Candace's decisions." He studied Wendell carefully to let it sink in. "Saybrook is, of course, a small community, and the Lancasters were rather public figures. There will be questions, curiosities . . . that sort of thing. Candace would like her business and family matters to be left out of any communications you might have, no matter with whom. Will you agree to that?"

Wendell did not know what to say. It was one thing to invite him here today and inform him that he was soon to be without a job. That he would need to stay on long enough to dismantle the very place that secured both his employment and peace of mind. It was another thing entirely to question his loyalty. Had he not just agreed to remain on-site and in his position for the duration while Candace took off overseas? And for a bonus that could never fill the gaping hole they'd just opened in his life? He was offended.

Suddenly, it occurred to him why: the girls didn't know. Huge plans were afoot, and no one had told them a damn thing. Their lives had already been irretrievably upended, and yet they were about to be even more. Wendell gazed at Candace now, realizing he'd underestimated her.

He cleared his throat. "I have spent the better part of my working years taking care of this place and the people on it, both before and after I returned from Afghanistan. I gave you my word, and my word is good."

Candace glanced at Geoffrey. "I believe we've reached an understanding."

Geoffrey produced a one-page contract from his briefcase and presented it to Wendell. He even clicked the ballpoint pen before handing it over. "If you'll give us your John Hancock here, we should be good to go."

As Wendell signed the contract, he knew he was signing away the future of White Pines along with his own. If he hadn't, they would have hired someone else to do the work. At least this way, he'd stay a bit longer. Do his best work, the way Alan and Anne would have wanted, even if it meant going against every grain in his being. There was some honor in that, he knew.

He set the pen down. "As I said before, my word is good. But I do have one question."

"Yes?" Candace's tone was impatient.

"When will you tell the children?"

Candace didn't flinch. "Children are resilient, you know. We'll tell them when the time comes."

Wendell did not know that children were resilient. And he strongly suspected Candace did not, either. How could she? Candace was a childless woman making life-altering plans for the daughters of her estranged only brother.

There was one thing Wendell did know: the Lancasters had loved each other and this place most of all. One week ago, Julia and Pippa had lost almost everything. And now they would lose the rest. "The sooner you tell them, the better," he said.

Outside the office door, there was a sudden scuffle. All three adults turned as the door flew open with such force that it banged back on its hinges.

It was Julia, a wild expression on her face. Wendell's heart sank at the sight of her.

"Tell us what?" she barked.

Fourteen

Julia

The men had fled the room like rodents off a burning ship, but Julia didn't care. She'd overheard enough from the other side of the door to know that it was her business and she had every right to know it. Mr. Banks had looked rather sorry as he gathered up his laptop and briefcase and said a hurried goodbye. And Wendell; what was he doing? At least he'd had the heart to ask about her and Pippa, but that didn't change the fact that he was in here with her aunt, plotting behind her back. Julia made sure to catch his eye and glare as he, too, headed for the door.

Her aunt was the only one who remained, an air of irritation playing at the corners of her otherwise composed expression. "You should knock first," she said as soon as the men exited.

"And you should tell the truth!"

"No one is hiding any truth from you," Candace said. She'd been holding the door for the men, and now she strolled back to the chairs she and Wendell had occupied for their little meeting. "Please sit."

"I will not," Julia said. She crossed her arms. "What's going on? What is this about my parents' property being sold?"

Candace clasped her hands, and Julia felt the air in the room shift. "You and your sister have suffered an unimaginable tragedy this summer, and I am so sorry for both of you.

"But you need to recognize that my life has also changed suddenly. I've had to return to the States to take care of your parents' affairs and to attend to you and Pippa."

Julia couldn't believe what she was hearing. Were she and Pippa merely *affairs* to Candace? Two new inconveniences to contend with? She knew her aunt had no experience with children, but she'd hoped that would somehow change with time. Julia didn't need another parent: she had a mom and dad, and no one could replace them. Besides, she was fifteen going on sixteen. Soon she'd be a real adult, and she'd be able to take care of both herself and her sister. Candace was merely a babysitter: someone to keep the house from burning down. Someone to drive them to orthodontist appointments, to make sure they had food in the fridge. She was no parent, that was for sure. "Is that what my parents' will says? That you had to come take care of us?"

"It does. Which I plan to do, rest assured."

"What else does it say? I have a right to know."

"Please don't be so dramatic, Julia. Mr. Banks and I have barely had time to review it ourselves."

Dramatic was her friend Chloe crying for two days after a bad haircut when the stylist cut her bangs too short. All Julia wanted to know was how much worse her already ruined life was going to get. "What does the will say?" she repeated flatly.

"Your father provided for you both beautifully. Mr. Banks is in charge of financial allocations, and over the years, you will receive disbursements."

So her aunt was not in charge of everything after all. Julia felt her insides relax just a little.

"There is plenty of money for your education when you turn eighteen. And there is discretionary money for your future when you turn twenty-five: for investment, for travel, for your first home. You're very fortunate in that regard."

And yet none of that would bring her parents back. Warily, Julia sat down. "I heard you say that you want to sell something."

"Yes. The will leaves me in charge of your parents' property."

Julia narrowed her eyes. "My parents have lots of properties."

"Indeed. Commercial properties, which will remain as investments for the time being. And this one, White Pines." Candace paused. "White Pines is the one we need to figure out."

"What do you mean, *figure out*?"

"As you know, I am your appointed guardian. As such, there are decisions I need to make on your behalf."

Just like that, Julia's heart started slamming against her chest. "What kind of decisions?" she asked.

"Decisions that are in everyone's best future interests. As you know, my life and work are in London. At some point, I will need to return. And as your guardian . . . as your *family*," she added, "I will have to bring you girls with me."

"To London?" Julia sputtered.

Candace pressed her lips together. "Don't worry, we can stay here through summer to give you girls a chance to pack up and say your goodbyes. I think mid-August will be best, so you have time to settle in and get to know the city a bit before you start school."

As her aunt spoke, Julia's mind began to spin noisily. Some of her aunt's words penetrated the noise: "museums," "theater," "Buckingham Palace." But the spinning continued, along with a fresh onslaught of images: Chloe and Sam laughing in the school cafeteria. Riding Raddy along the soft edges of the lake. Her parents. Her thoughts screeched to a halt there. Her parents were nowhere in London. Any remnant of her parents was here at White Pines.

Candace was still talking. "You can see much of the city from the London Eye—"

"No!" Julia leaped to her feet. "We're not going to London."

"Julia, please."

"Pippa and I are staying *here*." She glared at her aunt. She had to make her understand, right now, at this very moment. This was not a conversation she would even tell Pippa about. Because they were not leaving.

Candace cleared her throat. "I don't think you understand—"

"We'll find another guardian," Julia interrupted. And before Candace could open her mouth to protest, "Chloe's mom! Mrs. F will take us. She's known us our whole lives, and they're like family." She did not add, "unlike you."

"It's not that simple," Candace said. Though her expression had softened slightly, Julia could tell she was not wavering. "I am your court-appointed guardian. It's what your parents wanted."

"You didn't even know my mom and dad!"

Candace stood, too. "Julia, that's not fair. This is not easy for me, either. But your parents have appointed me, and I will not be turning you girls over to a stranger."

"Don't you get it? *You're* the stranger!" Julia could not stand there another second. And she couldn't risk Pippa, who she prayed was still playing Barbie upstairs in her room, hearing them. "I'm sorry, but we are not leaving our home. I'll figure something out." She halted in the doorway. "I'll talk to Mr. Banks if I have to. You can go back to your life in England, and we'll stay here in ours."

Then she spun on her heel and ran through the house and out the front door. Outside, she headed for her only sanctuary: the barn. When she got to Raddy's stall, she threw her arms around his neck and buried her face in his mane. She hadn't even asked about what would happen to Raddy!

There were plenty of other people who'd want them—*really* want them—in Saybrook. Not just Chloe's family but also Eliza! She had no kids of her own, and she'd known Pippa and Julia forever. Her parents had loved Eliza. There were others, too, she'd think of once she'd calmed down. Candace was not their only choice.

She pulled her phone from her pocket. The text between her and Sam was open, waiting for her reply.

The last message he'd sent was: "Please Jules. When can I see you?"

It was time. She stabbed at the screen with her index finger: "Midnight. Tonight."

"She can't just take you away," Sam sputtered as he paced back and forth in front of their rock. "Everything you know is here. Your home. Your friends and school."

"You."

He halted and looked up at her.

Julia smiled. If she'd had any doubts about her growing love for him, this cemented it. Sam was incensed, and that didn't just validate her feelings. It drove home her plan.

Sam clambered up on the rock beside her. "We can get you a lawyer. Or some kind of guardian from the court—"

Before he could say another word, she pressed her lips against his. It was *so good* to be with him again.

When they parted, there was only the sound of the peepers and their breath between them. "We will figure something out," he whispered.

"You said 'we.'"

They sat on their rock together, shoulder to shoulder. She'd been wrong about Sam. Seeing him had not brought back a flood of guilt, as she'd feared. Instead, for the first time since the accident, she felt a small piece of her old self. Suddenly, she didn't feel so alone anymore.

"I'm calling Eliza tomorrow," she told him. "She was my mom's assistant. But that sounds wrong—she's really like family. She's been with us for years, from holidays to birthdays to everything in between. My parents trusted her completely."

Sam wrapped an arm around her shoulders and pulled her against him. "Just because your aunt wants to take you guys away doesn't mean she can. Did you ever hear about those kids who get emancipated from their own parents?"

Julia thought a moment. "Yeah, there was that kid whose parents were anti-vaxxers and he got a judge to legally separate him."

"Exactly. What about something like that?"

Julia seized upon the suggestion. The idea went hand in hand with what she'd been thinking. Maybe she could appeal her parents' will. "But first I need to decide who would take us. It's not a small thing, taking in two kids."

"True. But you're not some poor foster kid lost in a system. You're Julia Lancaster."

The way he said it made her laugh. "So what?"

"So, there are tons of people in this town who know your family and care about you. I'm telling you: we'll find somebody."

Julia leaned in to him, letting the idea spill over her. It wouldn't be easy, but it might be possible.

Later, when they'd talked themselves into the deep darkness of night, Sam walked her home. As they crept across the yard, Julia glanced up at her aunt's dark bedroom window.

Even though their talk in her father's office earlier had been brutal, Julia had swallowed her pride and gone to find Candace shortly afterward. It wasn't because she had any intention of making peace; it was to protect Pippa and buy herself some time. Julia's biggest fear was that Candace would tell Pippa, who had already been through too much. Better to let her aunt think she was going along with the plan until she could figure something else out.

She'd found her aunt in the sunroom, slouched in a wicker chair with an iced tea. "Sorry about earlier," she'd said, even though she meant not a single word of it.

Candace regarded her curiously. "Julia, this is not easy for any of us. But it will be for the best."

"I know." Julia stared at her feet, hoping her voice was convincing. "But I have to ask you for something: please don't tell Pippa yet. Not until I get used to the idea and tell her with you. She's too fragile right now."

As drained as her aunt looked, this seemed to relieve her. "All right, I suppose that's fair."

After that, they'd had what constituted a normal dinner together, and later, Julia had helped Pippa with a bath. She'd tried not to watch the clock as each passing minute brought her closer to seeing Sam at midnight.

Now she and Sam ducked among shadows until they reached her front door. "You didn't have to come all this way," she whispered, reaching behind her for his hand.

"The hell I didn't," he said.

She turned to face him. "Thank you. For all of it."

Sam tilted his face down toward hers. In the faint light from the house, his jaw was strong, determined. There was no trace of the gangly kid she'd known in middle school. And if she'd ever been sure of any one thing, it was this: Julia Lancaster loved Sam Ryder.

"So, you'll call Eliza first thing tomorrow?"

Again, his worry for her made her smile. "You mean today. Yes, and you'll be first to know what she says."

Sam pecked her once more on the lips. "Good night, Jules."

She slipped inside and turned the lock on the door, holding her breath. To her relief, the house was still and heavy with slumber.

Through the front window, she watched Sam trot down the yard and slip effortlessly into the darkness. It occurred to her he'd done the same thing to her heart.

Fifteen

Ginny

There was nothing like having supportive parents, but one person's idea of supportive was another's of suffocating.

"Huh. That's not the welcome I was expecting." Her mother stood at the front door with her arms crossed.

"I'm sorry, but I wasn't expecting you to drop in."

"Well, maybe if I'd been invited, I wouldn't have to drop in."

Ginny was exhausted. It was Sunday afternoon, and what she wanted to do was close the door and crawl back under the covers, but that plan was scratched.

"Since I'm here, why don't you give me the tour."

"Mom. This was one of your summer rental listings. You know this place inside and out."

"Not since you moved in." Her mother stood on tiptoe, peering over her shoulder and into the cottage. "It'd be nice to see what you've done with the place." As if that were decided, her mother sailed around her and into the living area. Ginny pushed the door closed.

"Well?"

Her mother glanced around, frowning. "You haven't done anything with it."

"Exactly. I've been here—what—a handful of days? And I've been working nonstop."

Her mother pursed her lips. "Still. I'd have thought you'd get a throw pillow. Or something."

"Sorry to disappoint you. It's not like I've been lying on the beach all week." Which was exactly how she'd hoped to spend her first day off since arriving. Right after the nap her mother had taken her hostage.

But her mother had already moved on to the fridge and was peering at the contents inside. "Honey, there's nothing in here but wine and cheese. And this." She pulled out a half-eaten container of hummus and scowled at it. "This expires in a week."

Ginny plucked it from her hand, closed the fridge, and stood in front of it. "Mom, you stopped packing my lunches twenty years ago. I'm a grown-up."

Nina raised one plucked eyebrow and shrugged. "Semantics." Then she showed herself to the couch. "So, what's new?"

There was no chance Ginny was getting her day back, so she collapsed into the rocking chair. "Well, since you've seen I haven't redecorated the place yet, allow me to break the news that I have also neglected to procure a new fiancé."

Her mother did not find this funny. "Oh, please." And then, under her breath, "It's only been a week." But her expression grew serious. "I actually came by with some news. We've got an opportunity to land a new listing. A big one. It could really help the future of the Feldman Agency, if we get it."

Ginny thought back to all the properties Sheila had shown her at the office that week. There were plenty, but many of them were summer rentals, like her own cottage, or smaller starter homes without big price tags. As Sheila told it, the competing agencies in town, Sotheby's International and the Cramer Group, had become better known as the "luxury property" brokerages, scooping up all the high-end listings and courting out-of-town clients and urbanites, leaving Ginny's parents' agency the smaller family homes and seasonal lake rentals. It was enough for them to keep their head above water, but if they wanted to survive, they needed to land some of those coveted larger listings. "Where is it?" she asked.

Nina's face fell. "It's a sad story, I'm afraid, but business is business. Remember that beautiful estate up on Timber Lane?"

"White Pines?"

Her mother nodded. "The owners died quite suddenly a couple of weeks ago."

Ginny recalled her mother mentioning something about a recent tragic accident in town, but between her job loss, the breakup, and her move across the country, the details were foggy. "I didn't realize it was White Pines." What she didn't add was *"That's where Wendell used to work."*

"Yes. Apparently, an out-of-town family member has been assigned to manage the property, and she wants to sell. Her lawyer, Geoffrey Banks, reached out to us yesterday. I haven't dared to tell your father yet; no use getting him all worked up in his present condition. But I had a meeting with Sheila this morning, and we both think we have a good chance. If you take it."

"Me?" Ginny was both surprised and touched. "But I just got back. Nobody here knows me anymore."

Nina was already shaking her head. "Honey, you're young and sharp. And you're fresh out of the Chicago commercial market. This will be smooth sailing for you. Besides, from what Mr. Banks said, this aunt is all business and straight off a plane from London." She gestured to herself and smiled sadly. "Just look at me. Between your father's health and the business struggling, I don't think I can handle much more. I hardly look the part of luxury real estate tycoon."

"Mom, stop, you're doing fine." True, her mother looked older and more tired than Ginny could recall seeing her. And

Ginny was not used to seeing her in leisure attire, like the wide-legged capri pants and shapeless sweatshirt she sported today. But she was still a vital and competent woman who knew the industry in town better than anyone. "Mom, I'll do whatever you and Dad need me to do. But White Pines is going to be a big fish to land. What do you think it'll go for?"

Her mother swallowed. "Close to ten."

"Million."

"Yes. Million. She wants to subdivide it and has a developer lined up."

"What a shame," Ginny thought out loud. "That gorgeous estate chopped up." When she and Wendell had been together, before he left for the National Guard, Ginny had visited White Pines plenty of times to drop Wendell off or pick him up from work. It was a magical property, complete with all the natural elements: a small private lake, fields and forest. Being up there had always felt like stepping into a different world, and she knew how much Wendell had loved it.

"I hate the thought of it, too," Nina agreed. "But regardless how we feel, someone is going to get the listing. Why not us? Besides, it could save our agency."

Ginny sank back into the couch cushions. Working the local residential estate market was a far cry from the commercial work she'd done in the city. Back in Chicago, ten million and above wasn't out of this world for some of the downtown buildings she'd handled for developers and investors. But here, in a small New England town, it was a high-stakes opportunity. "I'll do it. We should probably get started today."

Her mother let out a hoot. "Really? That would be wonderful, honey. Because she's asked us to come by tomorrow. And we need to present our most polished marketing plan if we're going to land this." She lowered her voice. "Apparently, Sotheby's and Cramer already met with her. But don't worry! The last interview always stays freshest in the mind."

Ginny forced a smile. She wanted to do this for her parents because of all they had done for her over the years. And to help them out of the hole their family business was in that they'd been too afraid to tell her about. She had a lot of guilt over that one. Staying so far away for so long, she'd lost touch with the two people who should've meant most to her.

But she also felt a flicker of hope in her chest for herself. Her whole life had fallen apart in the last few months, and this was her chance. To distract herself. To brush herself off and get back in the game. Whatever you wanted to call it.

Ginny threw on jeans, swept her hair up in a quick ponytail, and grabbed her laptop. The Feldman Agency was closed on Sundays, outside of appointments to show properties, so no one would be seeing her. On her way over, she began crafting her pitch. All she knew of this out-of-town relative now in charge of White Pines was her name and that she'd flown in from London. As such, Ginny figured it was fair to assume she wouldn't know Saybrook or the market as well as a local. She'd probably also want to secure a quick sale and wipe her hands of it. The first thing Ginny would do was look up Candace Lancaster and try to put together a profile. The next thing she'd need to do was learn all she could about White Pines. She didn't have much time.

She'd been at the office for three hours when she couldn't ignore the growling in her stomach anymore. Nina had been right: she needed more in her fridge. Ginny glanced at the messy desk in front of her. Thanks to what she could glean from Google and town property records, she'd already filled several pages of notes about both the seller and the property. Candace Lancaster was a wealth management consultant for a private outfit in London, and her net worth was nothing to sneeze at. Ginny would have to bring her best game. As far as White Pines went, she had no idea what Candace would be asking, but in the case of Connecticut real estate, the sum of the parts was often more valuable than the whole, and if Candace wanted to subdivide, Ginny would need to see surveys and maps of the proposed division to properly assess the lots and come up with a final figure. There was still much to do, but she was starving.

The Feldman Agency was smack dab in the village center, bookended by the hardware store and the post office and directly across the street from Audrey's Café. Ginny glanced over there now, longingly. She hadn't exactly been eating well or taking great care of herself lately; a salad was what she needed, but a sandwich was what she wanted. As she slung her bag over her shoulder, she wondered if they still made that mouthwatering Reuben she and her dad used to split.

The second she walked through the door, Audrey spied her. "Wow! I heard you were coming back, but I didn't believe it." Audrey had been Ginny's childhood friend's older sister. Alice had moved to New York, but Audrey had stayed on and opened a family business with her husband. Now, she pulled off her apron and hurried around from behind the counter to give her a big hug.

"Back for the summer," Ginny said, aware that others in line for lunch were watching them curiously. "You look great!" Audrey was only four years older but had been Ginny's idol when they were growing up. She was the big sister Ginny never had, the one who taught her how to apply mascara, the first one to play spin the bottle, the one whose training bra Alice and Ginny had secretly tried on in a fit of giggles when they snooped in her closet. Now, though she looked no different than Ginny, the chasm between them remained: Audrey was a happily married woman with two kids and a successful business. Who, despite all that, managed to look fit, put together, and happy. "I have to confess, I'm here for the Reuben. Please tell me it's still on the menu."

Audrey laughed. "It is, but even if it weren't, I'd make you one." She went back around the counter and sent Ginny's order to the kitchen with a cute teenager in a matching striped apron. "I was so sorry to hear about your dad," she said quietly.

"Thanks. He's doing really well, thankfully. But I'm trying to help out with the business."

"Yeah, three realtors in one small town is tough. But your folks are the best. I'm sure you'll help them keep it going."

Ginny smiled tightly. So the word was apparently out that Feldman Agency was struggling. And that she was the one swooping in to help. Hopefully.

She thanked Audrey and stepped aside for the growing line while she waited for her order. She had a few new texts: two from work friends in Chicago, asking how she was settling in. And one from Thomas. Her heart caught in her chest. Despite the fact that she really did not miss Thomas, being alone all of a sudden was hard. A few times since arriving, she'd almost thought of calling him. She opened his message, wondering if he felt the same. "Forgot to ask if you have my stone mortar and pestle? I can't find it anywhere in the boxes I've unpacked."

Ginny scowled. Leave it to Thomas to inquire about his stupid mortar and pestle. This was something she did not miss about Thomas. His fussiness for routine, from making homemade guacamole every single Friday night after work to taking inventory of his kitchen tools mere days after she'd left. No, she had not lugged that heavy thing all the way home to Connecticut. And she doubted she'd tell him if she had. Clearly, Thomas was doing just fine, mortar aside. She was stuffing her phone back irritably back in her bag when someone called out her order: "Reuben sandwich."

"Here!" Ginny said, waving her hand. She stepped forward just as a guy behind her did so and said, "That's me!" at the same time.

Ginny turned at the same moment he did. It was Wendell Combs.

His eyes widened. "Ginny?" He looked as surprised as she felt.

"Wendell. Wow, good to see you."

The girl at the cash register held the takeout bag between them in confusion. "So, whose sandwich is this?"

Ginny could feel herself flush, and she cursed silently. In a town the size of Saybrook, she should not have been surprised to run into Wendell at some point. But today? She pushed her hair back. And looking like this?

Wendell answered first. "She can have that one. I'll wait." Then to her, "I see your taste buds haven't changed."

Flustered, Ginny glanced between him and the girl at the register. "I'm sorry, I didn't see you back there. Please, take the sandwich. You were here first."

"No, no. It's all yours." He looked her in the eye for the first time and smiled shyly. "I remember how you get when you're hungry."

"Right." Ginny smiled and thrust a wad of bills at the cashier. "Keep it," she told the girl when she started to count them out.

"But it's ten dollars, too much—"

"A tip!" Ginny said, grabbing the sandwich from the counter. She turned back to Wendell. Why was he staring at her like that? She glanced at the line behind her. Why was she blushing? "I should get out of the way."

"Your sandwich will be another minute," the girl told Wendell.

Wendell didn't seem to mind. He turned to Ginny. "Since you stole my sandwich, how about you wait with me a minute?"

"You insisted I take it!" she argued playfully, but she was happy for the excuse to follow him to doorway where it was quieter. Suddenly she wanted very much to catch up with Wendell Combs.

"I didn't know you were back. Are you visiting your folks?"

Ginny was surprised he hadn't heard. "My father—he had a heart attack a couple weeks ago. He's doing fine, but I wanted to come home and help out." She did not add that she had lost her job and her fiancé. She wondered if Wendell even knew she'd had a fiancé.

"I'm really sorry to hear that, Ginny." Wendell jammed his hands in his jeans pockets. "I've always liked your father. He's a good man."

Ginny got this response every time someone in Saybrook mentioned her dad. She'd forgotten how tight the community was and how much her parents were still a part of it. "He likes you, too," she said, regretting it the instant the words came out of her mouth. No point dredging up old memories. Especially not in the back of the café during rush hour, with her hair looking like this.

Wendell glanced at the counter, probably wishing his sandwich would appear. She stole a good look at him. There was the familiar line of that strong jaw. The dark hair that made such a contrast against his blue eyes.

"So, what're you doing these days?" she asked, feeling more in control.

If he'd been surprised to see her before, he looked downright stuck right now. "Well, that's a good question." He glanced at his boots, then back up at her. "I'm still up at White Pines, as head caretaker."

Ginny couldn't believe it. Her mother had mentioned he'd stayed in town, but Ginny had assumed it was in some sort of professional capacity, like the law school he'd deferred when they were last dating. White Pines had just been a college job. "That's great." She heard how hollow the statement sounded.

"Well, it has been. After everything . . ." He hesitated. "Well, when I came back, it seemed like a good place to start. I guess it never made sense to leave."

Ginny listened, trying to imagine Wendell working there all these years. It was a far cry from the plans they'd made as college grads. But then Wendell had changed.

"I guess you've heard about the accident," Wendell said. His eyes were deep pools of sadness when he said it.

"Horrible," she said. "Such a loss to the town, from what my mother said."

Wendell nodded. "Yeah. Worst of all are the two girls left behind. I'm not sure what's going to happen to White Pines or them. They're good kids." He sounded vested beyond the question of his job.

"I heard there's a family member taking over. Will you stay on?" She'd thought of Wendell as soon as her mother mentioned White Pines. Now she realized he was likely about to lose his job as well.

"For now," he said. "The plan is to sell it, eventually."

Ginny studied his expression. Aside from a few gray hairs and a slight weathering to his handsome face, Wendell looked largely unchanged. The proposal she was working on across the street at her parents' agency flashed in her mind. Should she mention it?

Just then his order was called. Wendell glanced at the counter, then back at her. He smiled. "I guess that one is mine."

Ginny smiled back, even though she felt a plume of disappointment rise up. "Better get it. You know how I am when I'm hungry." She was tempted to say something more.

"Good to see you, Ginny. You look well."

"You, too." She watched him stride through the lunch crowd before turning for the door. Seeing him had unsettled her in a way she couldn't put her finger on, and she felt the urge to leave before Wendell did.

Sixteen

Julia

The problem wasn't Aunt Candace, who wanted to return to London. Let her go! The problem was finding someone in Saybrook who would want them.

Julia's call to Eliza had been a disaster. "I have something I need to ask you, and I totally get it if the answer is no, but I'm really hoping it's yes." She paused, already out of breath. "But no pressure."

Right off the bat, Eliza sounded worried. "Jules, is everything okay?"

Julia groaned. Already she'd flubbed it. "Actually, it is serious." With as much maturity as she could muster, she explained the situation. Candace wanting to go back to London. Her plans to bring the girls. What leaving White Pines would do to Pippa. (For a second, Julia felt bad for exploiting Pips, but she had to pull out all the stops.)

Eliza listened in silence, and when Julia finally finished, adding Radcliffe for extra emphasis, there was a muffled sound on the other end of the line. "Eliza?"

"I'm here, honey." She sniffed a few times, and Julia realized she was crying.

"Oh, gosh, I'm sorry," Julia rushed to add. "It's just that you're the first person I thought of." She hesitated. "You love us."

"Of course I do!" Eliza said firmly. "I always have." There was a heavy pause, and Julia felt the floor begin to open beneath her. "Honey, I am so flattered and honored that you're asking me. You two girls . . . you're like family. I mean that. But I'm not a parent, and I can't pretend I have any business taking on a job as important as that. What you need right now is real family. And if your folks wanted you to be with Candace, there's good reason for that."

As soon as the words spilled from Eliza's mouth, Julia knew it was never going to happen. Eliza didn't want them. "Like family" was not family. There were probably a million other reasons, but there you had it.

"So, you knew all along," Julia said.

"I spoke with Candace a few days ago."

Julia felt betrayed. They'd discussed her future without her? "And you thought Pippa and I would want to leave White Pines?"

"I didn't think that, no. But being with Candace is what your parents wanted. They said so in their will, and I want to respect their wishes. But I'm still here for you girls. Always."

Julia swallowed hard. "But you don't want us."

"Oh, Jules. I need to come over there."

"No, I'll be fine," Julia said, trying to stifle her own tears, which were starting. "I'm sorry I asked. It's a big ask, I know."

"Listen, you can call me any time, day or night. I'm on your side, even though I'm betting it doesn't feel that way right now." Eliza sighed audibly, and Julia could hear her struggle.

When Julia hung up, a fresh loneliness washed over her. She crossed Eliza's name off the list in her journal with a permanent black marker. It seemed fitting. Chloe was next.

She answered on the first ring. "What's up?"

"Can you come over? There's something I need to talk to you about. Something big."

Chloe was a terrible procrastinator and always late to everything; intrigue might get her moving.

"Is this about Sam?" She was chewing gum loudly. "You've been very secretive lately. I had a feeling something was up."

"What? No. Not everything in my life is about Sam, you know," Julia said.

"If you say so." She cracked a bubble in Julia's ear.

"Just come over, and I'll tell you."

"Whatever you say, mystery girl. This better be good." But to her credit, she was there within fifteen minutes, a record.

Once they were upstairs in Julia's bedroom with the door closed, Chloe flopped on her bed and stretched out against her decorative pillows. "So, you've got big news? Spill." There was a hand-stitched embroidered pillow from her mother, and Julia's heart did a pitter patter as Chloe propped herself up with it.

"I need to ask you something. And I need you to be totally honest with me. I'll be okay if you say no."

Chloe's eyes widened as she listened, and for once she didn't interrupt. Julia told her almost everything, leaving out the fact that she'd asked Eliza first. Chloe could be sensitive. Now was not the time to deal with drama. "So, what do you think?" Julia asked when she finished.

Chloe was not just open to the idea, she was obsessed. "Oh my God—we could be, like, sisters!" Her face lit up. "It makes total sense. We're together all the time anyway. And my parents already know what it's like to have two kids. What's two more?"

Despite her nerves, Julia found herself laughing as her friend gushed. "Well, I'm not sure that's the way we should introduce the idea to your mom and dad. But you've got the basics."

"No, really! Think about it, Jules. You and Pippa would move into the guest room, which I know would kind of suck to share a room with your little sister, but we'd figure that out later. Wait—what if you and I shared?" She was off and running with the idea. "We already go to the same school. We're both on the tennis team.

I mean, it'd be two more mouths to feed, but you guys don't eat *that* much."

Unlike Eliza, an adult who thought things through perhaps too deeply, Chloe wasn't thinking seriously enough about it. Taking on two kids wasn't the same as an extended sleepover, no matter how she tried to spin it. "So, there's only one problem," Julia said when Chloe finally stopped talking. "How do we ask your parents?"

Chloe was adamant. "Let me do it. I know my mother, and she'll get all mushy and sad about your parents, and then she'll get all happy that you guys want to live with us. There will be crying."

"What about your dad?"

Chloe waved this away, as though Mr. Fitzpatrick were the least of their concerns. "He'll be all practical and probably have questions. But Mom always gets final say."

Julia wasn't so sure that was true. The Fitzpatricks she knew were a lot of fun, but they were both levelheaded people. And Chloe's dad wasn't exactly a pushover. "I don't know. I feel like I should be there, even though it's awkward. I mean, I'm the one asking this of them."

Chloe cocked her head as she mulled it over. "True. But let me break the news first. If it's in front of you, they might be more worried about being polite than really hashing out the pros and cons. You need an answer soon, right?"

Chloe had a point. And she was incredibly persuasive, some might say bossy. "Okay," Julia said finally, "but you have to ask them when they're together, and only if they're in a good mood. Otherwise table it."

"Got it," Chloe agreed. "My dad gets home at five. Give me until after dinner, okay?"

It was a long afternoon of waiting, but it gave Julia time to think things through more carefully. It would be okay to live with the Fitzpatricks, even though it would mean moving away from White

Pines. Staying in Saybrook was heaps better than the alternative; there was no way she was letting Candace drag them to London. No way in hell.

Just after six o'clock, she glanced longingly at her phone. She was trying to kill time, hunkered down on the couch with Pippa, watching *Shaun the Sheep*. What was taking so long? Maybe no news was good news. Maybe they were taking stock of the square footage of the guest room, trying to decide if they could fit two beds in there. Maybe they were making a pros-and-cons list, as Chloe had suggested they probably would. Whatever they were doing, the waiting was killing her.

At six thirty, the doorbell rang. Julia's heart leaped in her chest.

Candace was in the kitchen cleaning up from dinner. She frowned. "Are you expecting anyone?"

"Yes," Julia lied, jumping up from the couch. Pippa had barely looked up from her TV show. "I'll get it." *It has to be Chloe,* she thought as she raced through the foyer and pulled the door open. Maybe she wanted to deliver the good news in person!

Only it wasn't Chloe. It was Mrs. Fitzpatrick. And sitting in the car behind her was a sullen-looking Chloe in the passenger seat.

Mrs. Fitzpatrick smiled tightly. "Sweetheart, I wondered if we could talk?"

Julia bit her lip nervously. "Hi, Mrs. F. I guess Chloe talked to you." She held the door ajar.

It was a long conversation. If Candace was upset or angry, she gave no indication. Mrs. Fitzpatrick did most of the talking. By then Chloe had come in, her eyes red and puffy.

"I'm sorry," she whispered, taking a seat beside her mother on the opposite side of the dining room table. "I tried."

From time to time, Julia stole sideways looks at Candace, who listened and nodded, saying very little. In the end, the message was clear: the Fitzpatricks adored the girls. Loved them, in fact. But they were not in a position to adopt them or take them in. "I'm sorry, sweetheart, but I thought it best if we all sat down and talked this through together." She reached across the table for Julia's hand and squeezed it. "To make sure we're all on the same page."

Julia forced a smile, but on the inside, her bones ached. No matter what they said, no one was on her page. No one had any idea of the pain her page held.

Candace turned to her. "Well, I must say I am surprised by all of this, though I suppose I should not be."

"London isn't the only option for us," Julia said. "We don't want to go, and I was trying to figure something else out."

Candace thanked Mrs. Fitzpatrick. "I do appreciate you bringing this to my attention. It's been a very difficult time for all of us. There's a lot we need to work through."

Mrs. Fitzpatrick nodded sadly, but her eyes were trained on Julia. Julia could feel the weight of her sympathy boring a hole into her forehead. She wished she would look away. Instead she did the worst possible thing and came around the table to pull Julia up out of her chair and hug her. "Honey, I am truly sorry for all you're going through, but we love you. And given time, I really believe everything will work out okay."

Julia nodded, but she didn't believe a word of it. She couldn't bring herself to look at any of them when they stood to go.

Candace walked them to the door, and Julia made for the living room. Pippa was still glued to the TV, her thumb jammed in her mouth and Monkey in her hands. "Time for bed," Julia said, snatching the remote from the leather ottoman. She clicked the TV off.

"Hey!" Pippa wailed.

"I said time for bed," Julia snapped.

"Julia!" Candace stood in the living room doorway. Pippa began to howl. Candace crossed the rug and went to her. "It has been a trying night. Don't take out your frustrations on your little sister." She took Pippa's hand and led her out of the room. Julia flopped down on the couch, numb.

She wasn't sure how much time passed, but the sun had finally slipped behind the hills in the distance. Candace flicked on the kitchen lights, and Julia could hear the clicking of her sensible low-heeled shoes across the marble floor. She stood in the living room archway. "I think you should get ready for bed, too."

Julia didn't answer. The skyline was inky gray and dark. She imagined her insides the same color.

Candace came in and sat beside her on the couch, lowering herself cautiously a cushion's distance apart from Julia. "That stunt you pulled tonight was unacceptable. Calling up a nice family like that and worrying them to the point where they felt they had to come check on you. As if you were somehow in danger."

Julia sat up. "That's not what happened. I called them because I want to stay here. If you weren't taking us away, I never would've had to do that."

Candace looked tired but unwavering. "I know you're going through a lot. But you're fifteen years old, not a child. Your little sister is looking to you for guidance." She looked straight at Julia. "It's time you licked your wounds and cooperated."

Like her parents' death was a scraped knee? "How can you say that? It's—"

"The truth," Candace said, rising from the couch. "When my parents sent me away to boarding school from this very house, I, too, was angry. I felt like they were getting rid of me. I didn't want to go."

"My parents are dead," Julia said, standing, too. "And you're not sending me to boarding school. You're taking Pippa and me away from everything we know."

Candace was not finished. "The truth was, my parents knew what was best for me, even if I didn't. Moving away taught me independence. Resilience. I learned to count on myself, and I grew up."

Julia shook her head. "I don't need to grow up," she said, fighting back tears. "What I need is my life back!" Before Candace could say another word, she spun on her heels and ran for the door. Barefoot, she ran headlong across the yard. The grass was already damp and cold beneath her feet. By the time she reached the barn door, her heart roared in her ears. She tugged it open. Inside, she ran across the dirt and hay-strewn floor to Radcliffe's stall. He raised his head curiously and nickered in greeting.

"Oh, Raddy." Julia let herself in his stall and flung her arms around his strong neck. His mane was soft and smelled like hay and sunshine, and she buried her face in it, crying.

Radcliffe stood very still, as if he understood, until she let go. "I'm sorry, boy. I don't have any treats." He lifted his muzzle to her forehead and sniffed, the soft whiffle of his breath warm and sweet against her skin. Despite herself, she laughed. "Thank God for you," she told him.

Outside, the moon rose over the horizon line. She sank in the corner of Raddy's stall and closed her eyes. Images danced behind her lids: the sad expression on Chloe's face. The text Sam had sent earlier, "How did it go?" The look on Pippa's face when their aunt ferried her upstairs, as if Julia were the problem.

She pulled out her phone.

Sam picked up on the first ring. "So?"

"So, nothing. It was a bust."

"All of them?"

Julia tried to keep her voice even. "Every one."

"Damn." He paused. "I hope you don't take this the wrong way, but I was doing some research. Just in case."

"What kind of research?"

"Remember we talked about kids who emancipate themselves?"

She didn't want to get her hopes up again. "I'd still need a guardian, Sam."

"Not necessarily. I mean, I don't know for sure. But it turns out there is someone here who would know."

"In Saybrook?"

"Yeah. Her name is Roberta Blythe. Wanna know what the weird thing is? She lives on your road."

Seventeen

Wendell

Ginny Feldman had been heavy on his mind. Ever since he'd run into her in the café, Wendell tried to shake off the memories that threatened to flood—if he let them. He could not say how long she'd been gone from Saybrook, because that would mean thinking of Ginny. And thinking of Ginny was a dangerous thing. But it had been a long time. After Wesley died. After he'd told her she deserved better and should move on. For a while she'd stayed at Saybrook after Wesley's funeral. Each day that passed was unbearable, and one of the few times Wendell had prayed in his life, he'd asked God to give him the strength to wait her out, to convince her to go. When she finally did, he'd prayed to survive it. He'd heard from her only one time since, and that was when his father died, just six months after Wesley. By then Ginny had gone, out to Chicago, he'd heard. She sent a condolence card. When he'd opened the mailbox and seen her scroll handwriting, his chest had tightened. He still had that card, tucked in his top dresser drawer.

Seeing her the other day had rattled him. It was like seeing a ghost from his past, and his past was already littered with them. He'd lost his mother to cancer. Then Wesley to war, and then his father to what he was pretty sure was grief, despite the official cause of death as stroke. A man's heart could stand only so much. And though Wendell had done everything in his power to shut his own off, he was no different.

But he could not allow himself to go back. He would focus on work and try to push Ginny from his mind. She was here temporarily. He'd done it before.

So far, the morning was already a sticky one, shrouded in a heavy layer of fog. It was as if the estate had heard the news and was rebelling with a saplike humidity that slowed everything on the property to a near standstill. The apple blossoms had wilted and fallen. Oversize peonies, done blooming, turned brown, slumping on their stems as their once magnificent fragrance soured. Even the birdsong was muted, and Wendell spied the tall gray egrets still in the lake, as though their appetites had been diminished by the sun. He himself was slow-moving today, despite the long list of tasks Candace had assigned him.

Unlike Alan, who had taken joy in meeting him at the big barn after sunrise, Candace left handwritten lists on yellow legal-pad pages affixed to the barn door with a single tack. The sparseness of the arrangement, coupled with the precise angles of her handwriting, provided a start to his day that left no space for sentiment. Today's list of chores was nothing more than preparing the areas immediately surrounding the house that potential buyers would tromp across and inspect. Plumping the annual beds, weeding perennials, shearing hedges, applying a fresh layer of dark mulch atop that already bleached by the sun. To him, it was nothing more than fluffing pillows in a guest room.

Wendell was working up in the gardens around the main house when he heard a scream. He spun around, searching for the source. It seemed to have come from down below, by the barn. A bolt of fear ran through him. Wendell dropped his shovel and started downhill toward the barn quickly.

When he'd arrived, he hadn't seen any sign of the family. But now, as he crested the rise and scanned the view below, a very different scene was unfolding. A large silver livestock trailer was pulled up outside the barn. Outside the truck's cab stood a man wearing a baseball hat. In the barn doorway were two figures, and immediately, Wendell recognized Julia and Candace facing each other in some kind of standoff. Julia gestured urgently, her voice shrill, but Wendell could not make out what she was saying.

The truck driver turned, and seeing Wendell approach, shook his head.

"What's going on?" Wendell asked.

"All I know is we're here to pick up a horse. Didn't expect a scene like this." He nodded over his shoulder. There, behind the trailer, a woman held Radcliffe on a lead rope. Raddy's legs were wrapped for travel, a light fly sheet draped over him, just as if he were shipping off to a horse show. The woman seemed to be waiting uncertainly for Candace and Julia.

"You can't take him," Julia pleaded, hanging on to Candace's arm. "He's *my* horse."

Confusion enveloped the group in the barnyard, but Candace stood in the midst of it like a flagpole in a storm. "Julia, please." She freed her arm and turned her attention to the woman. "As I was saying, it's best if you load him up now. I'll give you his paperwork, and we can talk later today by phone. I apologize for this display."

Wendell hurried around the truck to where they stood. "What's going on?"

Candace turned. "Oh, good, Mr. Combs. We could use your help." She began to make introductions, but Wendell had eyes only for Julia.

"Tell her!" she cried, rushing up to him. "Raddy is a gift from my dad. She can't just sell him." Her eyes were like a frightened animal, and Wendell felt something rise inside him akin to the panic that so often found him in the night. He blinked, forcing himself to exhale.

"Ms. Lancaster," he said, turning to Candace. "There was no mention of anything about the horse."

Candace appealed to him as if she'd found an ally. "Thank you for coming to help." She gestured to the truck. "Litchfield Farms has agreed to purchase the horse, and they're here to collect him. Would you please help them load him in the trailer? I need to take Julia back in the house."

"No!" Julia grabbed Wendell's wrist and squeezed hard. "He will never help you steal my horse."

Wendell could feel all eyes upon him. Radcliffe paced nervously at the outer edge of their circle, and the sound of his hooves on the pavement was ominous. Julia's fingers on Wendell's wrist pulsed. He needed to think.

"Ms. Lancaster, when was this arranged?"

"We are preparing this property for sale," she said firmly. She turned to Julia, who was still holding on to Wendell's arm like they were on the same team. "Julia Louise, I am sorry, but we cannot take your horse to London with us. It's just not possible. So I have arranged for Litchfield Farms to take him in. It's a lovely place, and he will have excellent care."

"He has excellent care here! And I'm not leaving."

The situation had spun out of control. All Wendell wanted to do was send the trailer away, tell the woman to put Raddy back in the barn.

"Why don't we take a breather," he said, feeling the heat of Julia's grip. "Perhaps you all could sit down and discuss this further."

Candace narrowed her eyes. "There is nothing to discuss. White Pines and everything on the property is to be sold. Mr.

Combs, we have an agreement, and I am asking you to help us load this horse."

Beside him, Julia began heaving. "Don't let her," she begged. He dared a look at her and regretted it immediately.

"Julia, get back up to the house," Candace snapped. "You are making a scene." She nodded to the woman holding Raddy. "Load him up, please. *Now.*"

Wendell felt Julia's body coil like an animal's, and he braced himself instinctively against her. "No!" she screamed, buckling against him. "Don't take him! He's all I have left."

The woman looked torn but did as she was told. She circled Radcliffe to the back of the trailer as the driver hurried around and lowered the ramp.

"Please," Julia whimpered against him. He could feel all the fight leaving her, and as it did, something inside him failed.

Without thinking, Wendell wrapped an arm around her. There was the creak of metal springs and the thud of a trailer ramp hitting the ground. The obedient clomp of hooves as Radcliffe disappeared inside. "All clear," the woman called from within. Outside, the driver secured the partition and closed the gate. It happened in such swift unison, it reminded Wendell of a tactical exit strategy. He winced.

The woman exited the trailer through a side door and came to stand by them. She glanced between the three of them. "I'll call to let you know when he's settled." She turned to Julia. "I'm sorry this is so hard, honey. We'll take good care of him, I promise."

"Thank you," Candace interjected. "We'll let you be on your way."

Julia had gone limp in Wendell's arms. They watched the truck back away from the barn and turn down the driveway. When it disappeared into the grove of trees, Wendell turned to Candace. "Why?" he asked.

"Mr. Combs, this does not concern you. If you have a problem with how things are being run here, perhaps this job is not a good match for you." She looked at Julia, sighed, and turned back up to the house.

Wendell felt Julia stiffen. He released his arms, and she spun to face him.

"How could you?"

"Julia, please. I had no idea she was doing this."

Julia's cheeks streamed with fresh tears, making her look almost like a little girl again. "He was the last thing I have from my father. You knew that, and you let her do this anyway!"

"It was not my decision," Wendell said softly. "I don't agree with what she did. But what could I have done?"

Julia hinged forward, her face close to his. "My parents liked you," she sputtered. "Since they died, every adult I know has let us down. I thought you were different."

She may as well have spat in his face. Wendell took it all. There was nothing different he could have done, but he hated himself nonetheless.

"I'm sorry," he said. "I never meant to let you down."

When she took off toward the woods, Wendell watched her as the familiar dull roar began in his ears. Eventually, she reached the lake and ran along the sandy edge to the far side of the woods. He did not know where she was going, but as the sound in his ears heightened, he wished the woods would swallow him whole, too.

That night, unable to sleep, he lay prostrate as memories rolled through him. His mother, placing her hands on either side of his face. "Take care of your little brother," she'd said. Ginny, standing in line at the funeral and how he'd refused to meet her gaze. The way he used to avoid the Lancaster family and linger in the truck at White Pines until Anne and the girls had passed, so he would not become entangled in conversation or niceties. Wendell had not wanted to know them, to care for them. The arrangement was supposed to be about business: Alan's job gave him an escape; he gave Alan his trusted labor.

But that first spring, when the row of dogwood trees he'd convinced Alan not to dig up and discard the season before had come back in a fragrant flush of pink bloom, Alan had found him on the property one day, come up from behind, and clapped Wendell on the back heartily. "You did good," he said, like a father would say to his son. Or a staff sergeant to his private soldier. Words Wendell did not ever again deserve to hear. And he'd known then that staying apart would be hard.

When the sun streamed in through the windows the next morning, Wendell rolled out of bed and slipped into yesterday's jeans. He poured his morning coffee into a travel mug and headed outdoors. Behind the farmhouse was a small red barn where his father stored tools and lawn mowers. Wendell entered the barn and did not come out for two hours.

At nine o'clock, when the bank opened, he called Trudy to the truck. That morning he did not turn right out of his driveway toward work. As he headed north toward the village center, he adjusted the rearview mirror, glancing once at his reflection. He knew what he needed to do.

Eighteen

Roberta

No one ever knocked on her door. Maybe it was because she had no friends in town. After a friend like Charlotte, what was the point? Maybe it was because everyone else knew better than to bother her. Unlike Robert Frost, Roberta believed good fences did make good neighbors. She loathed dinner parties and would rather perish than "pass the potatoes" around some neighbor's table. She had no desire to break bread and listen to people chew it, or, worse, impart their mundane thoughts. No, Roberta did not call in on people, and she did not have people call in on her.

The last person to make that mistake was a fresh-scrubbed young man in a polyester suit who'd rapped on her door with his skinny knuckles and thrust a religious pamphlet under her nose. She knew those people had circled the neighborhood with some regularity in the five years since, but not once had one dared to stop in front of her house again.

So when someone stood at her door knock-knock-knocking like their life depended on it, Roberta was somewhat amused. They'd tire out soon enough, she figured as she turned the pages of her new book; they always did. But when the knocking paused and resumed, cruelly, she got annoyed. It did not matter who it was. Who did the caller think they were?

Book in hand, she peered out the window. It was not a religious pusher, as far as she could tell. Nor was it a delivery person. She squinted. It was a young girl. She softened a little. Maybe the girl needed help. Oh, hell. Roberta opened the door. "Yes?"

It was a girl, all right. A pretty blond teenager. She didn't recoil at Roberta's scowl. Nor did she step back as Roberta filled the doorway. Instead, she leaned in.

"Are you Roberta Blythe?"

Roberta sized her up. This one had pluck. "Who wants to know?"

"I'm Julia Lancaster."

Roberta's breath caught. It was one of Wendell's Lancasters. She held the door open.

The girl had gone through two cups of peppermint tea, but Roberta had not even sipped from her first. She hadn't had a chance.

"Let me see if I understand you correctly. You want me to help you emancipate yourself from your aunt and stay in Saybrook with your little sister."

"Yes." Julia's expression was level. She'd done some homework. And she was dead serious.

What Roberta couldn't figure out was how this girl had arrived on her doorstep. "Forgive me for saying so, but it's my understanding that you have means. There are plenty of talented attorneys out there. You could afford to hire anyone."

"I don't want anyone. I want you."

"How exactly did you find me?" she asked, expecting the girl to mention Wendell right off the bat.

"My boyfriend. I mean my friend, Sam. He found you somehow online. I think it was a newspaper article or something?"

Roberta's insides shuddered. Was she referring to the Bruzi

case? She switched the subject. "We actually have a friend in common."

Julia stared blankly. "Really?"

"Yes. Wendell Combs."

Immediately, Julia's face clouded. "He's no friend of mine."

Roberta was confused. She knew Wendell didn't let anyone get close, but from all the stories he'd shared of the Lancasters over the years, she'd come to the understanding that they had. And they'd liked him quite a good deal. "I'm sorry. I know he works for your family."

Ever so slightly, Julia shook her head. "Not for long. He works for my aunt now. And she's leaving."

"I see." All through her career, Roberta had to try to read people. It was part of her job. She could tell she'd hit a nerve with Julia; something had happened that she did not yet know about. But to guess from the look on the girl's face, she was not about to share what it was. "Well," Roberta said, "having heard all you shared today, I think you may actually have a case."

Julia brightened.

"But I am not an attorney. Nor am I a guardian ad litem, which is what you will also need." She stood and went to a small antique secretary desk in the corner. She pulled out her old Rolodex and riffled through it until she found what she was looking for. "What I can do is refer you to someone who is." She plucked out a business card and handed it to Julia. "Here. Someone who can really help you."

Julia blinked as though she'd not heard correctly. "But . . ."

"But nothing. You give her a call."

Julia read the card aloud. "Jamie Aldeen."

"She was just starting in a local firm when I was on my way out of the courthouse. But I worked with her a good deal on some family cases in my last two years. She's sharp. And she's passionate."

"Are you not those things?"

Roberta pushed her glasses up on the bridge of her nose. This child was something else. "Who I am is a retired judge. There is nothing I can do for you." Roberta pointed at the card in Julia's slender hand. "But she can!"

Julia looked deflated, but she kept the card. "On one condition."

Really, this child was too much. Roberta chuckled. "You're giving me a condition?"

"I am. I will call this Jamie Aldeen. But I want to be able to talk to you, too. As, like, a consultant."

Roberta considered. It would get this girl out of her living room for the moment, if not entirely out of her hair. Besides, once Julia met with Jamie, she could sink her teeth into Jamie, who would know how to handle her. Roberta couldn't blame Julia for being so bold, if uninvited and sitting here in her living room; the girl's life did depend on it. "Very well. I will take your calls. If," she emphasized, "you use the phone first and don't just pop by."

Julia found this amusing. "You don't like people popping by."

"I do not."

"My mother used to say that the things we don't like are often the very things we need."

Roberta raised her eyebrows. "Like broccoli?"

"Not exactly what I meant." Julia laughed. "But yeah. Broccoli works."

After Julia left, Roberta found she could not go back to her book. Nor could she sip the cold tea. Rather, she sat, feeling a change of energy about the room. It had been a long time since she'd allowed herself to think of anything to do with the law. Or family courts. But something about her unexpected visitor had filled her with an odd sensation. Odd but familiar. Eventually, Roberta did return to her book. And she spent the rest of the day the way she always did: cooking, walking Maisey, watching *Jeopardy!*

after dinner. But later, when the sky was growing dark and the first stars began to twinkle overhead, Roberta picked up the phone.

Wendell answered right away.

"I met a friend of yours today."

"Oh?" He sounded wary. "Who was it?"

"A real piece of work." She smiled, recalling the meeting. "Julia Lancaster."

Wendell sounded as surprised as she'd been. After hearing the whole story, he grew quiet. "She's a good girl, Bertie. I know you've put that part of your life behind you, but this kid has been through a lot. If there's anything you can do to help, she deserves it."

Roberta did not object, at least not out loud. "I've heard you out," was all she would say.

Wendell was not one for the phone, but to her surprise, he didn't seem to want to rush off. "Remember Ginny Feldman?"

It had been years since she'd heard that name. Oh, there were times she'd wanted to bring it up, but she hadn't dared. "Of course," she said, trying to keep the flutter of curiosity out of her voice.

"Apparently, she's home for the summer. We ran into each other at Audrey's Café."

"Well, that is a turn of events." To her relief, Wendell did not seem shaken by Ginny's surprise return. But she knew it must affect him on some level. "Maybe you should give her a call. Ask her to come visit."

Wendell was quiet for a long while, and she feared she'd offended him. Oh, she was so good at being so bad at conversations!

Finally, he spoke. He sounded tired, but there was a playful lilt to his tone. "Maybe you should focus on the visit you just had. Sounds like she got to you."

Roberta dismissed this. "I've got zero desire to get involved," she reminded him. "I referred Julia to an attorney over in Litchfield."

"And yet you're on the phone with me. Let me ask you something, Bertie. When was the last time you called me?"

She thought a minute. Once a month, they had breakfast at the café. Sometimes he stopped on the road to chat if he caught her in the yard. But they never called each other up. Ever. "I don't recall," she said, growing frustrated.

"Like I said."

"Good night, Wendell."

Before she hung up, she could swear she heard him laugh.

Nineteen

Ginny

To Ginny's surprise, the agency pitch for Candace Lancaster had frayed her nerves. Working at her old firm, she routinely courted big-name contractors and developers in the city. Whether it was a dinner meeting at a swanky downtown wine bar with investors or a precarious mid-construction tour on the top floor of a high-rise in hard hats, Ginny got deals done. Well versed in the back-door politics that dominated the commercial market and used to juggling the competing needs of tight budgets and big dreams, she could recall very few times when she felt rattled. She was a pro. But she was unprepared for the likes of Candace Lancaster.

It wasn't like she went in unrehearsed. By the time they met, she'd reviewed all the comps in the area and had designed a glossy mockup of a property brochure, along with a marketing plan for Web and print media. The night before her appointment, she'd even done a dry run in her parents' living room. Her father was out of bed and sounding much more like himself, she was relieved to see. "Your mother kept this listing from me all week!" he boomed as soon as she arrived. "Why the two of you think you need to protect me, I'll never know. I'm strong as an ox."

Her mother had rolled her eyes. "You want to know why? Just listen to yourself. Settle down, Irv. You'll get your ticker worked up."

"Bah." He waved his hand and sat down irritably, if gently, on the couch and was fairly well behaved until Ginny finished. "Perfection!" he shouted afterward. "You're going to nail this listing down, I know it. Our agency will be back on its feet."

Her mother seemed quite pleased, too, if more reserved. "Irving, don't put pressure on her. She's got enough to worry about."

Ginny had laughed it off. Sure, the competition was stiff. Sotheby's, in particular, put a lot of money into their marketing and had widespread clientele networks. But what Feldman Agency may have lacked in size and clout, it more than accomplished in local savvy and personal attention. As soon as they settled her father with the remote control and a bowl of cantaloupe and cottage cheese (after a protest for ice cream), she and Nina sat down in the kitchen. As her mother reviewed comps, Ginny took notes of all the big estates Saybrook had been known for and sold off over the years. Nina Feldman was like a vault: she remembered every detail of every listing, and Ginny incorporated it into her presentation. "You've got this," her mother told her as she kissed her goodbye on the way out. "I promise not to call you tomorrow. Let us know how it goes." She crossed her fingers on both hands, and Ginny felt a pang. What if it didn't work out? This was about so much more than landing a listing.

The next day, as she drove out of White Pines after the presentation, she was sure of one thing: there was no way Candace Lancaster was going to sign them.

From the beginning, Ginny struggled to get a read on her. All the woman wanted to discuss was money and timeline. "My goal to is develop the property," she announced the moment Ginny walked in, after giving her a firm once-over. "What I need is a broker to assist in the sales. Do you believe a developer is the way to go, or would you suggest individual building lots sold separately?"

From that moment, it was clear Ginny needed to dive in. She tried to steer the meeting, referring to the comps her mother had shared when Candace asked about listing price. Showing her the marketing plan when Candace inquired about procuring sales. But it all came down to the dollar.

"What is your marketing budget?" Candace asked.

Ginny hedged. In no way could Feldman Agency compete with the money that other firms poured into advertising. "The size of the budget is not as important as how that money is spent," Ginny declared. She spent the next thirty minutes explaining her ideas. A subdivision would garner the highest income, assuming they could procure a developer soon. Candace remained quiet, interjecting little, showing even less emotion. By the time they exchanged a curt handshake goodbye, Ginny was sure she'd been crossed off the list.

Now, driving home, all she wanted was to kick off her red sling-back heels and have a drink on the deck. She left a message with her parents, relieved when her call went to voicemail. The last thing she wanted to do was rehash the meeting.

No sooner had she pushed open the door to the cottage than her phone rang from inside her purse. She'd left the lakeside windows wide open, and a brisk lake breeze wafted through the house as she hurried to the couch. There was a new bottle of Riesling in the turquoise fridge, and she glanced at the fridge longingly as she slung her bag on the table and searched for her phone. She loved the rattan summer tote, but she really needed to get something smaller; it was an abyss. By the time she retrieved her phone, it had gone to voicemail. But the name on the screen caused her to catch her breath: "WC."

Ginny poured herself a glass of wine and stepped out onto the deck before she listened to the message. The water was a deep green-blue in the afternoon light, and she was tempted to walk down the hillside to the rocky beach below and dip her toes in. But there was that message. All these years, and she'd kept Wendell on her contact list. And he'd apparently kept her number.

The sound of Wendell's voice took her back. She'd always loved its gentle tone. "Hey, Ginny, it's me. Wendell." He paused. "It was good to see you the other day." Another pause. "Look, I'm not sure if you'd be interested in getting together, but I wanted to ask you over. There's something I'd like to show you."

Ginny replayed the message three times and refilled her glass once. What was Wendell asking? It *had* been good to see him. Better than she wanted to admit, in fact. But was he asking her out? Or was this the call of an old friend? Most curious was what he'd ended the call with: "There's something I'd like to show you."

One thing was sure. She'd had a rotten afternoon at White Pines, and she was pretty sure she'd lost the one gig her parents' agency really could've used. She needed a distraction. Fifteen minutes later, she'd changed into shorts and a T-shirt and texted him back. "How's now?"

When she pulled into his driveway, Wendell was waiting on the front porch of the farmhouse. He stood and came down the steps to meet her. "Thanks for coming by."

"I was happy to." Ginny smiled, unsure whether she should hug him; before she knew it, he'd wrapped an arm around her and drew her hesitantly against him. For a moment, her nose was pressed to his neck, and she inhaled: the scent of soap and pine, and something else, was a jolt of recognition. She pulled back quickly. "So what's the big mystery?"

He glanced over his shoulder at the red barn behind the house. "Would you like something to eat? A beer?"

She could tell it had something to do with that barn, and he seemed pulled to it. "Why don't you show me whatever it is first, and then I'll take you up on the beer."

He grinned. "Sounds good to me. Come on." It felt strange being back at the Combs' farmhouse all these years later. And yet nothing had changed. They passed the front porch they'd spent so much time sitting on back then. And his mother's perennial garden behind the house, by the patio. All of it was surreal, like stepping back in time.

"So the place is all yours now."

Wendell was walking just slightly ahead of her, and she had to hurry to keep up. He looked back at her. "It is. Dad left it to me, and I wasn't sure what to do with it at first. It's a big house for one."

She glanced back at the house. It was the stuff of a New England bed-and-breakfast brochure. "You've kept it up beautifully," she said. "I think it's nice you stayed."

They'd climbed the slope of backyard to the small red barn in the rear. Wendell stopped at the sliding door and turned to face her. "You're the first person I'm sharing this with," he said. Then added, "The only person, actually."

"Okay."

But there was more. "You know I work at White Pines. And you know about the accident. There were two little girls left behind."

Ginny nodded. "Yes, I heard."

"Their aunt, Candace Lancaster, has flown in from London, and she's not exactly a good match. For the children or the property. It's all kind of a mess."

Oh, she knew. She was about to tell him she'd just met Candace that very same afternoon, but something in Wendell's expression stopped her. He went on, "I don't like to mix business with my personal life. In fact, I don't really have much of a personal life anymore."

An uncomfortable feeling fell between them. Years ago, she had been part of that personal life. "I know," she said, averting her gaze.

"Candace has made a lot of changes since she arrived. She's selling the place and moving the kids to London. It's been hard to watch, let alone difficult to work with. But the other day, I couldn't stay out of it anymore."

Intrigued, Ginny met his gaze. "What happened?"

"I got personally involved."

With that, Wendell slid the barn door ajar and stepped to the side. Ginny hesitated in the doorway. Dust motes rose up around them, reflecting in the sunlight. Hesitantly, she stepped inside the barn. There, in the corner, was a horse.

She spun around to look at Wendell. "You have a horse?"

He shrugged sheepishly.

Ginny shook her head. "You have a horse." The horse nickered at them, and she went to pat it. "Hey, girl."

"Boy," Wendell said. "His name is Radcliffe."

"Radcliffe," Ginny repeated, running her palm down his silky forehead. None of this made sense. But the horse was beautiful, a deep red chestnut with a broad white blaze down his forehead. His coat was shiny with good health and his body muscled from training. Someone loved him. Ginny saw a bale of hay on the floor, and she pulled out a handful and fed it to the horse. Radcliffe snatched it gently from her fingers and bobbed his head as if begging for more. She laughed and turned to Wendell. "You have a lot of explaining to do."

They barbecued steaks on the back patio, where they had a view of Radcliffe in the small makeshift pen Wendell had erected with electric wire. He explained the whole story to her, from the fact that the horse had been a gift from Julia's now deceased parents to how she'd collapsed against him in the driveway and then turned on him for not stopping the aunt.

"It's heartbreaking," Ginny allowed. "But now what? You can't keep him in that forever," she said, nodding toward the small enclosure that the horse stood in.

"It's just temporary."

"And then?" She'd never had a horse of her own, but she'd ached for one as a child and knew enough about them, having grown up in Saybrook.

Wendell flipped the steaks and shrugged. "Then I'll enlarge the area and build a proper fence for him."

"What about Julia? If you tell her that he's here, I imagine she'll want him back. And in the meantime, you're stuck with a horse."

"I don't know what I was thinking or what to do now. All I know is that Alan gave her that horse," Wendell said. "And seeing her watch the trailer pull away . . . I had to do something."

Ginny sighed. Wendell Combs was still the Wendell she'd always known, even if he'd tried to put up walls. "I understand."

He pulled the steaks off the grill and looked at her. "I hope it's okay I called you. As nice as it was to bump into you the other day, I had no plan to reach out to you again afterward. But then this happened. And there was no way around it: you were the first person I thought to talk to."

Ginny was touched. And more. If she were honest, she was secretly elated to hear those words come out of his mouth. Even with all the years apart and the terrible way he'd pulled away from her after Wesley died and he came back from Afghanistan, here they were. "I'm glad you called," she said, taking the plate of steaks. "Come on, let's eat."

They took their old places on the front porch, in the same rocking chairs, and held their plates on their laps as the sun set. At first it felt so easy and so good. Ginny's senses flooded. From the rosy hues of the skyline to the cold beer in the bottle at her feet. Wendell's knee, adjacent to hers, brushing each time either one of them moved.

"Are these zucchini from the garden?" she asked, spearing a forkful.

Wendell nodded. "You remember."

What she thought was: *No matter how hard I tried to forget.* Instead, she popped the squash in her mouth and said, "Delicious."

When dinner was done, they sat quietly and watched the sun go down. But each passing moment filled her with questions: old questions that wound their way to the surface despite the years she'd hoped would cover them up. Why had he pushed her away back then? Did he regret it?

She glanced sideways at Wendell, and it was as if they were almost back there. His dark hair was still thick, though speckled here and there with silver. His lake-blue eyes still so earnest, if the corners were creased. It was possible Wendell was more handsome than before, a grown-up who'd retained the boyish smile but the posture and confidence of a man.

"I heard you were engaged," he said, eyes on the horizon.

So he had known. She looked at him. "I was. But I'm not now."

It was his turn to look at her. "How does that feel?"

She shrugged. "We were together a long time. Thomas was a great guy: smart, kind, hardworking. But I guess it turns out he wasn't my guy."

"I'm sorry things didn't work out for you," Wendell said.

"I'm not. It's hard thinking about starting over, and honestly, sometimes it can be downright paralyzing. But it forced me to take stock of where I was, and I realized I wasn't happy." She'd said this many times to friends and her parents. But here on Wendell's porch, for the first time, it felt true.

"So you're back home for now."

"If this still counts as home, then yes." Then she added, "For now."

He nodded. "Does it still feel like home?"

Ginny was sure it did for him. Aside from college, and then the National Guard, he'd never really had the chance to leave. And after . . . well, he'd no longer wanted to. "I don't know if it does," she said truthfully. "I guess I'm figuring that out."

Wendell did not press her, and he didn't pry for details; that had never been his way. She almost wished he would; it felt good to talk. It felt even better to talk to him. But she reminded herself that this was better. One summer day at a time.

When dusk fell, Wendell stood. She watched the muscles in his back shift beneath his shirt as he retrieved her plate from the porch floor. From behind the house, they heard Radcliffe whinny, and they locked eyes and laughed.

"Guess he's ready for bed," Wendell said. "I don't know what to do with that horse, but for now I guess I should clean up and put him in the barn for the night."

Ginny followed him inside. Wendell was a good man. That horse was not going anywhere.

In the kitchen, she turned on the tap.

"No, no," Wendell said. "Guests don't do dishes."

She smiled uncertainly. "Is that what I am?"

Wendell looked apologetic. "I hope everything tasted all right," he said, switching the subject. As he began rinsing dishes, she leaned against the counter and finished her beer. Her insides felt looser, like a part of her had given in to something. She didn't understand what all this business with the horse really meant, or why he'd included her after all this time, but she'd come to a decision about it. "Well, while you're trying to decide what the next step is, the horse is going to get loose and run off."

Wendell turned off the faucet, flipped the towel over his shoulder, and turned to face her. "Meaning?"

"Meaning you've got work to do. And you're going to need help."

For the first time all night, he smiled like he meant it. "Are you volunteering?"

That old familiar twinkle in his eye did something to her. There he was, still in there. "Maybe."

He looked her up and down, his eyes resting on hers. "It's strange, isn't it?"

"Me being here?"

Wendell pressed his lips together. "No. That part's nice. I meant us—talking like this. Back in my kitchen. Like old times, and yet . . ."

Ginny couldn't help it. She stepped toward him and rested her hand on his chest. Wendell looked down at it.

"You have a good heart, Wendell Combs."

He closed his eyes.

Ginny tilted her head up toward him and pressed her mouth, ever so gently, against his. It was more of a brush than a kiss. Wendell stood very still. She did it again, this time with intent.

"Ginny," he whispered. His voice was full of ache, though she couldn't say if it was for her or for the past. It gave her pause, and she took a small step back. But then his arms were around her, his chest pressed to hers.

"Ginny," he said again. "Please." But even as he said it, his lips were moving down her throat. When he got to the nape of her neck, he stopped.

"It's okay," she said, pulling him tighter. But already she could feel herself losing him.

They stood together, neither moving, in the center of his kitchen. "I'm sorry," he whispered just before he broke away from her. "I didn't mean for anything like this." His eyes were flooded with apology.

"Me, neither," she said, stepping back self-consciously. "I should go."

He walked her to the car and held the door open. "Thank you," he said. "For coming here. And listening." He glanced up at the red barn. "For everything."

"It was nice," she said, sliding behind the wheel. She wanted to flee; to get out of there as fast as possible. And yet the thought of driving away stung. "Do you still want a hand with the fence?"

Wendell smiled sadly. "I would love that."

"Good. Call me when you start. I'll come by when I can."

As she backed down the driveway, she watched Wendell climb the rise to the barn. He stopped beside the pen, and the horse came to him. Ginny watched as he ran his hand down the horse's neck. Radcliffe stood very still as Wendell ducked his chin and pressed his forehead to the horse's.

Twenty

Julia

Since the *incident*—as she now called it—with Candace stealing Radcliffe, Julia had refused to even look at her aunt. As far as Julia was concerned, the woman was dead to her. And that worked just fine; since she would be seeking emancipation, it was time to prove that she didn't need an adult to take care of them. She could do it all by herself.

As Roberta Blythe had instructed, she'd called the lawyer, Jamie Aldeen. When they'd spoken on the phone, Jamie had taken a lot of notes and asked a lot of questions. At first she'd sounded hesitant, but as soon as Julia told her that Roberta had recommended her and that they'd talked, the lawyer took her seriously. "When can you come in?" She'd promised to call Julia back before the week was over, after she did a little more research. But she had made one thing clear: Julia's chances would be a lot better if she found a guardian. "There must be someone you can think of," Jamie had said. But Julia had exhausted the possibilities, shy of asking Sam. Which was *not* going to happen.

They met in Jamie Aldeen's office at Cunningham, Blake & Aldeen. "Your name is on the sign," Julia said when Jamie invited her into a small glass-walled conference room.

Jamie smiled. "That's right."

"But you're so young." Right away, she felt like an idiot.

Jamie laughed. "Young, huh? Guess I should've scheduled this meeting sooner." Then, "Thank you, but I'm not as youthful as you may think. And yes, I am a partner."

Julia nodded appreciatively, hoping that meant Jamie was good at her job.

"So, let's get down to business." Already Jamie had compiled a large file. In the next hour, she explained everything about emancipation in the state of Connecticut. It meant Julia would be viewed as an independent adult: she'd be responsible for obtaining her own housing, paying for all living expenses, obtaining and maintaining a vehicle when she was sixteen. And that was all before any mention of Pippa.

"What about my little sister?" Julia asked.

Jamie set the file down on the sleek table and leaned forward. "Emancipation is going to be a challenge, Julia. Guardianship of siblings is another issue altogether. Let's fight one battle at a time."

Julia deflated somewhat. She'd looked it up; she'd known what it meant. Hearing it come out of Jamie Aldeen's mouth in the stark office lighting felt different. It felt impossible.

Jamie must've sensed Julia's concern. "If you decide to retain me, these will be my problems to try to solve. Not yours. For now, let's compile some information to determine if you have a case."

Jamie's questions were to the point: "What's your GPA in school?"

"I have straight As, and I'm in all honors classes. Well, algebra might have been a B-plus."

"Okay. Any history of mental health issues?"

Julia shook her head. "No."

"You've been through a lot with your parents' loss. Any depression, anxiety, any thoughts of self-harm?"

"No!"

"It's okay. It's not personal."

But it was.

"Ever smoke?"

"No."

"Use drugs? Or alcohol?"

"Never." She'd had a sip of beer last spring at a high school party that she and Chloe had gone to. Should she mention that? Would a court find out?

"What?" Jamie said, pausing.

"Well, I did go to a party with my friend. There was a keg."

"Did you drink?"

"Like a sip. It was gross." She made a face. "I don't get what the big deal is."

Jamie smiled. "Good. Keep it that way."

The meeting took over two hours, and by the end, Julia was drained. They'd reviewed Julia's background and what life used to be like with her parents. They covered the tension at home with Candace, and the anxiety and fear she felt about being moved to London. Pippa was discussed as well. "I'm going to need to compile school records, pediatrician files, witness accounts, and your parents' estate planning documents. It's going to require some digging. Are you prepared for that?"

Julia nodded. She gave Jamie a list of people who'd witnessed the distress at home as of late: the Fitzpatricks. Eliza. Wendell. After some thought, she added Sam, too.

"There's something else we need to discuss. Once I file with the court, the judge will schedule a hearing. As your guardian, your aunt will be notified of the filing and of the hearing date. How do you think she'll react to that?"

Not well, Julia thought. "Should I tell her?"

"That depends. Will it cause more strife in the household?"

Julia shrugged. "Probably. But it's not like I'm afraid of her or anything like that."

"So you feel safe at home?"

It was a terrible question that caused her some guilt. Candace was awful, but not like that. Julia had no fear of her acting out abusively. "Yes. She's not a good match for us, but she's not a bad person."

Jamie made some quick notes. "Good. I will also be requesting that the court assign a guardian ad litem. That person will be visiting your home and interviewing all of you. Plus friends, the therapist you mentioned, that sort of thing."

"Okay." It was a lot. "How long does all this take?"

Jamie glanced up from her notes. "A good bit of time. We want to do a thorough job if we're going to do it right."

Time was one thing they didn't have a lot of. But having a petition filed would force Candace to keep Julia and Pippa in the state until the court held their hearings and made their decisions. Julia felt an immense sense of relief for that.

"All right," Jamie said, leaning back in her chair at the end of their session. "We have a lot to do. But I will say this: I think you have a case."

"I do?"

"It's early to get excited. And I want to caution you to manage your expectations. This is a serious thing, to file a petition for emancipation. After everything we've discussed today, are you certain this makes good sense to you?"

Julia didn't hesitate. "More than ever."

"Okay, then. Any questions?"

"Yes." Julia paused. It was the one thing that worried her almost as much as the potential outcome. "How do I pay you?"

Jamie pushed a one-page contract toward her. "I'm not going

to charge you up front. If you sign this contract today, you will be retaining my services with a contingency clause. That means I will recoup reimbursement for my fees once we request that the court release some of your trust funds. Are you comfortable with that?"

"Yes. One more question. Where do I sign?"

When she got home, Julia did not tell Candace where she'd been. She needed time to think before she broke the news. One thing Jamie Aldeen had told her was that she had to demonstrate that she was capable of adultlike duties. That meant all kinds of domestic things like laundry, helping Pippa, and cooking. Which was how she found herself in the kitchen rummaging through the fridge to make dinner for herself and Pippa (it was just the two of them after all). There were a few basic dishes she could make if pressed. Tacos, spaghetti, and mac and cheese. So she was a little intimated by the slimy raw chicken breasts when she pulled the package out of the refrigerator. But she recalled her mother having dipped them in some kind of egg mixture and then dredging them in breadcrumbs before popping them in the oven to bake. That was a start; the rest was what the Internet was for.

An hour and a good deal of mess later, the oven timer went off. By then Pippa had wandered downstairs and Julia put her to work. "Here, Pips. You can help make salad."

When they were done, the meal was good, if not great. The chicken breasts were a little overcooked and dry (ketchup!). And the salad was quite soggy (neither had remembered the spinner, but at least it was clean). Despite having made the salad, Pippa didn't want any of it. Julia was at least able to get her to nibble some carrot sticks. The chicken she cut into small bites. "It's good," Pippa said, spearing one with her fork and popping it in her mouth. The kitchen island was a mess of raw egg and breadcrumbs, the sink full of pans and bowls. But when Pippa ate that first bite, Julia thought she might cry with relief. Being a parent was a lot of work.

Candace had made her way downstairs at that point. "What's this?" she asked, looking around.

"Dinner!" Pippa said, smiling. "Jules made it." Julia said nothing.

"I can see that." Candace picked up the raw chicken container, scowling. "Why didn't anyone come get me?"

Julia shoved a forkful of chicken in her mouth and kept her gaze trained across the table on her little sister. She handed her a napkin. "Here, Pips. Wipe the ketchup off your chin."

Behind her, Candace picked up a pan and set it down. "Julia? Is there any left?"

Pippa looked at her big sister curiously, but Julia just shook her head in silence. She'd make up a reason later. But she was not dignifying her aunt's questions, her comments, or her very presence. Dead. Dead. Dead.

"I see," Candace said. "So this is how it's going to be."

"You can have some of mine!" Pippa offered.

Julia shot her a look.

"No, thank you, dear. I will make my own supper. And clean up my own mess," she added.

Julia snorted. That was fine with her. She had every intention of cleaning up the mess from her cooking. It was *her* kitchen. Ignoring her aunt, Julia collected the plates and brought them to the sink. "C'mere, Pips. I'm going to wash the dishes. You can dry."

They worked side by side, and even though Pippa didn't do the greatest job drying, Julia put everything away in the cupboards. "All clean!" she announced to no one in particular. "Let's go for a walk outside." By then Candace was sitting alone at the table with a tiny sandwich. She'd turned the chandelier on and was reading the local paper. Julia wiped down the island, left the sandwich makings right where her aunt had left them, and hung the wet dish towel on the oven handle. On her way out, she flicked off the chandelier light.

Outside, the early-evening air was still hot. Pippa shaded her eyes, scanning the yard. "What're we going to do?"

"Let's get your bike out. It's time you practice without your training wheels."

"Nah," Pippa said, plopping down on the front step. "Don't wanna."

"You mean, 'I don't want to,'" Julia corrected. Attitudes aside, she wasn't about to let Pippa regress to full-on baby talk.

"I hate that bike."

Julia put her hands on her hips, and it occurred to her that was the exact stance her mother used to take when she was fed up. "Pippa, you're almost seven. All your friends ride without training wheels, and there's no reason you can't, too. I'll help you!"

Pippa wagged her head back and forth in the negative.

Julia reached down for her hand and pulled her up from the step. "Come on. We're at least going to try."

"We're moving to London," Pippa grumbled. "They have big red buses there. Aunt Candace said so. I'll take a bus."

"We are not moving," Julia told her. "So you'd better learn to ride this bike, because there aren't any buses around here."

If Candace got her way, Julia was pretty sure Pippa's pink sparkly two-wheeler wasn't going overseas on a plane with them. But it was the last gift Pippa had gotten for her birthday from her parents. And teaching Pippa to ride it had been something their mom had said she was looking forward to that summer. Julia recalled the excited look on her mother's pretty face: "Just think, Pips! We can bring your bike to Cape Cod. The whole family can ride the Rail Trail, and you can lead the way."

Julia had so little control over anything now. For some reason, that made it suddenly very important that her mom's wish for Pippa come true. She went to the garage, punched in the code, and waited as the door rose. There, in the corner, was Pippa's bike. The training wheels were on the shelf above it. Right where her mom had left them the day she took them off. Julia swallowed hard and wheeled the bike out into the sun.

"Not riding that thing," Pippa said, picking at a stray dandelion in the grass.

"Come on," Julia said impatiently. "It's hot out here."

As they were standing at the top of the driveway arguing, Julia heard the sound of a vehicle coming up. Wendell's truck pulled into the lower barn. *Raddy's barn,* she thought angrily. A plume of fresh resentment rose within her. She'd been in that barn only once since the day Candace stole him. Standing in Raddy's empty stall, his hay still half-eaten in his bucket, she'd spilled angry tears and vowed that she would not leave with that woman if it were the last thing she did. At that point, they could put her in the foster system before she'd get on a plane.

"Wendell!" Pippa shouted. She waved from the top of the driveway as he got out of the truck, but he didn't look up at the big house.

"He can't hear you," Julia told her.

Pippa scowled. "Hi, Wendell!" she shouted again. Julia covered her ears. For such a tiny person, she had a set of lungs on her.

Below, Wendell stopped and looked their way. He raised a hand in greeting. "Hello, Miss Pippa," he said.

Julia sneered. He'd always called Pippa that. She used to think it was cute. Now she thought it was stupid. Fake, even. What did he care what happened to them?

"I'm riding a bike!" Pippa shouted.

"Good for you," he shouted back. She had to admit it sounded like he almost meant it. *Good for you,* she thought.

But as she watched Pippa pick up her bike and swing her leg over the seat, it occurred to her that Wendell's visit was in their favor. If Pippa needed an audience to do this, even if that audience happened to be the traitor Wendell Combs, so be it. Julia had bigger fish to fry.

"That's right, Pip. Let's show him."

As Pippa scooted along the driveway on her tippy-toes, Julia hurried beside her. "Now, Pip, we're staying up here at the top. Back and forth. Whatever you do, keep the handlebars pointed straight. We're not going down the driveway."

Pippa shrieked delightedly. "I sure hope not!"

Julia couldn't help but smile; the transformation was ridiculous. Pippa could be so stubborn.

"All right. When you're ready, put one foot on the pedal and push off with the other. I've got you."

She waited while Pippa tried to balance. "But it's wobbly!"

"I've got you," Julia reminded her. She glanced down the driveway. To her surprise, Wendell was standing by his stupid truck.

Suddenly, Pippa pushed off. The bike wobbled left and right, and the handlebars turned. "Straight ahead!" Julia said, trotting alongside.

Pippa tipped, catching herself at the last second. They'd barely made it six feet, and Julia's toes had narrowly missed being run over. "Okay. Try again."

The next push-off, Pippa got her balance and made it almost all the way across the top of the driveway. "Okay, brake!" Julia called.

As directed, Pippa braked hard, and Julia steadied her.

From down below came the sound of clapping. Julia stole a glance. *He can leave now,* she thought.

But Pippa was thrilled. "Did you see?" she called down.

"You're a natural," Wendell shouted back.

"Let's do it again," Pippa said.

Just like the last time, they tried again, and again. Pippa was much more balanced this time. So much so that midway across the driveway, Julia let go. Pippa must've felt it, because she looked back sharply, turning the handlebars involuntarily as she did. Before Julia could stop it, the bike made a hard left and tipped, and Pippa went down with it.

"Pippa!" she shouted.

Pippa lay sprawled to the side, the bike tipped on top of her. Her lower lip trembled, threatening what Julia knew would be a good cry. "You're okay," she insisted. "This happened with Mom, remember? You got right back on."

At the mention of their mother, Pippa locked eyes with Julia, and her lip trembled harder. Julia lifted the bike off her and pulled her gently up.

"Everybody okay?" Wendell shouted up to them. Julia had almost forgotten about him. *He better not come up here,* Julia thought as she dusted Pippa off. Thankfully, there were no scrapes on her knees or elbows. "She's fine," she shouted back. She had this under control. "One more time?" she asked softly.

Pippa looked very unsure, her eyes shiny with the threat of tears. "You're doing so great!" Julia added. "Let's show this bike who's boss."

"Okay." Pippa's voice was so little, Julia felt like she might cry, too. Wendell was stationed at the bottom of the driveway, arms crossed, like some kind of sentinel. Did he think he was still in the armed forces? She was thankful that her aunt had not poked her head out the door to check on them. Or, if she had, she'd at least left them alone. It was unlike the busybody. *Maybe she choked on her tiny sandwich,* Julia thought, smiling to herself.

They went back and forth across the driveway not just once but five more times, until Julia was getting out of breath. Each time

Pippa did better. "Okay, break time," Julia said on the last lap. She bent over, hands on her knees, puffing. "You did good!"

"Mommy taught me," Pippa said, looking down at the pink streamers that fluttered from her handlebars. Julia ran her hand through them, thinking they felt almost like a horse's mane.

"I know she did, kiddo. She did a good job."

At the bottom of the driveway, Wendell lifted a hand and went inside the barn. Julia was still furious with him, but she found herself almost waving back. She wondered what he was doing in Raddy's barn at this hour and why he'd come.

As they wheeled Pippa's bike back into the garage, he came out, carrying something in a large black garbage bag. She stood in the driveway, watching as he walked around to the rear of the truck. Once he glanced up at her. *What is he doing?* she wondered. Then she caught herself. Whatever it was didn't matter. Raddy was gone. Her parents were gone. Wendell climbed in the truck and started the engine. *Let him go, too,* she told herself.

The truck headlights went on, and it backed away from the barn. As she watched it go, she realized she didn't feel the usual sense of loneliness. Instead, an idea sparked. An idea inspired by Jamie Aldeen's advice. So crazy, and such a long shot, that only a fool would bet on it.

"Hey, Pip," she called. "It's still early. What do you say we take your bike back out?" It was no longer about teaching her little sister to ride a bike. Suddenly, it was part of her plan.

Twenty-One

Wendell

In the middle of the night, a noise outside startled him awake. Wendell lay in bed on his back, his senses on high alert. It was not unusual for the nocturnal wildlife to make some pretty crazy noises. The scream of a fox or the howl of a coyote could send shivers down a grown man's spine. He held his breath, listening.

He heard it again. There was a sharp thud below his open window. Wendell slipped silently from his bed, muscles tensed. An evening breeze ruffled the curtains, and he moved quickly to the window, scanning the yard below. His father used to sleep with the front porch lanterns on all night, a sign to the town that he was always there, even in the middle of the night; but Wendell was not his father and did not like to waste electricity, so he'd not continued the practice after his father passed away. Now, squinting down into the inky darkness of the front yard and driveway, he wished he had.

It was probably a racoon messing around with the garbage can lid or some such, but he decided to check it out, just in case. From the floor, he retrieved his T-shirt and pulled it over his head. He was about to walk out the door when he heard a voice. Wendell froze. Yes, it was very clearly a human voice, not the sound of an animal. He turned, retrieved the metal baseball bat he stored under his bed, and headed for the stairs.

His National Guard training had taught him to keep a cool head, to think critically in a flash of a moment, to judge a situation before acting. It was something that had stayed with him all these years after active duty, and he knew it always would. But after Wesley's death, Wendell had never been able to recoup that sense of dead calm. In its place was doubt: about his timing as well as his judgment. There was no place for doubt in active duty, and after the loss of Wes, it had spelled the end of his military career. Now, as he stood on the bottom step with the bat in hand, images of Afghanistan flooded his mind. The white-hot heat. The desert dust rising up in his nostrils. The thud of bootsteps in sand during morning drills. It didn't matter that he was in the safety of his own home and not in a war zone; the familiar trickle of doubt began.

Wendell let his eyes adjust as they scanned the windows of the first floor. The sound had come from the front porch area, and he moved toward the front door, ever so lightly so as not to elicit a single creak from the hundred-year-old pine floorboards. As he crept toward the door, he was met with a noise from the other side. Wendell's blood froze. The desert images came again. He closed his eyes, willing his thoughts to clear, his heart to slow. But they had already gotten away from him.

Outside, there was a sound on the porch floor. Wendell gripped the bat harder and walked up to the door, keeping low. He was about to peer out the keyhole when he heard a voice. "Shhh," someone said. There was more than one person. He was about to reach for the outdoor light switch when the door handle creaked. Wendell looked down in horror as it began to jiggle back and forth. They were trying to get in, to surprise him. Well, whoever it was had their own surprise coming.

In one fell motion, Wendell flipped the lock, flung the door open, and raised the bat over his shoulder. From the other side of the screen came two screams. Wendell kicked the screen door open and leaped out onto the porch.

Two figures stumbled backward, much smaller than he'd thought. One fell down. Both screamed again. They were female voices, young voices. "Wendell! It's me."

Wendell let the bat fall to his side and stepped back, letting his eyes adjust. "Julia?"

The girls sat side by side at his mother's vintage Formica kitchen table, a crocheted blanket draped across their hunched shoulders. There were two steaming cups of tea in front of them, which neither had touched. Wendell reached for the one in front of him. What he really could've used was a shot of bourbon, but that wasn't happening. So he poured honey into his mug and began stirring it with a teaspoon.

"That's a lot of sugar, you know."

He looked up. Julia was staring at him. "Sugar? You just tried to break into my house. I almost swung a bat at you, and you're worried about my sugar?"

She glared back at him. "You scared us half to death."

"I scared *you*?" Wendell sat back hard in his chair and laughed. It came out as a sharp bark, and Pippa's eyes widened. "Sorry," he said, regaining composure. Then to Julia, "You have some nerve."

But he regretted it as soon as the words were out of his mouth. He was on high alert, still coming down, and it made him irritable. When he thought of the raised bat over his shoulder and the two little girls tumbling away, he shuddered. It could've ended so badly.

Julia picked up her cup of tea and blew on it. She glanced at Pippa, who looked heavy-lidded and exhausted. "Still too hot," she told her.

Wendell glanced at the wall clock: twelve forty-five a.m. "Does your aunt have any idea where you are?" Looking at the two of them, he already knew the answer.

"She's sound asleep," Julia said decisively. She set her teacup down. "We need your help."

Wendell was set on knowing what on earth could've brought them out here in the middle of the night. Whatever it was, it must've been bad. But first things first. "We have to call her," he said, rising and moving toward the old-fashioned phone on the wall. "She at least has to know you're okay."

"No!" Julia leaped from her seat and reached for his wrist, almost knocking over her cup of tea. It startled him, and the look on his face must've startled her, too, because she let go before he could jerk away instinctively. He was a trained soldier trying to deescalate. She shouldn't be lunging at him like that. "Please, not yet. Let's talk first."

It went against his better judgment, but the night was already out of control, so he found himself sitting back down reluctantly. "You've got five minutes, and then we call her. I can't risk her thinking you're missing or maybe worse. It's not right." He didn't add the next thought that occurred to him: two little girls from the family he worked for, alone with him in his house in the middle of the night. He winced. "Hurry up and tell me, please."

Julia leaned forward, lacing her fingers together. Despite her young age, it was an authoritative posture of a person with far more years and confidence. "I have a proposal."

"Shoot," he said. Beside her, Pippa took a loud slurpy sip of her tea and smiled, shyly, across the table. "Want some honey?" he asked her. She nodded.

Before he could pass it, Julia grabbed the honey from him and thunked it down in front of her sister. "Are you listening?" she asked him. "Because this is important."

"Yes." Wendell sighed. "Go on."

"You've heard my aunt's plan for White Pines."

It stung, being reminded. Wendell nodded.

"And you liked working there, yes?"

"I do. I still work there."

"Not for long," Julia said.

He couldn't argue that. She paused, glancing around the farmhouse kitchen. "This is . . . homey, I suppose," she said in a tone that sounded like she was being generous.

Wendell frowned. "What does my house have anything to do with your being here?"

Julia lifted one shoulder. "It has potential," she went on as though she hadn't heard a thing he'd said. "Anyway, I know White Pines is your only job."

"For now."

"My father liked you. You're a good caretaker. He never would have let you go from this, your one job." Her blue eyes were steely with intention.

"Can you please get to the point?"

Julia glanced sideways at Pippa, whose head was tipped back, her nose in the teacup, as she drained it. "You know what 'caretaker' means, right?"

Wendell was losing patience. "Julia, I'm not sure what you're getting at."

She rushed on. "It means 'taking care.' How would you feel staying on at White Pines and taking care of it for good?"

"That sounds nice, but it's not possible."

Julia shook her head, a slow smile creeping across her face. "But it is. You can stay on at White Pines and continue to take care of it. With one condition."

Wendell had a bad feeling. "Which is?"

She sat back in her chair and crossed her arms. "You take care of us, too."

Wendell couldn't help it. He laughed. Loudly. And as soon as he did, he found he couldn't stop.

Julia's expression soured. "What? What exactly is so funny?"

Wendell wasn't sure if it was humor or relief or the two mixed together with the late hour and the frightening close call they'd all just had. But he couldn't stop laughing.

"This is not funny," Julia said, pushing her chair back. "This is serious. *I'm* serious."

Wendell had to turn away, he was laughing so hard. "I'm sorry," he managed finally. "It's just . . . I don't know. Ridiculous."

Julia scowled at him. "Ridiculous? This is my life." Gone was the decisive and demanding young woman who'd been seated across the table as if it were her house and she were interviewing him for a job. Her lower lip trembled. Sensing a turn, Pippa looked between the two of them anxiously. If he weren't careful, her lip would start, too.

"Wait, I'm sorry," Wendell said, pulling his chair back in. "I don't think that at all. It's just . . . I was your dad's caretaker for a property. For barns and fields."

"And orchards and trees and, to some extent, Radcliffe. All living things. Things that require taking care of."

"Yes. But that's not the same as people. Especially little people."

"I'm not little. In three years, I'll be eighteen, the same as you and your brother when you could enlist."

The mention of Wesley caught him. This girl knew far more

than he realized. "Three years is a long time," he said softly. So much could happen in three years. The time it took to do basic training and be deployed to Afghanistan. For a soldier to be killed in action. To bury a brother and, not long after, a father. Wendell swallowed hard.

But Julia was not letting up. "Look, according to my lawyer, we need a guardian. And from what I learned about my trust, there may be enough money for me to keep White Pines—if I can find a guardian." She stared at him, waiting for it to sink in. "You need White Pines to keep your job. Everyone wins."

Wendell shook his head. So she'd gotten herself a lawyer. He was unsurprised, maybe even impressed. "Why now, in the middle of the night?"

"Because I don't want my aunt to know about this. And we're running out of time."

"Julia, you were furious with me a few days ago. Now you want me to live with you?"

She glared back at him. "That's exactly what I want."

Unable to stand the look in her eyes, he rose. Wendell could feel her desperation, and it was affecting. It was also not lost on him what a touching request she was making. But there was simply no way.

"Look, I can cook, I can take care of Pippa, and I can do laundry. All we need is an adult who can take care of White Pines so we can stay there. That's all."

"That's all?" He had to be firm, right here and right now, and not let this runaway idea take them any further down the road. "Julia, you have that person. It's Candace—"

"I hate her!" she snapped, eyes ablaze. "Look what she's done. Stealing Raddy. Selling our home. Taking us away to a place we've never even been."

This was getting too heated. Julia was livid, and Pippa looked like she might cry. It was time to get them back home, even if it was the last thing they wanted. But Julia was not done.

"Do you know Pippa rode her bike all the way here tonight? In the dark! She just learned to ride a bike yesterday. It took us an hour to get here." Julia tugged Pippa's hand lightly, and Pippa stood up. For the first time, Wendell noticed her right knee was skinned. There was a long red scrape covered with dirt.

"Pippa, you're hurt?" He knelt beside her, examining it. When he looked up, she was eye level. Her eyes were cornflower blue, just like her dad's. Wendell felt his throat tighten. "Can I help you clean it? I'll be gentle, I promise."

In the bathroom medicine cabinet, he found the small first-aid kit. It was a leather pouch, the same one his mother had kept all those years ago for the family. How many times had he and Wesley torn through it looking for Band-Aids?

He brought the kit out to the kitchen, but Julia held out her hand. "I'll do it."

Wendell handed her the kit and stood by, watching. Julia was so tender and so thorough. "You could be a nurse," he told her.

"Or a doctor."

He grimaced. "Or a doctor."

Pippa whimpered once as Julia ran an alcohol swab cloth over the knee, but that was all. "Very brave," he told her.

Before she stood up, Julia kissed Pippa's knee. "All better." Then she rose and handed the pouch back to him. "Thanks."

As he reached for it, she hung on. "Think about what I said," she urged. Her eyes were a mix of steel and something else: fear, he thought. "Please." Then she let go.

"We should call your aunt," Wendell said.

"Not necessary. We're leaving now."

It was almost one thirty in the morning. "It's too far, and it's not safe. Let me give you a ride."

"We don't need your help," Julia said, taking Pippa's hand. "Thank you for the tea." As if they'd just come to visit on a summer day instead of attempting a break-in during the middle of the night.

"I know you're mad, but I insist." When she glared at him again, he added, "Or I call your aunt. Your choice."

"Fine." Julia gave in.

"Come on, we'll put the bikes in the back of my truck."

Outside, the sky was pitch dark, the half-moon the only sliver of light as they moved away from the house floodlights. He could hear the spin of the bike tires as the girls pushed their bikes up the hill behind him to the barn that served as a two-car garage. What a night. What a crazy proposal.

He had just slid the garage door ajar when there was a distinct kick from across the yard. "What was that?" Julia asked. Both girls spun around.

Wendell's heart began to race. He'd completely forgotten about Radcliffe. "Nothing, just an animal. Better get in the truck."

Radcliffe nickered.

Shit. He must've heard Julia or sensed her somehow. Wendell reached for Pippa's bike and began talking loudly. "Here, let me help you put this in the truck, kiddo."

But Julia knew what she'd heard. Of course she did. She turned to face him. "You have a horse?"

Wendell's thoughts raced. If he said yes, she might want to see it. He couldn't have that. "No, it's probably coming from the neighbors. They have cows."

But it was too late. Julia set her bike down in the middle of the driveway. "That was a horse. And it came from right over there. In that shed."

Wendell lifted Pippa's bike into the bed of his truck. "Julia, it's late. Let's go."

But Julia was already halfway to the barn with Pippa trailing behind. Wendell felt all of his reserves drain as their shadowy figures drifted away.

Julia had reached the barn. "Can I go in?" she shouted back to him.

It was over. No matter what he said. He began walking in their direction.

Radcliffe was on high alert now, and Wendell could hear the horse rattling the stall door from within. He groaned in frustration and cut in front of Julia. "Here." He swung the door open. The scent of horse and hay met them in the doorway.

Julia froze, peering inside. "Oh my God. Is that . . . ?"

Wendell nodded grudgingly. "Go on," he said.

Twenty-Two

Roberta

At first she thought she was seeing things. As she drove by the Combs house Saturday morning on the way home from a trip to the garden center, she noticed a teenager standing outside. She slowed the car.

Yes, she was right. At the top of the driveway was a girl with a long blond ponytail. She was pushing a wheelbarrow toward the little red barn behind the house. Roberta paused at the end of the driveway. It was absolutely none of her business, but she had been worried about Wendell. And she hadn't heard a peep since that phone call they'd had. Plus there was the matter of the casserole dish she'd brought for dinner a few weeks earlier. Usually, Wendell returned things straightaway, but this time her baking dish was still sitting somewhere in his kitchen.

She parked the car at the top of the driveway. The girl was already gone from sight, but the garden cart was parked outside the barn door. Roberta slid her sunglasses up on her head and strolled over. "Hello?" she called out.

There appeared to be some activity in the barn, but no one answered. As Roberta drew closer, she called out again, "Wendell, are you home?"

A girl popped her head out the door. "Hello!"

Roberta halted. It was Julia Lancaster.

"Hi, Roberta. Want to meet Radcliffe?"

"Who?" This was not what she was expecting. Roberta swatted at a fly and followed Julia into the barn and across the dirt floor. It was a small barn, once used by Wendell's mother as a potting shed. The wall-to-wall sliding door at the far side was wide open, letting in full sun and a scene that took Roberta's breath away. There was Wendell standing in a small grassy enclosure beside a pile of wooden fence posts and rails, holding a post-hole digger. Beside him was a woman. And behind them stood a big red horse. "My Lord!"

Wendell smiled sheepishly when he saw her. Like he was twelve years old again. "Bertie."

"Wendell." Roberta looked between the four of them. She needed a minute.

"Hello!" The woman approached with her hand extended, and Roberta did a double take.

"Ginny Feldman!" Well, this was even more of a surprise than the horse. "How nice to see you."

But there was no time for handshakes or greetings. Julia motioned to a wheelbarrow in the corner. "I brought another load of dirt," she said.

"Bring it over here!" Wendell called back to her.

Roberta barely had time to step out of the way. "Coming through," Julia said, wheeling it narrowly around Roberta.

Roberta stood there staring while they went on about their business as if she weren't even there. What on earth was going on? Apparently, no one here was going to tell her; she may as well have asked the horse, who looked at her now, swished his tail, and snorted. Well. Roberta cleared her throat just like she used to before delivering a courtroom verdict. "Wendell? A word?"

They stood outside the barn door at the edge of the patio, discussing the matter in hushed tones. "So you've got yourself a horse.

And a work crew that includes your old girlfriend. And you're all building a pasture." Roberta glanced at the busy scene on the hill behind her. Had Wendell lost his mind?

"Not a pasture," Wendell corrected. "A paddock."

Roberta looked at him. "Paddock." She let the quiet settle between them. There were so many questions batting around her head that she had no idea where to begin without embarrassing Wendell or sticking her nose in further. "I came for my casserole dish," she said instead.

"Right. Sorry, Bertie. I've been meaning to return that, just with the last few days and all . . ." His voice drifted. She waited as he went inside and emerged a moment later with the dish. "It was delicious. Thank you."

"You're welcome." She took the dish and held it against her chest, eyes on the barn. "So what exactly is the plan here?"

Wendell ran a hand through his hair. "Honestly, I don't know. I wanted to help somehow, and rescuing that horse seemed about the only thing I could do."

"Uh-huh." Roberta cocked her head. The Lancasters were a family of means. Everything they did in Saybrook was top-quality. "How much?" she asked.

Wendell frowned. "Excuse me?"

"You know what I'm asking." She nodded in the direction of the barn, where the horse stood outside swishing his tail in the sun. "How much did that rescue cost you?"

Wendell let his breath out. "More than you want to know."

Roberta hugged her dish tighter to her chest. "That much."

"Yes, ma'am."

Wendell was a man of modest means. Sure, he'd inherited the beautiful farmhouse, but aside from a small military stipend and whatever savings he might have been able to squirrel away as a caretaker, she imagined all his assets were wrapped up in the property she stood on now. That horse probably cost twice more than her car. "I best be off," she said finally. "Good luck with the fence. And the horse." She turned down the flagstone path to the driveway, even though she was leaving with far more questions than she'd been able to find answers to since pulling up the driveway. And she didn't like that one bit.

"Roberta."

She paused and turned around. "Yes?"

"They want to live with me."

There was no way she'd heard right. Cupping one hand over her ear, she walked back toward him. "Excuse these old ears, I didn't quite catch what you said."

Wendell's expression was grave. "The girls. They sneaked over here in the middle of the night and asked me to be their legal guardian."

"Their guardian? You?"

He shrugged. "I know, it sounds ridiculous."

"No, no, I didn't mean that. But those girls have family, and I can't imagine their aunt, from what you've told me, would even hear of such a thing."

"Things at their home are pretty volatile at the moment. Julia hired herself that lawyer. And her lawyer called me yesterday."

Roberta could feel her judge's robe settling over her shoulders as she processed this information, trying to keep her expression and opinion neutral. "I see." She studied his expression, looking for some clue as to what this meant to him, if anything.

"I told the girls there was no way I could do this, Bertie. But when Jamie Aldeen asked if we could meet, I agreed to. I figure I at least owe it to Alan and Anne to have the conversation. Even if I don't think this is the solution."

Roberta shrugged. "Well, solutions to problems come in

many forms. A change in guardianship depends on many factors, and in this case, the first being the aunt's desire to release custody of the children. And more important, your desire to obtain it." She narrowed her eyes. "Wendell, do you have such a desire?"

He flushed. "No, Bertie. I would love to help Pippa and Julia. But I don't think I'm cut out for this."

"Right." Still, Roberta sensed some hesitation. "Because that would be a tremendously life-changing thing, taking guardianship of two children. It's a commitment that many view as a life calling. And it could be forever."

"Like I said, I'm going to the meeting to share all these very points. There may be another way I can help the girls, but that's not it." He glanced uneasily up the hill. "Speaking of, I need to get back up there."

To her utmost surprise, Wendell leaned in and gave her a quick peck on the cheek. It was something he'd not done since he was a little boy.

Back at home, Roberta called Jamie Aldeen's office. "So I hear you've met my young neighbor," she said.

Jamie chuckled. "We've had a phone conversation and a meeting, neither short."

Roberta began to wonder if she'd made a mistake sending Julia Lancaster to Jamie. Now she was involved. And so was Wendell. "From Julia's conversation with you, she's gotten it in her head that she would do best by finding a guardian."

"That's true," Jamie said. "I think a judge would be hard-pressed to give a fifteen-year-old custody of a minor as well as control over her life. She can't drive. There's the matter of a residence. It's complicated, to say the least."

"But you think she has a chance?"

Jamie sighed. "You know we attorneys don't like to play the

odds or give our clients false hope. If she pursues this officially, I think it's going to be an uphill battle. But yes. I do think she has a chance. In fact, I filed the motion for a hearing with the court today."

Roberta sucked in her breath. So things were already in play. "The reason I ask is that the guardian the children have in mind is a family friend of mine."

"Ah. Small world, that town of Saybrook," Jamie said.

"You don't have to tell me," Roberta said, trying to keep the conversation light.

Jamie said, "I also don't have to tell you about attorney-client privilege, but I can confirm that a potential guardian is joining us for our meeting tomorrow. I think the best place to start is to make sure everyone wants the same thing and has a firm understanding of what this really involves."

"Right you are. Well, I wish you luck. And if you've any questions at all, please don't hesitate to reach out. With your clients' permission, of course."

"Thanks, Roberta."

When she hung up, Roberta felt a sudden wave of fatigue. Wendell was right. Whether any of them had wanted to be or not, they were all involved. She wondered about the meeting tomorrow: if Wendell really meant that he was going just to support the girls and set the facts straight. Or if there was some small part of him that was going because he might actually be considering the girls' request.

It was ridiculous, in so many ways. Wendell was the closest thing Roberta would ever get to having a child of her own to worry over. As such, she felt protective of him, first. He'd lost so much in his young life, and since, he'd worked hard to keep himself from heartbreak. For years, he'd stayed that course, pushing friends and loved ones away. Forbidding himself any real joy or connection, as if he had to punish himself for something. It had broken her own heart, watching him do that. But she'd come to accept that whatever small way he'd let her in, she would grab ahold of. Wendell had built firm boundaries; he let almost no one through.

But today there were facts that spoke to a break in those boundaries. The fact that Ginny Feldman was at his house. And he'd pulled that crazy stunt and rescued the horse for Julia. No wonder the girl had set her sights on him as a guardian. In her mind, Wendell had acted heroically. Finally, there was the fact that Wendell was going to meet with Julia's attorney.

But there were other facts, of the commonsense variety, that rang out louder. No one knew better than she how many things could go wrong when shuffling children between custodial relationships. As challenging as their situation might be with their aunt, the best thing that could happen to those girls might be to remain with family. They would be cared for and go to the best of schools, and the subsequent travel and adjustments might just make them more resilient.

Roberta told herself these things as she walked Maisey that afternoon, and later, as she dined outdoors by her garden. People often got notions about what they thought was in the best interest of a child. As a judge, she was armed with more than notions.

But as she got ready for bed that night, staring at her reflection in the mirror, she could not shake the fact that those children had gone to Wendell in the middle of the night. They had sneaked from their house, ridden their bicycles through darkness, and pulled him from his bed to ask such a question.

One thing she knew from all her years as a probate judge in

the district family court: no matter what outsiders or child development experts or even the courts might think, there was one oft-overlooked barometer for determining what might be best for a child that was truer than all the rest. And that was the wish of the child.

Twenty-Three

Julia

Her gut had been right. Of course it had. She'd felt it the night Wendell had watched her teach Pippa to ride her bike, which was what had led to the two of them sneaking out and going to his house. But the second she saw Raddy in Wendell's barn, there was no doubt. Wendell Combs was the guardian they needed.

Chloe and Sam, however, had not shared her conviction.

"Are you out of your mind?" Chloe sat cross-legged on Julia's bedroom rug, braiding Pippa's hair. "You basically asked a stranger to take you in."

"Wendell's not strange," Pippa whispered.

"You mean he's not a stranger," Julia corrected.

Chloe made a face. "He's probably both."

Julia ignored this, distracted momentarily by her best friend's hands moving deftly through Pippa's fairy-spun hair. Just as her mother had. But what reminded her most of their mother was watching Chloe section off pieces of hair, quickly and expertly. Julia used to howl when she was that age and her mother tried to braid her hair. What she would give to take that back.

"So he's quiet and kind of serious," Julia argued. "But he takes care of this place like it's his own. And let's not forget he saved Raddy." She glanced out the window at the empty barn. "You just don't know him."

Chloe affixed a sage-green bow to the end of Pippa's braid and turned to Julia. "Do you? I mean, really, Jules. How well do you know this guy? And let's remember—he's a *guy.*"

Julia couldn't dismiss that point. No matter how you looked at it, there was a big difference in having a male guardian versus a female, especially when it came to caring for two girls.

Sure, she had doubts. What if they didn't get along? Worse, what if they grew really close but he changed his mind? Then there was the matter of Wendell actually having a life of his own beyond them. There was Ginny, whom he'd introduced as an "old friend" but clearly seemed to be more. How did she, or any other future woman, fit into the picture? The bottom line was, so much could go wrong.

Sam had shared some of her darker concerns. "Jules, this sounds kind of crazy to me. What if he's a predator?"

This made her leap to the defense. "Oh, please. My father knew Wendell for years while he worked here. He even went to Wendell's house a few times, and I don't recall any mention of bodies buried in the backyard."

Sam was not letting her off the hook. "My mistake. No shallow graves guarantees he'll be a super stand-in parent."

"Look, my dad was a good judge of character." She paused, trying to lighten the moment. "That's why I never introduced him to you."

Sam scoffed. "Hilarious. But seriously, Jules—this guy could be a total delinquent."

"I don't think so, Sam. He served in the National Guard. In fact, my dad told me he saw active combat and even got some kind of medal."

"Well, that's pretty cool. But I've also heard that going to war can give people trauma. It can mess them up."

"Mess them up, like becoming an overnight orphan messes someone up?"

Sam shut up as soon as she said it. "Shit. I'm sorry. I didn't mean—"

"It's okay. Just forget it." This was what always happened. Death found its way into conversations, no matter whom she was talking to or what about. All around her, the veil of her parents' loss loomed.

The one person she did not tell about Wendell's rescue of Radcliffe was Candace. It was too risky. Candace had not been happy when Wendell delivered them back home the other night. After being woken by the ringing doorbell, Candace had looked aghast, seeing the three of them standing in the doorway. Wordlessly, she'd sent the girls up to their rooms, but Julia could hear the fury in her tone as she spoke with Wendell.

"I'm very sorry to have woken you with such a fright," he'd said. "I told the girls I'd have to bring them right home."

"What on earth were they doing there?" she'd cried.

Wendell sounded chagrined. "They asked me if I would consider being their guardian."

"Good Lord. Not this again."

At first Julia feared she'd gotten Wendell in trouble, but luckily, Candace blamed only her. As she ferried Pippa up the stairs to bed, Julia overheard their conversation below. "Mr. Combs, please forgive the terrible interruption of your night. That child has been asking every Tom, Dick, and Harry to adopt her in her efforts to stay here. She is out of control, I'm very sorry she's dragged you into this."

The next morning, to Julia, she said, "This idea of finding a new family has taken over your judgment. You're becoming a negative influence on your little sister, and now you're interfering with our neighbors and with Mr. Combs. This must end here."

There was no way around it: she had to tell Candace the truth. "It's actually just beginning." When Candace looked confused, she added, "I told you Pippa and I don't want to leave, but you didn't take me seriously. So I found someone who will. I hired a lawyer."

Candace actually laughed. Julia couldn't believe it; adults had the strangest reactions to serious news. "Mr. Banks? I'm afraid he's the family attorney, Julia. He cannot represent you or your foolish notions."

"Not Mr. Banks. Her name is Jamie Aldeen, and she's a family practitioner. I met with her yesterday. I filed for emancipation."

This time Candace did not laugh. Not even close. "You cannot be serious." Her voice was icy.

Julia bit her lip. She thought back to what Jamie had asked her about feeling safe in her home. "I wanted to tell you, but I knew you wouldn't like it."

"Well, you're right. I don't! Do you have any idea what you've done? You're dragging all of us into court, and all our personal business will be fodder for the public."

"It's confidential," Julia said, trying to keep her voice even. "I'm a minor."

Candace jabbed one manicured finger in the air between them. "Which is exactly why you need a guardian!" She shook her head angrily. "Now I have to call Mr. Banks. I'm calling your therapist, too. Maybe she can talk you out of this nonsense."

Candace had called both, and that afternoon Julia found herself once again sitting across from Miss Lottie, who looked sad-faced but concerned when they met.

"Julia, if you are serious about emancipation, you do realize I would likely be asked by the courts to weigh in?"

Julia had thought of that, and it had seemed like a good thing.

Lottie spoke softly but firmly. "Your recent behavior, despite the valid reasons you state for it, could be considered rash and not in the best interest of Pippa. You must realize going out in the night like that, alone, could've ended very badly?"

Julia's mind flashed to Pippa's skinned knee, her anxious face at Wendell's. "But I'm doing this for her," she argued.

"I believe you," Lottie said. "And I know how desperate you feel. But from now on, if you want to make a case to a judge that you are mature and responsible enough to be considered for emancipation, your actions need to demonstrate that. Let your legal counsel advise you. And stop taking matters into your own hands."

Lottie made perfect sense. But what Lottie, and others, could never understand was how much was at stake. What Julia did not tell Lottie about was Wendell buying Radcliffe. Although he hadn't told Julia to keep it a secret, she knew that if Candace found out, she would probably fire him. And after all he'd done for her and Pippa, she couldn't risk doing that to Wendell.

After her appointment with Lottie, she vowed to be more careful. More sensible. In order to see Raddy, Julia covered her tracks. She made up stories to tell both Pippa and Candace, that she was going bike riding with Chloe. Or to the town beach. Pippa had been sworn to secrecy about Raddy being at Wendell's house, but if she knew Julia was going to see him, she'd want to come, too, and Julia couldn't risk Pippa accidentally giving the secret away. Luckily, Candace was so entrenched with realtors and the lawyer that she barely paid attention. It gave Julia a chance to spend more time with Wendell and put to rest any doubts that lingered.

"Wendell, why did you take the job at White Pines?" she asked. It was the afternoon of the meeting with Jamie Aldeen.

He looked confused. "It's a good job. Your folks were good people." He returned his attention to the post he was setting.

"That's not what I mean. I see the way you are when you're there. You appreciate White Pines maybe as much as I do."

Wendell looked up at her. "Maybe." He stepped back to eyeball whether the post was level while she held it. "Tip it a little to the right. No, that's left. One more inch . . ." Wendell's militant perfectionism was starting to wear on her. But there was Raddy, grazing happily in his pen, so no way was she about to complain. She held the post tight as Wendell shoveled gravel into the base of the hole to help stabilize it. Then he packed it with dirt.

"What about White Pines do you love?" she asked.

" 'Love' is a strong word."

Julia groaned.

"I can tell you what I like about it. I like the peace and quiet of it, working in the fields, knowing that I don't have to talk to anyone or bend or flex for anyone all day."

"So you hate people," she said.

"No, I just like being alone."

"What about White Pines? Everyone who visits says it touches them, that it's a magical place. Does it do that for you?"

"You sure do ask a lot of questions."

"You sure do try to avoid them," she told him. "Come on. Don't be a sissy."

He threw her a look.

"I'll stop talking if you answer," she said.

"I doubt that." But she could see from his expression that he was picturing the property. "I guess I like the way the place can change so much each season but still remain itself."

"Like how?"

"The way the sun hits the orchard in the late afternoon on a fall day, and the way the edges of the pond freeze into these sparkling slivers where the water meets the land, one layer stretching over the other like silver-blue threads. Thousands of them, if you look close." His eyes twinkled as he told her.

"Remember that spring we found the baby bird?"

He shook his head. "You found the bird. Then you made me climb up the tree and find its nest."

Julia loved that memory. "You didn't seem to mind."

"Nah, I guess I didn't."

He was coming around, and she could feel it. "See, you do love White Pines, even if you won't admit it. If you came to take care of us, you wouldn't ever have to leave it."

"Julia. Your aunt is selling White Pines. You know that."

"Not if I stop her. My lawyer said that she needs to review the will first, but who knows? There could be a way around it."

Wendell sighed and set down the level he was using. "So now you're not just going to emancipate yourself, but you're going to stop the sale of White Pines?"

"There's no guarantee, but I have to try."

Just like that, the spell was broken. Wendell dropped the shovel in the wheelbarrow and headed to the last post hole. "Julia, I'm going to that meeting. But it's because your attorney, Ms. Aldeen, called and asked. I don't want you to read into this any more than that. I've told you how I feel about your request."

Julia kept her eyes trained on the ground as she trailed him to the last post. "I know, I know." But it didn't mean she'd stop trying. She'd never stop trying.

Twenty-Four

Wendell

He had always prided himself on honesty, and every time he saw Candace Lancaster and thought of the horse he was hiding in the barn behind his house, he felt like a liar.

Wendell was a man of his word not just from his National Guard training; his own parents had raised him as such, long before his days in the military. He understood the value of a person's trust. If Candace asked about the horse, he would tell her the truth, even if it meant losing his job or ending Julia's secret visits to his house. There were good reasons he'd done what he'd done. But there was also good reason to face the consequences of your decisions. That was life.

He hadn't been in the main utility barn for more than a few moments that morning when he heard his name called from outside. But it was not Candace. Geoffrey Banks stepped out of his car. Wendell hadn't seen him since the meeting up at the house two weeks earlier.

"Good to see you again," Geoffrey said, extending his hand. "Do you have a moment?"

"Of course. How can I help?"

"The surveyors have completed their work, and I wanted to go over the maps with you. Candace would like to identify them for prospective buyers."

Inside the barn, Wendell invited Geoffrey over to a sweeping worktable. Geoffrey paused, looking up at all the tools hanging on pegboards, the equipment covered and stored in the corners. He ran his hand over the worktable surface before unrolling a large white survey map. "This space is better kept than my office."

"Thank you. Alan took a lot of pride in taking care of things around here."

Geoffrey scanned the barn interior appreciatively. "And you still do. So, here's the update. The engineers have subdivided the estate into eleven different parcels. As such, Candace's broker will be showing each of the separate lots to interested clients. But ultimately, she'd prefer to sell to one developer."

Wendell scanned the map. The estate had indeed been divided. What Geoffrey did not know, and could never understand, was that the divisions on paper represented something entirely different to anyone who knew White Pines. Wendell knew the land intimately, as one vast parcel from forest edge to waterline. From the rise of the orchard hill to the dip of the wetlands. The only divisions he knew were natural: watercourses, elevations, rock formations. The tree line that jutted out against the horizon. The depression of swampland where beavers and egrets and old mother snappers made their habitats. Those were the divisions of the land that he worked with and worked around, respectfully. As his gaze left Geoffrey's pointed finger and followed the topography and elevation markers, he recognized every nook and cranny of White Pines. It was the land he traversed by footstep and measured by stride. The only divisions were made by Mother Nature, by habitat and by season. He worked his tongue around his mouth in silence, taking it all in. Reluctantly, Wendell's gaze followed Geoffrey's hand tracing the subdivision. A gold signet ring flashed on his pinkie finger in the narrow band of sunlight slipping through the barn window, as unnatural and vulgar as the subdivision it traced.

Geoffrey stabbed a finger at the largest parcel in the northeastern corner of the map. "Over here, we have what will likely command the largest price. It's got a great view, or so I'm told."

"That's the peach tree grove."

"Is it? Well, it's going to have to come down, for whoever buys it. Best view on the estate. Candace wants the buyer to have a three-hundred-sixty-degree sightline."

"She wants it cut down?" Wendell's stomach turned. "That orchard is almost a hundred years old. Her grandfather started it in the thirties." In all his years on the estate, Wendell had worked hardest and longest on the peach orchard. Since he began, he'd already turned over and replanted half of it. Alan had loved not only the knotty crooked trees that defied orderly rows but also the fruit. The scent in August. The honeybees attracted by the peaches and the shady view beneath the branches. How many times had Wendell spied the family under those boughs, enjoying a picnic lunch? It was the stuff of children's storybooks and old movies. And now they wanted to dig it up to build a structure that would likely jut out garishly against the natural backdrop, a stain against the bow of terrain and flush of fauna.

"That depends on who the buyer is."

Wendell could picture it: an unimaginative boxy neighborhood, with alternating colors, vinyl-sided with faux chimneys and composite shutter. Attached two-car garages on each construction. Wendell stepped away from the worktable. "How does this change my management of the property?"

"Candace hired a broker. They've decided to attempt to attract a developer first." Geoffrey pointed to several proposed driveway locations. "The broker feels it's important that we visually mark the property divisions so potential buyers can envision the actual lots."

"So they can imagine their yard. Where to put the trampoline or swimming pool," Wendell muttered.

Geoffrey looked confused. "Right. Anyway, our idea is to add to the existing stakes laid by the surveyors. Candace would like it if you could walk the property lines and mark the proposed driveway entrances with different-colored tapes. The broker has lined up showings in the coming days."

"Days," Wendel said. But it would take mere hours for the backhoes to come in and desecrate the peach trees. He imagined the wildlife habitats, undisturbed in their present state, being knocked down, dug out, filled in. He ran his hand roughly through his hair, shaking his head. "Alan would have hated this."

Geoffrey glanced down at the map, then at Wendell. "I know. But Alan is no longer with us." He looked truly sorry, and Wendell could hear the empathy in his tone, but it did not change the fate of White Pines or what he was asking Wendell to do. Geoffrey put a hand on Wendell's shoulder. "So, are you on board?"

Through the barn window, Wendell caught the wild flash of greenery over the shoulder of Geoffrey's suit jacket. "I'll start today."

For the rest of the day, he drove the Gator around the property, marking the proposed driveway entries for each lot on the map. Wendell was not an engineer or surveyor. What he felt like, standing back and looking up at the colored lines of tape fluttering against the fields, was an executioner.

Finished with his grim work for the day, he was locking up

the lower barn door when he heard voices floating down from the house. He glanced up. Candace was talking to a woman in the driveway, but she was hidden from view behind the family car. No matter; he'd seen enough that day, and it was time to go home.

Wendell was about to climb into his truck when a VW Beetle rolled down the driveway and pulled up beside him.

"Ginny?"

She smiled ruefully. "Hey, Wendell. Just finishing for the day?"

Wendell nodded. "Long one. How about you? What brings you to White Pines?"

Ginny was dressed nicely, but she looked uncomfortable. "I had a meeting."

Wendell glanced up at the house as it dawned on him. "A meeting."

"Yes. Candace Lancaster just signed my parents' agency to list White Pines." Even as she shielded her eyes from the late sun, he saw the flicker of remorse. "I wanted to tell you the other night, but I never thought we'd get the listing. It just seemed pointless."

Wendell's mind rolled back to the dinner they'd shared on his porch, like old times. To the moment in the kitchen. And the next day, when she'd returned to help build the fence with Julia. "It seemed pointless to you?"

Ginny put the car in park and got out. "Please let me explain. Candace called the agency for an interview, but it didn't go well. At all. I started to tell you that night at your place, but then you shared how upset the sale of White Pines made you. I didn't want to upset you even more, especially since I never thought we'd land it."

"Were you going to tell me now that you landed it?"

Her expression twisted. "Yes! Right after I told my parents. You have to understand, this is big news for them. Their agency has been floundering, and my dad had the heart attack. If we're successful selling this place, it will change everything for them."

The conflict in her voice was genuine, but he was too caught off guard.

"It's okay, Ginny. I get it." There was no point in making her feel bad. But he didn't want to hear anymore.

Ginny wouldn't let it go. "Someone would've sold it, Wendell. This is so hard for me, knowing what this place means to you. But it means something so different for my family."

"I said I get it." It came out harsher than he'd meant, and he instantly regretted it. There was the familiar flash of hurt in her eyes. Just like all those years ago. Wendell stepped toward her. "Ginny, wait. I'm sorry."

But she was already getting back in the car. "That makes two of us." Before he could say anything else, she put the car in drive and was gone.

Wendell spun around to the barn. There was a bucket by the door filled with the tape he'd used to mark the fields, and he grabbed it now and slung it at the barn. It hit the wall with a crack and spun away to the ground, spilling its contents across the driveway. He glanced up at the house. Agreeing to stay on at White Pines had been the worst decision.

The dark mood stayed with him back at home, and when he turned his lights out late that night, he knew sleep would not come. He had been wrong to accept the job offer from Candace. Despite the bonus. He'd have been better off cutting his losses and taking a position on a contractor's crew or in the hardware store to tide him over until he found a position like managing White Pines. Only he knew the truth: there was nothing else like it. But this was worse. Worse than leaving or letting go, worse than giving up the sanctuary-like peace of the estate and his work among the wild fields and animals. He'd have been better off working the counter at a fast-food joint; the constant din, smells, and influx of demanding customers sure to trigger his PTSD from Afghanistan. It was a terrifying thought for a man who fought every day to buffer himself from such episodes. But even that would have been better than systematically dismantling the place that had saved him.

At some point he fell into a fitful slumber, and for the first time in a long while, he was with Wesley. Not the Wesley who haunted him, from their last year together, serving in the Guard. But Wesley as a child. They were running, across the upper yard behind the farmhouse, where the horse was now living. Their mother's garden was in its full glory beside the red shed, a tangle of tomato vine tinged with robust orbs of fruit. Tidy rows of frilly-leafed red lettuce. Trellises covered in green beans. Wesley was chasing him in some kind of game, and Wendell could feel his sturdy legs pumping beneath him, his heart pounding in his ears. His little brother was lithe and fast, and despite Wendell's age and height advantage, running was Wesley's claim to childhood neighborhood fame, not his. As Wendell rounded the corner of the garden and sprinted across the open yard, he could hear Wesley catching up. He ran faster, his legs straining. But then he stumbled, catching the toe of his sneaker in a divot in the grass, and he almost fell. He was done for. Wesley would surely have him now. But just as he turned, prepared to be face-to-face, Wesley closing the gap, his little brother was not there. The sound of his breath behind Wendell had faded, the pounding of heels in the grass distant. Wendell slowed to a walk and spun around. Wesley had fallen back, drifting as if a tide were pulling him away. He was running, arms pumping, but drifting backward. "Hey!" Wendell called out. "Where are you going?" But Wesley did not answer. He ran faster, despite his reverse direction, and then he tired, slowed, and simply stood. Wendell watched helplessly as his brother receded into the distance, a vision above the fields. Before he disappeared, he lifted one hand. Wendell screamed his name.

He was upright, his chest pounding. It had been a dream, he realized now, catching his breath. Wendell looked around the room, disoriented. A lazy breeze stirred the curtains; the night outside his window had gone quiet. He fell back against his pillow. There was a sound outside, a scratch across the porch floorboards. Wendell was wide awake, but his limbs would not work to let him cross the floor to his window to look. It was probably nothing. What followed was a low moan, unlike the first sound. It reminded him of his dream, but he was awake now; it didn't make sense. When he heard it again, this time he got up.

The porch light flickered when he turned it on. Through the window, he saw a small figure curled up in one of the rocking chairs. He unlocked the door and tugged it open. A child in striped yellow pajamas was tucked into the chair, her knees pulled to her chest, thumb jammed in her bow-shaped mouth. It was Pippa. Wendell tiptoed outside and stood over her, watching her little chest rise and fall. The child was fast asleep. He looked left and right, across the porch. There was no sign of Julia.

Not wanting to disturb her, he knelt. How long had she been out here? He placed his palm against her back; to his relief she was warm, not chilled, despite the cool temperature. Wendell had never spent much time around children, especially small ones. They made him nervous. But something about Pippa's sweet, sleepy expression got to him. A tendril of blond hair had fallen across her eyes, and he gently tucked it back behind her ear. It was so soft. At the touch of his fingertip, her eyelids began to flutter. Slowly, she turned her head in his direction. For a start, Wendell feared he'd scared her. But Pippa just stared back at him sleepily.

"Come on, Pip," he said. "Let's get you inside."

Without warning, she lifted both arms and draped them around his neck. She was light as a feather, and she wrapped her legs around his waist. "Oh, okay." Gently, he carried her inside.

But Pippa didn't stir again. Almost immediately, she tucked her chin against his neck, her breath warm and heavy. He had barely made it into the living room with her in his arms when he felt her body grew heavy. She was already sound asleep.

Slowly, Wendell carried her to the kitchen and lifted the phone with his free hand. Without meaning to, he turned, and his nose brushed the back of her hair. He recognized the smell instantly. The scent of baby shampoo that his mother used on him and Wesley when they were small and took baths together. Wendell closed his eyes and dialed Candace.

As he waited for them to come, he sat with Pippa on his lap on the couch. The weight of her against his chest, and the smell of the baby shampoo, and something else—the sweet smell of a child—filled his senses. By the time Candace's car rolled into the driveway, Wendell was sound asleep with Pippa still tucked against him. Upon hearing the slam of a car door, he started.

Pippa was sitting up in his lap, watching him intently. "Can I see Raddy?"

Wendell met Candace at the door, Julia in tow. Julia blew right past him. "She rode here all by herself?"

"She's in the living room," he said, but the screen door had already slapped shut behind her.

Candace remained on the porch. She looked completely out of character in a blue bathrobe and tennis shoes. "I don't understand. What is she doing here?"

It was what he wanted to ask of her. Both girls coming the other night together was one thing. But Pippa venturing here alone in the dark was entirely different. "Did something happen at the house?" he asked.

Candace looked offended. "Of course not. They were sound asleep in their beds."

"That may be, but a six-year-old doesn't run away in the night for no reason." He glanced over his shoulder, where Julia was rubbing Pippa's back on the couch, and a wave of protectiveness rose within him.

Candace was not having it. "There is nothing wrong except for the fact that these girls are out of control."

Julia joined them with Pippa, but she stayed on the inside of the doorway. "We want to stay here," she announced.

Candace looked between the three of them, her eyes flickering. "Enough is enough, young ladies. Get in the car." She strode across the porch and down the steps.

Wendell felt hesitation about sending them home, but it was best to let everyone sleep on it and circle back in the morning. "It's late," he told the girls. "What you need is to go home with your aunt and get some sleep."

Pippa whimpered. "But I don't want to."

From the driveway, Candace flung the car door ajar. She screamed with such force, Wendell jumped. "Get in the goddamn car!"

Wendell had never seen her lose control, and to judge by the girls' reactions, they had not, either.

Pippa started to cry. Wendell took her hand. "Come on, Pippa. I'll walk you out." He didn't like being in the middle of this. But he didn't want to stand aside and let things get any worse, either.

Julia bit her lip but did not budge. "Julia," he said, turning to her. "Listen to your aunt for tonight. We can figure this out in the morning."

"No. Pippa's upset, and I'm not making her go. Let us stay."

Tears sprang to Julia's eyes as she said it, and Wendell felt himself bend. It was all becoming too much.

"Julia, now is not the time to push things. I promise I'll come by in the morning."

But Julia had other ideas. "He has Radcliffe, you know!" she shouted across the porch.

Candace came to the bottom of the steps. "What did you just say?"

Wendell let his breath out. "Julia."

"What? She might as well know everything." She spun to face her aunt. "After you stole my horse, he went and bought Raddy back. He's here in the barn. Go see for yourself."

Wendell closed his eyes.

Julia was on a tear now. "And I've been coming to see him every day," she went on. "You think you know everything, that you're in charge. But you're not."

Wendell couldn't even look at her. Julia didn't realize it, but she had just cemented her aunt's ire. He walked to the porch railing to face Candace.

"Is this true?" she sputtered.

He didn't know which part of the story she meant, but he supposed it didn't matter anymore. "Yes, ma'am. All of it." He would not say he was sorry.

"What were you thinking?"

"I felt badly about the horse being sold. The kids had been through so much."

Beside him, Julia crossed her arms as though she'd won the battle. But the war was Candace's, Wendell already knew.

"Your judgment is baffling," Candace said finally. She turned to Julia. "I'm leaving, with or without you."

"Please?" Julia begged at his elbow. "Can we stay with you now?" But if she'd been expecting an ally, she did not have one.

"Julia, it's time to go," he said.

"I had to tell her. This way she'll see that we have this under control. We don't need her."

Wendell shook his head. "Listen to your aunt."

She would not budge. "Whose side are you on?"

"There are no sides, Julia."

Candace got in the car and started it.

Julia glared at him, and Wendell could feel the heat of her disappointment. Then she took Pippa's hand. As she stomped down the steps, she called back, "I thought you were different. Some hero you are!"

It was a blow effectively targeted and expertly delivered. He took it, dead on.

Candace rolled down the window. "Mr. Combs, we will talk in the morning."

Wendell leaned against the railing. "I only bought the horse as a nod to Alan; he was my friend." As the words came out, Wendell realized he meant them. He had never admitted it before, and yet when Alan had died, a friend was exactly what he'd lost.

Candace stared straight ahead as the girls clambered into the backseat in a flurry of disarray. "We'll discuss this tomorrow morning. First thing." He was going to be fired.

Wendell stood on the porch until the taillights rolled down the driveway and turned into the darkness. There would be no sleep for him tonight. He sank down in the rocker that he'd discovered Pippa curled up in.

Wendell was used to feeling numb. It was a state he'd spent years chasing. But tonight he felt too much. Sadness. Regret. Loss. He sat, rocking, until the first light came over the horizon. He thought of the girls, driving away in the backseat of the car, and wondered if he'd made a huge mistake. Of Ginny, driving away from him that afternoon. He thought of Dr. Westerberg, who had told him that he needed to let himself feel the good parts along with the bad. But what happened when everything good left?

When the sun made its slow climb over the hills, Wendell stood up. There, at the bottom of the porch steps, was a tiny pink bicycle with sparkly streamers on the handlebars. He went inside and shut the door behind him.

Twenty-Five

Roberta

Julia Lancaster was a hell of a pain in the butt, that much she was sure of. What Roberta was not sure of was whether or not she could help the girl.

Roberta had been working in her kitchen on a pie crust when there was a knock at the door. Blueberry season had come early, that first week of July, due to the long spring and warmer weather. Nothing, it seemed, was as it should be that summer. Not the season, not the sense in Saybrook. But an early crop of blueberries, she would welcome. She'd just begun rolling out the crust when Julia Lancaster showed up.

Now, perched on Roberta's living room couch, wringing her hands nervously, Julia looked to be in that aching stage between little girl and young woman. It tugged at Roberta's heart.

Julia cleared her throat. "I'm sorry to barge in. But we have a situation at my house."

"Oh?"

"I tried to reach Jamie. She's pretty cool, by the way. But apparently, she's in court all day?"

Roberta leaned back in her chair. "I'm glad you like her. She's very good. Okay, so this is not uncommon. Lawyers are not usually reachable by phone right away, but I'm sure she'll call back as soon as she can." She paused, knowing that by asking more questions, she would further involve herself. Which she did not want to do. "What is the situation at home?" She could not help herself.

"Things are bad. Last night Pippa ran away."

Roberta shook her head. "Good grief, you girls are a couple of night owls! Again?"

"Yes. To Wendell's."

"I see." Wendell was surely having a time of things. Roberta would have to check in on him next. "What happened?"

"Pippa and I don't want to stay with our aunt anymore. We don't want to leave our home, but as long as she's in it, we can't stay. I filed for emancipation. I just didn't think it would be this ugly this fast."

Roberta felt for Julia, but she wanted to ask the girl what she'd expected. This was how it went. People took so long getting to the end of their rope, making big decisions. And by the time they did, often things had broken down so much they couldn't stand to remain under the same roof as the courts tried to make sense of it all. "What is it you want to do?"

"Jamie said a guardian ad litem was being assigned to us. I want that person to come sooner than later. We need them."

Well, she knew what she was talking about. And it was not an unreasonable ask. What was unreasonable, unfortunately, was the time these things seemed to take to process and get going. Nothing involving the state was ever fast.

"There must be someone you can call," Julia said hopefully. "An old judge friend?"

Roberta raised one eyebrow. "Old judge? Like myself?

Julia flushed. "Sorry. I didn't mean it like that."

"In any case, I can't get the wheels of justice spinning any faster than anyone else. But I suppose I could make a call and at least inquire. I do know the probate judge for Litchfield County; he's a good man."

"Would you please?" Julia looked grateful.

"Yes, but in the meantime, you need to share this with Jamie as soon as you hear from her. What you need is legal counsel. Not talking to a retired judge in her living room."

"While she's in the middle of baking a pie."

Roberta glanced over her shoulder into the kitchen, where the pie crust waited on the counter.

Julia shrugged. "I saw the blueberries. And the dough. Pippa loves blueberry pie."

For a terrifying second, Roberta almost invited her back to the kitchen. It would not kill her to hear this girl out further. To weigh in. To *get involved,* as she'd told Wendell.

Instead, she smiled tightly and ushered Julia to the door. "Yes. There is the matter of the pie."

With Julia gone, she returned to the kitchen. As she'd feared, the darn dough was warm. When she balled it up to roll it out again, she dropped it. It wasn't the slipperiness of the dough so much as the shaking of her hands. The last thing Julia had said before leaving: "I knew you'd know what to do."

There was a time when Roberta was foolish enough to think so, too. But no longer. The truth was, Julia Lancaster was calling up old memories. Memories she'd rather not allow back in the corners of her mind.

The Layla Bruzi case had been complicated from the beginning. Jenny Bruzi was a twenty-three-year-old single mother of two children, Layla, age five, and Dominic, age two. The children were fathered by different men, neither of whom married Jenny, but she lived with Dominic's father, Austin Hicks, with both kids. At age seventeen, Jenny had dropped out of high school, just one semester before she would have graduated, to have Layla. She'd never gone back. Layla's biological father was not in the picture, at least when Jenny Bruzi had been brought to the probate court's attention by Layla's maternal grandmother, Edith Warren.

From the start, Roberta had seen red flares. Edith Warren was appealing for custody of both her grandchildren, but it was her claims about Layla's physical well-being that concerned Roberta most. Edith felt that Layla was in some kind of danger being around Austin Hicks, though there was never any evidence of that.

In documents obtained by the Department of Children and Families and the New Milford Police Department, there were two domestic violence calls made, one by Jenny in September 2012 and one in November by her mother, Edith, against Austin Hicks. Austin was arrested on each incident and later let go. Charges were filed and then dropped both times by Jenny.

Sadly, it was not uncommon for women in situations of domestic abuse to bravely make the call for help, and file a charge, but later drop it. The reasons were many: financial strain, lack of stability and support, fear for their personal safety or the safety of their children. At the end of the day, Roberta knew the ugly truth: no restraining order was going to provide any real protection for a woman and her children if someone was determined to cause them harm. There were shortcomings in the law, just as there were shortcomings in people. As much as she believed in the law, and some might say loved it, it was on a judge to make case-by-case determinations to provide the real protections needed for those most vulnerable, in this case, a five-year-old girl.

At the first custody hearing in Roberta's courtroom, Edith Warren claimed that Austin had a nasty temper, and though he and Jenny fought often, it was Layla who she felt was most vulnerable. "He's real jealous. It's not good for either child to be around him when he and Jenny get into it, believe me. But Dominic is Austin's biological son. He treats him different."

Roberta wanted to hear more. In her experience, third-party witnesses were often reliable and made sound contributions to completing the picture she was trying to piece together. "Please give the court some examples of your concerns if you can, Mrs. Warren."

"Well, I haven't seen him hit her or nothing. At least not in front of me. But when he gets fired up, he looks at her funny." Her voice broke then, and she paused, looking as if she might cry. Roberta felt for Mrs. Warren. It was not easy for families to show up and testify under oath, even if they were doing it for what they thought was the right reason. She waited as Mrs. Warren collected herself.

"Layla reminds him of Jenny's ex and the life she had before him. He doesn't like having Layla around, I can tell."

"Can you elaborate on your fears, Mrs. Warren?" Roberta needed specifics to point to, as much as she hated to ask and feared the answers. In her experience, there had been cases of domestic abuse that, statistically, the women seemed to absorb the most. But she'd had a case of a child with a broken arm who'd gotten pulled too hard by an angry stepmother. Another, just a six-month-old infant, who'd been shaken but, thank God, survived. In her small country courthouse, it was not common. But it happened everywhere, even in the forested hills of Litchfield County, where the front yards were manicured, the schools were good, and the playgrounds were full of happy, healthy, cared-for children. It happened everywhere. And if Mrs. Warren was suggesting she had good reason to believe it was happening now, that Layla Bruzi might be in some kind of imminent danger, Roberta was going to flesh it out. "If you could give us any examples of something Mr. Hicks has said or done to warrant your fears, that would be helpful." She watched the conflicted expression on the grandmother's face as she looked over at her daughter, Jenny. "Anything at all," Roberta encouraged.

"When he drinks, he goes after Jenny sometimes. Twists her arm. Pushes her down. She tells me these things, but then he gets in her ear afterward, and suddenly, the story changes."

Roberta looked at the young mother, who stared at her lap. Roberta had seen and heard plenty of disquieting things in her years as judge, but it was often the inanimate details that got her, like now: the aisle of still space between mother and daughter. A grandmother on one side of a courtroom, her daughter on the other. Divided, in this case, by a man. Beside Jenny, as Edith Warren went on, Austin Hicks maintained a calm expression Roberta could not read.

When Jenny Bruzi stood before her, Roberta couldn't help but feel the nerves beneath an otherwise angry demeanor. "This is all ridiculous," she protested. "Austin is a real good man, and he's the only dad Layla has ever known. Her own sure isn't around." She glanced at Austin, and Roberta wondered if this had been rehearsed.

In the case of Austin Hicks, it was clear to Roberta the first time he opened his mouth that, despite his limited education, he was intelligent and unswervingly charming. He spoke confidently in her courtroom and with respect. Despite his admission of one incident of physical altercation between him and Jenny, and a subsequent verbal disagreement as reported by their neighbors, there were no reports of any endangerment or neglect to the children.

When questioned, Austin Hicks did not deny his responsibility or try to avoid accountability. Rather, he admitted openly that he had what he referred to as a "complicated" relationship with alcohol, and he had, in fact, lost his temper and his better judgment on occasions around Jenny and the children in their apartment. "I'm not denying it. Our fight got out of hand, but the kids were asleep. I would never do that again. I would never do it in front of the children."

"Mrs. Warren is concerned about your ability to care for the children, Mr. Hicks. Can you tell the court what your plans are for employment and providing for rent, groceries, and living expenses?"

Austin Hicks shared that he'd recently applied to multiple local businesses, including Walmart, Home Depot, and a restaurant. "I used to work at my brother's garage as a mechanic, but it went out of business."

There were records to support that claim, and Roberta knew these things happened. "I advise you to pursue a new job with vigor," she told him in no uncertain terms. "And I wonder about anger management classes in the interim." He did not look pleased, but he did not protest, either.

Roberta questioned Jenny Bruzi methodically and thoroughly. "Ms. Bruzi, do you understand that, statistically speaking, once there is assault in a family home between two partners, it is more likely that the children will eventually be on the receiving end of such?"

Jenny nodded and insisted that was one time and that it had never happened again. Roberta believed it neither then nor for the future, but she repeated the gravity of the situation. "Raising children in a home where the parents are at odds, even verbally, is psychologically damaging to the children. Even at their young ages, they are processing this, whether or not they understand it. Do you wish to raise your children in a home where fear and aggression are being modeled?" It was not her intent to shame Jenny Bruzi, but Roberta was going to drive home the worst-case scenarios to her there and then, in the hope that it might somehow sink in that she was on a very dangerous path if this behavior and this relationship continued. Roberta indicated to Jenny's mother, across the aisle: "Just appearing here today in front of me, as a family divided, I would argue that damage has already been done."

There would be another hearing. And more visits from DCF to the apartment, which would result in reports being submitted to the court and recommendations for Roberta, as judge, to consider. But at the end of the day, the decision fell across her shoulders. And to this day, how she ended up ruling on the Bruzi case still weighed on her.

Twenty-Six

Wendell

Two things had happened. First, Wendell received a phone call from an attorney named Jamie Aldeen, followed shortly thereafter by one from Roberta. His presence at an emergency hearing in the petition for emancipation of Julia Lancaster had been requested.

The second thing that occurred was that for-sale signs went up at White Pines. He'd had time to reason with himself, and he was glad that the work had gone to Ginny and her parents. They were good people. But even though it may have been irrational and more than a little bit unfair, it stung as a betrayal. Ginny should've told him she was trying to land Candace as a client. As he drove past the Feldman Agency sign at the mouth of the driveway, he tried not to grit his teeth. Since Julia had blown the whistle on all of them, it was time to face Candace.

As promised, Candace waited for him outside the barn.

"This may surprise you, but I don't want to discuss anything about the horse," she said, approaching the truck before he'd even had a chance to shut the door. She seemed rushed.

"All right." This was a big surprise, and a relief, but Wendell needed to clear the air. "If I may, there's a clarification I need to make."

Candace lifted her chin.

"I'm not sorry for buying Radcliffe. It still strikes me as the right thing to do. But I am very sorry for the apparent confusion and hurt this whole situation has caused the girls. I know you have your hands full, as you said."

This seemed to satisfy her. "I could have fired you, you know."

Wendell swallowed. "You still could."

"I don't have time. And I sense you know that." She indicated to the trucks parked along the edge of the field that he had not noticed until now. "The surveyors and engineers are back on-site today, finalizing some line changes. And I already have showings with two developers. That said, I propose we move on."

So she was going to forgive him. Sort of. Wendell wasn't sure if he was relieved or not. There was an even more complicating factor. "I received a call from Julia's lawyer. And a hearing notice from the court."

"As have I." Candace looked worn, and Wendell actually felt bad for her. It wasn't her fault that Alan and Anne were gone. She was not a mother and clearly had no feeling for White Pines. "It's my understanding the girls have brought this about without any input or suggestion by you. Is that true?"

"That has always been the truth," Wendell said firmly. "From the beginning, I told Julia that this was not an idea I supported, and I had no place being involved." He paused. "But to stay truthful, I also have to admit that whether I like it or not, I am involved now. And if there is something I can do to help, without interfering, I am trying to stay open to that."

"Are you able to continue to work here on the property?"

"I am," Wendell said. It would be hard, but he couldn't leave now.

"All right, then. I propose we move forward as our contract stipulates. As for the children, I have no choice but to let this play out. It is a tremendous distraction and expense, and I am not happy about it. But I have faith a judge will dismiss this out of hand, and that some sense of order will be restored. Julia is just going to have to accept that."

Wendell wasn't so sure, but he did not say this. For now, he still had a job. And there was a lot to do.

All morning he tried to keep his mind on his work as he carried the trimmers up to the ornamental trees by the main house. From the distance came the sound of voices every now and then. Candace was walking the property with a team of surveyors. It was impossible to make out what they were saying, and for that he was thankful.

The night before, Wendell had caved. Against his better judgment, he'd parked himself in his father's old study and pulled the chair up to the mahogany desk to check the broker's listing. "Pristine Connecticut properties in the hills of Litchfield County. Unique opportunity to design your own country haven. Just one hour northwest of the city!" Wendell had shut down his computer, staring at the blank screen a long time after it went dark. It was happening faster than he'd thought.

Now, at work on a row of edges along the main driveway, he had full view as the group made their way down the grassy hillside. As per Candace's instructions, he'd meticulously mowed the fields down to lawn height. "Easier for buyers to walk," she'd said. Usually, Alan let those fields grow tall in summer, mowing a single narrow path through the wavy grasses to the orchard but leaving the rest in its natural state. Twice each season, he'd invited the local dairy farmer from Happy Acres Farm to come hay those fields, free of cost. Wendell liked that natural balance struck: between town and property, from wild clover to domestic herd feed. This year there would be no haying for the dairy farm. He wondered idly where they'd source their feed for the year and what it would cost them.

Wendell looked up as the surveyors drew closer. There was a group of four, in casual attire and work boots, carrying equipment. Behind them, Candace walked with a well-dressed man and woman, deep in conversation. Wendell identified the woman immediately: it was Ginny. Even at that distance, he recognized her graceful figure and the way she moved her hands through the air when she talked with zeal. Seeing her walk down the grassy paths he'd mowed was a fresh hurt. Despite the heat, Ginny looked crisp in tailored white pants and a sleeveless coral top. She was speaking to the man in their trio. Like him, Ginny was here to work.

Wendell imagined the pitch she was making, the words spilling from her lips like a cool stream through the sun-drenched field: "lakefront property," "private enclave," "natural environs." As they approached, the man tipped his head toward her, seemingly hanging on to Ginny's words. Wendell watched as she directed his gaze east then west, surveying the view. After further discussion, they shook hands and Candace and Ginny departed to the house, leaving the man to see himself out.

Hoping to avoid interaction, Wendell returned his attention to trimming the base of the hedge, but it was too late.

Wendell looked up from his work to see a pair of driving moccasins in some kind of reptilian leather.

"Say, there. You work here?" the man shouted over the noise.

Wendell cut the trimmer's power. "Affirmative."

The guy slid his sunglasses up onto his head. "Nice place. How long have you worked here?"

Wendell did not like crouching at this guy's feet. He stood, swiping at the dirt on his knees. At full height, he looked him directly in the eye. "Can I help you?" he said instead.

The guy had a toothy smile. He extended a tanned hand. "Scooter Dunham. Prospective developer."

Wendell knew about Scooter Dunham. For every parcel of

open space Alan and Anne had purchased for the town land preservation trust over the years, Dunham Corporation was often the opposing bidder. They turned wild land into residential developments. Alan had hated the Dunhams. But Alan had been polite. Wendell shook his hand.

"So you knew Alan Lancaster," Scooter said.

"I did."

"Alan belonged to Quaker Hill Country Club with me." He flashed his teeth again. "Never was much of a golfer, but he was charitable. I always meant to attend one of his fundraisers, but I never did make it. A real shame."

Wendell wasn't sure if Scooter meant the deaths of Alan and Anne, or the fact that Scooter had missed the opportunity to visit White Pines until now. He sincerely doubted the man had ever been invited. "It's all a shame," Wendell replied. He nodded to the group of engineers. Scooter had asked him enough; now it was his turn. "Are you planning to bid on the estate?"

Scooter chuckled. "I keep my cards close." Then, "We'll see. There are nicer properties I've got my eye on. In fact, I'm going to see one now, an old farm by Quaker Lake."

Wendell knew the property. A childhood friend had grown up on that farm; his elderly parents still lived there. "I didn't know that place was for sale."

Scooter Dunham lowered his sunglasses. "Everything is for sale."

Wendell had heard enough. "Excuse me," he said. He flicked the button, and the trimmer buzzed to life. Wendell swung the machine in a clean arc over the top of the boxwoods, shearing off the top layer in one sharp swoop. Scooter hopped to the side as a jet of shorn twig and leaf sprayed the air between them. When Wendell was young, listening to his father talk about the working of town politics, about governing boards and committees, regulations and rules, it all sounded so honorable. But as Wendell grew up, he learned the truth. No matter the might of the rules or regulations, or the value of the things they stood to protect, what Scooter Dunham said was not wrong: for the right price, almost everything was for sale.

The day turned unbearably humid, and by the time he finished work, he was filthy and fatigued. All he wanted was a shower and a cold beer. But both would have to wait.

He saw them the moment he pulled into his driveway: up at the barn, a group of kids. Julia turned and waved. Wendell waited in the truck as she jogged to his window. "Hey," she said, a huge smile on her face.

He was irritable and tired, his conversation with Candace fresh on his mind. "I'm not sure your being here is a good idea right now. After the other night. And now with the hearing coming up. I have a job to keep."

Julia ignored this. "Oh, good! You got the hearing notice."

Wendell pushed the truck door open impatiently. "I still don't understand why I was summoned. We've already been over the guardianship thing. The person you need is not me."

"I know, which is why I'm still looking for someone else," she said. "The judge just wants to talk to everyone involved."

"*Involved*. Exactly what I was trying not to be."

Julia switched the subject. "So, I brought some friends to help today." She turned and pointed as if he had not already seen the two teens loitering outside his barn.

Wendell followed her gaze. "Help with what?"

"The barn," she said. "The paddock came out so well, I figured we could help you build a better stall for Raddy. He needs a real door. I saw some plywood in the corner, and Sam brought a set of hinges he found in his garage. I looked online to figure it out. See?" She held up a sketch.

Wendell glanced at it but kept walking. "Too hot today," he said.

"But they're free today. And we biked all the way over."

Wendell spun around. "Julia. I said not today."

"But—"

"But nothing! That's hard work, and it requires all kinds of supervision. They're just a bunch of kids. And I'm not a babysitter."

"There's just two of them, Sam and Chloe. She's my best friend I'm always telling you about. Anyway, Sam is really strong, and they're both hard workers. We can do it all, if you're tired, and you can just watch from the patio or wherever. Or not at all."

"Dammit, Julia. I said no."

Her face fell. Instantly, he regretted it. But he could not give in. All around him, the things he'd built to ensure his work, secure his house in this town, and protect his peace of mind were coming down. What he really needed was to be alone. "Now, please, tell your friends I'm too busy, and take them home."

He left her standing there and stalked up the walkway and up the porch steps. As he sat to unlace his work boots, he could feel her staring at him. Too bad she hadn't been at the house when Scooter Dunham was standing in her front yard; even he couldn't have withstood the withering look of a teenage girl. "You're a real grump, you know that?"

Wendell tugged off his boots. He just wanted to get in the house. Turn up the air-conditioning.

"Fine," she said finally, hands on her hips. "I'll tell them you're ungrateful and they should go home. But I'm building a stall."

"Build whatever you want," he said, rising and pulling the screen door ajar. "Just leave me out of it."

He let the door slap shut behind him with a loud creak. Upstairs and finally free from Julia, the shower had never felt so good. Wendell turned the knob until it ran cold and tipped his head back. Even behind his closed eyes, he could see the look on Scooter Dunham's face. And on Julia's. Maybe he should sell this house and get out of Saybrook. Maybe he should start fresh somewhere else, doing something new. It was a terrifying thought that he toyed with only in times of great stress. Likely, he could never go through with it. But now he wondered.

When he'd toweled off and dressed, he peered out the window in the direction of the barn. The horse was grazing quietly. The kids were gone.

Later, when he'd finished dinner and a second beer, he went to the kitchen to clean up and let Trudy out one last time for the night. He was standing on the back patio waiting for her to get her business done when he heard the sound of hammer on board. The barn lights were dim but on.

"Christ." Slowly, he made his way up the hill to the red barn. In the doorway, he paused. Julia was standing in the corner of the barn, her back to him. She'd nailed up one side of lateral boards to a corner post. Even from a distance, he could see they weren't exactly level, but as he stepped closer and examined her work, he noticed the nails were sunk tight. She spun around, hammer in hand. "Jesus! You scared me."

"Sorry," he said gently. Her face was sweaty, and there was a smear of dirt across one flushed cheek. "I didn't know you were here."

"Yeah, well, after you kicked my friends out, I had to do this alone." She turned back to her work. "But I'm doing it."

"I can see that." He looked around the stacks of wood and tools, then at Radcliffe, who stood with his head low in the corner, as if waiting for his bed to be made. Wendell felt bad. "Look, I'm sorry about before."

Julia said nothing but resumed her hammering. He winced as she missed and struck the edge of her thumb. The hammer fell to the dirt floor, and she gripped her nail. "Dammit!"

"You okay?" He stepped forward, but she spun around, eyes flashing.

"I'm fine!"

"Oh, okay. Sorry." But he could see her thumb was red, if not bleeding. "You're going to need some ice on that."

"It's not my thumb. It's this. It's . . . everything." Then, without warning, she spun his way. Wendell feared she might lash out, and he started to hop back, but instead, she fell against his chest. His breath escaped him as she wrapped her arms tight around his waist. The muffled sobs were hard, and she shuddered against him.

Wendell did not like to see other people cry. It was too private, too intimate. It wasn't that he found them weak but, rather, the opposite; it made him feel helpless. "It's okay," he said. He held his arms out from his sides awkwardly, afraid to touch her but just as afraid not to.

Pressed against his chest like that, Julia Lancaster was so much smaller than she seemed in life. Or maybe she always had been; it was that she seemed larger because she was so fierce. But now, her face buried in his arm, she felt as fragile as a bird. Not unlike the one they'd rescued together all those summers ago, in the orchard. Wendell was tired of thinking. Of escaping memories, of chasing clarity. This time he did not wonder what to do. He let his arms fall around her gently. He let her cry against his chest until she was all cried out. When she was done, he reached into his back pocket and handed her his blue bandana.

After, when her tears had stopped, she pulled away and looked up at him, suddenly bashful. "I'm sorry." She wiped her nose and looked away.

"Nothing to be sorry about." Then he picked up one of the boards from the floor. "Let's get this stall done," he said.

Twenty-Seven

Ginny

Wendell had every right to be upset with her, but there were things he didn't understand. At least that was what she told herself at first.

What she later realized what that she was wrong. Nobody understood better than Wendell Combs.

Wendell knew exactly what it was like to watch your parents struggle with their health. The poor man had lost both of his. And he knew too well what it was like to fear for your career. His position at White Pines was soon to end, and she was the one working to make it happen.

What an idiot she'd been. She cursed herself as she navigated the log steps down the steep hillside to the lake. Ever since she'd arrived, she'd sat on the back deck staring at the water, wishing she had a spare minute to jump in. Wishing it were a little warmer. Or the path less rocky. What it really added up to was that she was afraid to jump in. Candlewood Lake was one of the best parts of growing up in Saybrook during her childhood. And right about then, she needed a good dunk.

The water's edge was rocky, as she'd known it would be. Ginny kicked off her flip-flops and tiptoed across the stones that bordered the grass before the sand took over. Where the shoreline evened out, her feet sank into the soft earth, and Ginny gasped as she stepped into the water. It was cold but not freezing, and she scanned the horizon as she allowed herself to enjoy the refreshing coolness against her skin.

So much had happened so quickly. She tried to focus on the lone power boat across the lake. Her cottage was nestled along a strip of shoreline that was densely wooded, with no immediate neighbors. To the left was a narrow peninsula of rock outcropping and cedar trees. To the right, a spit of sand and rock jutted out into the lake, creating a small cove. The water was too shallow for a dock or boat but perfect for what she needed: privacy and peace of mind. It felt so good. Without hesitating, she waded in and dove under, allowing the lake to envelop her.

Ginny kicked to the bottom, touching the sand with her fingertips for good luck, just as she had as a kid. When she burst to the surface, she scanned the lake. The motorboat was gone, the only sound the faint quack of ducks around the edge of the peninsula. She rolled onto her back and floated, letting the gentle bob buoy her. This was everything she needed.

If Wendell had not been happy, her parents had been thrilled. So much so that it scared her when her father popped out of his chair and leaped up to hug her. "Careful!" she'd laughed, wrapping her arms around her dad and inhaling the familiar scent of Old Spice. "Oh, stop," he'd said, holding her at arm's length, a delighted smile on his face. There was color to his cheeks, and he was looking more like his old self. "This calls for celebration. Nina, break out a beer."

"But the cardiologist," her mother began.

"Pshaw. What he doesn't know."

They'd toasted on her parents' deck: white wine for Ginny and her mother, and a lone bottle of beer that she noticed her father savored.

"Let's not get ahead of ourselves," she warned them. "We've got the listing for a few months. Now we need to sell it."

They'd been in the business long enough to know. But even her mother, the more pragmatic of the three, seemed lighter. "This is good news. I've already put out the word to a few colleagues in Westchester County who have clients with deep pockets. I have a feeling we can wrap this up by summer's end."

"Actually, I think we may have a developer in the wings."

"Really? Who?"

"Scooter Dunham."

Her parents exchanged a look.

"What? Is there something I don't know?"

Nina was encouraging. "Well, as a buyer, he's a solid option. Dunham Corporation is aggressive, and they've done well in recent years."

But her father shook his head. "As a person, he's an ass."

Ginny wasn't surprised, even from her limited time with the guy. Scooter had been a bit obnoxious. Already downplaying the property's value, finding fault in the lot sizes. And she was put off by his overcomplimentary style: the way he'd held on to her hand too long when shaking it. The wink he gave when they said goodbye. The guy was clearly fond of himself. But she'd navigated these kinds of creeps before, and she wasn't deterred. "I can see that. But haven't his residential developments done well in town?"

"They have, for him," her mother allowed. "Which means good business for us if he works out."

"Then what's the problem?"

"They're downright ugly." Her father set his bottle down, and Ginny realized it was empty. "Look, his developments run high on price and low on quality. Not the typical New England attention to detail and craftsmanship we like as residents of Saybrook. But as realtors, we know a sale is a sale."

Her mother agreed. "Your father's right. The guy is known to be a bit of a jerk. But you can handle him, honey."

"Stay on top of him," her father advised. "If he's serious, stick it to him and get the deal done. We want a sale. It doesn't have to be the perfect buyer."

The news of Dunham Corporation took a little of the celebratory edge off, Ginny could feel. But even though Ginny agreed with wanting a top-notch development for such a beautiful place as White Pines, she couldn't argue their bottom line: beggars couldn't be choosers. Besides, she'd just gotten the listing. Maybe there was time to find a better developer. Candace Lancaster wasn't going to give them agency all summer; she'd made it clear she wanted to move fast. If Ginny didn't produce, she'd replace her in a heartbeat.

But in spite of all the work she'd done both in the office and in marketing, it wasn't White Pines that stayed with her in quieter moments like this, as she stared up at the sky from where she floated. It was Wendell.

What had happened during the time she'd gone over to help build the fence for the horse had been fluttering around the edge of her mind since. First, there was the fact of the horse and the girl, Julia, whom she'd met that day. Ginny still couldn't believe how deeply Wendell was getting involved. As much as it heartened her to see, and as much as she believed this was good for him, she couldn't help but worry. It stemmed from loss, and Wendell didn't need any reminders of what that felt like.

The other thing that pressed against her thoughts even more than the girl and the horse was what happened to Ginny when she was around him. If she'd been asked a year ago whether she had any regrets about Wendell Combs, she would have firmly said no. And she would've been telling the truth. Sure, she had a hard time letting go of him and the future they'd mapped out together. Wendell had been her first love. That meant something. But years had passed, and miles between had filled them. In that time, Ginny had grown up. She'd built a solid career. She'd fallen in love again. And her relationship with Thomas, though ill-fated, had been a grown-up relationship. Even though it hadn't worked out, Ginny knew what it was like to live with someone. To buy that first house together. To share everything from how their day at work went to tubes of toothpaste and the ups and downs of family and friends. She had not been a starry-eyed teenager living at home in her childhood town as she had been all those years ago when she was with Wendell. She'd carved her own path in the world, and she'd enjoyed walking it. So if anyone wondered where Wendell Combs factored in to her adult life, Ginny would have had one answer: the past.

Now she wasn't so sure. Seeing Wendell was a nice surprise. He looked good. Better than most guys her age. The hard work and being outdoors at White Pines had maintained his athletic build, and he looked strong and sure of himself. Unlike so many of the husbands of her friends back in Chicago, who fought potbellies from desk jobs and fatigue from young children, Wendell was vigorous. He carried himself like the young soldier who'd enlisted with the Guard. And despite the sadness in his demeanor, when they'd joked while working in the barn, she'd spotted that glimmer in his eye. Julia had chatted nonstop; boy, that teen could talk. It made Ginny laugh and Wendell roll his eyes, but as she carried on about Radcliffe and her friends, it gave the two of them a chance to share conspiratorial looks. "Was I that chatty?" she'd whispered. "What?" Wendell had said, cupping his ear. She'd punched him playfully in the arm. And she'd shaken her hand, not so jokingly, after. He *was* still so strong.

Something undeniable was happening to her when she was around him. Like she was right where she was supposed to be in that moment: something she'd tried to feel but never really had even in the good days in Chicago with Thomas. And coupled with that familiar warm feeling was another: fear. That she was getting too close to someone who had made it clear he was not able to get close to anyone ever again. Even to her. Especially to her.

Ginny rolled over onto her stomach and began a slow stroke to where the warm shallow cove met the deeper open span of lake. For a moment she treaded the darker water. The sun was bright and high. She dove under, then circled back toward shore. Swimming helped to clear her head. But there were some thoughts she just couldn't still.

Ginny stood under the outdoor shower a long time, tipping her head back as it ran from her cheeks to her toes. If there were places on earth that were heaven, a hot outdoor shower after a brisk lake swim was one of them. She was enjoying the rush of water on her spine when her phone rang from the deck. Ginny grabbed her towel and went to retrieve it from her shorts pocket on the Adirondack chair. She checked the screen. "Scooter Dunham." Well, well. She swallowed hard and answered.

"Ginny, it's Scooter." So they were on a first-name basis. "I've thought it over, and I think I'd like to make an offer."

"Hello, Mr. Dunham. That's great to hear. What're your thoughts?" Ginny wasn't playing games. She cut to the chase.

He chuckled. "As you know, I specialize in subdivisions. For this property to make any sense for me, I need confirmation on buildability."

They'd discussed all this already. Geoffrey Banks was in the process of obtaining building and zoning permits from Saybrook town hall. "I believe we should have final word from the town planning and zoning office later this week," she reminded him. "Our attorney doesn't have any concerns about it being passed."

"Well, that may be. But my attorney does. Something about a wetlands walk?"

Ginny ran through the facts of her last discussion with Candace and Geoffrey. "Yes, that's correct. I can confirm when that will be, but it's supposed to be a formality."

Scooter chuckled again. "Formalities have a way of turning into problems," he mused. "This isn't my first rodeo. So, while I'd like to make an offer, it is of course contingent."

Ginny wrapped her towel tighter around herself. Her refreshing swim and water were already wearing off. "Contingencies are part of my business," she replied, making sure to keep her voice chipper. She really wished he'd get around to the offer. It was like a game of cat and mouse. "Are you making a verbal offer now, or should I wait to hear from your attorney?"

Scooter paused. "I handle my own offers. Eight point five. Contingent upon permits and buildability. The offer is being faxed to your office now."

Ginny let her breath out. It was just south of full ask. And it was the first offer after mere days on the market. Candace would take it, she was sure. Her parents were going to flip. She cleared her throat, willing her tone to remain professional. "Very good. I will share this with my client and get back to you."

"One more thing. It's a twenty-four-hour turnaround."

Ginny glanced at her watch. "No problem. You'll hear from us by then."

As soon as she hung up, she spun around in her towel and shrieked. Birds from a nearby maple took off. She called Candace first.

"Are you free to discuss this?" Candace asked. She didn't mean over the phone.

Ginny began gathering her clothes from the deck and hurried inside. "I can be there in half an hour."

. . .

Ginny didn't know if Geoffrey Banks had other clients besides Candace, though she suspected he did. But there he was again, sitting in the home office next to her. He stood when he saw Ginny.

"Ginny. I hear you have good news!" He smiled and shook her hand.

Candace's greeting was cool. "Let's take a look at it," she said, gesturing to the wing chair across from her.

Ginny shared copies of the offer and walked them through it. "It's a solid offer. Twenty percent down in cash, thirty-day standard closing. But if permits come through before then, he can close as soon as two weeks."

Geoffrey nodded approvingly, pointing out certain clauses to Candace as they ran through it.

"What about other offers?" Candace asked.

Ginny was dumbstruck. They had almost full asking price in under a week on the market. Hadn't Candace said she wanted this deal done quickly? "Well, I have another developer lined up for tomorrow afternoon. That is, if you don't want to accept this offer. It's a twenty-four-hour-only."

"Is the other developer available sooner? Perhaps you should check."

Geoffrey shifted uncomfortably in his seat. "Candace, you have that option, of course. But I would caution against it. This is an excellent offer and in good time. Is there something about it you object to?"

Ginny could feel her nostrils flare, something she'd done when stressed or upset when she was in second grade. Her mother used to tell her to stop it. She couldn't remember the last time it had happened. She rubbed her nose now, then caught herself. "I can reply to Mr. Dunham with changes, if you've any in mind?"

Candace shrugged. "Well, if this offer is this good and this soon, why isn't there reason to think there will be better?" She turned to Ginny. "Surely you've handled a bidding war before?"

Ginny exchanged a look with Geoffrey. "I have, yes. A few resulted in over-offer asks. But others resulted in my buyer accepting a higher offer with more risk, and that resulted in the deal falling apart. Unfortunately, by then the remaining bidders were turned off or had found other properties. I'm not sure you want to risk that, given the time sensitivity of your situation."

They were the magic words. Candace sat up straighter. "Very well. As long as Geoffrey thinks these contingencies are standard and acceptable."

If Ginny wasn't mistaken, a flash of concern flickered across his face. But he recovered quickly. "Why don't I review this with Candace, and we can get back to you later this afternoon. Let's say three o'clock?"

Ginny sensed a shift in the room; clearly they wanted to discuss this alone. She stood up. "I'll have my cell phone on, whenever you're ready."

Candace nodded. "I'll walk you out."

"No bother, I'll leave you two to discuss things. Thank you for meeting on such short notice." Ginny gathered her files and stuffed them in her leather bag, feeling the slightest unease. She'd been fully expecting them to sign the offer to purchase right there. No matter. It was a big deal, after all. And she wouldn't rush them.

Outside, the sun was high and hot, and she shielded her eyes as she walked to the car. Two little voices caught her attention. Down the yard, under a big tree, sat Julia and her little sister. "Hello!" Ginny called, waving.

Julia recognized her and smiled. "Oh, hi. This is my sister, Pippa."

"Hello, Pippa!"

Pippa came right over. She was holding flowers in her hand.

"What's that?" Ginny asked, kneeling. If Julia was beautiful, her little sister was a smaller version. Same gold-spun hair and blue eyes but cute as a sprite.

Pippa smiled shyly. "A daisy chain." She stared at Ginny. "You're pretty."

"Oh!" Ginny laughed. "Well, thank you. You're creative. May I?"

Pippa handed her the chain of flowers. It was so delicate, Ginny worried it might fall apart in her hand. But then Pippa took it back, and before Ginny knew it, the little girl had reached up and settled it on her head.

"Leave her alone, Pippa," Julia said, coming up to them. But she was smiling, too.

"Thank you!" Ginny turned left and right. "How's it look?"

Both girls seemed pleased. "I haven't seen you at Wendell's," Julia said.

"Oh, right. Well, I've been very busy." Ginny indicated to the house. "Your aunt has me working hard. Not that I mind!" she added quickly.

Julia snorted. "I'll bet. You should come back. Wendell . . ."

Ginny removed the daisy chain delicately and set it on Pippa's head. "Beautiful." Then she turned to Julia. "Wendell—what?" she asked gently. She could tell Julia was worried about something.

"Nothing. We haven't seen him lately. My aunt won't let us. Until the hearing."

Ginny had heard about the hearing from Wendell, when they were still talking. "Is it soon?"

Julia nodded. "Tomorrow."

"I see. Well, that sounds important. I wish you good luck."

The girls seemed okay, but there was a heaviness she hadn't noticed at all in Julia that day at Wendell's. Ginny was about to say her goodbyes when she realized she didn't have her phone. "Shoot.

I think I left my phone in your house. Do you think it's okay if I go back in?"

"Sure. I'll take you."

Ginny felt bad interrupting their play and, worse, having to go interrupt Candace and Geoffrey after she'd just told them she'd wait to hear from them. How would this look?

Julia showed her in but stopped at the kitchen. "You know where the office is, right?"

"Sure, thanks!"

Ginny was halfway down the hall to the office door when she spied her phone on a console table. Of course—she'd stopped there to zip up her briefcase and must've set it down. Relieved not to have to knock on the door, she was just reaching for it when she heard Geoffrey speak. Despite the heavy wooden door, his voice was loud and clear. "I don't know, Candace. It's a risk that could blow up the deal."

Ginny froze.

"I disagree. The wetlands commission is just a small local board. Unless they find one, there's nothing for them to report. And the permit will sail through."

Unless the commission finds what? Ginny wondered.

"It's not that simple. If the town hall files go back far enough, and if the commission does its due diligence, they'll find the old reports. In which case, the Department of Environmental Protection would get involved. And that could delay or, worse, halt the entire project."

Despite the fear of being caught, Ginny found herself leaning in toward the door. So there *was* something they didn't want her to hear.

There was a long pause. Then Candace spoke. "It's just a bunch of stupid turtles. How can that upend a multimillion-dollar project?"

"It almost happened before. When Alder Combs was first selectman."

Ginny's breath caught in her chest, and she had to steady herself. Alder was Wendell's father.

"Well, it didn't then, and we won't let it now. Keep the report buried. Whatever it takes."

There was a rustle of movement on the other side of the door, and Ginny leaped back, almost dropping her phone. She caught it just in time, and clutched it to her chest, and half-ran down the hall.

Julia looked up from the kitchen island as she rounded the corner. "You okay?"

Ginny glanced at the kitchen counter: at the bowl of cut-up strawberries and the red spotted stains they'd left on the cutting board. Pippa smiled, her lips bright red. "Want one?"

"No, but thank you, girls." She had to go and fast. "I'll see you soon."

By the time she pulled the front door closed behind her, she was sweating. As a broker, Ginny was obligated to disclose any and all issues with a property she was handling. It was the law. If there was some kind of report that had any bearing on the property, and if she knew about it, she was obligated to disclose that information to the buyer. On the other hand, if she didn't know anything about it, there would be nothing to disclose. God, she hated the moral compass her parents had instilled in her. The thought of her parents caused her more angst. They needed this sale!

She hurried down the driveway. She was in her car before the next awful thought came. It wasn't about what Candace and Geoffrey Banks were trying to conceal. It was about Wendell. She'd already made so many mistakes with him. Should she tell him?

Twenty-Eight

Julia

The morning of the hearing, Julia dressed carefully. She'd known exactly what she would wear from the date the hearing was announced. It was the mint sundress her mother had bought her for the gala. Until then, she'd been unable to look at it hanging in her closet. It had not been to the dry cleaner, but she didn't care; wearing it to court seemed fitting.

She studied herself in the mirror, thinking of all that had changed since she last pulled this dress over her head. There were hollows under her eyes, and despite their bright blue color, they looked flat. Anyone else might see a young blond girl in a summery dress, but she may as well have dressed herself in grief. So much wrong had happened. Today was her chance to right some of it.

She was about to turn away from her reflection when she noticed something stuck to the bottom of the hem. It was a tiny spiky twig with one dried green leaf. She examined it; it must've come from a prickle bush that she'd passed in the woods that night as she sneaked out to meet Sam. A single thorn, curved like a hawk's talon, poked sharply from the stem. She pressed the tip of her thumb against it until the pain pierced. When she jerked her hand back, a satisfying drop of red bubbled at the tip of her thumb. *There,* she thought. *This is happening.*

Jamie Aldeen picked Julia up an hour beforehand. "Remember, the judge is going to ask you a number of questions. Just answer them as honestly and thoroughly as you can." They'd gone over this the day before. But now the thought of speaking before a judge made her mouth dry and her stomach flutter.

Candace drove separately with Pippa. When they arrived, Candace sat in the opposite corner of the probate court. She did not speak one word to Julia on the way in. To Pippa she said, "This is the meeting I was telling you about, Pippa. Your sister and I will be going into a room to talk with a judge. There's a nice lady who will wait with you." She thrust a coloring book and a packet of crayons in to Pippa's hands.

The clerk checked them in. "Is Wendell Combs here yet?" Julia asked, glancing around nervously.

"Not yet." Wendell was never late to work. He wouldn't be late for this.

Julia took a seat beside Pippa. The courthouse smelled familiar, much like her middle school hallway: the recirculated air, the linoleum floors. It felt like it, too. Serious. Echoey. A place where adults ran the show. Beside her, Pippa squiggled on the bench impatiently. "When can we go?" she asked.

Julia had packed snacks for her in a lunch box. She handed it to her and lowered her voice to a whisper. "I need you to be really good and patient, today, Pips. Okay? I'm trying to work on plans for us. Remember what we talked about?" She glanced at Candace, who was staring at them.

"Okay, but hurry," Pippa said. She dug into the bag and pulled out some pretzels. The door leading outside swung open and Julia's chest gave. Wendell! But it was Geoffrey Banks, who nodded at them all and joined her aunt on a bench.

Moments later, the chamber doors opened. A young woman in a suit addressed them. "Are you here for the Lancaster hearing?"

Jamie stood and motioned for her to come. Julia's heart began to pound. "Be good, Pippa," she said.

Judge Eliot Bartlett looked far friendlier than Julia had pictured. He was somewhat older than her father and had a neatly trimmed dark beard. He smiled at her as soon as he saw her. "Good afternoon!" Then he adjusted his glasses and glanced at a clock on the wall. "Rather, good morning. Goodness. I don't even know what time it is!"

The clerk laughed, as did the judge, and Julia felt her insides relax. This was a good sign. But where was Wendell?

"Please, have a seat while I review your file." This was not the courthouse Julia had seen on television and in movies. It was much less formal, like an office. The judge sat behind a separate desk, facing them. Julia followed Candace's cue and sat opposite her aunt. Both turned to face the judge, who opened a manila file and began looking through the documents inside it without comment. As he did, the clerk offered water to both Julia and Candace, which Julia didn't really want; she just wanted to get started. It seemed forever that he read through the file before he looked up. Gone was his smile.

"Ms. Aldeen, you are the counsel representing Julia Lancaster in this petition?"

"I am, Your Honor."

"And I see we have two Ms. Lancaster's here." He looked up at Candace. "You are Candace, custodial guardian and aunt to Julia and Pippa."

"Yes, your honor. This is the family attorney, Geoffrey Banks."

The judge nodded. "And I see we are also expecting a Mr. Wendell Combs?"

There was a pause, and Jamie stood. "Mr. Combs is an interested party, and I wonder if we might give him five minutes, please?"

The judge did not look pleased, but suddenly, there was a noise at the doors. The clerk poked her head in. "Mr. Combs is here."

"Send him in."

Julia's insides flushed with relief. Greetings were made, Wendell sat down in the corner, and then Judge Bartlett turned sharply to Julia. "So, you are Julia Lancaster?"

Julia nodded. "Yes, sir. I mean, Your Honor."

The judge pushed the file to the side, clasped his hands, and leaned in as though prepared for an intimate conversation. "Let's talk about what we have going on here. Julia, I know Ms. Aldeen is representing you, but I would like to hear from you first. In your own words."

Julia cleared her throat nervously. "Well, Your Honor, I filed for emancipation."

"I see that. Can you share with me what led you to that decision? It's a serious one, and I want to hear how you arrived at it."

Julia glanced at Candace, who merely raised her eyebrows as if to say, "Go on. You're the one who dragged us here."

She took a breath, hoping her voice was steady. "I filed for emancipation because my parents died earlier this summer."

"I am very sorry to hear about that. The loss of any parent to a child, let alone both, is a trauma. My sincerest condolences." His brown eyes were kind, and indeed, he looked very sorry as he said it.

"Thank you, sir. I mean, Your Honor." She could feel her cheeks flush, and that made her annoyed at herself. There were so many reasons she was here, all of them just and right and good, and she needed to pull herself together and get them out or this judge was going to think she was as incapable and idiotic as she was presenting herself to be. She took another deep breath. "When my parents died, I thought that was the worst thing that could happen to me and my little sister, Pippa. She's only six, and she's outside in the hallway now," Julia added, gesturing to the double doors behind them.

The judge nodded for her to go on, and she could tell he was listening carefully.

"But then I learned that our aunt, a person we had never even met before, was going to be our guardian, and that she wanted to move us away from our home in Saybrook all the way to London. A different country." She said the last part so it would sink in.

The judge only smiled. "Indeed it is."

"Pippa and I have spent our whole lives here, outside of when I was really little and lived in New York with my parents. Pippa was born here, and Saybrook is our home. It's where we go to school. It's where all of our friends live. Everything I love and know is in Saybrook. To move us away from all that, to a place we've never been, with a relative we barely know, is like another death all over again." She was so nervous she'd run completely out of breath, but she'd gotten most of the important stuff out. She reached for the glass of water, suddenly grateful for it.

The judge waited as she took a few gulps, his hands still clasped thoughtfully. "So, this move to London has come as a surprise to you?"

Julia set the water glass down. "A shock, to be perfectly honest."

He nodded. "I like perfectly honest." He turned to Candace. "I imagine this has not been easy for you, either."

"No, Your Honor, it certainly has not."

"Would you please share with the court what has transpired between you and Julia and her sister since you arrived?"

Candace was sitting slightly behind her, but Julia did not turn around. "I arrived two days after the death of my brother. I agree with Julia, it has all been a shock."

Julia swiveled to look at Candace. There were plenty of synonyms for shock; that word was hers.

The judge continued, "I imagine it's been quite a strain for everyone involved. And I would like to hear how the three of you have been getting on since your arrival here in the States. But first, having heard what Julia has just shared with the court today, what are your thoughts about her petition for emancipation?"

Candace sighed, somewhat dramatically, Julia thought. "My thoughts are that she is grieving too hard to know what is best for her right now." Candace looked over at her. "Julia is correct that we do not know each other well, but that is something time can take care of if she would be willing. Her father and mother's wishes were to appoint me as guardian, and it has not been easy for me. But it is a wish I feel obligated to honor and uphold." She paused. "Besides, Julia is a child."

Julia scoffed, and Jamie gently put a hand on hers and squeezed. "It's okay," she whispered.

The judge made a note in the file. Julia did not like that. Nor did she like Candace's word choice. Where was the honor in selling a child's horse out from under her? "Excuse me, Judge Bartlett."

The judge looked up. "Yes?"

There was another squeeze from Jamie, but Julia went on. "I feel it important to share certain facts, since you ask about what has taken place since my aunt arrived." Her heart was racing, but she needed to set the record straight.

"All right, please go on."

"I had a horse." Julia ignored her aunt's audible groan behind her. "A horse that my father gave to me as a gift. Radcliffe is his name, and he was the most important thing to me in the world besides my family. Radcliffe and I competed in shows and competitions all around New England. He wasn't just a pet; riding is my sport and a huge part of who I am. Two weeks ago, my aunt called up a local stable and arranged to sell him without my knowing. I just happened to hear a commotion and look out my bedroom window to see a stranger leading my horse out of the barn and away." She paused, catching her breath. "I ran outside to stop them.

I begged her not to. But she ordered them to load him up and take him away." She turned to face Candace. "That was the last part of my father I had. And she took that part away from me without even having the guts tell me first. I didn't even get to say goodbye."

The judge's brow furrowed. He looked to Candace. "Is this true?"

"It is, Your Honor. But not quite as it is being portrayed. With our plans to sell the family property and move overseas, I had many decisions to make in a short amount of time, and there was no other choice but to sell the horse as well. It's not like we could load it on a plane and take it with us. Had it been a dog or cat, I would have been happy to. But a horse?" Here she threw up her hands, and the jangle of her bracelets echoed in the small room.

The judge cocked his head. "I'm curious why Julia was not informed of this decision. Wouldn't it have been kinder for her to have a chance for closure?" *Kinder*. Julia's hopes rose. He was seeing in Candace all the things she lacked. All the things Julia and Pippa would need.

Candace nodded. "For that I am sorry. At the time I thought it would only upset her more, and it also was not made clear to me when the stable was coming to pick him up; their communication about transporting him was a bit spotty, so I didn't want the horse lingering and therefore drawing out her upset. I did, however, make a lot of calls and get the best recommendations for a stable who would take excellent care of the horse and ensure a good home." She flashed a look in Julia's direction, but instead of seeing sorrow, Julia saw only competitiveness in her aunt's eyes, as if she had just scored some kind of point. Julia hoped the judge saw it, too.

"So, you feel you did your best to find the horse a good home, given that you could not possibly bring him with you." The judge repeated this as Candace nodded along, and he made another note on the file. He looked up at Julia. "It sounds like your aunt did try to find a suitable home for your horse, given the difficult circumstances and the timing. Still, it's little consolation to you, I suppose."

Julia shook her head. "It is no consolation," she said firmly.

The next hour, the judge posed a series of questions, including input from both attorneys, about the current custodial arrangements and the tensions within the household. Julia breathed with relief as Jamie reported the two instances of Pippa running away to Wendell, once with Julia and once on her own. Jamie discussed the trauma of parental loss coupled with what would be a second trauma if the girls were moved away from their childhood home, school district, and friends.

Next it was Geoffrey's turn. He shared Candace's work in finance back in London and the details of the large house she kept there, which would accommodate the children. The way she'd dropped everything to come to the States to care for Pippa and Julia. The difficult decisions she'd had to make, including selling the horse. Julia glared at them. How could they use Raddy to argue their case?

After the attorneys presented, the judge had more questions. He asked Candace about the obligations she had outside of her career, considering she was now guardian to two children, and how she planned to balance parenting with her work and personal life. "Given all I have heard today, Ms. Lancaster, it seems you have crafted a neat and successful life for yourself in London. Are you certain you wish to maintain guardianship of these children, in light of the sacrifices you would need to make?"

Julia held her breath. She knew in her heart that Candace was doing this because she had been told to, not because she wanted to. Maybe she had some lifelong regrets about her poor relationship with her brother, Julia's dad. Maybe she was just used to getting her way, and even if she didn't want them, as Julia largely suspected, she wasn't about to let a fifteen-year-old dictate that she would not have them.

Candace answered calmly and carefully. "I have never planned to have children, if that is what you're asking, but I am well equipped to provide and care for them in all the ways a child needs. Indeed, I would say they would have many more opportunities and advantages living with me in London. Certainly more than if Julia emancipated herself and attempted to live as an adult before she was ready to." She paused. "Especially since that would mean the children would likely be split up."

At this, the judge turned to Julia. "Julia, I have reviewed the financial arrangements made on behalf of you and your sister by your parents' estate. They are in a trust at the moment. Do you understand how that works?"

"I do. Mr. Banks, my dad's lawyer, explained it all to me. He is the custodian of the trust, and I won't have access to any of it until I'm eighteen. And even then it's only given to me in small amounts over the years."

"Correct," the judge said. "Your situation is quite unique. Rather fortunate, I would say, in that you have a large sum that will eventually be at your disposal to care for yourself, get an education, and afford future living expenses. That works very much in your favor in regard to your petition for emancipation."

Julia couldn't hide her smile. "My parents took good care of us. My wish is to take care of myself, as they would have trusted me to, and to obtain guardianship of my little sister, so that we can remain together." She made sure the judge was looking at her before continuing. "They would want us to be together. I know it in my heart."

The judge nodded. "I do not doubt that. But obtaining guardianship is an entirely different process than emancipation. There is no guarantee that you would obtain guardianship of your younger sister."

"I understand. But I'm not going to give up without trying."

"There is one question I have. Your aunt is clearly willing to take care of you, despite your feelings about moving. Is there anyone else in your life whom you'd prefer to live with who has the willingness and capacity to care for you and your sister that you'd like the court to know about?"

"There is, actually. His name is Wendell Combs." There was the scrape of a chair behind her, and Julia turned to look at Wendell. "He's a good family friend," she added. "My mom and dad liked him very much."

Suddenly, Candace stood. "I'm sorry, Your Honor, but this man Julia is referring to is the caretaker of the estate. I am his employer. He's a *gardener*."

The judge looked between them. "Do you feel there is a close relationship between this gardener and the children?"

"Only of a professional nature," Candace replied. "Though Julia wishes it were otherwise."

"That's not true," Julia interjected. "He has known us our whole lives, and he was close to my parents. They treated him like family. And he has become close to us." She stuck her chin out. "He went to the farm my aunt sold my horse to and bought him back because he knew it broke my heart to see Radcliffe taken away. He was there that day. And I think it broke him a little bit, too." She turned to Candace. "*That's* how well he knows us."

"All right, all right, let's settle down," the judge intervened. "I am not making any suggestions or recommendations, simply trying to find a middle ground given the amount of trauma the children have already endured. Outright emancipation gives a minor adult freedom but also adult responsibilities. It is to be granted neither lightly nor easily. As such, I wish to explore all options." He motioned for Wendell to come forward. "Mr. Combs, I would like to hear from you."

Julia watched Wendell make his way to the front of the room. He took a seat beside her, which felt right.

"Mr. Combs, would you please describe the nature of your relationship with the Lancaster family?"

Wendell looked nervous, but he spoke clearly and with conviction. Julia listened as he detailed his early years working for her grandfather when he was just a teenager and during his college summers. Wendell had been at White Pines since he was just a couple years older than she was now! How had she not realized that before?

He described his relationship with Alan and Anne and how he'd enjoyed working for such good, fair people. But he didn't stop there. Wendell told the judge how he'd seen the girls grow up, and how close the family was, to both each other and the connection they had to White Pines. "I can't do it justice," he said softly. "White Pines is the kind of storybook setting every child dreams of growing up in. And the Lancasters gave their daughters that kind of life there."

But Judge Bartlett wanted to know about his relationship to Pippa and Julia.

"To be honest, I feel like I've known the girls almost their whole lives, even though our interactions were, as Candace noted, of a more professional nature. But everything changed since Alan and Anne passed away."

"How so?"

Julia listened with her heart in her throat as Wendell told about the night they'd biked to his house. How surprised he'd been. And later, how concerned. How he'd wondered if he made a mistake by sending them home with Candace that second time. "I didn't fear for their personal safety," he explained carefully. "But I saw the hurt. There was so much hurt." He glanced uncertainly at Candace. "For all three of them."

The judge thought a moment, glancing between the parties in front of him. He had one final question for Wendell. "Thank you for sharing so eloquently, with the court, all of that. As you heard Julia say earlier, she wishes for you to be awarded custody at this time. What are your wishes regarding that request?"

Wendell did not answer right away. In fact, he hesitated for so long that Julia feared he would not. She fought the urge to leap up, to pinch his knee. *Say* something, she pleaded silently. Finally, he spoke. "Your Honor, I have no children of my own. And though there was a time I once thought I would, after my time in the military, those thoughts changed. Julia and Pippa Lancaster are remarkable little girls. Anyone here today can tell you that. I don't know that I have the qualifications for taking care of them. I'm not nearly as equipped as their parents were. And I lack any and all experience necessary."

No, Julia wanted to scream. *That is not what you're supposed to say!*

"Are you suggesting guardianship is not in their best interest?"

"What I'm suggesting is that I am good at many things, but parenting is not one. I may not be the most qualified person for this job. But if you and the court decide that I am a good candidate for temporary custody, I feel that taking care of them would be an honor."

Julia sank back in her seat. Hot tears streamed down her cheeks. "Thank you," she mouthed to Wendell.

But it was not over. The judge was clearly torn. "This is an emergency hearing for the petition for emancipation. However, it has become clear that there are more pressing matters. I believe the court needs to consider immediate custody issues before any determination of emancipation is made."

Jamie looked at Julia and nodded. This was what she'd hoped for.

"It is clear the current living situation for the children with their aunt is not in their best interest during this time of transition."

Julia could sense that he had arrived at some juncture, and her heart began to pound.

"This is a challenging decision for any judge. Julia, you are quite capable and clearly very bright. You have means to support yourself that most others do not. And you have made your wishes to stay in Saybrook very clear." He stopped. "However, you are only fifteen. That is one year below the age our state deems acceptable for emancipation. Which is not to say it cannot be done, or that your departure to London cannot be delayed until such time as you are of legal age to be emancipated. But age alone is not the determining factor."

Julia's heart began doing its flip-flop thing again, and she wondered if the whole courtroom could hear it. "I will be sixteen in just nine months."

Jamie threw her a look.

"I know the math," the judge said. He closed the folder and looked between the two of them once more. "Given the current strain in the home, and taking into account the child's wishes and the potential guardian's willingness to care for the children, I propose a temporary joint custody arrangement."

Candace sucked in her breath as Julia did the same. She didn't want part-time custody. She and Pippa wanted to be free of her!

"Ms. Aldeen, you have requested a guardian ad litem for the children."

Jamie nodded. "Yes, Your Honor. I feel it will provide the court with pertinent information and protect the interests of both girls in the meantime."

"I agree." Judge Bartlett addressed Wendell next. "Mr. Combs, effective immediately, I propose that Julia and her sister, Pippa, move in with you for one week. This will give everyone a cooling-off time. Starting next Monday, I then wish to set a schedule in which the girls will be with their aunt Monday at noon through Thursday at noon. At which time they will transition to your house for the weekend. Are you able to accommodate them while also working?"

Wendell looked to Candace. "I work Thursdays and Fridays. But perhaps they can come with me? And stay on the property, but leave with me at the day's end?"

Candace shook her head. "Forgive me, but this is silly. The girls can come home. In fact, they can stay home."

Judge Bartlett cleared his throat. "Ms. Lancaster, it is my opinion that both you and the children need a break. You are in the process of selling the home and property, yes?" She nodded. "Then, if this is not objectionable to you, and you can continue to be available to them during the workdays as you have been, I think this is a good compromise.

"In the meantime, a guardian ad litem will be meeting with all of you. Please make yourselves available to them and share as openly as you're able. This is an important part of informing the court's decision. I call for a continuation, to be scheduled in two weeks."

A hearing date was set for two Mondays out. Judge Bartlett stood, adjusted his robe, and stepped down from the small platform on which his desk sat and sailed out through a side door. Julia felt her insides flutter like the hem of his robe.

Twenty-Nine

Wendell

It was move-in day. There was no other name to call it. Wendell watched at first with amusement, then doubt, as the girls loaded up his truck with their "belongings."

"Just a few things to make your place feel more homey," Julia explained as the girls came out to meet him in the driveway. "After all, the judge said we're staying for a week."

Wendell shook his head as Pippa dragged a sparkly purple duffel bag larger than she was down the front steps. "Exactly. A week. Not a year." He stooped to help her with it and lifted it into the bed of the truck. "Good grief, Pippa. What did you pack in here?"

He was serious, but Pippa giggled in delight. "Just my stuffies."

"Her stuffed animals," Julia translated. "Like about a hundred of them."

Wendell shook his head again. "Will we be needing one hundred stuffies?" Then, as he walked around the truck to help Julia with her equally large bag, "Does *anyone*?"

But they weren't done. "Where are you going?" he asked as both girls ran back up the steps.

Pippa halted. "To get the rest."

Wendell waited outside, noting that Candace was markedly absent. He wasn't surprised. He also wasn't about to let himself inside the house, though from what he'd seen so far, the girls weren't light packers and could've used a hand.

Two more trips later, the bed of his truck loaded, the three climbed inside the cab. Wendell started the engine and looked over at them. Pippa was sandwiched between him and Julia. She rested a small hand on his leg.

"Ready?" he asked.

"Yes!" Pippa shouted.

Wendell was not entirely sure he was, but he put the car in drive.

Back at the house, there was more surprise. Roberta stood on the porch, waiting with a platter.

"Hello, Bertie. What's going on?"

She held up the platter. "Chocolate cake, that's what." She gave a look of mock horror as the girls began dragging their things out of the back of the truck. "Heavens. Are they staying for good?" But when Julia gave her a quick hug on the way up the porch steps, Wendell noticed her soften.

"That's so nice of you," Wendell said, climbing up behind them with a bag on each shoulder.

"Well, seeing as you're a Sherpa, I figured you could use a little cake. There's more." She nodded across the porch. There, in a corner rocking chair, was Ginny.

"Ginny."

She waved shyly. But there was nothing shy about the girls' greeting.

"I remember you!" Pippa exclaimed. Wendell had never seen Pippa so forward. She opened her purple bag and pulled out what appeared to be a striped tiger cat. "This is Fangs."

Ginny laughed and petted his head. "Fangs is lovely. Do you think he'd like to see his new room?"

Wendell set the bags down, immediately feeling uneasy. "Oh,

I figured I'd put the girls together in my childhood bedroom. I already vacuumed and made up the beds."

Ginny and Roberta exchanged looks. "I'm sure you did," Ginny said. "But we thought maybe the girls would like to personalize them a little?" Wendell noticed a bag of things at her feet. Three bags, to be exact. It was starting to seem like bags of things were going to be a regular occurrence, and he wasn't sure how he felt about that.

Julia beat him to it. "Ooh, this is so pretty," she said, opening one of them. She pulled out a strand of twinkle lights. Pippa abandoned Fangs and began rummaging through the others.

"It's just some bedding and decorations," Ginny explained, coming to stand beside him. "Nothing that will ruin the walls or anything. I hope you don't mind."

Wendell looked at the earnestness in her gaze. For the first time that morning, he felt his insides calm. "I don't mind at all," he said, softly. It was a relief to have Ginny and Roberta there. Clearly, there was a lot for him to learn.

Upstairs, Wendell showed the girls down the hallway. "This is my room," he said, opening the door to the master suite, where his parents used to reside. "And this," he said, continuing down the hall, "is your room. It was mine when I was a kid."

He stepped aside so both girls could peek inside, but neither went in. Wendell glanced around at the blue walls. The checkered curtains his mother had hung years ago. The baseball trophy sitting on the dresser. He'd worked so hard to vacuum and dust and had even moved Wesley's twin bed into the room so they could share, thinking Pippa might be afraid to be in a strange room all alone at night. Now, looking over their shoulders, he saw what they were seeing and was suddenly even more grateful to Roberta and Ginny. "Guess you'll want to unpack and decorate," he said.

He was right. No sooner had he and Ginny finished carrying

the bags upstairs than the girls had already half-decorated their room. The beds were moved side by side along the window. Both were stripped of their navy and red bedding and replaced instantly with floral comforters in teal and lavender. A basket Wendell had never seen before appeared and was just as quickly filled with dolls from Pippa's giant purple bag.

To Wendell's astonishment, the transformation was swift, if not seamless. Their questions came even faster.

"Do you mind if I run the new sheets through the washer?" Ginny asked.

"Where can my stuffies sleep?" Pippa asked, jumping on the bed.

He tried not to flinch when Julia asked, "Do you have a hammer?" And moments later, "I think we need spackle."

By the end of the afternoon, the room was no longer Wendell's childhood chamber, and two happy girls lay side by side on Julia's bed, gazing up at the twinkle lights that draped from the ceiling. Ginny leaned against the doorframe, looking pleased.

"I never could have done this without you," Wendell said to her.

When Ginny turned, her face was so close that Wendell could count the flecks of green in her eyes. "It's amazing what some sparkly lights can do," she said after a breath.

If Wendell stayed there a moment longer, he was afraid he would kiss her. He cleared his throat. "Who's ready for cake?"

After Ginny and Roberta left, there was a lull. They were all tired, and Wendell figured he'd better throw something together for dinner. He found the girls in the living room, flicking through channels on the TV.

"You don't have Apple TV?" Julia asked, frowning at the screen.

Pippa looked like she might cry. "How will I watch *Peppa Pig*?"

Wendell did not know who Peppa Pig was, and he didn't want to get sidetracked by streaming services. "Why don't you two go see Raddy while I make us some dinner?"

Pippa stared at him. "What's for dinner?"

Wendell smiled. "I got some pork chops at the market this morning. How's that sound?"

Both girls wrinkled their noses. "Uh, we don't eat pork."

"Oh." No one had told him that. "I suppose you don't like lamb, then?" he asked hopefully.

Pippa slapped a hand across her mouth. "You eat lambs?"

"Not lambs. Lamb." Though what was the difference, really? "Okay, so we'll skip the chops tonight." He hurried into the kitchen and scanned the fridge. "Do we eat chicken?"

Both girls shouted back: "Is it white-meat chicken breast?" and "I like it with gravy."

Wendell sighed and made a mental note. They'd have to sit down at some point and figure out meals. "How about spaghetti?"

To his great relief, both said yes.

After dinner, they went on a walk around the property. Wendell showed them his mother's perennial beds surrounding the farmhouse. "My mom would've liked this," Julia mused. Pippa was excited to visit Raddy, and Wendell was relieved that they'd gotten through dinner and almost to her bedtime without issue. But when they went back indoors, she started to look unsure.

"Are you okay, Pippa?" he asked.

She looked to Julia, her eyes wide and sad. "What's wrong?" Julia said.

Pippa didn't want to say. She whispered in Julia's ear while Wendell waited. This was not a good sign.

"She's tired," Julia explained, but Wendell could tell that wasn't what Pippa had shared.

"I've got ice cream," Wendell suggested. He'd intended to save that for tomorrow, but it was becoming clear that he needed to pull out all the stops on their first night.

The ice cream worked and they ate together in the parlor.

Wendell let the girls take the rocking chairs by the fireplace and he perched on the edge of the couch.

"Is that an antique?" Julia asked.

"Actually, it is. It was my grandmother's."

Julia nodded and looked around. "Is this whole house antique?"

Wendell followed her gaze. He'd always thought of his house as homey and well appointed. His father had been a simple man who'd grown up in the farmhouse with simple furnishings, but his mother's eclectic urban touch had electrified it with pops of color and interest. But as his eyes traveled over the parlor room and beyond, into the kitchen, Wendell understood the question. The parlor was a dated formal wallpaper. The Oriental rug was a bit shabby and worn, its mahogany and gold colors faded. The bookshelves were lined with dusty hardbacks, books that Wendell hadn't read or touched since his own childhood. And the kitchen—well, it was straight out of the eighties. "I guess you could say that," he allowed. "It's an old house," he reminded them.

"Yeah. But so is ours."

That was true. Julia's great-grandfather had built theirs probably not long after Wendell's house had been built. But what a difference on the interiors. The White Pines house was open and airy, painted in pale earth tones and white trim. The lighting fixtures were modern; the furniture was crisp and white and plush in its newness. The chestnut floors had been redone and gleamed in the sunlight that spilled through the windows. Wendell looked around at his farmhouse, which also had large windows, but the drapes were heavy and dark. For a beat he felt a little ashamed. And then protective. "Do you not feel comfortable here?"

Pippa tried to stretch out on his mother's Victorian fainting couch. "It's nice," she said. But her face contorted as she switched positions until she gave up. The house was not, Wendell realized with some consternation, a kid-friendly house.

Suddenly, he was very tired. "Well, at least your rooms are done up really nice. Let's get cleaned up and ready for bed."

Julia frowned. "It's only eight thirty."

"What time do you go to bed?"

"Ten. Pippa goes down around now, though."

Wendell brightened. "I figured since it's your first night, and you're sharing a room, maybe this once you can go to bed a little earlier so she feels comfortable. You could read. Or . . . look at your phone a bit?"

Julia shrugged. "Okay."

Upstairs in the hallway bathroom, there were more problems. "How does this work?" Julia asked. The girls were standing with toothbrushes in hand. A dribble of paste lined Pippa's mouth.

"What's wrong?" Wendell asked.

She pointed to the toilet. It had an old-fashioned pull in the center to flush.

"Oh. Here, let me show you." He demonstrated, and Pippa laughed. "What's so funny?"

"You pull the gold chain and down it goes!" She was getting giddy, whether from fatigue or from the toilet, Wendell couldn't say.

"Okay, okay. Time for bed."

When both were in their pajamas and washed up, Wendell knocked at the bedroom door. "May I read you a story?" he asked.

Pippa nodded sleepily. She was a tiny thing under the new comforter set and looked snug as a bug.

"What's the title?" Julia asked.

Wendell decided to sit on Pippa's bed. There was more room, and he didn't want to crowd the teenager. "It's an old book. One my parents used to read to me. It's called *Corduroy the Bear*."

Julia groaned. "Another antique?"

Wendell swatted the edge of her bed playfully with it. "Yes. Another antique." But this time she giggled.

Despite her cynicism, Julia stretched out on her bed and turned in his direction as he began to read. Beside him, Pippa's eyelids fluttered. When the book was done, Julia smiled. "That wasn't so bad." She yawned. "Actually, it was kind of cute."

Pippa was quiet, and when Wendell pulled the corner of her blanket away from her face, he saw that she was sound asleep. Her expression filled him with a deep sense of accomplishment. Very gently, he pulled the covers up around her and eased off the bed. As he tiptoed out of the room, he glanced over at Julia. "You can stay up a while, if you'd like. But be sure it's not too late."

"Okay. But one more thing."

Wendell paused in the doorway. "Yes?" It was such a strange sight, the two girls in his and Wesley's old beds, under his roof for the night. Despite the unfamiliarity of it all, it was also really nice.

Julia whispered, "Sometimes Pippa wets the bed." She looked worried.

"Oh." Wendell thought a moment. "If that happens, come get me. I'll change the sheets, and maybe you can help her change pajamas."

"You won't be mad?"

Wendell shook his head. "Of course not. You know, my little brother, Wesley, used to do that sometimes. But my parents understood." He shrugged. "Accidents happen."

"Right." Julia smiled. "Thanks, Wendell."

He smiled. "Good night, Julia. Sleep tight."

As he headed down the hall, Wendell paused outside the closed door of Wesley's room. Until that day, Wendell rarely went inside. Now he opened the door and looked around. Aside from the missing bed, it was just as Wesley had left it when he enlisted. On the closet door hung a David Ortiz Red Sox jersey, and over his desk was a Green Day poster. The bookshelf in the corner was lined with novels he probably never read for his high school English classes, a stack of music CDs, and a couple of middle and high school basketball trophies. His old Converse sneakers were lined up by the foot of the bed, toes pointing out. Wendell shook his head. Despite the years, it felt as if Wesley could just walk back in the door at any time. Ask Wendell to borrow his car. Give him a hard time about what a softie he'd become.

Wendell leaned against the doorframe. "What would you think of me taking in these girls?" he whispered to the empty room.

Thirty

Ginny

Ginny prided herself on being a people person. Normally, she enjoyed working with clients and developing relationships with them; it was a critical factor in doing her job well. But Candace was a vault. She was not going to open herself up one bit.

As surprising as the development had seemed initially, now that the Lancaster girls were staying with Wendell, Ginny thought it wasn't such a bad idea. For a man who preferred complete solitude and avoided relationships the way most people avoid contagions, the mere idea of him taking care of two orphaned girls was preposterous. After Wesley died and Wendell returned to Saybrook, he'd made one thing clear: he wanted to be left alone. She, more than anyone else, knew that.

But there was something about this new arrangement that was breaking through to him. In the little time she'd gotten to know them, she couldn't deny it: Julia and Pippa's story was heartbreaking, and the two were so sweet, only a person with a stone-cold heart could help becoming attached. Wendell Combs was not immune, and that said everything.

But Candace was. And for the life of her, Ginny could not figure it out. White Pines was one of the most beautiful places she'd ever set foot on, and since she'd grown up in picturesque Saybrook, that said a lot. However, Candace remained unmoved by both the family estate and the children. There had to be a reason why. But it was not Ginny's job to figure it out. Her job was to remain professional with a woman who was difficult to please and whose property could mean the survival of her parents' agency. Which was why Ginny decided to keep her connection to Wendell and the girls separate from her role as broker.

Still, it felt strange having come from Wendell's house, where she'd helped to decorate the bedroom for Julia and Pippa over the weekend, to meet with Candace on Monday morning. More than once she was tempted to mention that she'd seen the girls and they were doing fine. She realized Candace might not appreciate that. Or, worse, might not care. So she kept her mouth shut. Besides, there was the matter of the conversation she'd overheard between Geoffrey and Candace in the office the previous week.

Ginny had called Candace and offered to drop off documents that morning. The offer to purchase White Pines had been accepted, and Scooter Dunham's deposit had been received. What remained was one contingency: the estate had to be approved for subdivision by the town's planning and zoning department, so that Scooter could be assured of his development plans. And that included approval from the Inland Wetlands Commission. Otherwise, the deal would fall apart. And there was too much at stake, for Ginny as well, to let that happen.

As she pulled up to the house, she noticed a group of people in the distance, walking through the upper fields. When she knocked, Geoffrey Banks opened the door. She imagined the poor man practically lived at White Pines these days. He invited her in. "Come, join us. Candace and I were just wrapping up an estate meeting."

They were seated around the dining room table this time, and Ginny couldn't help but notice the girls' absence. The quietude made the sprawling house feel especially empty. "Now that we've got Mr. Dunham's documentation, I'd like to get an update on his contingency request. Do we know where things stand with the application for zoning?"

Geoffrey shared a copy of the application with her. "The commission met last week and reviewed our application. The zoning inspections have been done. And the Inland Wetlands Commission folks are conducting their walk as we speak."

"Ah, that's who I saw out there," Ginny said. "So, assuming today's walk goes well, we should expect approval for our permit to build?"

"Yes," Candace said. "Assuming." She glanced at Geoffrey. There: Ginny saw something in her look.

"Is there anything you're concerned about? Anything that might turn the approval process in the other direction?" Ginny was pressing, but that was her job. If something hadn't been disclosed, she needed to dig it up now.

"Well, there are lots of wetlands on the estate," Geoffrey allowed. "Which means that the commission is going to investigate things on their site walk."

"What kinds of things?" Ginny asked.

"Setbacks. Species of plants and animals, that sort of thing. The engineers have already come in and done soil tests to determine where the wetland boundaries are. The site walk is more of a formality."

"Nothing to worry about," Candace interjected firmly.

But that wasn't entirely true. While the Inland Wetlands Commission may have been a small one, if there were species or soil areas that could not be disrupted by excavation, they could stop a build. Which could mean that one or more of the lots created with the surveys might not be buildable. Unless an abutting property owner wanted to purchase it for privacy, a nonbuildable lot had pretty much zero value.

"Are we still marketing the lot?" Candace asked.

"Yes, of course. The listing remains active until the sale."

"Good. I think it's best to keep marketing it aggressively and keep others on the hook. I have a good feeling about Mr. Dunham, but one never knows."

Ginny did not have such a good feeling about Mr. Dunham, but for reasons other than the one Candace was suggesting. "Well, I should get back to the office."

Back outside, she noticed the group of commissioners getting into their cars down at the lower barn. They must've completed their walk. She waited as they pulled out before she drove down, so as not to disrupt them. When she passed the barn, there were two cars still there. One was a Subaru wagon. The other was a red sports car she recognized right away. But neither driver was around.

Ginny wondered idly if Wendell was there, working somewhere. As she pulled past the barn, she glanced back, looking for his truck. What she saw instead were two men, standing by the side of the barn, speaking closely. One of the men was Scooter Dunham. The other must've been a commissioner. Ginny slowed, watching as they shook hands. Scooter looked up just as she drove by, and she pulled her gaze away. Whatever they were doing, Scooter shouldn't have been talking to a commissioner. She wondered if Candace knew he was on the property.

Ginny glanced in her rearview mirror. The other man was getting into his car. But Scooter was watching her drive away.

There was a lot of work waiting for her, but Ginny didn't go back to the office.

Instead, she went to Saybrook town hall.

"Well, if it isn't Ginny Feldman!" Mrs. Hawthorne, the town clerk, stood up from behind her desk and trotted around to give her a hug. "You look no older than your high school graduation."

Mrs. Hawthorne's daughter was an old school friend of Ginny's. "Good to see you, too," Ginny said. Being home in a small town had some perks.

"What can I help you with, honey?" Mrs. Hawthorne asked.

"I'm representing a client on Timber Lane."

Mrs. Hawthorne nodded knowingly. "The whole town is talking about it. That beautiful place is going to be dug up and turned into a suburban eyesore." She clapped her hand over her mouth. "But that's just my opinion. Between us, of course."

Ginny laughed. "Of course. I was wondering if I could see the file on the property."

"You must mean the property card. Is there something in particular you're worried about?"

Ginny knew it was somewhat unusual for a listing agent to review town property files, but her gut was telling her she should. What she'd overheard of Geoffrey and Candace's discussion earlier that week suggested that something wasn't quite right. "I wanted to check on its zoning status and take a look at the history of permit applications." When she got a funny look, she added quickly, "I'm just crossing my t's and dotting my i's."

Luckily, that seemed to satisfy Mrs. Hawthorne. "I'll walk you down the hall to the building and health department for that. If you need anything else, come back and see me."

Ten minutes later, armed with the property file, Ginny settled into a small meeting room across the hall and began reading. There was nothing out of the ordinary that she could find. There were applications for a new septic back in the twenties, probably filed by Alan's grandfather. Several property maps were included in the file, showing how the borders had changed when the family purchased neighboring land to increase the estate. An old black-and-white photo, of a donkey pulling a cart with two children in it, a girl and a boy, was tucked between two of the maps. Ginny pulled it out and studied it. She wondered if the children were Candace and Alan. But there was nothing out of the ordinary in the file; after going through the entire thing and coming up empty-handed, she gave up her search.

She stopped at the town clerk's office to say goodbye. "Thanks, Mrs. Hawthorne. Say hi to Alison for me!"

Mrs. Hawthorne looked up from her desk. "Did you find what you were looking for, honey?"

"No. But then I guess I don't really know what I was expecting to find."

"Maybe I can help."

Ginny didn't want to stir up any trouble. Her job was to get the transaction done for her client and get the deal done for her parents' agency. But she also had an ethical code of conduct to follow. "Well, there was one thing. There's been a lot of talk about the Inland Wetlands Commission. I was just curious if there was a history of issues I should be aware of. But it's probably nothing," she added quickly.

Mrs. Hawthorne looked thoughtful. "Well, I don't recall any issues off the top of my head, but Saybrook has a lot of wetland properties, and protecting those areas has become a bit of a big deal with the state. Tell you what, I'll dig around a little if you like."

Ginny did like that idea, even if she was reluctant to pull strings. "That would be great. But promise not to spend too much time on it—I don't want to trouble you."

"For you? You bet! Now, if you were one of those bossy out-of-town developers, probably not." Mrs. Hawthorne winked. "I'll let you know if I find anything, sugar."

As much as Ginny hated to admit it, her mother had been right. Again. Working in a close-knit community had its advantages. She was on her way out of the town hall when her phone dinged. It was Wendell. Since she'd gone to the farmhouse to help settle the girls in, things between she and Wendell had seemed to settle. Ginny wasn't sure what, if anything, she felt for Wendell beyond curiosity and the desire to help him. But she took comfort in the sense that he seemed to have forgiven her for not telling him about listing White Pines from the beginning. She found herself smiling as she read his text: "The county fair is tonight."

"You hate the county fair," she replied. It was true. She'd dragged him to it every summer, and every time he'd gone. Even though the Ferris wheel made him dizzy and the smell of cotton candy turned his stomach.

"These girls don't hate the county fair."

"What's to hate?" she replied.

"Crowds. Noise. The Ferris wheel." There was a pause. Then, "Want to come?"

Ginny laughed aloud and texted back: "Meet you at the Ferris wheel."

The Saybrook County Fair was a midsummer highlight for everyone in town. It was a traditional New England event complete with livestock, music, games, and food. When she was growing up, Ginny's favorite had been the animal barn, where you could pet the farm animals and see who won best in each division. Her parents joked that they could drop her at the animal barn, then go on every ride and play every game, and she'd still be commiserating with the bunnies or baby goats when they came back to find her. Little had changed.

"You girls will love the bunny tent!" she told Julia and Pippa.

Pippa's eyes widened. "There's a whole tent of bunnies?"

"Technically, they share it with the chickens and turkeys. And the pigs and goats, too. But there are *a lot* of bunnies."

"Some of my friends show their horses here," Julia said, looking in the direction of the riding rings and barns. "I used to, too."

"You can ride Radcliffe any time," Wendell told her.

Julia just shrugged. "Thanks. But it's different now that I'm not training and showing."

Ginny exchanged a look with him. "Let's get something to eat first. They've got the best fried chicken and corn on the cob. And a meal isn't complete unless you also get a fresh-squeezed strawberry lemonade to wash it all down."

Julia brightened. "I am kind of hungry."

The four ate their way through the food tent, starting with chili dogs and corn and ending with watermelon ice cream. Pippa talked them into riding the carousel three times, until Ginny could tell Wendell felt dizzy. Julia wanted a tattoo at the henna artist's tent, and even though Wendell made a face, Ginny elbowed him gently. "Go on. It's not like they last."

Grudgingly, he relented, and while they were gone, Ginny took Pippa to pet the farm animals. Twenty minutes later, Julia ran up to them with a smug look on her face.

"What'd you get for a tattoo?" Pippa asked. Julia angled her wrist so they could see: it was a small outline of a tree. The branches curved skyward like elegant arms; like something out of a fairy tale. "That's beautiful," Ginny said.

"Wait till you see what he got." Julia pointed at Wendell, who was coming up behind her.

"No way!" Ginny said, laughing. "You got one, too?"

All three girls began reaching for his arms, trying to see where his henna tattoo was.

"Hey, get outta here," he said, batting them away playfully. "Personal space!"

"Go on," Julia urged. "Don't be a sissy."

Reluctantly, he pulled up his shirtsleeve, revealing a small brown animal. Pippa gasped. "A pony?"

Wendell scowled. "Not a pony! A horse. A big strong horse, like Raddy."

Pippa was already howling with laughter. "No. It's short and fat. It's a pony! Wendell got a pony."

Ginny couldn't help it; she burst out laughing. The girls were beside themselves, and it was clear that Wendell was enjoying every second of it. In fact, she'd never seen him like this.

"Let's go on the Ferris wheel," she suggested. Before he could complain, the girls each grabbed one of his arms and dragged him toward it.

"You're all going to be sorry!" he warned.

Toward the end of the night, the crowds thinned and the sky grew dark. Carnival rides and game booths blinked in neon as they made their way down the main strip. Julia, who'd gone off with some friends earlier, was meeting them at the exit gates. It was time to go home.

Pippa was so tired, Wendell had long ago picked her up and swung her over his shoulders. Now she slumped atop them, a half-eaten cotton candy in one hand, the other resting atop his head.

"There she is!" he said, pointing. Julia stood by the base of the Ferris wheel with a boy Ginny recognized from building the fence at Wendell's house a few days earlier.

"Oh, oh," Ginny whispered, leaning in. "Look at that."

Wendell's relaxed expression shifted. "Sam's a good kid. But he's standing too close."

Ginny shrugged. "I think he's fine. Besides, Julia's the one who just reached for his hand."

"What?" Wendell said, squinting into the distance.

"Relax, I'm kidding," Ginny joked. She had to admit, Sam was cute. And she could tell by the awkward way they stood together that they liked each other. "To be young again," she said softly.

When Wendell glanced at her sideways, she pretended she didn't notice. But before they got any closer to Julia, she grabbed his hand and squeezed it, then just as quickly, she let it go.

"Come on, Julia," he called, waving. "Time to go."

Ginny almost added "home" but caught herself. She wondered what the girls thought of as home these days. And she wondered what it was about tonight that had almost made her say it out loud.

All night, Ginny couldn't help but notice the looks they drew as they walked together through the fairgrounds. Saybrook was small, and although many of the people they passed smiled and waved to them, Ginny was sure they were at the heart of a lot of chatter. What did people think when they saw her walking with Wendell and the girls? What kind of picture did they paint?

She stole a peek at Wendell now, as he carried Pippa and listened to Julia's excited chatter, noting the fatigue at the corners of his eyes. But also something else: the crinkle of happiness.

As they walked to the truck, Wendell asked both girls if they'd had fun.

"Yeah," Julia said, glancing back at the carnival lights. "Tonight was a good one."

Pippa nodded groggily from Wendell's shoulders and murmured something incoherent.

With the bright lights and noise behind them, the sound of peepers began to fill in among the shadows. In the darkness, Ginny felt the warm press of a hand in her own. She glanced up at Wendell. "Tonight was a good one," he said.

Thirty-One

Roberta

Jamie Aldeen's call came early that morning. "The court appointed a guardian ad litem, and she's meeting with all parties this week," she explained, "but I could use your advice on something in the interim."

From what she'd seen firsthand, Roberta had been truly surprised by how well it seemed to be going. Wendell was a good man with a good heart, she knew as well as anyone. But he'd shut himself off from so much for so long. Roberta had seen some wild things happen in the court over the years, but in her wildest dreams, she wouldn't have predicted the series of events rapidly unfolding in his home. Now, hearing the concern in Jamie's tone gave her pause. "I'm all ears."

Roberta listened as Jamie explained her concerns. Julia's file for emancipation was a two-part process. While her first wish was to be emancipated, her ultimate goal was to obtain custody of Pippa and to raise her. "As we've discussed, the emancipation is enough of a challenge. I don't see the judge giving her full custody of her little sister. Despite her age of almost sixteen. Despite the family funds available to support them both and well. Not at age fifteen."

Roberta had warned Julia of this very fact herself. But she'd understood why the girl wasn't deterred. She wanted to fight for this.

And she couldn't change her age. "I share those same concerns. What have you come up with to make your case?"

"Well, the guardian ad litem has already interviewed Candace Lancaster and Wendell. She's meeting with the girls next."

"Have you any sense of her reports thus far?" Roberta knew they'd go to the judge, but sometimes attorneys communicated with the GALs and could discern some sense of their findings or leanings during those interactions.

"Not really. I wanted to get your sense about Mr. Combs."

Roberta had thought Jamie would be focused on Candace and making a case for the tensions at home. The lack of a former relationship. The woman's residence overseas. Courts liked to keep the children in circumstances as close to their normal lives as possible, assuming those were safe and fit surroundings. "What do you need to know about Wendell?"

"This is personal. Please know that I plan to reach out to him directly, but I wanted to get your sense first. If the emancipation request is denied, do you think he has any interest in custody of the girls? Because from what I've heard from Julia, it's been successful so far. And that was her initial wish."

Roberta sucked in her breath. She could not speak for Wendell, of course. But she knew what Jamie was asking: she wanted to know if following this trail would be a waste of their precious time or if there was hope. "You think the children would do best with him?"

Jamie paused. "Let me put it to you this way: I think he is their best shot at staying here in Saybrook."

Roberta had to be careful. Wendell was sacred ground. She'd known him almost his whole life. She was all he had for what might constitute family. And she'd made promises to his mother. He was not like everyone else. Wendell was as strong as they came on the outside. But on the inside, he was as fragile as Charlotte had been.

And she often felt that she had to protect him from himself. What Wendell might be willing to do out of duty might not be what was best for him.

Roberta understood the intricacies of this case Julia Lancaster had looped them all into. She knew that time was critical and that the children's options were limited. And despite her wish to remain neutral, she felt for those two girls, more than she'd ever wanted to. But her loyalties were to Wendell. "There is something you need to know."

"What's that?" Jamie asked.

Roberta hesitated. Wendell's losses were his business. Just as the way he handled them was. Over the years, he'd made that very clear to her. If they were to stay friends, she had to respect his privacy, and he respected hers. For many years, this approach had served them both well. She would not trespass against him now. But she did need to share one thing. "Wendell is a veteran, as you already know. And he has suffered more loss than most in his thirty-nine years. His involvement with these girls is a surprise. But his loyalty runs deep. Whatever you ask of him, be aware that every man has his limitations."

Jamie listened without interruption and took a moment after, when Roberta finished. "I understand," she said. "Let me please clarify one thing. Do you think any of that makes him unfit?"

Roberta held her breath. She thought of the old medical doctrine: "First, do no harm." And then she thought of Wendell. Of his losses and the years of therapy he'd undergone. The deep circles under his eyes and the sleepless nights that she knew he endured to this day. "That's not for me to decide," she said finally. "But I ask you to weigh it against any requests that are made of him on behalf of the Lancasters."

When she hung up the phone, Roberta's head throbbed. What had she just done?

She took two pills from the ibuprofen bottle in her medicine cabinet, tossed them back, and lay on the couch with a cold washcloth across her forehead. It wasn't that she didn't want to help Jamie Aldeen, a lawyer she both admired and trusted. Or those poor Lancaster girls, who deserved every bit they could get. As a judge, she'd taken an oath: "To faithfully and impartially discharge all the duties incumbent upon me under the Constitution and laws of the United States. So help me God." And in her mind, she'd failed.

It had been almost a decade since Roberta had walked away from her appointment as judge of the Housatonic Valley probate court but when she allowed her mind to drift back to the painful months leading up to her retirement, it seemed like yesterday.

Edith Warren's application for sole custody of her two grandchildren had brought Jenny Bruzi, her daughter, Layla, and her son, Dominic, to Roberta's court. But it was Austin Hicks, the biological father of little Dominic, who had held her attention.

There had been incidents of domestic disturbance between the adults, and Roberta had explored all evidence and findings from reports related to those events. But the matter at hand for her to hear was the custody of the children, and removing two children from the custody of a parent was no small matter. There had to be a compelling reason to do so.

After interviewing the family members during the initial hearings, Roberta had concerns. She addressed those concerns using every tool available to her.

She'd ordered that DCF visit the family weekly and that Austin Hicks and Jenny Bruzi apply for jobs; another hearing was scheduled for four weeks later to hear updates.

Austin had found and maintained a job at a local auto parts

center, where he worked the cash register and stocked shelves. He had taken only two sick days. He made his rent payments on time. According to DCF, there were groceries in the refrigerator, if not all the healthiest kinds. Layla was in a special program called Head Start, and her attendance was intermittent. Jenny was quick to blame the lack of a car: there was one vehicle for the household, and she claimed Austin needed it to work. When asked why she could not drop him off at work, since it was often for eight-hour shifts, then pick him up, thereby allowing her use of the car, she would look to him and remain silent. This was where Roberta's red flares began to spark. She didn't like it when a person questioned in her courtroom deferred to another, often woman to man. It was a sign of a power struggle, of a person's fear to speak freely for herself. Roberta made note of these, and many other details, in her file. She watched Austin Hicks like a hawk, but she watched Jenny Bruzi even more closely. It was what Jenny did not say that caught her attention.

Edith Warren had a lot to say. But none of it was proving useful to Roberta's attempt to build any kind of case for what the grandmother was requesting of the court. Mrs. Warren was convinced Austin Hicks was a threat to her daughter and grandchildren, and as the judge presiding over the matter, Roberta made every effort to delve into those concerns and determine their warrant. During the final hearing, she pressed Mrs. Warren for details.

"To your knowledge, has Mr. Hicks ever physically or verbally caused distress to either child?" She waited as Edith Warren considered this. Even if it was something as seemingly benign as taking a child's hand too roughly or yelling, as she knew many parents did at some point, Roberta wanted to hear it. In her position, she counted on the people who came through her courthouse doors to provide the details, no matter how small. That was their job. Hers was to sift through them all and decide whether or not they were relevant. And right now, if what Mrs. Warren was claiming held any water, Roberta needed something to go on.

But Edith Warren could not produce any evidence of distress. "No, ma'am." She shook her head sadly. "All's I can tell you is that he don't like little Layla. And if he's around her when he gets angry, like he does more and more, I can see him going for her. Something real bad will happen. I can feel it in my bones."

DCF was ordered to maintain their weekly visits to the house. Eventually, with those reports showing no change in status quo, they became twice monthly. By January 2013, with no new incidents reported or charges filed, and the children appearing at doctor appointments in good health, Roberta felt she had no reason to deny them from their mother. Both Layla and Dominic were returned to their mother in full custody. At the hearing, Edith Warren wept. When Roberta asked if there were any changes or any evidence to support her concerns for the children's well-being with their mother and Austin Hicks in their apartment, Edith Warren said simply, "I know him, Your Honor. You don't know what he's capable of."

Roberta Blythe loved the law. While there were cracks in the system, and loopholes where areas became gray, she believed that was where a judge's role came into play. It was her job to examine those cracks and fill them. To provide safety nets when needed. To support, to protect, and ultimately, to keep families together. And so she did. She extended the DCF visits and reiterated her concerns and hopes for the Bruzi-Hicks family arrangement. Beyond that, with no new evidence to present to the court, she could not under the law remove Layla Bruzi or Dominic Hicks from the custody of their mother and award guardianship to Edith Warren.

Before she stood to deliver her verdict, she felt the ominous weight of Edith Warren's stare. "I feel it in my bones," Edith had warned.

As Judge Roberta Blythe made her ruling that Jenny Bruzi should maintain full custody of both her children on April 13, 2013, she believed in *her* bones that she had done her due diligence.

Three weeks later, on May 2, Roberta received a phone call in the early morning. The night before, Austin Hicks had taken his son, Dominic, from his crib, poured a gallon of gasoline around the bed he shared with Jenny, and lit the apartment on fire. Paramedics and rescue volunteers responded to a 911 call shortly after two a.m. Jenny Hicks was pulled to safety from a second-story window, suffering from smoke inhalation but pronounced alert and conscious on the scene. Minutes later, five-year-old Layla Bruzi was also pulled from a window. She was unconscious. She had suffered third-degree burns on 40 percent of her body.

Just fifty-two miles away, in Hartford County, Austin Hicks was pulled over by Connecticut state troopers on Interstate 84. He was arrested for attempted murder.

Thirty-Two

Julia

The week with Wendell had gone fairly well. There were issues, of course. The house was no White Pines. It was dated and kind of dark, and the relics that Wendell called antiques were kind of ugly. The TV was ancient. The Wi-Fi was terrible. She missed her bedroom and all her belongings, despite the nice things Roberta and Ginny had done to make them feel welcome. Wendell didn't know what to make them for meals, but then again, neither had Candace. "Are you sure you don't want to come for a sleepover?" Chloe had asked. But Julia knew she couldn't. "I have to show the judge I can handle this," she explained. "Wendell is the only one who has agreed to take us in for now. I've got to make it work."

But it was a far cry from home. Outside, Wendell's place was beautiful, and of course, there was Raddy, but she missed her view of the fields and the knowledge that her parents' bedroom was just down the hall, even if they were not in it. Even after they got used to staying at the farmhouse, they couldn't shake the feeling that they were houseguests.

Most of all, Julia missed the security of knowing what the future held in store for her. The hearing at the probate court couldn't come soon enough. Julia needed to know what was next for them.

Now, back at White Pines, Julia wanted nothing but to run down to the lake and meet Sam. There was so much to tell him. Like how Candace had welcomed them back politely that morning. If her aunt was mad or felt betrayed, she did not show it. She was too busy with the family lawyer and was already on the phone. Candace's attention was on the buyer she'd apparently secured. A heartbreaking fact that Julia had to tell Sam right away. "I'm going out for a walk," she told her aunt, who barely looked up from her laptop at the kitchen island.

"Very well. But be back at noon." She didn't elaborate, and Julia didn't ask. All she wanted was to go find Sam.

She'd hoped to see him standing near their favorite tree by the egret nest. Or waiting by the edge of the woods, at the mouth of the path. After all, he knew that she was coming home that morning. To her disappointment, he was in neither place. Julia walked along the edge of the lake, scanning the sand for a sign. There was nothing.

"I'm back," she texted him, wondering if he was home and could come meet her. But she already knew: they had no reception by the water, and that was part of the thrill. Sometimes their meeting up was left to chance.

She sat on their rock, scanning the ground for a sign. There was no message on the beach. Nothing written in the sand; no treasure left on the shore.

But then she saw it. There, at the base of the rock right next to her foot, was a small pile of stones stacked just-so. Julia hopped down. They were perfectly smooth, flat on each side. Perfect for skipping. She looked up, half-expecting to see Sam watching her from some hidden spot. "You remembered," she said aloud. She scooped one up and held it in her palm, enjoying the cool weight of it. Then, the way her father had shown her, she skipped it. The rock bounced once, twice, then plunked beneath the surface. "Damn," she muttered. She tried another. This one sank immediately. For no reason at all, tears pricked at her eyes.

She'd been good at this. She'd told Sam so. Was everything her parents had taught her or done for her fading already? Julia grasped the last rock and let her gaze rest on a spot in the distance. Then, with the flick of her wrist, she released it. The stone flew parallel to the lake's surface, hitting the surface once, twice, three times. Then another. "Five. Six!" she shouted as it skimmed across the surface before sinking with an audible *plunk*. With just the birds for spectators, Julia did a quick bow. "Thank you!" she shouted across the lake.

Back at the house, at noon, Pippa and Candace were in the kitchen. With them was a young woman with short curly hair and an ugly striped brown skirt. Candace had on her "company face" but was wringing her hands. *This* was interesting.

"Here she is!" Candace said, motioning her in. "Julia, this is Miss Blake, and she is here to talk to you and Pippa about some things."

Julia glanced between the two women and put her hand on Pippa's shoulder. "Things?"

Miss Blake was not about to have Candace speak for her, and she stepped forward, extending her hand with a huge smile. "Hello, you must be Julia. You can call me Katy. I was asked to come here by Judge Bartlett, remember him?"

Julia nodded warily.

"He's asked me to come and speak to you girls today. I was hoping we could sit down together and get to know one another." She glanced at Candace. "Just the three of us."

Instantly, Julia forgave her for the bad skirt.

Katy invited them to sit with her in the living room, and Julia liked her take-charge attitude straightaway. She was soft-spoken but direct. "I was sorry to hear about your mom and dad," she began once Candace stopped hovering and finally left them alone. "It must be a very sad time for you girls."

Pippa nodded. "I miss Mommy. And Daddy."

"I'm sure you do. There is no one better to take care of you." Katy paused. "It's very nice your aunt Candace is here to help care for you now. Family is very important. But sometimes there are other people we know and like who might help take care of us."

Both girls nodded. Julia watched as Katy pulled a pad of paper and a pen from her bag. She also pulled out a sketchbook and a box of Crayola crayons. Irritation rose within her. Julia was tired of therapists and court systems. She knew all their tricks. Katy was probably going to ask Pippa to draw a stupid picture of her family and analyze it. But she put aside the art supplies and set the pad of paper on her lap.

"I hear you have a lot of good people like that. I wanted to ask you about one of them. Can you tell me about Mr. Combs?"

To Julia's surprise, Pippa piped up. "Oh, you mean Wendell. He's our friend. He lives here a lot, but he also has his own house. He takes care of Raddy."

Katy glanced curiously at Julia. "Is that the horse?"

She had really done her homework. "Yes," Julia said. "He rescued him for us."

"I see." Katy made some notes on her pad. "How much time have you spent with Wendell?"

Pippa shrugged. "Some. A lot. But not every day."

Clearly, Julia needed to chime in. "He works here, so he's here every day. Actually, he's known us since we were really little. Since Pippa was born." At that, Pippa started nodding exuberantly. She liked when the conversation turned to her. "But we never really spent a lot of time with him, just us. Until recently. Until our folks died and our aunt came." She paused. "He's the only adult I like spending time with these days."

Katy looked up at her. "That's very helpful." She turned to Pippa. "So what about Wendell do you like?"

The meeting continued another hour, and then Katy did give Pippa the art supplies. "Pippa, can you draw me a picture of you and Aunt Candace?"

"Why?" Pippa asked. "I'm really good at butterflies." Julia had to hide her smile.

"I would love a butterfly!" Katy said. "But right now I need two pictures. They don't have to be fancy or big. They can be simple. But they need to be on a different page." Julia watched as she pulled two sheets off the sketchbook and labeled one "Pippa and Wendell" and another "Pippa and Aunt Candace."

While Pippa worked, Katy motioned Julia aside. "I'm a little thirsty. Maybe we could get a drink of water in the kitchen?"

Again a trick, but Julia followed. She liked Katy and wanted to trust her, but she was not going to lay any more hopes in any basket the state of Connecticut was holding. "What do you want to talk about?" she asked, cutting to the chase.

Katy took it with no offense. "Mr. Combs has petitioned the court for temporary custody. I assume you know that?"

So he had gone through with it. Julia nodded, ignoring the flutter in her chest. She would not let herself go there. Not yet.

"It's procedure for me to come out and meet with children and get a sense of what they want. At Pippa's age, of course we want to talk with her and hear about her feelings. They're important. But she is also very young, and we typically give more weight to older children, like yourself. You have more experience."

"And more say?" Julia interrupted.

Katy smiled tightly. "No one has all the say. That's why I'm here, to listen to everyone and then combine everyone's wants with what is best for their needs. Is there anything you'd like me to add to your thoughts today that perhaps you'd feel more comfortable sharing alone?"

Julia did have more to share, but since her experience in the courthouse during the hearing, she didn't trust Katy or anyone else to take her seriously. She glanced back at Pippa in the living room. As she did, her eyes fell on the family portrait above the fireplace. Painted just two years ago, from a photo taken at her mother's forty-fifth birthday celebration. It was the four of them posing at the edge of the yard, with the orchard in the background. Each one connected by a hand here, an arm there.

"Anything at all," Katy urged her. "Speak from your heart."

And Julia began.

Thirty-Three

Wendell

Wendell had not liked being in court the first time, just a few weeks ago. He liked being there even less that morning. But he wouldn't have missed it for the world.

Judge Bartlett got right down to business. "Good morning, everyone. I have a full docket today, so let's get started." He looked up. "Since our last meeting in the petition for emancipation for Ms. Julia Lancaster, the girls have split their time between the home of Mr. Combs and their family home with their aunt, Ms. Lancaster. I want to hear how that has gone. Ms. Blake has been assigned by the court to report on the children's behalf." He looked up at the GAL and removed his glasses. "Ms. Blake, would you please share your findings with the court?"

As Katy Blake stood before them, sharing the details of her interviews with everyone involved, Wendell's ears burned. He listened with an intensity that belied the calm look he knew he wore. And as he listened, memories pulled at the corners of his mind. Wendell thought about the kind of parents his own had been. About his childhood with Wesley and how much had changed at the loss of their mother. How Alder, a man of such physical fortitude and moral direction, had been reduced in both size and capacity. As a first selectman to Saybrook. As a father to Wendell and Wesley. And later, to just Wendell. He watched the blond back of Julia's head as she sat listening in the seat just in front of him, beside her attorney. He noted the erectness of her posture. The rigidity of her gaze when she turned to whisper to Jamie or glance at Candace, several seats over. Wendell wondered how she could sit there knowing that everything said in this room on this summer morning would make up the next few years of her young life. It was these thoughts that kept him glued to his seat when every other fiber in his being told him to run. Wendell cared too much, he realized. He was here not just out of duty to a man who'd taken him under his wing and hired him. Nor out of a sense of longing for the family he had lost. He was here because of what the girls meant to him. For the first time in years, Wendell was doing something for *himself*.

"Will you please show the court?" the judge asked.

Wendell watched as Katy Blake stood before the room holding two pieces of paper, one in each hand. He squinted. They were drawings.

"I asked Pippa to illustrate two pictures: one of her and Wendell Combs, and one of her with her aunt, Candace Lancaster. This is the result."

In one picture were two stick figures, standing apart. The larger one's arms draped by its sides. The smaller one held a flower. There was a blue sky.

In the second picture were the same two stick figures, large and small. There was also a third figure, medium-sized. And what looked like a big brown dog but Wendell realized was a horse. A rainbow streaked overhead. The hands of all three stick figures were linked.

As Katy Blake sat down and Jamie Aldeen stood to speak, Wendell found himself unable to hear. He was too busy trying to swallow the hot tears that were spilling down his cheeks. He swiped at them, trying to focus. Jamie was saying something about the wishes of the children. Wendell already knew those wishes as if they were his own.

When Candace was questioned, Wendell felt his insides simmer as they did before an episode. He cleared his throat and made two strong fists. He had to keep the panic at bay.

At some point, Wendell heard his name. By then, sweat was seeping through his button-down shirt, drenching his underarms. He shook his head, collecting himself. "Excuse me, Your Honor?"

Judge Bartlett was staring at him. Candace and Jamie Aldeen had turned to look at him, too. Julia did not.

"I asked, Mr. Combs, if you have anything you'd like to add."

"To add, Your Honor?"

"Yes. Is there anything you'd like to tell the court about the custody arrangement this past week?"

Wendell cleared his throat. "Yes, Your Honor." He looked at the back of Julia's head, then at Judge Bartlett. "Both Julia and her little sister did very well at my house, I thought. The first night was a little bumpy, as Pippa felt homesick. But each day was easier. We set up a bedroom for them, and they decorated it nicely. They slept and ate well, as far as I could tell. They seemed comfortable, and we spent a good deal of time together."

"Very good. How was your time spent?"

Wendell thought of all they'd done. "During my days off, the girls spent time outside, hiking the property with me. We went to the county fair. As you know, Julia's horse is on the property. We finished building an enclosure and stall for him, and the girls seemed happy to participate in that." As the words tumbled from his dry mouth, Wendell realized how clinical this all sounded. A list of things done. Nowhere in there was how he or the girls felt.

"Thank you, Mr. Combs. The court appreciates your investment of time and energy in helping to decide the best course of action." Judge Bartlett riffled through papers, and Wendell caught his breath. It seemed his role was done. At that point, Julia turned around. "Thank you," she whispered. Wendell nodded. For the first time, his breathing steadied.

"The court would like to take a short recess while I confer with the guardian ad litem. I ask everyone to remain close by."

Unlike the others, Wendell remained in his seat. Jamie ushered a very worried-looking Julia out, assuring her this was all normal. Candace and Geoffrey stood and conferred quietly in the corner. Despite the air-conditioning, the room was suffocating, but Wendell feared if he got up to leave, his legs would be jelly. He stayed put until the judge returned and everyone was called back.

"All right," Judge Bartlett began when everyone had been seated. "The court has heard a number of compelling accounts regarding the emancipation case for Julia Lancaster." He looked directly at Julia, and Wendell felt his heart rate increase, as he was sure hers had. "You are a remarkable young woman who has proved herself to be bright, determined, and capable, despite a shattering hardship that has fallen on you this year.

"That hardship is what I believe has propelled you to file for emancipation. A serious decision with serious consequences. That said, you are a unique young woman with a unique set of circumstances that afford you the financial security to care for yourself."

Wendell felt the air in the courtroom shift. Why couldn't the judge just announce his verdict?

"While I empathize deeply with your plight, and while I understand your wishes to emancipate yourself, I cannot discount the nature of your situation. You have just lost your parents. A difficult loss for any adult, let alone a child. And for the intent of this proceeding, you are still recognized by the state of Connecticut as a child.

"You are grieving, Ms. Lancaster. As you have every right

to do. That is a healthy course of things. But given your recent loss and the depth of what I imagine your grief to be, this court cannot in good conscience saddle you with the responsibilities of adulthood at the tender age of fifteen and especially during this difficult time. Nor can it consider your further request to take on the additional responsibility of raising your sibling, who is significantly younger and will, as a result, require significantly more care."

Wendell's eyes flashed from the judge to Julia's back. She remained in her seat, but he could see the shaking of her shoulders.

"With that in mind, unless another opportunity for guardianship is presented to the court, it is my recommendation that you return to your family home with your sister and reside with your aunt. While your trust will remain as deemed by your parents' estate to both you and your sister, your custody will remain, as they set forth, with your aunt."

The judge drew a deep breath, looking pained. "Please know the court sympathizes with your situation. Deeply. But as such, I'm afraid the petition for emancipation of Julia Lancaster is denied."

Wendell did not hear what was said next. Nor could he have recalled, if asked. There was the whoosh of air moving around him. The rising of Julia in front of him. All eyes turned as she leaped up, her skirt billowing. And then there was silence. What Wendell would remember was that nothing came from her mouth. She simply sank to her knees.

And then there were hands. Jamie Aldeen's, reaching down to her. Candace, who came to stand beside her, speaking with her hands. Geoffrey Banks, who jammed his hands in his pockets, looking as if he would rather be anywhere else. And Wendell's. His hands reached for Julia, past all the others who'd come to stand around her. And when he made contact, she spun around and fell into his arms.

. . .

It had been years since he'd pulled in at the Spigot. Since the night Alan had sought him out and sat down on the stool beside him. Wendell was not an alcoholic so much as he was turning to drinking to numb himself. He could handle a beer, as long as he was in therapy and managing his PTSD. That was what he told himself as he parked the truck and pushed the door open.

Nothing had changed. Not the darkness or the stale murky air. In the corner, three guys stood around a pool table. An old jukebox blinked uncertainly in the corner, the music flickering on and off, though no one seemed to mind. He sat down on a spare stool, not far from the ones where he and Alan had talked, and ordered a beer. It would be just one. He needed to think about the hearing.

Down the bar, someone raised a hand. "Combs. Where you been?" Wendell looked over. It was Ronny Perkowski, whom he'd grown up with; Ronny now did caretaking for the Dunhams. Wendell raised a hand in greeting and kept his head down. He wasn't here to socialize.

The first beer went down too quickly, and he felt an actual thirst. So he ordered another. By then a couple guys he recognized from the town works department had come in. Bill Hardings was nice enough, but he was with another guy Wendell didn't particularly care for, Owen Miller, who was a bit of a blowhard. "Wendell, good to see you," Bill said. Wendell nodded and kept to his beer.

He tried not to listen as the guys talked about their work week and who was leading the men's softball league that summer. None of it mattered to him. But his ears pricked at the mention of Scooter Dunham. Ronny Perkowski was talking. "He's buyin' the Lancaster place. All of it. Going to turn it into a subdivision." He ran his hand over the stubble on his chin. "Big money."

"No way, I heard it was going to be open space for the town."

"Nah, that sister came over from London and took over. It's hers to do with what she wants. Ain't that right, Combs?"

He could feel their heads turn in his direction.

Wendell shrugged. "I don't know anything about it," he said.

"That's not what I hear." Ronny Perkowski slid off his stool and came around the side of the bar. He was smiling, but Wendell didn't like his tone. "I hear you're still working up there. You must see and hear all kinds of things. What's that Brit got you working on these days?"

Wendell took a swig of his beer. "It's just business, Ronny. Why don't you mind yours."

Ronny came up beside him. "Didn't I hear you've got a horse now?"

The hair on the back of Wendell's neck prickled.

"Yeah, I think I did hear that. Wasn't that the older girl's horse?"

The men started to snicker behind him. Ronny leaned in close. "What'd she do for you to get that horse?"

Wendell was off his stool before Ronny could finish his sentence. The first punch landed on the bridge of his nose. When Ronny regained his balance and popped back up, the next punch went to his gut and sent him sprawling backward to the ground. He lay on the filthy floor, holding his face, and cursed.

"Don't you mention those kids ever again!" Wendell shouted as he stood over Ronny. He spun toward the others, who'd moved closer and now stepped back.

Bill Hardings held up his hands. "Easy, Combs. Nobody wants to fight."

Wendell stared down at Ronny. "What about you? Anything else you want to say?"

Ronny's nose gushed behind his hand. "Jesus Christ," he hissed as Owen Miller helped him up.

Wendell took another step at him, and he jerked back. "Nothing else?" Wendell said between his teeth.

Ronny shook his head and leaned on the bar. "Get me some ice, dammit."

Wendell threw two twenties down on the bar and got the hell out of there. His hand throbbed, and outside, he examined it in the growing darkness. Nothing appeared to be broken, but his knuckles were an angry color and scraped. He sure hoped he'd broken Ronny's nose.

On the way back, he drove straight past his house. He didn't slow until he turned sharply into Roberta's narrow driveway, gravel spitting beneath his tires. She met him on the doorstep, a look of alarm on her face. "Wendell. Is everything all right?"

"I need your help."

Thirty-Four

Roberta

The Housatonic Probate Courtroom had once been hers to preside over. Standing outside its double doors felt like stepping outside her body and back in time. If it weren't for Wendell, she wouldn't be here.

Inside, she took a quick seat on the bench while Wendell went to see the clerk about filing the papers they'd worked on together. She wondered what Charlotte Combs would say about her son's decision. Roberta was pretty sure it'd be a lot.

Roberta was not the praying kind, but at that moment, she prayed that neither Judge Bartlett nor any attorney she might know would walk by. She was relieved that she didn't recognize the clerk. As soon as Wendell filed, she could get out of here.

As she waited, Roberta closed her eyes and let her mind wander. Being back at the courthouse was unnerving. The room was warm, and her memory was too long to keep her thoughts in check. She thought of something Charlotte had told her long ago. "Life is just a giant Ferris wheel, spinning through time. We're on it for the ride, and all we can do is hang on." Roberta pictured herself seated at the highest point of the wheel, the courtroom the cog. As she dipped down, she saw her past rising up to meet her from ground level. There was Charlotte, her dear friend. Perhaps her only true friend, who had found her that day in the IGA market with the two little boys in tow, and rescued her. Charlotte, who gave her a sense of family, who invited her to birthday parties and holidays, and made her laugh when she felt like crying, and saw her as she was and where she was in her station in life, and decided she was worthy.

After Charlotte, came the boys, Wendell and Wesley, both young. They were fast and squirmy, and on rare occasions, she could catch one and pull him onto her lap. Oh, they smelled like little boys: sweat and heat and shampoo, all mixed together with something earthy. She let them go, and as they ran, she knew they were running headlong into futures that would shake them both. And leave one behind.

Roberta felt the dizzying pull of centrifugal force as the wheel swung skyward and she swept by faces on the ground. Faces of those she'd worked with. Attorneys she'd fought against and some she'd fought for. Families she'd come to know, along with all the dark details that had brought them to her courtroom. And among those faces, little Layla Bruzi.

Roberta closed her eyes, picturing her before the apartment fire. Her strawberry-blond bangs cut crookedly; her smile bow-shaped and uncertain. Layla's stubborn young mother, Jenny, and little Dominic. And the man whose name she would not permit her lips to utter. The largest of all her regrets, which she could never let go of. Regret that had kept her shuttered away, alone in the shadow of life.

As the wheel crested, she pictured the Lancaster girls. Two unexpected vibrant faces, full of hope and sorrow. Who had, just maybe, given her a second chance.

"Bertie?"

Roberta opened her eyes, startled.

"Are you okay? I thought you might be sleeping."

Roberta put a hand to her face, then smiled. "No, no," she said, collecting herself. "I was just daydreaming. Are you all done?"

Wendell held his hand out to help her up. "I am," he said. "Let's go home."

Thirty-Five

Ginny

It had been a crazy couple of days at the office. Since the Feldman Agency had listed White Pines, business had picked up, and her parents were thrilled. Ginny wasn't sure if it showed a local increase of confidence, their having landed such a big listing, or if more people were noticing her marketing efforts and were being reminded of her parents' business. Regardless, they'd had a busy week, with two new listings, both nicely appointed homes in private communities, and a contract with an out-of-town young family looking to move before the school year began. "Keep it going," her father told her on the phone. She'd been so swamped at the office, she'd barely had time to visit her folks. Let alone enjoy some downtime at her cottage. In fact, being back in Saybrook had kept her so distracted that she hadn't given Thomas or Chicago any thought.

On top of that, she got a call from Scooter Dunham's attorney. He wanted to finalize the contracts and closing details for White Pines. Ginny had tactfully reminded him that the permits had not officially come in from zoning, and his contingencies had not yet been satisfied. If she were a less ethical broker, she'd have scheduled it and hoped they'd forget about the contingency.

But the attorney didn't seem concerned. "Mr. Dunham would like to sign the executory contracts and get the closing on the calendar anyway. He's expecting the permit approvals shortly, so we can go ahead and pencil in a date."

Ginny was surprised. It was Scooter Dunham himself who'd so vocally objected to moving ahead with the deal at White Pines before his subdivision feasibility was secured by the town. "Is there new information from town hall?" she asked, wondering if she'd somehow missed a relevant update.

"No. Mr. Dunham is just confident things are moving in the right direction."

Ginny thought back to the morning of the site walk. How she'd seen Scooter Dunham pacing in the driveway when she'd arrived to meet with Geoffrey and Candace. How strange it had seemed that he did not join them inside but, rather, remained by his car on the phone while the commissioners conducted their site walk on the property. And how later, when she was leaving, she'd seen him speaking privately to one of the commissioners by the side of the barn.

"I'll reach out to my client and check her schedule," she told Scooter's attorney, now. "We'll be in touch shortly."

Candace seemed delighted when Ginny called with the update. "I have an executory contract to drop off for signatures," Ginny told her. "Are you available this morning?"

"Yes, bring it by any time."

When Ginny pulled up the driveway at White Pines an hour later, the first thing she noticed was the red sports car parked in front of the main house. What was Scooter doing here, now?

Ginny was just stepping out of her car when the front door opened. "What fortuitous timing." Scooter came down the front steps to greet her as if the place was already his.

"Good morning, Mr. Dunham," Ginny said. "I'm here with executory contracts for my client. Copies were just faxed to your attorney's office for review as well."

Scooter looked pleased as punch. "Good to hear you're on top of things."

"Thank you for bringing those by, Ginny," Candace said. Then, "I'm going to walk Mr. Dunham out, but there's fresh coffee in the kitchen if you'd like. Help yourself to a cup."

But Ginny did not help herself to coffee. She lingered on the other side of the open doorway, pretending to check phone messages as Candace walked Scooter to his car. Their voices were low, but she caught much of what they said.

"The final report should be available in the next day or two," Scooter said.

"And you're confident things are in good standing? Mr. Banks still has concerns about that item we discussed earlier."

"That item has been taken care of," Scooter stated. "And there's no need to loop Mr. Banks in further."

Candace glanced up at the house, and Ginny stepped back out of sight. "That's a relief. We can keep this between us."

"Agreed."

By the time Candace joined her, Ginny had made sure she was in the kitchen pouring herself coffee. "Busy morning at White Pines," Ginny mused, wondering what exactly they'd been meeting about. It was most unusual for a seller and buyer to meet, especially without their agents present. That was Ginny's job.

"It is," Candace agreed.

Ginny couldn't shake the feeling she'd interrupted something. "Is everything all right with Mr. Dunham?" As Candace's agent, she certainly had the right to ask.

"Yes, of course. He wanted permission to walk the property with one of his contractors."

Ginny sipped her coffee thoughtfully. "It's a bit premature for that, isn't it? As your agent, I'd advise that you continue to show the property and operate under the assumption that it's not sold until the closing is finalized."

"I'm not worried. If Mr. Dunham wants to move ahead, that only works in our favor."

Indeed, but it still didn't add up. Maybe she was missing something. "Have you received the report from the Wetlands Commission site walk yet?" Ginny asked.

"I believe Mr. Dunham said it would be ready in the next day or two," Candace replied.

There was no way Scooter Dunham would know when the report was being issued. Only the commission knew that information. Was that what they'd been discussing in the driveway?

"Well, hopefully, it's good news." Ginny checked Candace's face for any clue but could find nothing. "Here's the contract for Geoffrey to review with you. You may wish to make changes, in which case we'll need to share those with the other side. He'll know what to do." She handed Candace the file with the updated contract, but Candace was more interested in next steps.

"Thank you. When are we thinking for closing?"

"Assuming all goes well with the commission report and the mortgage guarantee, it sounds like Mr. Dunham's attorney wants to schedule before thirty days. He suggested two weeks out."

"That's perfect timing," Candace said. "We'll be heading back to London soon after."

Ginny bit her lip. Candace had said "we." Unless Julia or Pippa had told her, Candace was unaware that Ginny had any knowledge of her legal issues with the girls or the hearing that had just taken place. Candace certainly didn't know her involvement with Wendell. So that made it impossible to press about the sudden change of plans for London. "So you have a return date set?" Ginny asked casually.

"Once this sale is finalized," Candace replied. "It's the only thing left for me to take care of here in the States."

Which could mean only one thing. The judge had reached a verdict. And it didn't sound like it had gone in Julia's favor.

As soon as she got in the car, Ginny called Wendell. Each time it went to voicemail. Finally, she drove over to the farmhouse straight from work to look for him. But his truck was not in the driveway. When she drove through the village center, she didn't see it parked in any of the places he might be. She even tried the Spigot, the old dive bar that he used to frequent when he came home from Afghanistan. She was relieved not to see his truck in the parking lot.

Just as she was pulling out, her phone rang. It was a local number, but she didn't recognize it. "Ginny? It's Gail Hawthorne calling from town hall. I wanted to reach you before I left work for the day, if now is a good time."

There was something different about Gail's tone. "Now is good," Ginny said.

"I may have found something. After you brought up the Wetlands Commission, it triggered some memories. I knew something had gone on in town years ago, but I couldn't recall the details. So I pulled the files of the properties abutting White Pines."

"That was smart," Ginny said, wishing she'd thought of that herself.

"Turns out there was an application back in the eighties to expand some farm buildings on one the of the lots neighboring White Pines. The application was denied because of a turtle species they discovered."

"A turtle?" Ginny almost laughed.

"Apparently, a turtle that was on the state endangered species list was found up there. They were a protected species at the time, and the whole project was halted as a result."

Ginny grabbed a pad of paper from her bag on the passenger seat. "Can you tell me what species is was?"

"The red spotted turtle. That rang another bell, and I looked it up online. As it turns out, by the eighties, their population had made enough of a comeback that they were taken off the list. When some meadows in town were bought for development, there was a big hoopla. Even the first selectman got involved."

Ginny exhaled. "Alder Combs?" That was Wendell's father.

"That's him. He tried to make a case that the species was still too fragile, but the town pushed ahead and the DEP okayed it. The story goes on from there, since they ended up being back on the endangered list after that, but I can send you the links if you'd like."

"Please do." Ginny's heart raced. "Gail, do you happen to know if those turtles are still on the endangered list for the state?"

"Sorry, honey. I'm a town clerk, not a wildlife biologist."

Ginny laughed. "You've done more than enough. Thank you."

"You bet. I'll email you the rest."

When she hung up, Ginny let the car idle a long time as she tried to piece together all Gail had shared. Just because the turtles had been an issue back in the eighties didn't mean they would be now. And there was no indication that the turtles even lived on White Pines property. But given what she'd seen of Scooter Dunham during the commission walk, and what she'd heard between him and Candace, she thought it was enough to delve into. Now she had even more need to find Wendell.

She tried his phone once more, but there was no answer. By then she was tired, her clothes were rumpled, and she wanted nothing more than to go home to the cottage and grill something for dinner on the deck. Pour herself a much-needed glass of wine.

There was already a vehicle in her driveway when she pulled in. Wendell opened the truck door and got out just as she pulled up next to him. "There's something I have to tell you," she said. "I think something is going on . . ."

Wendell circled around to her door and reached for her hand. Instead of just helping her out, he pulled her. Right up against him. "There's something I have to tell you, too. But first I have to do this."

Then Wendell's mouth was on hers. Ginny dropped her bag in the driveway and threw both arms around his neck. They kissed with an urgency she hadn't thought possible. They paused only once, when Wendell kicked her car door closed with the toe of his boot. Then, still kissing the whole way, they stumbled to her front door. Once inside, they halted in the doorway, out of breath.

Over Wendell's shoulder she spied her bag still lying in the driveway. Her unlocked car. She pushed the door closed, anyway.

Then, very slowly, Wendell pulled her up against him.

"Ginny," he whispered, pressing his lips to the nape of her neck. Running his hands up the back of her shirt. She shuddered beneath the swirl of his fingertips.

"Wait." She stepped back and very slowly unbuttoned his shirt, running her hands across the breadth of his chest and down the washboard of his abdomen. The man before her was not the same boy she'd loved in high school. There was a strength and solidity to him that was wholly new to her, and yet Wendell still felt so familiar. So safe.

Wendell cupped her chin and kissed her. "Ginny, please."

"Yes," she said.

The years between them melted away as they slipped beneath her sheets. Wendell moved artfully, savoring every inch of her skin. With his fingertips, his mouth. He moved over her like water, lapping the edge of the shore, flooding her senses until she cried out. Afterward, they lay in each other's arms, holding on to one another.

"I don't remember it ever feeling like that," Ginny whispered.

"Me, neither." Wendell rolled onto his back, and she rested her chin on his chest. "I hope it was okay. Showing up like that. And . . . this." He smiled at her.

"It was perfect," she said, pressing closer. "All of it." Then, "I needed that."

Wendell kissed her head. "I needed you."

Later, as they sat on her deck with a bottle of wine between them, Ginny tried again. "When you got here, you said you had something to tell me?"

He turned to her. "You first."

When morning light flooded her bedroom, Ginny stretched luxuriously. Beside her, Wendell roused. She watched him blink, then turn to her. She smiled sadly.

"What's wrong?" he asked, rolling toward her.

"I have to go the Wetlands Commission. And ask about the turtles."

It would be unethical to keep it to herself. But the truth was, it didn't just halt the development of White Pines. It also halted a deal that could change the course of her family's struggling business. Without the boon of that sale, Feldman Agency might not survive.

Wendell pulled her against him. "Did I ever tell you about those turtles?" he asked.

Ginny shook her head.

"My mother used to take Wesley and me hiking at the town meadows when we were really little. To the ponds and the wetlands to search for frogs and turtles."

Ginny smiled. "I can't picture that. From all the photos you've shared, she looked so dressed up. So stylish."

"She was. But she loved nature." He paused. "During my dad's term as first selectman, we stumbled across the red spotted turtles on one of our hikes. She loved that we'd found something thriving that had once been almost extinct. I still remember the uproar it caused my dad during a reelection year."

"What happened?"

"The town wanted to sell the meadows to a developer. My mother got pretty bent out of shape; she wanted my dad to fight it. And he did. The trouble was, he was just one vote on a board of selectmen. And it was while my mother was fighting breast cancer."

Ginny sucked in her breath. "So he wanted to fight it for her?"

"And he did. For a long time." Wendell shook his head sadly. "That was my mother. Dying of cancer and still trying to take care of everyone else around her. Me, Wesley. The damn turtles."

A tear spilled from his eye, and Ginny pressed her fingertip to it. "I wish I'd known her. I wish she was still here for you."

Wendell propped himself up on his elbow and looked at her. "That's the funny thing. Those turtles are back now. It makes you wonder."

It was eerie and yet seemed somehow fitting. "I don't know if the turtles will change everything for White Pines, but reporting what I know is the right thing to do." Ginny let a long breath out. "Whatever happens next, I guess we'll all have to find our way through it."

"We will. We are already." He pulled her closer, and Ginny pressed her forehead to his. "I didn't think I'd ever feel sure about anything in my life again."

"But you're sure about the girls."

He nodded. "There are two things I'm sure of in this world. The girls are one."

"And the other?"

Wendell leaned over and kissed her once, then again. "This."

Thirty-Six

Julia

After the judge denied her petition for emancipation, Julia felt her insides give in a way they hadn't done since her parents died. All along she'd been tensed and ready to fight. Her fists clenched, her body coiled. She'd felt a steady course of adrenaline that had served to drown out the grief for some time, both protecting her from its pull and propelling her forward to do what had to be done.

Gone was the fire in her belly that had driven her through each day. Gone, too, was the hope that somehow she'd remain in Saybrook. She holed up in her room, until Pippa trotted in and begged and fussed and pulled her from the safety of her bed. Julia had sat obediently on the bedroom rug, packing boxes that Candace brought in. There were two kinds: one to bring to London and one to donate. Surrounded by all her things, Julia was too numb to differentiate between the two. What did it matter anymore?

Chloe cried with her on the phone when she broke the news. But Julia refused to let her come over. Sam was harder. He was beside himself. "Meet me at the lake," he texted. "There has to be another way."

Although she longed to see him, to hug him tight and inhale that intoxicating scent of sunscreen and lake water and Sam-ness that clung to his skin, she couldn't bear to. From here on, her days at home were numbered. Each time she saw him, she'd think of it as "the visit before the last one" as she counted down to yet another heartbreak. Instead, she turned her phone to Do Not Disturb.

The judge's decision that day had sealed their fates. Unable to sleep, Julia stayed up all night listening to the playlist Sam had made her until the sun broke through her curtains. By then, eyes dry as husks, she'd decided it was best to let go of him, too. She pulled a sheaf of pages from her journal and grabbed a pen.

As the sun rose with fiery color, Julia crept out of the house and down to the lake where the surface glittered like garnet. Barefoot, she walked carefully along the sandy edge to the tree near the egret's nest. In the sand, she drew an arrow pointing to the weeping willow. On its trunk she tacked her handwritten note. "I think I loved you, Sam Ryder. Thank you for all you've done for me. Please respect my wishes now, and let me go."

Somehow she limped through the rest of the day packing boxes and counting the hours until bedtime, all the while wondering if Sam had found her note. When she did not hear from him by nightfall, she exhaled with relief and then cried herself to sleep.

Late that night, Julia was awakened by the crack of pebble against glass. At first she wondered if she'd imagined it. There, she heard it again. She sat up, startled.

Hesitantly, she pulled her curtain aside and peered down into the darkness. She could make out a figure on the lawn, and her heart leaped at the sight of him: Sam.

Once outside, she barely had time to pull the door closed behind her when he stepped forward. "Jules, how can you just cut me off like that? Without even saying goodbye?"

She let herself be pulled into his arms, and there was that

all-comforting scent of Sam that filled her senses and made her knees go weak. "I'm sorry," she whispered, wrapping her arms around his middle. He felt strong and sure, and she ached with having missed him all this time. "I'm glad you came. I was wrong."

Now, with Sam holding her tight on the front step and the moon overhead, Julia gave in. Together they stood a long time, the rise and fall of the peepers' song echoing around them until, reluctantly, they parted. "C'mere." Julia took his hand and pulled him to sit beside her on the front step.

"I can't believe you're going," Sam said. He shook his head, and in the blue light of the moon, she watched his boyish flop of hair fall forward. He pushed it out of his eyes. God, she would miss him.

"Neither can I."

"But we'll stay in touch. That won't change." Beneath his earnest words was a truth she already knew but did not want to articulate aloud. Everything *would* change. She'd meet new people there, he'd continue on here. Their lives would be pulled in different directions, and apart was apart, no matter the miles between.

Sam had no idea how lonely it was not to have a family. "Maybe Pippa and I can come back for Thanksgiving with your family or the Fitzpatricks."

He smiled in the darkness. "That would be great."

They sat and talked until their eyelids and limbs grew heavy with sleep and they had almost run out of things to say, and then they sat shoulder to shoulder like they had those first nights on their rock in the field, saying nothing. Suddenly, Sam pointed skyward, and she followed his finger in time to see a silver streak through the sky: a shooting star. Sam turned to her. "Julia Lancaster, you're my girl."

Her eyes filled with hot tears. "I am."

They kissed goodbye. It began tenderly. But then became urgent. Julia felt her insides stir until they ached, and Sam pressed against her with what must have been the same desire. Then she pulled away. "This is too hard."

Sam placed his hands on either side of her face. Julia felt so small and Sam's hands so large, as if he could hold all her worries and wants in those soft strong palms. "I got your note down by the lake. The one that said you thought you loved me."

"I don't think it. I know it," she told him.

"Well, I loved you first."

Julia pressed her lips to his. Then, before her body or her heart gave in, she turned and dashed back up the steps.

Through the window, she watched Sam go, unable to hold back her tears. It was the summer of goodbyes. To all the people she loved. To the life she'd known. To the person she used to be. No matter what happened, Julia vowed she would not say another goodbye.

Thirty-Seven

Wendell

After he'd left the courthouse with Roberta, he had wanted nothing more than to go straight to Julia and Pippa with news of what he'd done. But Roberta had cautioned him that the court proceedings might take time, and worse, getting the girls' hopes up again would not be fair. There was one person, however, whom he had to tell.

The next morning, he walked up the steps to the front door. Candace opened the door before he could.

"Good morning," he said, pulling his cap off his head. "I'm sorry to come by so early, but it couldn't wait."

Candace looked distracted. "I've been up for hours as it is; don't worry." Then, after regarding him more carefully, "Is everything all right?"

Wendell swallowed hard. "I wanted to tell you in person. I applied for guardianship of Julia and Pippa."

Candace's mouth fell open. "You did what?"

"As you know, Julia came to me with this idea a long time ago. And like you, I thought it made no sense."

"It doesn't!" Candace said. She glanced behind her, then stepped outside, lowering her voice. "Have you lost your mind, Mr. Combs?"

Wendell stared at his hat in his hand. "That may be," he allowed. "But I feel it's the right thing to do. The girls and I have become close, and I believe I can help them have the life they want. Here in Saybrook."

Candace scoffed. "Let me guess. With my dead brother's money."

Wendell shook his head sharply. "No, it's not like that at all. I know that money is in a trust for the girls, and I have no interest in a single dime of it. In fact, I'm pretty sure I can provide for them comfortably all on my own, until they're old enough to inherit. By then they can spend it as they choose."

"It takes money to care for them comfortably, and if you think there is any in it for you, let me reiterate, you are mistaken. As for the girls, I question your intentions, and I will fight this, Mr. Combs. I will fight it all the way, and I have the means to do so."

"Please," Wendell said. "It's not like that. I knew Alan. Better than you, perhaps."

He watched this register on her face, but Candace said nothing.

"These are great kids. They came to me. They asked me to take care of them. And though I wasn't sure at first, I am now."

"You are?" Behind them, Julia stood in the doorway. Her eyes were wide with distrust. "You're sure?"

Candace spun around. "Julia, this is a private conversation."

"This is about me," Julia snapped. "I should be part of it." She faced Wendell. "Do you mean what you said?"

Wendell wished he could push Candace aside; wished he could apologize to Julia for taking so long to figure it out, and call to Pippa. But this was it. "Every word of it," he told her.

Julia's expression was not one of glee, as he'd hoped. Instead, she burst into tears. "So you do want us?"

Wendell swallowed hard. "I do. It's why I'm here now." He

looked at Candace. "Please, can we sit down together? I think this is a solution that would benefit everyone, if you'd just hear me out."

Candace held up both hands. "Please leave this property. Immediately."

"But—"

"Now!" Candace barked. "I will send you your last week's pay. And you will be hearing from my lawyer." She ushered Julia back inside.

"Wait, let's hear what he has to say!" Julia protested.

But Candace was furious. "Inside, now. We will discuss this with Mr. Banks." She slammed the door behind them.

Wendell was left holding his hat on the stoop, his chest pounding. He had expected no less, but still, it came as a shock. He was fired.

Behind him, the door opened. Julia rushed outside. Before he knew what was happening she threw her arms around him and hugged him.

"Thank you, Wendell."

"Easy now." He clapped her on the back gently, then stepped back. "Nothing is decided yet. It's up to the court."

"In the meantime, be nice to your aunt, and whatever you do, let's not tell Pippa yet."

Julia squeezed him once more and let go. "Promise." Then she ducked inside and closed the door.

Wendell turned around, his gaze resting on the lush rise and fall of White Pines, the open fields dotted with Queen Anne's lace and cornflower. The shade of the wetlands and the glassy reflection of the pond. The birds were in full song as the sun made its daily climb overhead. Wendell put his hat back on his head and went to his truck. As he steered down the driveway, his heart in his throat, he had no regrets.

. . .

It was a full week later until the hearing was called. Each day Wendell worked on his property, trying to stay busy. Trying not to think about the courthouse or the girls. He made calls to old friends in and around town, putting out the word that he was looking for work. When Ginny came by, he tried to be present for her, but he knew it was unconvincing. Luckily, she seemed to understand. "You're a good man," she told him. "Trying to provide a family for those girls. Your parents and Wesley would be proud."

Wendell had turned away, hiding his grimace. What Ginny didn't understand was that that was the last thing he wanted to hear. Over the years, Wendell had finally come to accept the loss of his family. What he wasn't sure of was whether he could stand to lose another.

The morning of the hearing, Wendell dressed in his best suit and drove to pick up Roberta. They rode in silence the whole way to the courthouse. When he parked the truck, she reached over and placed her hand over his. "Whatever happens, you did all you could. And you are deserving."

Wendell could not reply, but he squeezed her hand back. He hoped she knew what he felt.

When they entered the courtroom, Judge Bartlett looked flushed. It was an unusually warm Indian-summer day, and Wendell, too, was feeling stifled and uncomfortable in his suit. It was déjà vu, all the players back in their places. Julia and Pippa were there, along with Candace and Geoffrey Banks. Jamie Aldeen sat between the girls, only this time, it was Wendell's hearing. He did not have a lawyer. He had Roberta.

"Good afternoon," Judge Bartlett said finally. He rolled his sleeves up and clasped his hands, as he had that first hearing. Wendell found himself mimicking this, willing his hands to stop shaking. A bead of sweat ran down his shoulder blades.

"This application has been a challenging one," the judge began. "I have been assigned not one but two children, who have lost both parents, and who have only one surviving family member to care for them.

"Add to that, the older child petitioned the court for emancipation because she did not feel it was in her or her sister's best interests to reside with their appointed guardian." He wiped his brow. "Now we have an application for guardianship." He looked at Wendell, who nodded. "Who is not family, and does not have a family of his own, but who claims he possesses a family bond with said children."

As Wendell listened, he had to remind himself that the judge was describing him. And to his ears, told as such, it did not sound like a promising situation. He took a deep breath, pushing the thought away.

"It has always been the position of the court," the judge continued, "to keep families together when possible but, ultimately, to rule in favor of what is in the best interests of the child. In this case, children.

"Traditionally, blood relatives were given preference. It did not matter where they lived, how far the children might be forced to travel to relocate, or, often, how the children themselves felt about the relatives awarded custody of them. Family was family, and if it existed and could be located, that was where the children went.

"These days, however, the definition of family has changed. The state still recognizes the significance of biological family. That said, we also recognize the preferences and needs of the children. Attempts are therefore made to keep children in what I like to think of as the least restrictive environment. In other words, to keep their lives as normal and familiar as possible. In this case, Mr. Wendell Combs's application for guardianship, we have a man who resides in the same town as the children. Who can keep them in their same school district and maintain their existing bonds with friends and neighbors and community ties. This is also a man who has known the family for most of the children's lives, a man whom they clearly feel comfortable and safe with, and a man who has expressed a sound desire to care for them until they are of adult age." Here, Judge Bartlett addressed Wendell. "Am I correct in those statements, Mr. Combs?"

"Yes, Your Honor. I stand by all of those statements."

"Very good. There are, however, challenges. You are a single man, which the court does not hold against you, but it does place added burden in that you do not have a partner or spouse with whom you can share parenting responsibilities."

Wendell nodded, but his will began to sag. All of his years of staying away and staying alone might not be to his detriment alone.

"You have no children of your own, and I don't think I need to tell you, Mr. Combs, that parenting is the toughest job you'll ever love. As a parent of four, I cannot imagine doing it alone, or starting out as a brand-new parent, not of a baby but of a teenager and an elementary-aged child." The judge held up a piece of paper. "Plenty was reported about you from the guardian ad litem. But I have only one question. What have you learned about parenting during this process?"

Wendell had answered this question before: during interviews with the guardian ad litem, with DCF, with Bertie, when she tried to help him prepare for this moment. But now he found himself speechless. "It will be a challenge," he managed finally.

"Is there anything else?"

Wendell cleared his throat. "What I can tell you is that when I served my country in the National Guard, which is its own sort of institutional family, I learned basic principles to survive. The first was teamwork. I can only do so much as one. But as a team, I have members who count on me, as I do them, and who make me stronger as a result. When I returned from Afghanistan, I rejected that notion. I had lost loved ones, and I didn't want to feel that pain again. So I cut myself off from the rest of the world. And as I was doing so, I came to meet the Lancasters.

"They wouldn't let me cut myself off. Sure, they respected my privacy, but over time, Alan and Anne invited me in. And their girls—Julia and Pippa—well, they just wouldn't take no for an answer. They would follow me through fields when I worked, or call on me to help when the horse bucked them off. No matter what I did, they were always hanging around, asking questions, telling me stories, testing my patience. Somewhere along the way, they got under my skin. They grew on me. When Julia asked me to be their guardian, I thought it was crazy. I thought I was better off alone and they were better off without me.

"But now, after all I've been through with them, I don't want to be alone. I like the commotion and the chaos they bring. I like the quiet moments when Pippa grows heavy against my chest right before she nods off. Even the angry moments when Julia cries foul because she disagrees with a decision I've made. It's raw and real. And hard. And now that I've had that experience, I can't imagine spending the rest of my life without it."

Judge Bartlett listened to all of this, his face expressionless and still. Finally, he pushed his chair away from his desk, but he did not get up.

"I think I've heard all I need to. I will recess for fifteen minutes and deliver my decision."

As the courtroom emptied, Wendell remained seated. He wasn't sure whether he'd said the right thing or not, but he'd told the truth. He was not seeking guardianship of the girls out of honor or a sense of duty. He needed them.

Thirty-Eight

Ginny

Six Months Later

Wendell Combs was always a private man, but she suspected he had very little privacy these days. He was also a traditional man who did not like change. But he had no hope of avoiding that any longer, either.

Wendell Combs had moved out of his family's farmhouse on Weller's Road for the first time since the day he came home from the hospital as a newborn in his mother's arms. Ginny never thought that she would see it, and she was pretty sure if you had asked him, Wendell would have said the same. But Wendell had grown up and grown out in ways she also could not have imagined, and in doing so, he had finally outgrown his childhood home.

When Wendell brought Julia and Pippa home that fall, it was not happily ever after. First there was the before, and then came the after. At first Wendell was granted temporary guardianship of the Lancaster girls while their aunt sorted out the affairs of the estate. There were many to attend to, most notably the presence of a certain turtle in the wetlands.

When the development for White Pines eventually fell apart,

the deal did, too. Scooter Dunham did not walk away from the deal; he ran. The main house was swiftly removed from the Feldman Agency's representation and listed with another broker in town. But the market had slowed with the arrival of fall and then winter, and eventually, Candace pulled it altogether.

Ginny's parents had been disappointed by the loss of the White Pines listing, but they also understood it was the right thing to do. "Your mother and I have been thinking of retiring for a long time now," her father tried to reassure her. "Maybe this is a sign."

Nina did not argue, though Ginny couldn't help but feel she'd let them down. "You drummed up some good business for us this summer," her mother insisted. "You reinvigorated the agency, even if we don't stay open."

But Ginny had another idea. "What if I stay on?" she asked.

"In Saybrook? Or with the agency?"

"Both." She'd had a lot to contend with that summer, from the closing of one chapter in Chicago to the opening of another back in her hometown. And revisiting a page from the past with Wendell. Now that page had new additions, with the Lancaster girls. And Ginny was still not sure exactly where she fit into all of it just yet. But she knew one thing. She wanted to stay a little longer to find out. Whether that meant what was unfolding between her and Wendell or taking over the agency, she could not say. She would make only one promise, and that was to herself: "I'd like to stick around awhile. And let things unfold."

The agency remained open, and she and Sheila would continue to work there for the time being. Just as she'd continue to rent the little cottage perched on the lake. Finally, she'd gotten around to turning it into something more like a home. As her mother had suggested, she'd put her personal touch on things. She'd even let her Nina buy her some throw pillows for the couch.

Meanwhile, Wendell had his hands full, and while Ginny

sorted her own life out, she gave him space to do the same. The girls moved in with Wendell full-time, and Candace returned to London. For the first time in seventy years, White Pines stood empty. There was no crew to manage it and no caretaker to oversee it. Wendell found a new job on the Saybrook town crew, working regular hours that allowed him to be home when the girls returned from school and on weekends. The girls put their own stamp on his farmhouse. Some of the antiques were put in the basement in storage. There was a comfy new couch, and the walls were painted in light colors. The heavy drapes on the windows were taken down, allowing light to spill in. The kitchen cabinets received a fresh coat of white paint, the ancient appliances updated. Wendell was no longer living in the past. Julia and Pippa had launched him firmly in to the present, and he had no time for second guesses.

In the end, it was not the loss of two young parents or the arrival of an estranged relative with an ax to grind. Nor was it about the greed of a developer or the attachment of a veteran soldier to a place, and ultimately the people in it. In the end, it was the plight of the turtle that ended the chapter of upheaval at White Pines. The same brown turtle with the garnet-spotted shell that had once delighted a young mother and her two sons who liked to walk along the riverbank in the town meadows. And later, the turtle who climbed slowly up the side of the rock that two teenage lovers sat upon, too shy to confess their feelings. The odd-looking creature that had once lived and swum and reproduced in the lush wetlands of a small corner of western Connecticut and later become endangered. Who had almost slipped into extinction, as easily as it slipped into its shell, had it not been for the cool moss and the shadowy shoals that hid it, protecting one generation enough that it could survive. Go on. Plod forward.

Around Christmas, Geoffrey Banks came to see Wendell. He brought with him some paperwork. Candace Lancaster, who'd long since returned to London, had no sentiments toward White Pines. As a child, she did not possess good memories of her summers there, as her brother, Alan, had. But in the end, she did possess some heart. The house had always been part of the estate, which was managed by Geoffrey Banks and herself, as trustees, and since the proposed development had fallen through and it had languished on the market, she did not have further interest in procuring a sale. If the children wished, the house could remain as part of the estate until they turned of legal age to decide what to do with it themselves. It was a burden Candace wished to relieve herself of, and if it served the girls as well, so be it.

And so, with much discussion and some guilt over the fate of his own childhood home, Wendell listed the family farmhouse for sale. By the New Year, the Lancaster girls were set up back in their own childhood bedrooms. With Radcliffe back in his barn. And Wendell settled into a room of his own.

Wendell Combs did not take Alan's seat at the head of the table. Ginny had been invited to enough family dinners since then to know that. Nor did he claim any interest or ownership in White Pines, though she knew it gave him great solace being back in the wilds of the estate he had loved. But he did begin to sleep through the night. And for the first time in years, he was able to go to the movies without fear of his PTSD being triggered, though that may have had something to do with the girls' preference for Disney. But what Ginny noticed most about Wendell Combs was that he was finally content.

When she pulled up to White Pines one January morning, Ginny could hear them the moment she stepped outside the car. She zipped up her coat, scanning the frozen landscape. The estate was no longer as austere; the fields and forested areas had returned to their wild state without a crew on site to tame them. In no time the tall grasses had taken over, sweeping across the once-closely clipped expanses. Over the summer, wildflowers had filled in barren spaces, and now, in winter, were the color of dried wheat. The silhouettes of shrubs and hedges were more rangy than sharp. In a way the landscape had softened, as had the man who now lived there.

Ginny could see him now, a handsome figure in a brown coat in the distance, walking through the orchard. There were no leaves on the trees, only snowy trails along the boughs and branches. The whole property was blanketed in white. Suddenly, a small figure in a bright red jacket popped out from among the trees. Darting after Wendell. Ginny watched as the man bent and scooped the little girl up and threw her over his shoulder. As they ran toward the lake together, peals of laughter broke the winter silence and rolled across the snowy expanse between them. Ginny could not wait a moment longer; she grabbed her skates from the passenger seat and ran after them.

Down on the lake, a handful of teenagers skated slow circles across its milky surface. They took turns pulling each other along. Stumbling. Teasing when someone fell. All bundled up, Pippa teetered across the ice toward them, holding tight to Wendell's hand. When he saw her coming, Wendell gave a hearty wave.

"Come join us," he called, his words turning to white puffs on air.

At the edge of the lake, Ginny sat down on a stump and kicked off her boots. Her fingers worked quickly against the cold as she hurried to lace her skates. When she was done, she stood, and took one tentative step on to the ice. Wendell's voice closed the frozen expanse between them. "Don't look down," he called.

Ginny looked up. Despite the bitter cold, the scene warmed her.

Out on the ice the skaters made slow sweeping arcs, their sharp blades scraping rhythmically. Someone laughed. A bluster of wind, and a wool mitten tumbled across the surface. Beneath them all, nestled in deep somber layers, the spotted turtles slept on.

ACKNOWLEDGMENTS

If 2020 has taught me anything it's about the depth and magnitude of gratitude.

The past year has changed all of us, there is no getting around that. Professionally, it changed the nature of how my book found its way out in to the world. Gone were the book tours and Indie bookstore events. Gone were the gatherings where I get to meet readers face to face and hear their own stories. Gone were book talks and getting together with other authors to celebrate, commiserate, talk shop. For many months, we couldn't even walk in to a bookstore and pick a book off the shelf. And yet those were small things.

For many, it has been a year of loss. Personally, my family lost a beloved member during the year of Covid. My children were home from school. It was a year of the great unknown as the world distanced and waited and hoped.

Yet, there were heroes. From those in hospitals to those who taught their students from their own living rooms to those who drove delivery trucks and stocked grocery store shelves and picked up garbage. Every day heroes all around us.

The publishing industry also pivoted. We swapped book tours for Zoom events. Bloggers and reviewers hosted online book talks. Authors rallied. Indie bookstores delivered and did curbside.

Books were still shared. Pages were still turned. Readers, like you, were still there for us. For all of these reasons, I am indebted and grateful.

Thank you to my brilliant editor, Emily Bestler, who gathered her team to brainstorm, share, and collaborate. To associate editor, Lara Jones, always of good cheer and forward thought. To Isabel DaSilva, associate marketing manager, who bolstered publicity and inspired me to do the same. To publicist, Gena Lanzi, for getting the good word out. To Sonja Singleton, production editor, and copy editor, E. Beth Thomas, for their careful review and keen eyes. To art director, Jimmy Iacobelli, and designer, Emma Van Deun for the gorgeous work, once again. To Atria publisher, Libby McGuire and associate publisher, Dana Trocker, and managing editor Paige Lytle. A village, indeed!

Tremendous thanks to my beloved and creative indie bookstore owners, my author friends, the countless reviewers and bloggers and big-hearted hosts of book events who continue to spread the good word, share the book, and connect us authors with our treasured readers. You came together this year, and in doing so you kept all of us together.

To my friends, who know who they are and why, I am grateful beyond words. If a person's worth is measured by her friends, I am one rich girl.

Finally, thanks must always go to my family. To my parents, Marlene and Barry Roberts, whose encouragement and love is endless. To my brother, Jesse, who has long supported my aspirations and always put up with me. To John, who continues day after day, and year after year, to show up and fill me up in ways too numerable to count. And always, to Grace and Finley: my eternal reasons for everything. I love you all, and not one page in this crazy, raw, beautiful life story would be worth writing without you in it.